About the Author

S.E. Falconer is an Australian author who began writing on the online platform wattpad, where two of her stories reached over a million reads. After graduating from university and working in her chosen field, she decided to pursue the publication of her books. Beloved Murderer is her first published novel.

Beloved Murderer

S.E. Falconer

Beloved Murderer

Olympia Publishers
London

www.olympiapublishers.com
OLYMPIA PAPERBACK EDITION

A CIP catalogue record for this title is
available from the British Library.

ISBN: 978-1-80074-891-0

This is a work of fiction.
Names, characters, places and incidents originate from the writer's
imagination. Any resemblance to actual persons, living or dead, is
purely coincidental.

First Published in 2023

Olympia Publishers
Tallis House
2 Tallis Street
London
EC4Y 0AB

Printed in Great Britain

Dedication

To my family, for always being there for me.

Acknowledgements

Thank you to my family for supporting and believing in me; without your support I wouldn't have been able to write and edit this book. To my parents for always being there for me, for supporting me so I had the time and ability to spend my days writing. Thank you to Olympia Publishers for believing in this book and giving it the chance to become a published novel. And a special thank you to my wattpad readers, to the readers who loved Mason and Elora from the very beginning. Your encouragement, support, and requests for updates, were the reason I wrote this book. Your love for the story is what gave me the motivation to purse publishing. This book is for you because it wouldn't exist without you.

Chapter 1

My hands were covered in blood. Crimson liquid trickled down my wrists and through the webs of my fingers. A drop of blood fell from a cut engraved on the skin on the lateral aspect of my eye and dripped down my cheek like a tear. It splatted onto a bouquet of red roses that was previously positioned elegantly on the table I had just destroyed, staining its beauty with my blood. Just like how I stained everything.

My hands were shaking and my chest was heaving from the rage still burning through my veins. Glass had shattered everywhere from slamming my hands down onto the glass table so forcefully it crushed into a million pieces. As the anger diminished, and I saw the destruction that I had caused, in its place materialised a desolate emptiness and despair. Following in the wake of the blood stain, a trickle of water descended my cheeks.

My psychologist, Dianne, wasn't expecting my outburst and she froze, staring at me with wide scared eyes. Her sudden fear towards me helped me return to reality and calmed me down a bit, but not completely.

"It's okay to feel sad you know. It means that you are starting to realise the effect that your actions have had on others. This is a huge step on your road to recovery." She soothingly reassured me pragmatically. I hiccupped my grief.

"So, when he told me he always wanted me around he was only referring to work?" I mumbled, covering my face with my bloodied hands.

"Yes, you unknowingly ignored the personal boundaries he put in place and only focused on the words and actions that you wanted to hear, the things that made it look like he wanted you too," she explained. I kept my eyes downcast, ashamed. "How does that make you feel?" she questioned when I didn't reply.

I couldn't believe I had been so deluded. The entire time he was running away from me and not towards. I growled out my frustration; tears were freely falling down my face as I scrunched my eyes shut.

"What is wrong with me?" I bellowed, throwing my hands up in the air. I pushed my fist into my forehead forcefully, trying to release the anger at myself.

"Elora, there is nothing wrong with you. You are just different to other people and together we are helping you to identify these differences and give you strategies to react in a more positive way when you feel this compulsion overcomes you again. I can clearly see your progress from when you started, you are much healthier now." Dianne spoke calmly with benevolence. I snapped my narrowing eyes towards her; how dare she speak like she knew what this hell was like inside my mind?

"Don't you see that I will always be deluded? I'm messed up and you can't change that," I shouted, stomping my foot. Dianne stood up, her back rigid and held out her hands in a calming gesture.

"Please just calm down, Elora. Sit down and take a deep breath. Feel the weight of your breath rising and falling on your chest." There was unmistakably a quiver of fear in her tone.

I sat down and did as she asked. I listened to her because I wanted to be normal and she could help make me normal. I steeled my mind and started to work on a grounding technique she taught me.

It was true that I was much better now compared to a year ago before my treatment but maybe that was just because I hadn't become obsessed with anyone yet. Maybe it won't even happen again, maybe the therapy and medication might actually work. I just hoped with everything in my being that I never became obsessed again.

I concentrated harder than I ever had in one of my therapy sessions and I processed everything she said critically. I knew I needed the help. I didn't want to be the person that I used to be any more.

Following the session, I refused to look at anyone I passed on the street, not trusting my ability to understand people anymore. I kept my eyes to myself when I stepped on the bus back to the small town where I had moved a month ago.

It was a long gruelling two-hour journey from the busy city into the quiet mountainous town of Everbrook. I only ventured into the city for my therapy sessions or else I would never bother with the draining journey through nothing but pine trees. I seated myself near the back of the bus, hugging my coat tighter as the cold wind continued to stream through the opened bus doors.

Following our departure, I stared out at the flourishingly viridian forest through the window and released a deep sigh as I thought about what I was driving back to. The tiny town I now lived was situated in the mountainside and it was constantly encased in a beclouded mist from the low hanging clouds that gave it a gloomy atmosphere. Everbrook was settled at the bottom of a mountain right next to the ocean and was known for its high cliff faces and the brook that ran right through the centre of town flowing into the sea.

The town citizens were disgustingly friendly, and everyone

knew everyone. So, when I moved here a month ago, I was the talk of the town. Or more like the new freak of the town. I don't know how but they had learnt about my past. And I don't think they'd had anyone like me in their perfect little town before – someone with a criminal record.

I lived in foster homes all my life, never really knowing who my real family were. I didn't really care much for them either. I found my own people to love – those who cared about me – but as unfortunate as it was for me my social worker somehow tracked down my grandmother.

Apparently, my gran had no idea I even existed, or that her son had a child out of wedlock, or that he gave me away when I became his problem after my mother died of an illness three years after my birth. The only reason I agreed to stay with Gran was because she insisted that she hadn't seen my father since I was three years old when he moved away with his other family, and because I couldn't secure a job due to my criminal history, living with my long-lost grandma became my only option.

I must admit, she was a nice lady and had tried her hardest to keep me happy. She even assisted me in finding a full-time job through her friend who ran the local library. But I couldn't help the resentment I felt towards her; her son was the reason I was this way.

Why couldn't I have had this family from when I was born twenty-one years ago? Maybe then I would be normal. I ran my hands down my face to distract myself from those distressing thoughts and began practicing mindfulness training.

The bus became crowded as we picked up travellers from the surrounding towns whilst driving towards Everbrook. Some of the people on the bus I had seen before but most of them I didn't know. I was glad about that fact; I had no desire to talk to anyone.

14

Another benefit of being a town pariah was that I didn't need to worry about anyone talking to me – they were all scared of me.

If by incidence anyone did glance my way, they would pull their noses up at me or their eyes would bulge in fear and they would look away hastily. The one behaviour they all had in common was that they didn't venture anywhere near me. It's not like I was a murderer or anything, I just had a bad past, but my one saving grace was that no one knew about my mental health condition.

As the bus became overcrowded, I started noticing their avoidance of me more prevalently. People would choose to stand up rather than sit in the seats near me. I hunched my shoulders from the sting of pain this caused and I couldn't help the welling of tears in my eyes.

As I tried to ignore the restrictive tightening in my chest, I noticed something even stranger – I realised with fascination that I wasn't the only person they were avoiding. There were approximately six seats in this bus that were unoccupied and only three of those empty seats were near me.

The other empty seats were situated around another person. It looked like a male by his tall and muscled stature and the black clothes he was wearing. I couldn't see his face because it was covered by the hood of his jumper, which was shadowing his features.

He was sitting a few rows behind me on the opposite side of the bus at the very back. I maneuvered my position so I could sneak a better look at his face, but it was a difficult task as his face was angled so that it was inclined towards the window. I tilted my head to the side as I stared at him in fascination – his behaviour was so strange. There really was no need for a hoodie to be pulled up in the now warm bus.

15

What could this man have done that would make everyone so avoidant of him too? I rubbed my chin, I was immensely curious. I switched seats, slipping into the one beside me, and swirled my head around as inconspicuously as possible trying to look at him again. He was still staring out the window but at this angle, I saw the side of his face more clearly.

He had a strong jaw line and noticeable dark shadows under his eyes. My eyes drifted along his form and they were drawn to a book he had clenched between his tightly fisted hands. He was angry about something. Actually, now that I looked closer, that strong jawline was so pronounced because his jaw was clenched too.

Suddenly, he grabbed the seat in front of him and clamped it between his fingers. The empty seat constricted under his strong grip. His sudden movements shocked me, and I quickly snapped my gaze away from him. My mind was whirling with questions. Why was he so angry? Who was he?

Feeling reckless, and loving the slight thrill that it gave me to watch him, I slowly inched my head back towards him again. I glanced at him out of the corner of my vision with wide, intrigued eyes. His hand was back on his book again and he was looking forward now, not out the window any more.

His tight fists had unclenched and his jaw had relaxed; he seemed to have calmed down. I inched my eyes back to the front unwillingly so he didn't catch me blatantly staring. But just as I did, I caught sight of his fingernails which were now red and raw with blood. My eyebrows pinched together in confusion; what a strange human being.

It was now clear why he was such a town pariah by the way he presented himself, but what exactly had he done?

I shook my head trying to push him from my mind; I didn't

really care about the workings of this town. When I saved up enough money and secured a job somewhere else, I would move away and start a new life.

Suddenly the bus jolted as we transitioned from a smooth road to ascending a steep cobblestoned trail towards the town centre. The sudden change from the sleek ride we were experiencing before was unexpected for those who weren't seated. Many flew backwards from the shockwave that wracked though the bus and almost everyone was able to right themselves, but there was one lady that had nothing to stabilise herself with.

She was flung backwards with a surprising amount of force, and her back smashed into the chair behind her. I watched cringing, as her leg twisted under the metal bar at an abnormal angle. The crunch of snapping ligaments echoed throughout the bus and was shortly followed by a cry of pain. She crumbled to the ground in a mess of tangled limbs, bleeding cuts, and bellows of agony.

Everyone watched on with either horrified wide eyes, or their mouths covered in distress, except for one person. For some reason, for some strange odd reason, after the woman was hurt, I looked behind me. I guess I knew that this would divert his attention away from the window and I would be able to see his face.

My heart nearly jumped out of my throat when I saw him; he had angled his face completely towards the commotion and his hood was pulled down. I gasped in surprise when I saw that his facial features were visible to my intrigued eyes. I still couldn't see his entire face but what I saw of it was striking.

He was gorgeous. His features were chiselled, his strong jaw line was prominent, and his nose sat at a crooked angle like it had been broken in the past. He had dark lashes framing bright blue eyes and dark chocolate brown hair that fell over them. His hair was parted to one side and styled in a fringe that flowed down towards the opposite side of his face in an elegant curl. Protruding from the bottom of the concealing strands of his hair was a very noticeable scar that ran down his cheek.

His attention was completely immersed in the scene unfolding before us; he didn't even notice me staring back at him. The strangest thing about what I was seeing wasn't his unexpected beauty, but the expression that was on his face. His lips were lifted up at the sides into a sinister smile.

Everyone looked upon the woman in either distress or sympathy but he was smiling. He was enjoying watching her in pain. I cocked my head to the side so the loose strands of my hair fell out of my ponytail whilst I gazed at him intently. At that exact moment, his intense eyes flickered at me. My stomach knotted and my eyes widened as panic flooded my veins.

My obvious staring was not discrete, and he caught me watching him while everyone else's attention was directed to the woman at the front of the bus. A strange flicker of fear crossed his face before it manifested into a deathly glare. His dark blue eyes bore into mine with a lethal intensity that knocked the breath out of me. His head was lowered, and he had dark circles under his eyes that made him look menacing. From this new angle, his dark hair had fallen away from his face and I noticed that the deep scar on his cheek ran right up to his eye.

A chill ran down my spine causing goose bumps to rise on my skin, but I couldn't look away. His glare captured something alluring inside me that I didn't want to disappear. The woman at the front of the bus let out a painful scream and only then he closed his eyes tightly and twisted his head away. I quickly averted my gaze when his eyes broke contact with mine, feeling a faint blush taint my cheeks at his strong hate directed at me. I didn't understand what I did wrong, but I suspected that I saw something he didn't want anyone to see.

Only after a few minutes, I realised that my hands were shaking in my lap. It felt like my entire body was alight with fire from the adrenaline that was pulsing through me. I had completely forgotten about the woman at the front and didn't notice when the commotion died down; a doctor on board had strapped her leg up. For the rest of the bus ride, I didn't dare look back at him and hid my face in my blood red hair, twisting my ponytail into my neck.

The rest of the bus trip passed agonisingly slow. I was constantly aware of the glare that I felt burning into the back of my head. I tried to ignore it but the hairs on the back on my neck were standing up and sending waves of heat through my blood. I found his glare exhilarating. It was a glare so hateful it felt like I was going to die at any second – like he was going to send a bullet into the back of my skull. My heart was pounding for the first time in a year; since my last obsession.

I savoured the last few moments of the bus ride as we pulled up into the town square. I sprang off my seat quickly before he could pass me, so I didn't have to face his glare again. I waited patiently in line as the others pilled off the bus. My knees were trembling, so I held onto the railing to steady myself.

As I stepped off the bus and onto the concrete surface of the station my chest relaxed – I sucked in a deep breath of the cold mountain air and felt like I was back to reality. It didn't last long though as someone tried barging past me.

They knocked me over and sent me flying to the floor. I placed my hands in front of me as I fell and braced for the inevitable crash with the concrete. Unexpectedly, a strong arm circled around my waist and lifted me up against a strong body.

Unconsciously, I wrapped my arm around their torso to prevent myself from falling. When I realised that I was safe and wasn't going to crash face first with the floor, I finally glanced up to the person who had me pulled up into their chest. My heart stuttered and a pulse of attraction ran through me; it was him.

An electric jolt ran through my body in fear as well as desire at our proximity. Being so close to his deadly stare set my body ablaze. His face was so close to mine that I felt his breath on my cheek and his warm body rested up against mine. Neither of us let go as soon as we should have.

As I stared into his beautifully dark face mesmerised, I noticed I needed to angle my chin up to see into his eyes as he was so much taller than me. He had dazzling blue eyes that were imbued with something more than just hate, something sinister. Something I wanted more of. A strong shiver shuddered through me all the way to my toes.

I couldn't help it, I leaned closer towards him. He gasped and his features became riddled with panic; abruptly he heaved away from me. My arm slipped from around him and hung limp by my side. The thrill I felt before was gone with him.

"Sorry." But it wasn't him who spoke those words for pushing me over. It was me. Something flashed in his eyes for a moment before it was gone and returned to the same dark glower that he had sent me the entire bus ride.

"Stay away from me," he warned darkly. His voice was gruff, deep and alluring like honey. I just stared at him as he yanked his hoodie over his head and stormed off down the street. I stood immobile as I watched him walk away until long after he disappeared from my view.

When I pulled myself together, I started the twenty-minute

walk back to my grandmother's cottage. I liked the peaceful walk; once I reached the edge of the town the rest of the walk was beside the blooming forest. But today's walk was different to any other – it was completely dominated with vehement thoughts of him.

Just thinking about him sent a flush to my cheeks. I knew I shouldn't feel like this, given he just looked like he wanted to murder me. He was the strangest man I had ever met and yet there was something intriguing about him. I wanted to know more about him.

He was just like me, a town pariah, but he was so beautiful I didn't understand why people would want to be away from him. There was something I didn't know about him and I was sure it had something to do with the way he stared at that woman when she fell in pain. There was something not right about it, not right about him.

Before I knew it, I was trudging up the cobblestoned path into my grandmother's cottage. It was a paltry little house that was constructed from a dark chestnut coloured stone and was covered with ivy leaved plants that overgrew the brickwork. The tiled moss-covered roof was angled into a pyramid shape and on the peak of the roof sat the stone chimney of our modestly sized fireplace.

The cottage resided inland from the town and was established right at the base of the mountain that overlooked Everbrook. It was very secluded due to the umbrous forest and colossal mountain face that surrounded it.

As much as I liked the cottage, I didn't like the owner who was looking out of the front window at me. I noticed Gran immediately from her wildly bushy grey hair and pink frilly robe. Grandma's face broke out into a wide smile and she waved at me when she saw me. I quietly groaned at her ardour and waved back at her unenthusiastically.

As soon as I opened the door, she hugged me and gave me a kiss on the cheek. I attempted to not cringe back away from her, but it was hard. I hated physical contact; especially the loving way my grandma was towards me. But my psychologist said that I should try to allow my grandma into my life. She said I needed to know what real parental love felt like.

"Hello, Elora. How was your day?" My grandma greeted cheerfully. I forced a smile back at her begrudgingly and only when she finally let go of me, I breathed out a sigh of relief.

"Fine." I shrugged. Those lethal blue eyes flashed in my mind and I realised what a lie that answer was, it was exhilarating.

"How was yours?" I asked to be polite.

"It has been a wonderful day. I have been cooking a roast dinner for us." She answered enthusiastically as she led me towards the kitchen. I breathed in deeply, admiring the ambrosial smell of the seasoned vegetables.

The cottage had an open plan layout situating the lounge, dining and kitchen all in one room. The furnishing was your typical olden styled Granny chic decor, with frilly flower cushions and kettle warmers. Luckily my grandma and I had our own room and bathroom. I was happy to have my own space to retreat to when being with another person became too much for me.

Grandma already had the vegetable dishes laid out on the kitchen counter top and the sight of it looked more enticing than any food I had ever seen. If there was one thing I had to admit about my grandma, it was that she was a brilliant cook. She checked her stopwatch that hung around her neck at the end of her necklace before asking me to take out the roast potatoes from the oven.

"It looks great," I admitted to her. She beamed back at me, accentuating the wrinkles around her eyes.

Dinner was a draining event; my grandma badgered me with questions that I mumbled vague answers to. After dinner, I excused myself and closed the door to my bedroom. The last of the sun's aureate rays were visible in the crepuscular light, setting my room into a dark sanctuary. Alone, I was finally alone.

I released a deep breath as I slid down the back of my door until I reached the floor. I closed my eyes, picturing those beautiful blue eyes and the breathless feeling of his striking face being so close to mine.

The only problem was that he told me to stay away from him, but it felt more like a warning than an order. I pursed my lips in dismay that he didn't want me anywhere near him. I didn't care though – there was something about him that drew me in.

I wanted to see him again and I was going to do everything I could to make that happen.

Chapter 2

I spent the next day in my grandmother's garden tending to her vegetable plants with her. It was a beautiful Saturday afternoon and the icy cold wind was refreshing. My eyelids fluttered against the enlivening breeze that swirled my hair away from my face and cooled my cheeks.

I loved how my grandma lived right on the edge of the undulating mountain. I smiled as my gaze set on an eagle that glided between the mist coated array of pine trees that sheathed the mountain eminence.

"Grandma, are these tomatoes ready to harvest?" I asked inquisitively as I looked over at Gran. She was watering her strawberry plants humming a happy tune. She glanced up from her plants and over towards the tomato's giving them a speculative look.

"They are perfect, very bright red all over. You can harvest them if you wish, Elora," Gran answered, smiling warmly. I had never known someone to smile as often as her.

I began picking them carefully, trying to preserve the natural state of the tomatoes. It took me an hour but when I had finished, a satisfying sense of peace lifted my lips as I beheld the freshly picked tomatoes in the wooden basket. Finally, something I could do right. Gran moseyed up behind me and glanced over my shoulder, peering at the tomatoes.

"Do you want to sell them at the market?" she suggested, tweaking a tomato between her fingers.

My heart started pounding viscously at the thought as fear clenched my stomach. Being around all those people and having to engage with them, I felt claustrophobic already. My fast heart rate missed a beat when I thought about him – he could be there. If I wanted a chance at a normal life, I needed to start doing normal things, and to do that I needed to step out of my comfort zone and not allow anxiety to rule my life.

"Okay," I relented ambivalently and with barely contained alarm. "I'll go." Gran beamed back at me as she held out the basket of tomatoes I had picked.

I trudged through the dense and dripping forest along the trail towards the town, the gravel crunching beneath my feet. I was rugged up in my thickest coat, but I still shivered through the warm material. The tomatoes were safely packed in the basket hanging off my elbow.

When I reached the edge of the town my breathing became shallow. I breathed in deeply in an attempt to calm down. Nothing was going to happen to me; nobody was going to murder me.

With lumbered steps, I arrived at the town square where the markets were thriving with life. The square was packed with cheers of families talking and laughing and clangs of activity. Stalls lined the street selling various objects from jewellery to cupcakes.

As I delved deeper into the square people started to notice me. Those who did either sent me warning glares or they spun away from me with accusation in their eyes. I lowered my gaze in an attempt to avoid attention, but it didn't seem to help. My hands were shaking and sweating so severely that the basket started to slip from my grip.

I subtly tilted my head up to search for the stall that was selling the vegetables. My eyes locked with a woman laughing as she interacted with her two children. When she recognised me, her smile slipped and she looked at me with wide fear filled eyes. She turned her children away from me and scurried in the opposite direction.

I squeezed my hands together between the basket trying to hold myself together. This was why I didn't want to do this. I noticed people walking as far away from me as they could and refused to meet my eyes.

I didn't know why they reacted this way. I mean, I wasn't going to hurt anybody. But I guess they didn't know that because somehow, they found out that I had spent the last year of my life in jail. Luckily, they hadn't discovered the reason why I was there. Although, I have come to realise that this might actually be a negative thing because it's caused people's imaginations to run wild. But I didn't want anyone to know. It was in my past and I wished it to stay there.

Dianne was the only reason I had recovered from my past. When I was first admitted into jail, she was assigned to me as my psychologist. She helped me diagnose my problems, understand them, and finally accept them. Only then was I able to heal.

During my sessions with her, I was diagnosed with an Attachment Disorder and symptoms of Obsessive Love Disorder. My condition causes me to believe that I am in love with someone and become, well, obsessed with them. In my experience, they don't usually feel the same way back, but there is something wrong with me that makes me think that they do.

My thoughts and actions become completely revolved around my one obsession and it's painful to think about anything else other than them. I have come a long way since then and combined with the therapy, my medication has helped greatly.

"Hello. You are Evie's granddaughter, aren't you?" I heard someone inquire, bringing me out of my thoughts. I glanced up to find a teenage boy behind a Japanese antiques stall. He had black messy hair and a noticeable birth mark on one cheek. I never understood the attention males gave me and I never really cared, I only ever wanted the attention of the person I was obsessed with.

"Hi, yes I am." I greeted him and subsequently swivelled to scurry away, but he called after me.

"Welcome to Everbrook," he shouted, flashing a massive grin and enthusiastic wave.

"Thank you." I smiled back and then quickly lowered my head, hurrying off. The inconsequential interaction caused sweat to break out on my brow. I just needed to find the vegetable store and get out of here. I shook my hands out to release the built-up anxiety that continually compounded after being around so many people.

I noticed the vegetable store ahead and my lungs deflated in relief. There was an old man with noticeably long grey hair that was parted between a widow's peak behind the stall. He had round glasses sitting on the edge of his nose and he was reading a magazine while perched on an ottoman. I approached his stool apprehensively, just hoping he wouldn't treat me horribly.

"Hello," I announced gingerly. The old man glanced up from his magazine, pushing his glasses up his nose and his features broke out into a friendly smile.

"Hi there, how can I help you today? My name is, Bill," he greeted me with a pronounced Scottish accent. His friendly greeting allowed me to loosen my tight hold on the tomato basket, my knuckles returning to a more natural colour.

"I was just wondering if you wanted any of my grandma's

tomatoes we recently harvested?" My voice quivered from nerves. Bill's eyes lit up in eagerness and he stood up from his stool craning his neck to take an inquisitive look at the basket.

"Brilliant. I'm in need of some tomatoes. Let's have a look then," he urged cheerily. I handed the tomatoes over and he took them eagerly peering into the basket.

"These are beautiful tomatoes." His comment made a smile rise on my lips, all that careful harvesting was worth it.

"I can give you fifty dollars for them if you would like?" Bill offered.

"That is perfect, thank you." I smiled, and in return, he gave me the money.

"You have a good day," he delighted.

"You too." I waved him goodbye with a genuine smile. He was a nice man and that interaction wasn't as bad as I had imagined. I released a strained jagged breath in relief as I walked away. Grandma would be delighted to hear that she had earned so much money for her tomatoes. I walked home with a strange sense of pride in what I had achieved.

I didn't notice how late it had become until the swaying foliage of the trees had transformed into dark swirling shadows. The storm clouds above veiled the remaining light of the day, embedding the forest into a tenebrous twilight.

I quickened my mosey steps into a stride as I increased my pace. Walking through the forest in the dark put my nerves on edge. I was already feeling jittery from such an emotionally filled experience in town, so the rustling sound of the wind gusting the tree leaves made me flinch at every shadow.

The umbrage of the tree branches felt like they were jumping out at me in warning. I entered the trail that connected the main road to the lane my cottage resided on. I instantly felt claustrophobic as I was enraptured by the tree trunks and their foliage.

The snap of a twig caused my muscles to freeze, and a yelp of fright to leave my lips. My eyes snapped to the direction of the noise to see two glistening bright eyes of a small animal cocooned between the shrubbery. As it ran off, I noticed that its fur was dotted with blood. My face blanched; I shuddered to think what had happened to it in this very forest. I continued on at a brisker pace.

The strong wind gushed against the back of my neck and I tightened my jumper around my shoulders – I must be close to the end of the trail now. Another twig snapped along with the crunch of leaves crushing under foot, and the noise approached – louder this time.

Suddenly, someone emerged out of the trees and a black figure stalked towards me. My knees trembled and I placed my hand over my mouth to prevent the scream that threatened to surface. I stood there frozen in fright as the figure descended upon me.

As the figure casually strode towards me it gradually moved into a stream of moonlight that shone through a break in the clouds and canopy above. My eyes bulged as a jolt of fright ran through me when the figure's features were illuminated, sending a shiver of fear down my spine.

It was him. Only, it didn't look like him.

He had blood covering his hands and clothes. There was so much blood that it was dripping off him in gruesome splatters. My eyes followed the trail of blood as it dripped down his arm and only then did I realise that he had a knife dangling from his grip.

The knife was coated in blood too. A drop of blood dripped

down the blade until it pooled at the end and then splattered onto the leaves on the forest floor. I was hypnotised by it – that feeling of something dangerous but enticing inside me sparking up again in his presence. It was similar to the rush of being accelerated and twisted through the air on a rollercoaster, exhilarating but accompanied with the heightened fear of knowing that if one thing went wrong you could die.

The tingling of want I felt when I was near him was only intensified by his current dark state. I looked up into his face with a vigilant gaze to see his cheeks had blood streaked across them as well. His features were dishevelled; his dark brown hair was sitting messily over the side of his face, and jutting out from the bottom of his hair was the deep scar that ran down his cheek. His eyes were wild with something animalistic. He didn't show any signs of fear from me seeing him like this; it was like he was in some sort of trance.

He shifted a step closer to me and a strong current of terror shot through me, paralysing my muscles at our close proximity. Beads of sweat formed around my quivering lips. My eyes darted towards the blood-soaked knife that was still hanging in his hand.

"You again," he growled acidly. The grumble of his dark menacing voice set something alight deep inside me and raged through my body. I glanced back up into his inscrutable eyes to see they had lost some of their wildness, but they gave nothing away. I didn't say anything, I couldn't, my mouth was stagnant as I bit my bottom lip.

He stalked a menacing step towards me. I didn't move a muscle, allowing him to come closer.

"What are you doing here?" he demanded. A cold sweat rushed through me and it took me a moment to understand his words, as my mind was in turmoil.

"Selling tomatoes," I mumbled inaudibly. But he seemed to understand as he stared at my mouth. He tilted his head to the side as he searched my features; his mind racing until his eyes flashed in consequence of the decision he made.

This would be the time when I should run for my life, but as he sauntered another step towards me, his chest brushed up against mine causing my lips to part and my blood to rush to my head. I was stunned to the ground – he had me at his mercy. He raised his free hand and ran his bloody fingers over my cheek leaving a streak of blood on my clear skin.

My heart sped up even faster as he touched me and the nausea of having blood on my face was overridden by the butterflies that swirling in my stomach from his touch. He leaned into me and his lips almost bushed mine. My lips tingled in want of his and my spine arched towards him.

"You know too much," he murmured into my cheek, the sound reverberating in his chest. He trailed his lips across my cheek just above where his blood-soaked fingers ran moments prior. Goose bumps rose up on my skin where he touched me.

Then I felt the cold tip of the bloody knife settle into the skin of my neck, but not hard enough to puncture it. A shock of fear shot through my blood causing my muscles to freeze but I also felt something else – a dark thrill of attraction. His lips were so close to mine; if I was going to die then I was going to die kissing his lips.

The moonlight illuminated his bright blue eyes as they stared back into mine with an intensity that drew me in. His dark hair was a swirling mess in the wind and fell partly over his eyes, obstructing my view.

He was so beautiful. He was so close already. His lips were slightly parted as if asking me to come closer. He callously pushed the tip of the blade deeper into my skin and it spurred me into motion. I leaned into him slowly and our lips almost touched, my heart beating out of my chest in anticipation.

But suddenly in a gust of movement he was gone and so was the knife against my throat. I slanted forward into nothing; the cool fresh air of the night whisked against the bare skin on my neck.

"You need to leave, now." He was standing stiffly a few steps away from me. His eyes were haunted and his tone held such urgency that it scared me. His insistent words sparked realisation back into my dazed body. My spine straightened as I finally comprehended that I was nearly just murdered.

"Go. Before you get hurt," he warned solemnly, his eyes blazing with vitality. The honestly of his words was evident in his eyes because I also saw conflict there, like he was having an internal fight with himself. As if at any moment he might change his mind. I knew that I wouldn't just be hurt if I stayed any longer, I would die.

I backed away from him and swirled away to sprint as fast as I could down the track. The clomp of my footsteps on the gravel echoed through the trees as I ran. My feet tangled in roots from the forest floor causing me to trip multiple times, but I prevailed on until I reached Gran's cottage. My breath was heaving out of my lungs and my knees were wobbling as I stopped to unlock the front door.

I slammed the door shut behind me and leaned my back against it. My heart was hammering and adrenaline was running through my shaking body. I locked the door behind me and only then did a sense of safety finally return to me, but that wonderful electrifying feeling also disappeared along with it.

Chapter 3

"Are you ready for church Elora?" Grandma called through the cottage. Gran had been asking me if I was going to attend all weekend and my only response was a reluctant maybe. She desperately wanted me to attend because she owned the church and explained it meant a lot to her and our family, but I didn't care about our family at all.

It was only last night, when I was recovering from what happened, that I realised there was a possibility he could be there. When Gran mentioned that most of the town goes on Sunday mornings my decision was made.

The church was secluded from the rest of the town – it was situated at the top of a hill and the forestation that lined the hill's slope was untouched by urbanisation. Gran drove us up the winding cobblestoned road towards the church and parked in the clearing outside the building. The door creaked as I climbed out the car into the icy wind that swirled my hair away from my neck.

I couldn't deny the church was beautiful. It had colossal moseyed windows that lined both sides of the building and the main entrance consisted of two glass mosaic doors expanding to the ceiling. Anteriorly, the roof stretched higher than the rest of the ceiling into a rectangular clock tower where the clock chimed every hour. It was large enough to comfortably seat everyone in our small town, and that thought made me want to bury my head underneath the church's tiled floor.

Grandma and I strolled up the small pebbled path leading

towards the front entrance. It was surrounded by a flower bed of white and red roses and lines of bird cherry orchards stretching up into the sky; it gave an ostensive indication of how old this church truly was.

Inside, most people had already arrived and were standing around chattering. As we walked inside the soft buzz of voices disintegrated and they turned their heads to stare at me.

"Don't mind them darling," Gran whispered into my ear. The people around us started to disperse and I heard my name being spoken as they whispered in outrage about the girl who was just released from jail. I squeezed my eyes shut and tried to ignore it, but my hands were trembling as I interlaced them.

The priest walked up onto the stage and asked us all to be seated and I breathed out a sigh of relief. The sooner this was over the better. Gran and I sat on the bench right at the back and nobody sat next to us. The people in front of us shifted uncomfortably because they were so close to me, but they didn't move as most of the seats were now occupied.

I nervously glanced around again to make sure no one was looking at me, but as my eyes flittered around the room, I noticed him. Instantly, my entire body shot into alertness and every nerve ending ignited from his presence. My eyes widened and my jaw fell open.

He was also sitting on the very last bench at the back of the church on the row opposite me. He was listening intently to the session and he was sitting on the edge of his seat with his head tilted forward. His face was smooth, displaying not an inkling of the anger that was on his features yesterday; it had all melted away. I couldn't believe my eyes, as much as I had hoped, I would never have thought I would find him here.

When I could breathe normally again, from having finally

overcome the shock of seeing him, I noticed something else about him. Everyone was sitting as far away from him as possible, in the same way they were avoiding me. He had the entire two back benches to himself. People seemed more scared of him than they were of me. I bit my lip as my curiosity skyrocketed, just who was he?

I needed to know more about him.

In that moment, when I was intently staring at him, he flickered his eyes towards mine as if sensing someone watching him. His eyes flashed in recognition when he saw me, and became hooded as they set on me with a deadly malevolent glare that sent my stomach fluttering. His hate-filled glare sent a shockwave of adrenaline through my blood causing my limbs to shutter. My muscles were tense, and my eyes were locked onto his like a deer caught in headlights. I had never felt so alive.

He glanced away from me after a few thrilling seconds and back towards the front of the church. My eyes refused to move from him, and I was left gaping after him with my mouth hanging open in shock and desire.

I didn't take my eyes off him for the rest of the session. I couldn't – he was so beautiful. His gaze was glued to the front of the room and he had his chin propped on his fingers as he intently listened to what the priest had to say.

That electrifying deathly glare he had sent my way earlier was still seared into my mind and caused my heart rate to remain alarmingly high. I knew that his glare should be enough to send me running out of here screaming but all I wanted was to move even closer to him. I wanted to read every aspect of his features to decipher just exactly why he was in the woods covered in blood, and why he seemed to hate me so menacingly.

As I stared at him for longer than I should have, I started to notice some of his natural movements. He had a habit of continuously clenching and unclenching his knuckles and he raised his hand as if about to pull his hand through his hair, but he was refraining. My eyes lowered and I noticed that he was dressed formally with black dress pants and his shirt was tucked in.

He was dressed in all black which wasn't a surprise; I was growing used to that colour on him. I quite liked the style on him; it made his eyes shine a brighter blue and suited his dark demeanour. His hair was formally styled today; his dark locks which usually fell over his eyes were jelled back into a curl over the side of his head. The style made the scar down the side of his face more noticeable.

I was brought out of my thoughts when the session ended and those around me began to take their turn at communion. I decided to stay back; I didn't want to make a spectacle of myself by being in perfect view of everyone.

"Are you coming, Elora?" my grandma asked hopefully from beside me.

"No, Grandma, I will stay back here," I declined with a shake of my head. Her shoulders dropped, and she tried to hide her disappointed expression, but I saw it clearly. I turned my head away from her in annoyance, crossing my arms. I heard her sigh as she has begun to reach for me but she changed her mind, lowered her hand, and walked off.

I dug my fingernails into the palms of my hands as I stood resting against the wall in the corner. I hoped that, if I could wish it enough, the stares of those around me would go away. To distract myself I glanced around the room trying to find him. It seemed like an almost automatic reaction for me to look for him now.

My eyes easily caught on the dark curl of his hair as his tall stature propped him above the rest of the town's heads. His skin was almost transparent like he had never seen the sun. That same strange thrilling feeling rushed through me as I glimpsed him again – I was addicted.

He was speaking to the priest at the front of the church and I strained my ears to hear what they were saying, but they were too far away for me to make out any words.

I watched him intently like a hawk, my eyes following his every movement. He turned around, pulling his hood over his head, and sauntered back down the aisle towards me. His head was lowered and his hood obstructed his eyes. He was walking with such confidence and grace that it surprised me.

The only other time I had seen him around other people in the town, he was extremely stoic and kept to himself. His new air of confidence was surprising, but I realised as he fleetingly glimpsed around the room that it was because of the people he was around. It was like he was putting up a barrier so that no one would talk to him. He wanted them to be scared of him.

I knew he could feel my stare burning into him but he didn't glance up at me – he was refusing to look at me. I waited anxiously for our eyes to lock; I was aching to run over and talk to him. He disappeared in the crowd of people and I was released from the taut hold he had over me. Breathing out heavily I fell back against the wall, my tight muscles relaxing. I had been straining forward towards him and I didn't even realise it.

I closed my eyes for a moment and let my head rest back onto the wall behind me, tapping my boots on the floor. How on earth did he do this to me?

The other town members had started to gather towards the back of the church where they had refreshments laid out. They had moved into their cliques and were chatting amongst themselves. Grandma still hadn't returned, so I remained where I was and waited for her.

I stayed well away from everyone, but I did watch them with quiet curiosity. My eyes followed a dark-skinned woman who's name I had overheard was Victoria – the town mayor. She had most of the town members flocking around her as she told them about the fair that was coming to town. Her dyed blonde hair was tied back slickly into a bun at the bottom of her head and she was dressed immaculately, giving her an air of superiority.

A loud squeaky laugh reverberated from beside the woman; I cringed backwards as a young girl about my age laughed at something a boy said next to her. Her face was caked with makeup and her hair was dyed a fake white blonde and pulled back into a high ponytail. She had strikingly similar looks to Victoria, just a younger version; she was clearly her daughter. But the younger girl had a lighter, olive skin tone, a round face, and was slightly on the overweight side. I couldn't help but express my disgust at how normal their relationship was as she smiled up at the boy with doe filled loving eyes.

As I was glaring at her display of affection for the boy with a blonde buzz cut – her eyes darted to mine. Her expression morphed into a glare of her own as she noticed me scowling at them. She released the attention of the boy as she turned to Victoria.

She whispered something in her mother's ear and then Victoria's eyes cut towards me. A strong, crushing feeling of anxiety built up inside my chest causing my breathing to falter. I realised I had just warranted their unwanted attention. I searched around frantically for Gran, but she was nowhere to be seen.

Abruptly, Victoria started stalking over to me, with the

younger girl and the buzz cut boy close behind her heels. My breath clogged in my throat and my lungs constricted on itself – I coughed. I placed my hands on the wall for support as if I could push the wall down behind me, but I was cornered.

They stopped in front of me with Victoria and her daughter peering down their noses at me like I was filth on the bottom of their shoes. Victoria spoke up first.

"I'm sorry but who said you were allowed to come here?" She spoke with a velvet sweet voice, but there was an undertone of abomination. She was sneering down at me; her disapprobation of me was clear in her obnoxious expression.

I kept my mouth locked shut and pressed in a flat line. All the judging eyes around me were boring into my soul and setting a deep pain alight in my bones. I couldn't handle this.

"This is a place for those who are pure, not for sinners and we all know where you just came from." She smiled mockingly and pointed her obnoxious nose up at me. I blinked up at her wide-eyed; a wince formed on my features.

My breathing spiked into hyperventilation and I placed my hand onto my chest to hold myself together. The walls around me started to spin and I wanted to scream and cry.

"Are you really tormenting the church owner's granddaughter?" drawled a deep lazy voice from beside me. I snapped my eyes towards the voice, along with everyone else, to see him leaning against the wall. He was casually standing against the same wall as me with his arms crossed against his chest with an alluring expression like he didn't have a care in the world. He diverted everyone's attention towards him and away from me.

My breathing altered from hyperventilation to absolutely nothing; I couldn't breathe with him so close. His voice sent a wave of warmth flooding through my blood which caused my body to relax at his presence.

Everyone watching suddenly turned their gazes away from him as if they were afraid of him. Everyone except Victoria.

"If I want to protect this town from something evil then I will," she snarled at him, holding her chin higher. Suddenly, Mason pushed off the wall and stormed over to us so he was standing in front of me. He stood so close to me I could feel his hand slightly slide over mine.

"You have no idea what evil truly is," he growled at Victoria threateningly with a ferocious intensity. I stared at him dumbfounded, my mouth dropping open. My stomach fluttered as a warm light feeling rose in my chest as I watched him defend me. It diminished all my anxiety having his strong frame blocking me from all the staring, judging eyes.

Surprisingly, Victoria did back off. As she spun around on her heel, she shot Mason a revolted glower as if he was worth less than the dirt under her feet.

"Let's leave these freaks alone Melissa," Victoria spat with a vindictive tone as she placed her hand onto her daughter's shoulder and steered her away from us. The others followed close behind them, scurrying away as if they couldn't get away from him fast enough. Why were they all afraid of him?

A muscle twitched in his jaw as he watched them retreat. His body was positioned in front of me like a barricade and he stayed unmoving for a long moment as if he was waiting to make sure they wouldn't return. He didn't turn around to face me but he hadn't walked off either. I felt like I should thank him. I placed my hand on his arm to gain his attention, but he jumped so high from my touch I must have shocked him. Without turning to me or even a backwards glance he marched off towards the exit.

"Wait." I called after him pipingly but all I saw were the doors sliding closed behind him in his wake. I stood there immobile; my muscles were frozen trying to comprehend what had just happened. Why did he just defend me? I thought he hated me?

I needed to know who he was and why he just did that.

"What's going on?" Grandma spoke up from beside me with her eyebrows pinched in worry. I narrowed my gaze at her flatly, unimpressed, so now she decided to turn up.

"Elora, I want to introduce you to my friends, Bill and, Henrietta." Gran smiled, gesturing to the man from the vegetable stool who had the long grey hair with the widow's peak. And then to an older plump woman in a wheel chair with a bald head.

My breathing was still ragged and my cheeks were flushed from what had just occurred. I didn't want to talk to anyone right now other than him. So, I turned my back on Gran and stormed off in the same direction that he went. My hands were in fists at my side; I couldn't believe she left me alone, that she forced me to come here in the first place.

The doors slammed shut behind me as I stomped out of the church, my temper flaring. Instantly, the cold breeze washed across my face sending a shiver through my body. I pulled my scarf tighter around my neck and searched vigilantly around for him, craning my neck to see into the trees beyond, but he was nowhere to be seen. Disappointment settled heavily on my chest and deflated my lungs.

I wasn't going back inside so I decided to walk around the church building towards the flower garden. But as I rounded the corner into the garden my vision suddenly became blurry as smoke blew into my face. I coughed and spluttered for a moment before my vision cleared and the figure in front of me revealed itself.

My heart jumped when I saw him leaning up against a pillar smoking a vape. His head was resting against the stone pillar, and one of his feet was propped up against the pillar behind him whilst he looked down at me with heavy lidded eyes.

His eyes were boring into mine with a dark intensity, and the side of his mouth was pulled up into a smirk. His formally styled hair was now tousled – as if he had run his hands through it multiple times. I wanted to run my hands through it. He looked so relaxed and sure of himself.

My eyes lowered, and a cold chill ran through my trembling limbs as I caught sight of one of his hands that was covered with blood. Blood was dripping down his hand and through the webs of his fingers.

My heart stopped in fear; why did he have blood on his hands?

Chapter 4

I glanced around the church to find no bodies or any reason for blood to be on his hands. I flickered my wide panicked eyes back up to him as he quickly tucked his hand into his pockets.

And as easy at that, his blood coated hand disappeared like it didn't even exist. But left in its place was a heart pounding darkness and trepidation in my soul that I couldn't disguise.

"Sorry, love," he drawled with a smirk. He then went ahead and took another drag of his vape, blowing the puff of smoke into my face.

I was left standing there staring at him with my mouth agape. He was still smirking and my eyes focused on his mouth. I noticed he had a long and narrow dimple that formed on one side of his face when he smirked like that.

He didn't take his intense gaze away from mine and it caused a dark shiver to run through me. I remembered his eyes last night when they were wild and about ready to kill me. That thought made the shiver a permanent residence.

Shouldn't I be running away from him and not following him? Then again, I have never been normal. He suddenly closed his eyes releasing me from his hold. He exhaled a deep breath filled with smoke; his chest deflating and forehead smoothing like he was relishing in the quiet. I didn't understand this strange calm mood he seemed to be in.

My eyes scanned his features and followed down his strong jaw where I noticed that deep scar along his cheek ran all the way to his collar bone. It wasn't an ugly scar, just a white indentation indicating a previous wound. I wondered how that happened – it must have been painful.

"Didn't I tell you to stay away from me?" he declared with a velvet tone. I peered back up to his face to see him staring straight at me; his features were void of hate, more curious, and it caused my heart to leap. I shrugged - I didn't know what to say. I feared I would say something stupid and then he would never want to speak to me again.

I just continued to stare at him and relished in the excitement of being this close to him, and having him looking at me – especially with the lack of hate burning from his eyes. I noticed the way the iridescent light from inside the church shone through the mosaic windows, making his blue eyes scintillating. He blinked and scratched the back of his neck.

"Are you going to say something or just stand there staring at me?" he questioned with raised eyebrows. His tone was amused rather than annoyed which helped me control the redness that fanned my cheeks. I realised that I had to say something or else he would leave. And I didn't want that.

So, I asked him the most burning question I had for him. The thing I wanted to know the most.

"Who are you?" I stammered and clumped a shaky step closer to him. He watched my movements warily with eyes like a hawk. When I didn't take another step forward, and he was sure I wasn't going to move again, his eyes slid back up to my face.

"Someone you're unfortunate to meet," he admitted hauntingly. His dark ready-to-kill eyes flashed in my mind and I knew exactly what he was talking about. I wouldn't say unfortunate, quite the opposite actually. I titled my head to the side as I searched his face for more information, but I didn't understand him at all.

My blazing curiosity was not sated by his answer; it only caused more questions to arise. Although there was one thing, I was sure of – I didn't want to call this beautiful man him any more.

"What's your name?" I whispered ardently, my tone a loudening crescendo – I couldn't conceal my urgency; I needed to know. I leaned forward as I asked and my lips parted in eagerness. I watched as he seemed to automatically lean his head back away from me. He inhaled another drag of his black vape and I noticed that his hand was shaking. Could I have caused that? Did he feel this strange attraction too?

"Mason Blackwell," he slurred. My world rocked; I repeated his name in my mind over and over again. I never wanted to forget it, or him. With twinkling eyes, I glanced up at his beautifully dark face and felt an overwhelming urge to tell him my name, and to make sure he never forgot me.

"I'm Elora," I burst, excited for him to know my name, and then remembered that I had a last name too. "Emsworth." He stared at me intently for a long moment not breaking eye contact. I gaped back at him hypnotised by his blue eyes – I never wanted to stop staring at them.

He blinked and turned his head the other way as if he was dismissing me, but I wasn't having it; I shuffled my stance, so his face was in my view again. A hint of a smile lifted one of his lips as he watched me.

"Why did you interfere before?" I tilted my head to side as I examined him curiously.

"You didn't want me to?" Mason responded resentfully with a scowl. Panic flooded my chest; I didn't mean my words to sound that way.

45

"I meant, why did you help me?" I stammered appreciatively with a warm smile. He eyed me warily out of the corner of his eye.

"That's none of your business." He dismissed me evasively.

"I would like it to be," I breathed out, without thinking. Mason snapped his eyes to mine and they widened at my confession. He continued staring at me shocked, his mouth opening and closing, lost for words. I straightened my posture and stood confidently; I wasn't ashamed of my admission, that was the truth.

Abruptly, out of nowhere, he leaned his face towards mine. My breath hitched and my lips fell open in surprise, but I didn't move a muscle. My heart jumped out of my chest and into my throat; I was absolutely electrified by him. His face neared so close to mine that I could feel his breath on my cheek.

Mason raised up his hand that was in his pocket, the one covered in blood. His hand reached up towards my face and his fingers widened as he neared my skin. His blood coated hand skittered towards my cheek as he moved to cup it. He didn't touch my skin, but he was so close that his hand swished along the hairs on my face and caused a shiver to run down my spine.

I didn't move, even though his hand was covered in blood. I didn't care if it meant he was going to touch me. I leaned my head into his hand, inching ever closer towards him.

Then just as quickly as he had neared me, he was gone. His skin didn't even brush mine. Disappointment dropped my lips into a frown. He stepped back and flopped himself back against the wall into a relaxed pose, his bloody hand jamming back into his pocket. I was left frozen, gaping after him like a fish out of water in a state of electrification.

"So why did you go to jail?" he asked, drawing on his vape

46

in nonchalance as if he hadn't just been inches away from my face a moment ago. I ran my hands down my face as I thought over his words. Instantly, I flushed, the heat rising up my neck and I ground my teeth together as acrimony rolled through me. I couldn't help but feel angry from being reminded of my past.

"That's none of your business." I folded my arms against my chest and pressed my lips together. His eyes twinkled as he leaned closer to me.

"But, I would like it to be," he drawled seductively, mimicking my previous words and drawing his lower lip between his teeth. Butterflies set flight in my stomach causing my eyelids to droop; he wanted to know more about me. My anger slipped away as a small smile formed on my lips.

"How did you know I went to jail?" I countered, deflecting his question. He raised an eyebrow.

"They call you the criminal you know, the entire town." Mason smirked, running his hand through his hair before locking eyes with me.

"But I just don't understand how the criminal that everyone is so afraid of, to me, looks like someone who couldn't even hurt a fly," he opined, waving a hand to gesture to my small frame and shy persona. My hands balled into fists at my side to rein in the sudden blaze that streamed through me from his accusation.

"Maybe you're just too deluded to see what's right in front of you." I raised my chin, pouting. One of his lips pulled up as he ignored my anger and continued on.

"I can see what's right in front of me all right and it's not someone who would ever hurt anybody deliberately. More like someone who is trying too hard to be accepted, to be loved," he assumed. He was completely right, and I hated it.

"You don't know anything about me," I objected, narrowing

my eyes. His lips lightly curved up at the sides – the start of a smile. I turned my back on him.

"Oh, but I do. If I didn't then you would be dead," he proclaimed into my ear; his breath fanned down the back of my neck. My body shuddered violently and I didn't know if it was from the coldness of his breath or his ominous words. I spun back around like a tornado and my mouth fell open from his abrupt and bold admission.

I didn't realise Mason had moved so close to me, so when I spun around and his face was right in front of mine my heart skipped a beat. His eyes were haunted as they stared into mine, and his expression had lost that playfulness, turning sombre. Still, I didn't feel any fear towards him, even after being reminded how I was in real danger from the man standing right in front of me now.

"Why?" I demanded assertively.

"Because you would have told someone about what you saw yesterday." A shudder crept through my skin as I thought about that – If I had made the decision to tell anyone about what had happened, I would be dead.

"You're not going to explain yourself then, for your actions yesterday?" I urged.

Mason scoffed at my words, "Now why would I do that? You haven't told anyone what you saw and you're still here talking to me, aren't you? Even without an explanation," he challenged. He was right, I once again had to consider how mentally unstable I must be that, even after everything, I still wanted to be closer to him and not run away.

"I can go and tell someone now," I provoked him, as I stepped towards the church entrance. His face remained blank, inscrutable, giving absolutely nothing away.

48

"You won't." Mason spoke with conviction – he sounded extremely sure of that fact.

"You're sure about that?" I straightened up as I faced him again.

"Certain," he declared, and stared straight into my eyes. I gaped back speechless and neither of us looked away for a long moment. Only when he dropped his eyes from mine did I feel released from his hold.

"Oh, and by the way." Mason tucked his vape away in his pocket before he glanced back up to me again. His expression was dark and his eyes hooded as he looked at me from under his eyelashes, just like last night in the forest.

"Don't ever speak to me again," he threatened, his previous teasing was completely diminished and replaced with a sombre warning. My gaze flew to him as I winched, and the skin bunched around my eyes in pain.

"What?" I managed to sputter out in shock. I thought he just saved me, I thought he wanted me in his life now. Mason didn't break his piercing gaze from mine and I saw the staidness filled intensity burning behind it. He wanted me to see how serious he was about this. But why?

"Elora?" I heard my grandma shout; her tone was infused with panic. Mason stepped away from me just before my grandmother rounded the corner. I was still in a ragged state of shock and wasn't able to move my focused glassy eyes away from Mason as Gran faced us. I wanted an explanation from him.

"Elora, what are you doing?" Gran questioned deploringly. I finally turned away from Mason to direct my attention at Gran; her lips were turned down into a frown as disapproval had clouded her features.

"Talking," I answered, in a clipped tone. Her eyes flicked

between the both of us for a moment before they settled on me in a hard glare.

"We're leaving," she stated firmly and gently touched my shoulder, and tried to lead me away from Mason. I frowned and flinched away from her; I wasn't leaving him.

"No, I haven't finished my conversation," I disagreed, pulling out of her touch. I turned my back on Gran to return my attention to Mason. But he had already disappeared leaving only one thing behind, my need to find him again.

Chapter 5

I glared at my grandmother from across the dinner table.

"You're making me feel uncomfortable," Gran announced, as she finally glanced up at me unimpressed from her dinner plate.

"Are you going to tell me why you interrupted today?" I snapped. Gran sighed deeply and placed her fork down on the table.

"You're not going to forgive me until I explain, will you?" she surmised, rubbing her tired eyes.

"No." I placed my hands into my jacket pockets and pressed my lips together in defiance. I wouldn't forgive her. I had been ignoring her all afternoon, refusing to even look at her.

"I already mentioned that Mason has a dark past," she started, and I scooted my chair closer to the table as I listened intently. The chair leg screeching against the tile floor.

"But I didn't mention just how dark," she admitted hauntingly. Her words caused the hair on the back of my neck to rise. I had already seen a snippet of how dark he was.

"Nothing can be worse than what I have seen in jail," I encouraged with nonchalance and a dismissive wave of my hand. My grandmother pinched her nose between her fingers as she leaned back in her chair.

"Believe me darling, this is probably the worst thing that I have ever heard in my lifetime, and that includes on television." She visibly shivered. "Mason Blackwell is a man that everyone

in the town stays away from and there is a reason for that."
Anticipation rose up in my chest like an inferno; I wanted to
know everything about him.

"What is the reason?" I urged eagerly, my breath
accelerating. Grandma's forehead puckered in worry and she ran
her hands over her curly grey hair. I bit my lip and shifted
uncomfortably when I saw that I was concerning her. She
couldn't know just how obsessed I already was.

"Elora, that man is evil," she stated acerbically, placing her
hand onto the table between us.

"Why?" My voice was soft. I made sure that I sounded
unperturbed.

"Mason was eighteen years old when his mother, father and
sister were killed," she explained, her eyes haunted as she looked
out the window into the dark forest beyond. I gasped, placing my
hands over my mouth. My poor Mason, his entire family was
dead.

"We don't really know exactly what happened that night. We
only know what Mason and his brother told the police, but the
whole town heard the screams coming from their house and a few
minutes later the entire mansion was up in flames." I noticed
Gran pull her jumper tighter around her.

"Two people emerged from the flames completely covered
in blood – Mason and his brother, Marcus. The two were treated
and taken to the hospital. The entire time, Mason was muttering
nonsense, like he was in a different world." Gran's chin trembled
as she recounted. My eyes widened in fascination; Mason was
just as mad as I was. My heart was pounding as I listened to his
bloodcurdling story.

"The two were questioned about what happened. They told
the police how their father was evil and had been torturing them

their entire lives. It was a shock to us all because their family were so friendly, and their father was the chief of police. We didn't know any more caring and law-abiding people," she described, with a shake of her head like she still couldn't understand how the story could be true.

"Obviously the police were suspicious about the story. So, they began to search the remains of the house. They had managed to save the bulk of the home as the fire brigade had extinguished the flames in time, and what they found in there was the most bone chilling story I had ever heard."

My pupils dilated as anticipation scorched through my veins. Grandma sucked in a deep calming breath and pulled her roseate scarf tighter around her head.

"The children had been kept in cells and were caged against their will, but the worst part was what the police found in the basement. Covering an entire wall was torture devices, and the entire floor and walls were covered in recently spilt blood. When the police tested samples, they couldn't get a direct match because the blood wasn't just from one person, it was a mix of multiple people." Gran grimaced and her tone was solemn. My hands began to quiver and my stomach churned in horror.

Grandma was right, I had never heard anything so horrific. My face reddened in fury and I ground my teeth together to hold in the pure loathing that was ignited by the thought of someone hurting Mason.

"The police were baffled. The blood must have come from somewhere. So, they checked the gardens and dug for any remains. They found hundreds of dead bodies scattered around the entire garden. In that house their father had killed hundreds of people and he got away with it because he was the chief of police. His family knew all about it – they were a part of it. That

53

was their lives," she explained hauntingly. Her eyes kept flickering around the house and towards the windows as if expecting a murderer to emerge.

"How did his parents and sister die?" I asked fervently. Grandma's scared eyes flashed back to me, narrowing, and she stared into mine for a long moment, contemplating.

"Mason said that his sister angered his father and he finally snapped, killing her and their mother. Mason said he managed to pick up a piece of pipe and hit his father over the head, knocking him out and escaped with his brother. He didn't know how the fire started but it was guessed that his father perished in the flames as his body was never found," she explained grimly. My breath caught in the lump in my throat; no wonder Mason was so mentally scarred.

"You would think having been trapped and locked up in that hell for all of that boy's life he would want to leave the house where it all happened. But he hasn't, not for eight years since his parents died. He lives by himself in their mansion up on the hill. We only ever see him leave at night or when he goes to church. Then he disappears from town for months at a time – I have heard that he runs his own security cameras and surveillance company." She shook her head as if disguised by his choices. I calculated the math in my head, that meant Mason was twenty-six years old, five years older than me.

"Everyone stays away from him and from his house," she declared, with warning lacing her tone. She leaned towards me and stared straight into my eyes with her eyebrows pulled together in seriousness.

"That house is haunted. Some nights you can hear screams coming from up the hill and every night the lights are off like there is no one home. People wonder what he does up there all by himself. Some people say that Mason is just like his father and that he is a murderer too."

A shiver ran through me at her words, causing my bones to chill. A small part of me already knew that her accusations were true after I saw him covered in blood. My hands were sweaty when I clutched the table between my fingers.

"Elora, this is why I beg you to see reason. That man doesn't know anything other than blood and death. For eighteen years of his life that was all he knew. How is he supposed to have any moral judgment when he has never seen the normality of the outside world before? In his mind, murdering people on a daily basis is normal. You have to stay away from him or I will fear your life will be in danger," she cautioned with a sombre severity that sent my toes crunching.

"I can take care of myself Grandma." I brushed off her warning with a roll of my eyes. She was scared for me but she didn't know the half of my past. She didn't know that I lived on the streets for months with only one other person for company, my best friend at the time Annalise, and I made it out of that alive. Gran's eyes flashed and her lips pushed together in frustration.

"My sweet child, I don't think anyone can take care of themselves when they are faced with a murderer and if you get yourself drawn into his world your already hard life is going to be overtaken by more darkness," she warned imploringly, her features pessimistic with gloom.

I looked away from her stern gaze; I didn't want her to see my blazed excited eyes and know how far I had already been drawn into that world. And I especially didn't want her to see just how much I liked it, but being in the darkness was where I felt safe, where I felt at home. She didn't realise it but maybe the darkness was exactly what I wanted – maybe it was exactly where

I belonged.

***

The slothful whistles of the birds chirping accompanied me on my walk beside the forest to work the next morning. The luminous rays of sunshine were gleaming through the canopy of trees into my red-rimmed and heavy lidded-eyes. I was unable sleep last night as all I could think about was Mason's story.

When I reached the town rain started pelting down from the caliginous clouds that had descended, shadowing Everbrook with a tenebrous fog. I was hunched under my hoodie trying to avoid the water droplets falling from the sky, so I only looked up from the ground when I felt something boring into my head in my peripheral vision.

As my eyes flickered up, my heart skipped a beat when they landed on Mason. He was standing on the other side of the road watching me intently. His head was tilted to the side in concentration and his hands dug into his leather jacket pockets. Those piercing blue eyes hit me instantaneously sending a deadly fire of sparks searing through my veins.

Mason's dark hair was saturated from the rain and was sticking to his forehead. He looked like a dark angel standing there, filled with evil but so beautiful. As always, he was angry, his jaw locked tightly and his eyebrows were lowered.

My stomach fluttered in excitement from glancing into his eyes and I was overcome with the desire to run to him. My view of him was broken when a truck chugged past.

When the truck drove past, I saw a flash of Mason before a second truck advanced right behind the first, and what I saw there sent my body into a state of stupor. Mason was standing in the

56

same position, but he was dripping with lucent crimson blood and he had his knife dangling from his hands.

He pounced at me with a horrifying look of malevolency on his face. My heart stopped in fear and I gasped with a dry mouth, but just as suddenly as it had arrived, the vision and Mason vanished as the truck flew past.

I stood with shaking limbs for a few moments, breathing in deeply. I knew instantly that I was having a hallucination again. I have had them before – my psychologist said that they are a side effect from my medications. Why would my mind bring that up? Maybe it was warning me, warning me to stay away from him.

I shook my head, and snapped myself out of the horrible thoughts and tried to forget about the vision. Disconcerted and flustered, I ran the rest of the way to work.

The bell on the library door chimed as I entered the building and a gust of heated air hit me as I walked inside. I shivered as the warmness soaked into my skin.

"Good morning, Elora. How are you?" Belle, my boss, greeted me as I walked past her to sit at the front counter.

Belle was the manager of the library. She had straight black hair that fell just below her shoulders and was styled with a front fringe. Her pointy ears stuck out the sides from the confounds of her hair. She was born in Japan and still held a bit of her accent. Due to her patient and peaceful radiance I actually found myself comfortable around her.

"I am well. How are you?" I smiled, picking up the books from the overnight return pile. I expected her to ramble about her family like she normally did in the morning. I didn't mind though because I did love hearing the hilarious stories about her girlfriend and their two adopted children.

"I am exhausted." She ran her hands down her face as she

flopped her head onto the counter. "We had someone break into the library Saturday night. Like, who would want to break into a library? Why not the bank?" she gushed fretfully, throwing her hands up in the air. My eyes widened at her words.

"That's terrible. Did they take anything?" I inquired, my forehead plucking in perturbance. If they took any of my books, I was going to kill them.

"No luckily, I think the alarm scared them off," she reassured, and my worry lines smoothed.

"That's good," I breathed. I glanced away from her apprehensively and that was the end of our conversation.

Belle was just as quiet as me when she was working, so we spent most of our time in the library quietly completing our work. But because we were always in silence, I noticed the never-ending ticking noise that I only heard when Belle was around. She told me once that she had a pacemaker machine built into her heart because she was born with a heart defect. I liked that she wasn't so normal herself, just like me.

The day dragged on, but as closing time approached someone walked through the entrance that I was not expecting. Two police officers marched into the library with stern expressions on their faces as they stalked up to me. My lower lip quivered and beads of sweat broke out on my temple as they neared. Memories bombarded me of police officer's forcefully handcuffing me and arresting me.

"Hi Madam. I am Amanda Jones, The Chief of Police. Can I speak with Belle Lavan?" she asked austerely, staring straight into my eyes. She had a very authoritative persona with dark brown eyes that were narrowed into a sneer like she was suspicious of everyone. My eyes drew towards her large nose that looked too big for her face and bushy eyebrows. She was dressed professionally with light blonde hair pulled back tightly. She was noticeably young for a chief of police.

I wrapped my hands around my waist as my mind went blank and my breathing stopped. Chief Amanda's eyes squinted suspiciously as she watched me, but I didn't care as she had already started to sway in my vision.

"Hi, Chief, I'm here," Belle piped up formally, stepping beside me and placing a reassuring hand on my arm. My shoulders dropped their tension and I smiled at Belle gratefully. Chief Amanda finally moved her snake like eyes away from mine, releasing me.

"We heard that you had a break-in Saturday night and we were wondering if you had any video surveillance of the incident?" the chief queried Belle curtly. Rubbing her eyebrow, Belle gave the chief a tight-lipped smile filled with worry.

"I'm sorry, no." Belle shook her head and the officer's features remained stoic as ever. The chief then pulled out a piece of paper from her pocket and held it out to us.

It was a picture of a boy in a school photograph. I leaned my head closer to gain a better look. The boy was a teenager and had black unkempt hair; his most noticeable feature was a birth mark down one side of his face. I recognised him as the boy that talked to me from the antique store the other day.

"Have any of you seen this boy in the last forty-eight hours?" the male officer questioned us sternly. My eyes flickered to him and saw that he had a stocky build and his ringleted tangerine hair was styled formally.

"No," Belle replied, and I shook my head at them. Both their faces dropped slightly in disappointment and Amanda scowled.

"He was reported missing Saturday night around the same time as the break in here, and we were hoping that you might have seen anything suspicious?" the male officer wondered. My jaw gaped open in shock – he was missing? What could have happened to him?

"Unfortunately, I only heard about the break-in the next morning," Belle explained. The male officer's eyes deflated; they must have been hoping for some sort of lead.

"Well we all know who is guilty, don't we?" interjected an old man with an insinuating tone. We all diverted our gazes towards the man who was lounging in a chair reading the paper. I recognised him instantly, it was Bill the long grey-haired man with a widow's peak who bought my tomatoes. I squinted my eyes at him and rubbed my chin in confusion but everyone else knew what he was talking about.

"I can assure you sir; Mason Blackwell's house was the first place we searched after obtaining a warrant and it was empty. He is exempt from the investigation for now." Amanda assured the man crisply. As soon as Mason's name was spoken my heart surged to life. They thought Mason did this?

Bill grumbled something unintelligible under his breath and returned his attention to the paper.

"Do you mind handing out some posters?" Amanda asked, as she placed a stack of papers onto the front desk.

"Of course." Belle smiled sadly and pinned a poster up onto our notice board, right next to another crumpling poster announcing the date of the town fair. I picked up a poster to see permeating the majority of the poster was a picture of the boy, Ryan.

The photograph appeared to be a high school year photo with a reward at the bottom and a notice that if anyone had any knowledge of his whereabouts to contact the chief of police immediately.

As I regarded the picture it pulled at my heart strings, and reminded me of how happy and innocent he was at the market. I rammed a few copies of the poster into my bag so I could help handing them out.

"Thank you for your time. If you hear of anything suspicious or see this boy, please let us know," Amanda requested, her direct gaze searing into both of us.

"We will," Belle agreed, and held her hand out for each officer to shake. They turned languidly and made their way out of the room with their shoulders slumped in disappointment. As soon as the door closed behind them a weight lifted off my chest.

Belle seemed to notice my distress because she tapped her hand on my shoulder reassuringly.

"Don't worry about Amanda, she has always been the biggest grumpy old sob ever since she started that job a year ago. Don't take her grouchiness personally," she explained with a smile. I nodded back at her gratefully still trying to stabilise my racing heart.

The last hour of work passed entirely too slowly. I continually found myself gazing off into the distance instead of working; I couldn't stop thinking about Mason. I wanted to ask him about all this new information I had found out today. Were everything they said about him and his family true? Did this missing boy have anything to do with that night I saw him covered in blood? But he had said that he wanted me to stay away from him and after drawing on what I had learned in my psychology sessions I arrived at the conclusion that his words meant that he doesn't want me to turn up at his house or watch him sleep.

"Before you leave, do you mind going through the rest of the returns and placing them in alphabetical order?" Belle asked with a warm smile, bringing me out of my thoughts.

"No worries," I agreed, and began my work categorising the books. I had just begun chugging the trolley loaded with books upstairs to the shelves when a chime sounded indicating another book had been returned.

"Wait, there's one more," Belle called as she traipsed over towards the return box and picked up the book. When she glanced down at the book a grin of radiance overtook her features.

"I have been wondering when this would return," she remarked, showing me the front cover. The book was old and tattered like it had been read a hundred times.

"What is it?" I asked curiously.

"Our most popular book." She beamed and widened her hands above her head in theatrics of the great reveal.

"Why?" I pried, stepping up onto my toes to obtain a better look.

"The book was set in this town. The author who wrote it lived in Everbrook. It perfectly details the town so well. Everyone loves to read it." Belle flipped the book over in her hands to read out the blurb. It seemed interesting; it was about a deadly poison machine that was hidden underneath the church.

"Do you mind if I read it?" I queried feathery.

"Of course, I have been waiting for it to return to recommend it to you. I have read it myself a few hundred times," she urged enthusiastically with a laugh. She leaned towards me to whisper from behind her hand. "But it did cause a lot of controversy a few years ago as people tried to determine if there really was a machine hidden underneath the church. Evie, your Grandmother had to deal with that problem." Her eyes were lightened with excitement from the gossip.

"Teenagers used to break into the church in the dead of night.

Your grandma had so many vandalisms that she decided to have the place scoped out professionally to prove to everyone it was only fiction. Only then the break ins stopped," she explained. I found myself smiling as my eagerness mounted – I loved mysteries.

"Well I need to see what all the fuss is about, thank you, Belle." I gave her a small smile that actually reached my eyes.

"You will love it," she promised with a wink.

She was right, I was enchanted by the book; I spent all night reading it. I was so engrossed that my eyes had become red and puffy by the time I passed out mid-sentence. I woke up the next morning and spent all day finishing it.

The book was set during World War One and followed a genius named Henry who created a poison that would slowly kill those who were exposed. Henry targeted the enemies fighting in the war on the front line. Especially targeting those who were already weak and young in an attempt to kill off the enemy soldiers in a rapid and untraceable fashion. Henry and his colleagues travelled to our town for its unique resources, and with them he created a machine that was able to release the poison into the atmosphere in the form of a gas cloud.

The experiment went horribly wrong; once the poison was released on the enemy territory there was no stopping its flight and it eventually started infecting the entire population. This was covered up by the authorities as a virus which is now known as Spanish influenza. After they realised how dangerous the poison was, they locked it away in a vault forever and built the church around the vault.

However, in the desperation that the second world war brewed, they began testing the poison again. They found that at more potent doses, the poison could twist the mind of the person infused into thinking they needed to kill everyone around them and then that person would die. The English started using this to infiltrate rival organisations successfully and they wanted to distribute it into enemy territory.

They needed the poison to be administered in the gas cloud form so it could be distributed to mass populations and enemy armies but the cloud form held many flaws. The operation was shut down as they were not able to contain the cloud to just enemy territory once it was released. It would have spread and poisoned the entire world until the cloud dissolved naturally.

I was enthralled by the book's realism and the thought of someone actually building such a machine in those times. It reminded me of my previous interest in Biomedical Physics and I became absorbed in researching the physics behind it all.

I made a mental note to thank Belle for the recommendation, and the best part of it was that I was so absorbed in the story that I had no time to think about Mason. But that was all going to end very soon.

Chapter 6

I lasted another day without him, but it was a tough twenty-four hours; whenever I allowed my mind to wonder the thoughts and dreams of Mason would slip into my consciousness. I tried to focus on my renewed interest in physics and DNA structure since reading *Everbrook's secret*. The distraction didn't last long though as the longer I was away from Mason, the harder it became to think about anything other than how I was going to see him again.

I worked hard to push him out of my mind that afternoon as I was due for my session with Dianne. The one-hour session passed slowly; Dianne asked me how I had been since I last saw her. I didn't dare bring up Mason and my possible new obsession.

Evening had already fallen when I left the clinic casting the city into a darkened hue. The gloomy atmosphere was enhanced by the dark storm clouds that had emerged. The thickening onxy clouds gave the ominous impression that a storm was imminent and I hurried my steps towards the bus stop to avoid the downpour.

The entire trip back to town the gushing rain hurled against the windows and the howling wind whisked stray tree branches onto the roof of the bus. On the journey I was lost in my thoughts and fantasies about Mason. As we chugged closer to town, I decided I was going to walk past his mansion on my way home. I desperately wanted to ask him about all the information I had discovered and I couldn't keep fighting my curiosity any longer.

The bus doors clunked and squealed open when we arrived back into the town square. As I stepped out into the darkened street, my attention was caught when I saw someone turn a corner onto the road that led up to the church. Someone that had the same stature and dark hair as Mason.

My eyes widened and my heart started beating erratically from the possibility that Mason could be here. I didn't even need to seek him out, he had already found me. I couldn't help it; the compulsion was too overpowering. I followed him, my feet hammering against the pavement as I ran to catch up to him. As I rounded the corner my shoulders dropped when there was no sign of him. Rain started pouring from the sky and I slowed down to huddle under my hoodie. I wasn't giving up my search for him and trudged up the road towards the church; the cobblestones under my boots crunched in the rainfall.

A crash of thunder resounded through the empyrean followed by a lightning flash that lit up the town scintillatingly. I groaned, tucking my coat tighter around my body as I turned the corner into the winding dark street that lead up the hill to the church. He must have gone this way. I rushed forwards along the small buildings that lined the street, stray rocks catching under my shoes as I hurried along.

Suddenly, out of nowhere a haunting scream pierced through the crisp air of the hibernated night. My body froze mid-step as ice slid down my back. I circled my head cautiously towards the source of the scream. It originated from down a dark alleyway between two abandoned deteriorating buildings. Could that be Mason?

The feeling of knowing something wasn't right gnawed at me and I knew I had to investigate. My curiosity bit at me and I peered down the dark alleyway before taking a few steps forward with shaking limbs.

"No." I heard a man scream in agony and my stomach twisted anxiously. I crept towards the commotion warily with accelerating breaths. When I finally reached the end of the alleyway, I cautiously peeked my head around the corner. What I saw there nearly sent me crumbling to the ground from the horror that paralysed me.

A man was pressed up against the building's wall by his throat and had blood dripping down his face which splattered onto his ripped shirt. I saw gashes in his arms like chunks of his flesh had been cut out and his wrist was bent at an unnatural angle, no doubt broken.

A flash of lightning sparked in the sky to reveal that the man's expression was a grimace of torment as the blood gushed out of the cuts spanning over his body. There was a dark silhouette of another man that towered over him and held a knife up to the man's throat. Blood began trickling down the man's neck as the knife pierced his skin.

He was being tortured. This wasn't just some mugging; this was something more sinister. The man torturing him swivelled his head towards me just as another lightning flash struck and those dark features became illuminated. Instantly a thrill passed straight through me to the centre of my bones.

The torturer was Mason.

I slammed my hand over my mouth to prevent any noise from emitting and expeditiously lunged back behind the wall. My mind began reeling as I gasped into my hands. Just when I thought Mason couldn't get any more terrifying, I find him torturing someone.

"Are you going to talk or am I going to have to really start

67

torturing you?" Mason threatened in a belligerent hostile tone. His voice sounded different; it was deeper emanating his malevolence. There was ear-splitting silence for an awfully long moment and I held my breath in heart-stopping anxiety.

I heard a punch as knuckles crunched into bone and a resounding painful screech. I cringed into the wall further, squeezing my eyes together as I heard the sickening snap of a bone breaking.

"Okay, okay," the other man conceited, shouting out frantically in blind panic. Cautiously, I peeked my head back around the corner again to see Mason's knife situated inside the skin of the man's upper arm as if Mason had just lacerated his flesh.

I flickered my wide eyes back up to Mason who now had a smirk on his face; he was enjoying watching this man in pain. Mason yanked out the knife from the man's arm and he screamed out, baring his teeth as his face contorted in torment.

"Why did you send this?" Mason demanded; his profound fury was evident in his choleric expression. Mason pulled out a piece of paper from his pocket and wound his other hand around the man's throat. The blood that had stained Mason's hands smeared onto the white piece of paper. The man glanced down at the paper with bulging panic filled eyes, blinking rapidly.

"Marlemore made me. If I tell you any more, he will kill me," the man answered, gritting his teeth and managing to splutter the words between deep painful breaths through Mason's fingers. The man's features were languid from weakness and his face was distorted into an ashen shade. Recognition flashed in Mason's eyes; he must have heard the name before. But I hadn't, who was Marlemore?

"He is the least of your fears tonight. Who is he?" Mason

barked callously, and precipitously he slammed the man into the wall by the shoulders as if to emphasise his words. A shiver ran through me and I knew it was for only one reason, the thought of how attractive this powerful and authoritarian side of Mason was.

"He is someone that even I'm afraid of. You should do as he says," the man warned hauntingly. Mason's features remained vacant, unperturbed by the sinister threat.

"What does he want from me?" Mason demanded. The man sneered up at Mason with a spark of defiance on his features.

"Your secret." The man smirked with blood dripping out his mouth as he spoke. His dared to look Mason right in the eye with a quirk of his eyebrow. My own interest was spiked and I strained my ears to hear more, what secret?

Mason's face drained of colour and his jaw dropped open, in fear or shock I wouldn't know. As the shock wore off Mason's expression it turned lethal; his eyes manifested into snake like slits.

"How does he know so much about me?" Mason bit back in a desperate frenzy for information.

The man remained silent, pressing his lips together tightly with defiance set on his features. Mason plunged the knife straight through the man's shoulder socket. Blood and gore spilt out from it along with a bellow of pain. The sound of agony echoed throughout the entire alleyway causing me gasp out in horror.

Unexpectedly, so fast I wasn't expecting it, Mason's face snapped straight towards mine. My stomach jumped into my throat as panic rushed through me like a blazing fire and I yanked my head back behind the wall. My lungs were heaving so fast the streams of raindrops that were once clearly evident in the yellowing street light in the distance became nothing more than a blur. I closed my eyes tightly to relieve some of the panic, but I knew I was too late. Mason saw me.

I opened my eyes and what I saw there caused me to flinch back in terror. Mason's dark figure was towering over me, his piercing eyes set into a menacing glower that was directed straight at me. A lightning strike brightened the caliginous sky and irradiated onto his face revealing his dark features. They were set in a glare so rage filled that for the first time since knowing Mason I feared for my life. Before I could react Mason jumped towards me and wrapped a strong arm around my waist, using it to spin me around and pull me back into his chest.

A sharp knife was placed against my throat and Mason applied pressure causing my skin to splinter under its unyielding force.

"Got you," Mason growled into my ear with a menacing dark voice that sent a shiver down my spine along with a dark thrill straight to the heart of my being. I gasped against the knife that was piercing my throat.

Mason was going to kill me. I had walked straight into my own death. If I hadn't followed Mason, then maybe he wouldn't have found me here and had the urge to kill me.

"I'm sorry," I apologised quietly, with earnest sincerity. If I hadn't been so stupid, if I had headed his warnings this wouldn't have happened. I closed my eyes and waited for the inevitable.

The knife paused, and then was suddenly released from my neck. I exhaled a deep sigh of relief as I opened my eyes.

Mason grabbed me around the shoulders, turning me around and placed the knife back at my throat again. I craned my neck away from the lethal blade as he pushed me against the wall, so we became immersed in an argent ray of a street light. My back slammed against the wall with a thud as the air was blown out of my lungs.

Mason's dark features became illuminated by the shadowed penumbral light that shone around his head. It was only then that the light hit my features and he finally saw my face. Immediately, his tight grip on my shoulder slackened; his knife dropped and his nails dug out from my skin as he released me. He stepped back as recognition flashed in his eyes and realisation took over his features. His mouth fell open and he gaped at me with wide shock filled eyes for a long calculating moment.

I realised from his shocked expression that he hadn't been trying to kill me – he thought I was someone else. But who? Who else was he expecting to be here?

"Elora," he growled darkly. In a flicker his eyes darkened as he glared at me and his strong jaw clenched cholerically as he ground his teeth together. He stalked a menacing step towards me. I instinctively moved to stumble a step away from him, but I was already anchored against the wall.

Mason's lethal face was right in front of mine, and his piercing eyes set into a glower that was directed straight at me. His menacing glare sent a deadly fire of sparks searing through my veins. The fear he evoked in me wouldn't deter me though; I couldn't take my eyes off him – he was so beautiful. His dark brown hair curled over the side of his face framing his stunning blue eyes. Everything about him made me want to go closer to him, not further away.

Mason stood rigid in front of me with his chest heaving up and down in deep breaths in an attempt to contain his boiling fury. The blood of the man he had just been torturing had smeared and scattered all over his clothing in gruesome trails. Some of the sanguine liquid had splattered over his face making his glare lethal.

My eyes skittered down to see his knife hanging at the end of his grip, dangling like a pendulum. His eyes were wide and I detected a wild spark in them like he was on fire and loving every second of it.

The sight of him in this dark state caused my stomach to squeeze in fear but also my heart to pump faster in excitement. Mason took another step towards me so he his chest brushed against mine and my breath hitched in reaction.

"Elora," Mason seethed in a menacing but alluring tone that sent an enticing shiver down my spine. I clenched my hands into fists at my side to contain my shaking limbs. My eyes were locked onto his which had sunken into his face, exasperating the dark bags that hung under his eyes. He leaned into me and I was trapped against the wall from his advance like a deer stuck in a car's headlights.

But the strangest thing about my reaction was that as much as I had the instinctual reaction to run away from this man that might hurt me, I also wanted to stay with him. I wanted to be closer to him and that desire was so much stronger now because I hadn't seen him for so long. Anything was worth being with him, even my death.

"Do you have a death wish?" Mason pronounced each word separately as he seethed them between clenched teeth. The fact that I'm here right now proved that I would rather him murder me than stay away from him.

"In one sense of the word," I muttered evasively. His eyes flashed and he raised his hand holding the knife. For a moment my body froze in fright, and a hot flush of pure panic shot through me. But then Mason carefully placed the bloody knife into his jacket pocket and not towards my neck. His manic eyes flashed up to mine and my heart pounded in my rib cage like it never had before. I stared back mesmerised as his gaze held mine in an impenetrable lock. Rain had pooled on his eyelashes, making them look longer and darker over his bright blue eyes.

"Have you been following me?" he accused bellicosely. I didn't move a muscle as Mason placed his hands on the wall beside either side of my face. My eyes flickered over his features, taking him all in and every feeling that he was able to evoke within me.

When I didn't respond he took one hand off the wall and flexed his fingers like he was releasing his anger. He lowered that hand towards my shoulder and placed one finger onto my skin. A sudden burst of heat rushed through me from the contact.

He pushed his finger down my arm smearing the blood that had tainted his fingers onto my skin until he reached my elbow. I cringed back in disgust from the unknown blood that now tainted my skin, but goose bumps also broke out on my skin from the thrill of his touch.

Mason's lip lifted up at the corner into a satisfied smirk – he was enjoying inflicting this mental torment on me. My hands balled into fists at my side from the degrading way he was treating me.

I yanked his bloody hand off me and his arm fell away from mine with a snap. His eyes followed my arm and when he looked up at me his features turned lethal.

"Did you not listen to my warning once again?" he barbed, and his words cut me deep. He thought I hadn't been staying away from him. I straightened my spine in defiance; I did exactly as he asked until I saw him. He needed to know this. He couldn't hate me.

"No," I objected in desperation. "I had been staying away from you. I just thought I saw you and then I heard a scream." I was shouting in outrage at his accusation.

Mason skewed his face to the side causing his rain-soaked dark hair to fall over his eyes as he observed me intently. I twisted my fingers into the material of my jumper to curb the anxiety that was threatening to break apart my chest. Would he kill me here and now?

His expression remained impassive, but he inched his face closer to mine. My breath hitched but I didn't move a muscle. Inch by inch he moved his face closer to my own and all I could do was stand there and watch him. I felt his breath feather my cheek as he touched his lips to my skin so softly it could have been mistaken for his breath. His close proximity made the truth spill out of my mouth.

"But then I saw it really was you and I wanted to stay here with you," I burst breathlessly. I felt the smile on his mouth as he pressed his lips more forcefully to my cheek and my breathing stopped. Feelings were rushing through me like tidal waves and I didn't want it to ever stop.

"You shouldn't ever want to be around me, soon you will be running away screaming," he warned darkly moving his haunting, mysterious eyes to mine. His tone had turned ominous but held a huskiness like he was breathless too.

Mason moved his lips towards my jaw line and as he did so his eyes held a mischievously dark glint. A smirk graced his mouth before he pressed his lips to the top of my jaw and flutters swarmed my stomach. The rough skin of his cheek brushed mine and made goosebumps rise on my entire body.

He ran his lips softly down my skin until he was halfway down my throat. I felt his touch all the way in my toes. My heart was hammering faster than it ever had before. His movements halted right where he had placed the knife to my throat earlier and now had a small red cut there. I wasn't sure what he was going to do next, kill me or kiss me?

After a long moment, he peeled away from me with a deep breath of resignation.

"This is the place where the monsters come out to play," he declared perilously and then pulled away from me completely. The warmth of his body vanished and cold air hit me like a cold bucket of water was thrown over my head.

Mason relaxed his threatening stance and the rigid cords in his neck dissipated as his features fell into a soft expression. That wild gleam in his eyes faded and all his anger disappeared as if I had flicked a switch. He took a step away from me and my tensed body fell back into the wall behind me in relief.

Mason opened his mouth to say something but suddenly snapped it closed as his eyes widened and urgency gripped his features. I had no time to comprehend the change in his demeanour before he leapt at me. He pushed his whole body into mine, squeezing me into the wall and placed his hand over my mouth.

Instinctively I inhaled air to scream and Mason clutched my mouth tighter and prevented me from making any noise. I felt the sticky blood that was lining his hands smear all over my cheek causing horror to sink into my bones. I flickered my eyes up to Mason in bewilderment asking for answers with them.

"Shh," he whispered exigently leaning his mouth into my ear, and his eyes darted around the corner as if expecting danger. I pressed my lips together and trusted him. The only noise intelligible was the sound of the rain droplets colliding with the pavement as we stayed frozen against each other.

Then I heard the voice.

Chapter 7

"Mason I'm waiting for you." The man's voice originated from around the corner, in a tauntingly winey tone. It was the man Mason was torturing.

"What are you hiding behind there?"

Mason's eyes darted to mine immediately, and they had something intense in them as he looked at me with his pupils dilated. Was it fear?

That thought caused my heart rate to skyrocket and I stared wide eyed back at Mason with a new distress in my eyes. Mason's eyelids fluttered and he glanced back at me softly in reassurance.

Materialising out the shadows sauntered the man. The sight of him made the hair on the back of my neck rise as horror sunk into my every pore. He had blood dripping down his face, arms, torso and from nearly every laceration that Mason had cut into his body. But the strangest thing was he didn't appear at all phased by the pain.

I pushed myself closer into Mason whose own body had tensed up. Mason spun around to face the man, hiding me behind his back. The tortured man's eyes zoned in on me and I watched in disgust as his lips curved into a satisfied smile.

"Look what pretty thing you have here," the man gibed in a condescending tone.

"Our work is done here, Kenneth. Leave now before I finish what I started," Mason threatened, his dark eyebrows lowering in warning, but Kenneth didn't move, all he did was lick his lips and keep his sparkling eyes locked on me.

"What changed your mind? Her?" Kenneth questioned, provoking Mason further. I stumbled a shaky step closer to Mason, leaving the shadows.

"Leave," Mason demanded ferociously and pushed Kenneth in the chest with so much force he staggered to the ground. Mason lurched a step back and grabbed my upper arm tightly in an iron lock. He tucked me into his side protectively. My heart screamed viciously from Mason's actions. He was protecting me.

"But I want her," Kenneth taunted in defiance as he jumped up again, his eager eyes not leaving me. I shrunk back from him in disgust curling my body closer to Mason's. But just as I did Kenneth's sneering face locked with mine as he leaped at me. He grabbed onto my arm and his grubby, sweat tainted nails sunk into my skin.

The feeling of such a nauseating and unwanted touch caused my vision to become blurry and panic to cloud my mind. Without thinking, I pushed him off me and lunged forward closer to safety, wrapping both my hands around Mason's waist. Mason became rigid but he didn't move out of my hold which made my heart soar even further. After a long unsure moment, he softly placed his arms around my back. His movements were hesitant like he didn't know what he was doing, like he had never been hugged before.

I dug my head into his neck and it calmed my breathing as I felt the fast beating of his heart within the vein in his neck against my cheek. Suddenly he tightened his hold around me and squeezed me to him. The panic and fear constricting my throat slowly decreased until it was non-existent. I didn't want to let go. I didn't ever want to let go of Mason.

I heard Kenneth growl and stand up behind me but my heart

rate remained steady now, I was with Mason. I honestly didn't know why I felt safe in Mason's arms when he himself had held a knife to my throat multiple times.

But Mason reacted to Kenneth and moved out of my touch to step forwards and punch Kenneth in the face with omnipotent force. Kenneth tumbled to the ground but not a moment passed before the gleaming whites of his eyes snapped back up to Mason.

"Get out of my way, Mason," Kenneth threatened from the floor; his previous smirk had been wiped off his face.

"No," Mason barked with finality as he stalked up to Kenneth. I watched Mason reach into his jacket pocket and pull out a gun, pointing the barrel right between Kenneth's eyes.

Kenneth didn't flinch, he just smiled wickedly revealing a loose tooth dripping with blood. Unexpectedly, Kenneth jumped to his feet and he punched Mason straight in the jaw with all his strength. Mason's head wrenched back from the powerful force, his dark hair flying out of his face.

A terrified noise left my mouth from watching him hurt my Mason. Blood dripped from Mason's lip and with his head still facing the ground, he flickered his burning with rage eyes back up to Kenneth.

But before Mason could react Kenneth's twisted gaze settled on me and he reached into his pocket, clasping something in his grip. He surged his hand back and threw something shiny straight towards my heart. A knife.

My vision wheeled into slow motion as I watched helplessly with frozen eyes as the knife streamed through the air. But just as the knife was a centimetre away from my heart an arm appeared in front of me catching the hilt of the knife in its bare hand.

Mason had moved over to me like lightning and had caught

the knife in his hands with expert skill. My eyes slid up to his and with a jolt through my blood I released that his stare was not in the direction of where the knife was thrown but rather at me. He had caught it without even looking. His blue eyes pierced into mine and something deep passed between us.

The moment was broken by Kenneth when we heard his feet slam into the puddles in the road. We both snapped our heads towards the noise to see him running away from us and down the alleyway at full speed.

Mason swore aggressively and swivelled to face me with urgency lining his features.

"Elora, get out of here. Take a taxi, don't walk home," he ordered as he reached his hand out to me, offering me his gun. My eye twitched as my stomach lurched and I glanced down at the gun uncertainly, twirling my hands together.

"Take this. If anyone tries to hurt you, shoot them." Mason's gripping eyes were laced with warning. I frowned down at the gun and even though it pained me to do so – I did as he asked.

"Please get to safety," he reiterated, almost in a beg. He urgently grabbed my shoulders between his hands. The warmth of his touch caused my nerves to calm enough to think clearly.

"Yes," I agreed breathy, the dry sound barely slipping past my lips. With one last languishing gaze Mason left me and ran after Kenneth. I stood immobile with my hands hanging by my side listening to the splash of Mason's footsteps until they dissipated into nothing but the splatter of rain hitting the building's tin roof.

A droplet of rain dripped from my hair and down the back of my spine, shocking me out of my stupor. With jerky movements I spun around and rounded back towards the town, running towards safety.

All of a sudden, my body was slammed back into the wall behind me with a deadly force that caused me to cry out. A figure appeared out of the sky, jumping from the roof above and wrapped its hands around my neck. I opened my mouth to scream but a hand was placed over lips, muffling my voice.

"Mason's biggest weakness is that he is too smart, it just makes him so easily deceivable," the voice of a snake muttered in my ear, and I felt the wind of the revolting remittance of his breath slide past my skin. My muscles seized up as I cringed against the iron lock of the person holding me hostage. My attacker leaned their head closer to mine, withdrawing from the darkness of the shadows to reveal Kenneth's slovenly features.

"Mason!" I screamed frantically into the night sky and thrashed against Kenneth's hold.

"He can't hear you. He is too busy chasing after someone else he thinks is me." He laughed wickedly, and I hung my head in defeat.

"It's just you and me." He grinned, illuminating a missing tooth along with blood gushing out of his gums.

He was right, I was on my own and I needed to protect myself. I steeled my mind from the agony threatening to spill out as I recruited my previously learnt self-defence knowledge.

I snatched my elbow out from behind my back and rammed it into his jugular vein in his neck which caused his tight grip on my neck to slacken. This allowed me to release my knee from the restriction of his body and I kicked him as hard as I could. He yelled out, hunching over and I utilised the opportunity to make my escape.

I tore frantically down the dark alleyway, but I wasn't quick enough to out-sprint his gun. A shot fired from behind me, rattling through the quiet night and skimmed through the skin of my leg. I lost my balance and crashed to the floor.

I wrapped my hand around my leg to find it bleeding but was relieved to see it was only a graze. I glowered up at Kenneth as he strutted up towards me and grabbed me around the throat. He slammed my head into the wall by the neck and I choked against his hold.

"You are going to pay for that," he threatened heinously.

"What do you want from me?" I demanded, with my chin high. He wasn't going to see me crumble. His warped mouth turned up at the corners in satisfaction like he was happy I asked that.

"I wanted to see why Mason has such an interest in you. He saved your life back there. And Mason doesn't save lives, he ends them," he declared, and his words made my stomach twirl with happiness at the mention of Mason's protection.

However, this also ignited my resolve; this disgusting excuse for a human would not get the better of me. I drew out the gun I still had stashed in my jacket pocket and aimed it directly at Kenneth's forehead, touching his skin. His eyes narrowed, but he didn't flinch.

"Your hands are shaking, you don't have the guts," he taunted satirically and I pushed the gun harder into his skin. But he was right, my hands and even my knees were quivering violently and the thought of even pulling the trigger caused my mind to black out like it was repressing terrifying memories.

Before I even had time to think through my next move, Kenneth slammed his hand into my elbow and snatched the gun right out of my hands. He took it from me easily due to my distraction and in the next moment, he had the barrel of the gun facing between my eyes.

"Too late." He grinned darkly, laughing villainously. I was

left completely vulnerable as my jaw chattered in fright. I cringed away and my upper lip curled up in disgust. But he still leaned his face that dripped with blood even closer to mine, moving out of the penumbral light.

From his close proximity it was the first time I had a clear view of his facial features, and what I saw there caused my jaw to drop; I recognised his ringleted tangerine hair.

"I know you," I shouted at him accusingly. His face jerked back and lost that playful gleam, and his eyes narrowed as he lowered the gun from my head.

"You're the officer that came into the library, you work for the police?" I realised with outrage. He just glared at me before he staggered a step away from me.

"Yes," he admitted solemnly, shaking his head as if he was greatly disappointed.

"You're a police officer, why are you trying to hurt me?" I stated in barbarism. His face remained impassive, but a satisfactory gleam entered his eyes. "Why is Mason trying to kill you?" I yelled louder in confusion, blinking repeatedly at the corruption of it all.

"Because I delivered a message to him," he finally divulged.

"Saying what?" I demanded crisply.

"What is the only excitement happening in your pathetic town lately?" Kenneth revealed darkly with a smirk. I wracked my brains to think back to my life outside of tonight.

"That missing boy, Ryan," I gasped, "But how does Mason have anything to do with Ryan?"

Kenneth laughed wickedly and didn't answer my question. My chest tightened up and I became ready to smash his head into the wall.

"Did Marlemore kidnap Ryan?" I commanded, frenzied. If

there was any chance of Ryan still being alive then I needed to find out.

"Let's just say, the person who kidnapped the boy. Their name starts with an M," he revealed with his crazed grin. I didn't understand who he could mean but if he was working for Marlemore then he might know where Ryan was.

"Where is Ryan?" I reached forward squeezing his neck between both of my hands. I pushed at his neck with all my strength, but he still had that wicked smirk on his face. I wasn't even hurting him at all.

He laughed, and in less than a flash he detached my hands from around his neck and slammed my head back into the wall behind me, turning my vision hazy.

"Stupid girl, why did you have to recognise me? Why did you have to ruin all the fun?" he groaned in annoyance and then smiled ghastly, making blood drip out of his mouth.

"Now I'm going to have to kill you," he promised, his dark macabre tone revealing the pure evil inside of him and what he had planned for me. "Really," he whispered, as he tilted his devilish face towards mine. "Really," he repeated, and my heart stopped from the panic-taking root inside my lungs. "Slowly," he breathed into my skin.

Using all the build-up terror streaming through my veins, I screamed as loud as I could, although it was soon muffled when Kenneth grasped my neck into his hands. But before he even had time to add pressure, we heard a voice from behind us.

"You shouldn't have threatened her," growled a furious voice that sent relief washing straight into my heart. I had never heard anything so mellifluous. Mason.

His dark figure appeared behind Kenneth and instantly I heard the squelch of flesh being cut. I gaped back up at Kenneth as his complexion sapped into a pallid hue, as all the blood left his cheeks and he hunched forward clutching his chest. His eyes were wide and crazed in disbelief as blood started trickling out of the side of his mouth. I looked down to see blood seeming from his stomach.

Mason had stabbed him in the stomach from behind. My gaze flicked back up to Mason to see that his eyes had twisted darkly and became hooded as he killed Kenneth. His eyes connected with mine and a fierce jolt of fire passed through me as I looked into his eyes as he murdered.

Mason yanked the knife out of Kenneth's back and my eyes zoned in on the silver flash of the knife covered in crimson blood. A small gasp left my lips as I watched Kenneth fall to the floor and his blood pooled around him on the ground. He soundlessly died.

"Leave now," Mason ordered dangerously and I jumped. I lifted my glazed over eyes up to him to see the deadly serious expression on his face. My heart was trying to break free in my chest and push me towards him as I gazed at Mason, at a murderer.

I knew I should be feeling some sort of fear or terror but the most messed up thing was that all I felt for him in that moment was a deep attraction. My skin was itching to be ignited by the darkness that tainted his soul.

But he didn't seem to feel the same way.

"Go!" he yelled again and this time I knew he was serious. With one last longing glance at his beautiful face, I gathered my composure and sprinted out of the alleyway.

I jogged up towards the closest taxi I could find and the entire drive home I was a shaking in the back seat. The anxiety that was churning my stomach made it the longest car ride of my life. When I arrived home, I walked into the cottage in a daze to find that Gran was already asleep so I snuck through the dark house and into my room quietly. I stood there shivering for a long time when the reality of the situation finally came crashing down on me.

Panic seeped its way into my heart as I remembered the way Kenneth's lifeless body sunk to the floor, dead. I just watched someone be murdered by the very man that I wanted with all my heart. Mason killed that man without a moment's hesitation and he knew exactly what he was doing.

Mason was a murderer.

Chapter 8

The whine of a door creaking pulled me from a deep sleep. It processed in my unconscious mind that there was something not right about that sound. Instantly alert, I waited stiffly listening to the sounds in my room, only hearing the soft willow of the wind through my curtains from the open window.

From that thought my breathing accelerated and beads of sweat broke out on my forehead. I had left that window closed. With fright paralysing my muscles I snapped my eyes open and what I saw there sent my heart jumping out of my skin in pure horror.

At the end of my bed stood the shadow of a figure glaring down at me. Glistening in the light that spilled through my window shimmered a silver knife that hung from the end of the grip of the figure's silhouetted hand. The figure's black clothes were dappled with red gruesome splatters of blood.

In that horrifying moment, the lightning that still raged in the sky struck and coruscated through my entire room blindingly for a second. The luminous light revealed the identity of the man standing before me.

It was the dark sinister glare of his blue eyes that I noticed first, causing my heart to stutter. The pure hatred that radiated from them set my very soul on edge. His untamed dark hair splattered down the side of his face and over his eyes making him look crazed.

Mason. The murderer.

Blinking rapidly in blind horror I launched myself away from him, hitting my back onto the bed head. What was Mason doing in my bedroom with a knife? The obvious answer to that question hit me like a battering ram.

"Are you going to kill me?" I questioned lifelessly as I courageously lifted my eyes up to his. My blood pounded when I saw he was already staring straight at me intently, fixatedly. His eyes flashed in surprise as if my statement shocked him.

His eyebrows knitted together and his jaw clenched. He stalked a step closer to me as another lightning bolt luminated the midnight sky. He was like the devil at the end of my bed, haunting my nightmares. I pressed my lips together to not let him see my quivering lips and the fear he had caused within me.

"That's what I came here for," he admitted solemnly, finally looking away from me. He closed his eyes tightly and squeezed them shut like he was in tremendous pain. I began to reach for him when suddenly his eyes burst open and zoned in on me with a frightening intensity.

"I want to kill you," he revealed with acerbic honesty; I saw that truth shine in his irises. He wanted to kill me. I grimaced as the fragile shards that made up my heart slowly started to crack and crumble. The pain of his words cut me deep but instead of feeling sad, my fists clenched as flames started to burn up my veins in anger.

I was sick of his games. I was sick of being on the receiving end of his hate. If he wanted me dead, then he had the perfect opportunity to kill me right now. I chucked my bed sheets to the side and leapt off my bed, so I was face to face with a shocked Mason. His lips had turned down at the corners, but his eyes were wide.

"Well then get it over with," I challenged leaning my nose

closer to his in frustration. Mason's eyes narrowed and my body jolted as I was suddenly pushed back against the wall behind me. My back hit the wall with a thud, followed by the cold sting of metal being placed against my neck.

My heart rate palpated and increased as my body rushed with fear induced hormones. Mason's eyes trailed up from my neck to look me straight in the eye as he applied more pressure on his knife to my vulnerable skin.

My lungs heaved up forcefully causing my chest to brush up against his. I strained my neck to lean myself as far away from the knife as possible as I glared down at it, but it was no use.

The knife broke the skin and I ground my teeth together to restrain a yelp of pain. My blood dripped down my neck and slid down the knife. I stared deeply into Mason's eyes in defiance and held my head high as he cut the knife into my breakable flesh.

I could stop Mason by applying some self-defence moves I had learned before I went to jail. It would be so tremendously easy to force him onto the floor when he was this distracted. But I just didn't care any more; I wanted to know for sure if Mason was capable of killing me.

I glared back into Mason's eyes in challenge, which were looking straight back into mine with a similar intensity. Mason's blue eyes were blazing with darkness as we stared each other down. Half of his features were shadowed, unreachable by the outside light and his dark hair had fallen loose from its usual curl, and partially fell over his eye.

Abruptly, his cold stare softened and his pupils un-dilated, so he was just gazing into my eyes tenderly. My breath hitched from the way he was looking at me so softly while he held a knife to my throat. Unexpectedly, the cold edge of the knife left my skin and my body was released. My knees wobbled and body sagged back into the wall forcefully for support.

"I can't." His voice was soft and his expression became agonised. I gasped for breath and touched my bleeding neck; it stung when my fingers grazed the cut in my skin. I looked at my hand to see blood coated on my fingers and through the webs of my hands. It was then that I noticed my hands were shaking violently.

Mason had his back to me as he faced the other side of the room. His head was bowed but I saw in the mirror that he was staring down at the blood-soaked knife in his hands.

"Why can't you?" I asked, and my voice croaked with emotion.

"I don't know," he answered in a whisper, so low I almost couldn't hear it.

"Why do you want to kill me?" I demanded more assertively, stomping my foot. Finally, Mason gradually turned his head around to face me and when I saw his features it almost sent me to my knees in shock. His whole face was riddled with guilt, his eyes were haunted with it. He heard my shocked gasp and turned his eyes away from mine, his jaw clenching.

"You know what I do, you saw me kill that man. You know too much about me and if you tell anyone there will be dire consequences," he admitted solemnly, his gaze directed downwards.

The tight coiled wire in my stomach unreeled as all my anger diminished from his admittance. The only reason he wanted to kill me was because of what I knew, not because he hated me. I exhaled a deep breath as relief rushed through me.

"You think I'm going to tell the police that you murdered someone?" I asked gently, shyly.

"Yes." He lifted his tense eyes to me, showing me the

vulnerability in them.

"I won't, I promise," I instantly assured him.

His eyebrows scrunched together in confusion as he stared at me in disbelief, but his eyes were alight with a spark of hope. He dropped the knife out of his hands and it hit the floor with a resounding clang.

I gazed at it mesmerised as it marginally bounced back up into the air again sending my blood flicking off the knife. When it stabilised, I moved my eyes back up to see that Mason had sat down on the edge of my bed. His back was hunched forwards as he looked down at his hands which were resting on his thighs.

"You can trust me," I ensured tenderly as I placed myself down next to him on the bed. His dark hair fell over his cheeks with his head bowed like that and I watched his jaw muscles contract and relax. His lips were pressed together; his expression was almost mournful. "I would do anything for you."

His head was still lowered dolefully but I noticed the slight dip of his eyelids when I said that. I had expected him to be horrified by my admittance but when he did turn to me his hair fell towards his ears revealing his features which were completely veiled. I wasn't prepared for when our eyes locked at such a close distance and my mouth gaped slightly from being so close to him.

"You're the strangest girl I have ever met," he declared flatly, looking at me impassively out of the corner of his eye. But I did notice the humour in his tone. He was running his hand down his black jeans repeatedly like he was digging his thumbnail into his skin.

"You're not so normal yourself." I teased back as I smiled up at him with doe eyes.

"Thanks." He graced me with his own closed-mouthed

smile, showing me his long dimple on one side of his mouth and crow's feet around his eyes. I didn't know why but I found his comment extremely amusing. I laughed loudly and my giggles didn't subside for a long time.

I started to worry that he might think I was crazy. But out of my peripheral vision, I noticed him looking at me with a strange expression on his face. His eyes were gentle and his tight jaw had relaxed into a small smile. His look sent butterflies straight into the pit of my stomach. That sobered me up and when I faced him, he was gazing at me with agonised eyes.

I searched his beautiful face completely mesmerised like he was the rising sun that I hadn't seen in a century. I noticed that he had a black bruise forming underneath his skin from where Kenneth had punched him and dark circles framed his light blue eyes.

My eyes landed on a cut on his cheek and the blood that was dripping from it. From the sight of Mason being hurt, I started to feel the butterflies climb up my oesophagus and bile rose in the back of my throat. Without a word I stood up and rushed out of the room as quickly as I could.

"Elora?" I heard Mason's frantic whisper from inside my room. Ignoring him, I quickly grabbed our first aid kit and a towel. I dampened the towel under the tap and headed back into my room.

Mason had remained sitting in the same position as I had left him in a brooding posture. Just at the sight of him still there in my bedroom caused my breathing rate to increase another octave. His beauty would never cease to amaze me, even when he was covered from head to toe in multiple people's blood, including my own. He was staring at me with confusion etched onto his features and his hands were fisted into my bed sheets.

"What was that all about?" He inquired fretfully.

"I got you some first aid supplies." I lifted up the box as evidence.

"I have had worse cuts than these in my time." He brushed it off with a flick of his hand. There was no way he was going to tend to those wounds himself.

"I will do it then." I plopped myself down on the bed next to him and in my haste, I sat so close to him that we were touching thighs. Immediately I felt the warmth of his leg soak into mine. A shudder of an alluring heat washed through me from the contact.

The best part about the small contact was that Mason didn't move away like I expected him too. My heart started to accelerate from being so close to him. I tried to ignore it though and with sweaty hands I placed the first aid kit onto my lap and opened the lid.

I pulled out the small towel and lifted it up to Mason's face to wash away the blood, but he suddenly grasped my wrist in his hand and yanked his face away from me.

"What are you doing?" He scowled grumpily. His eyebrows knitted together in innocent confusion.

"Washing away the blood." After a long moment his grip on my wrist slackened, releasing me. Gingerly, I reached forward until the cloth was pressed against Mason's forehead. He didn't move away this time and his eyelashes fluttered. I slowly wiped away the remains of the blood that stained his skin.

He kept his wary eyes on me constantly; I felt them boring right into my face and following my every movement. His intense scrutiny caused my body to become a quivering bundle of nerves.

I continued to sweep the cloth over the line of his jaw and

the cloth soaked up the blood on his face easily which revealed his stubble and the scar that ran down one of his cheeks. My heart was burning from his non-wavering stare; I never wanted his gaze to ever leave me again.

"Does that not affect you?" Mason asked suddenly breaking the deathly silence in the room. I gulped the lump in my throat, taking a moment to process what he had asked.

"The blood?" I glanced at him and he was staring straight at me with his head tilted to the side like he was observing something remarkable, and it made my heart skip a beat. He was gazing at me with that strange look again. I didn't know what it meant but it seemed almost soft.

"The blood of a dead man – the man I murdered," he retorted with a deadpan look and unblinking eyes. I stared openly right back at him, so he could see that I was not distressed by his words.

"No, it doesn't affect me," I admitted. Mason leaned his face closer to mine, running a hand through his fringe and away from his eyes. The longer hair of his fringe didn't remain in place and fell over his eye again. His deep blue eyes that were framed by his black eyelashes were boring into mine and all I could do was blink back at him.

"Why?" He pressed, his eyes burning with curiosity. I was crumbling under his charm; I wanted to tell him. I lowered my head, looking back to the cloth in my hands and started wiping away the blood that had dripped down his neck.

I cringed when the cloth wiped over the scar that ran all the way down his neck but it didn't seem to hurt him. I noticed the skin of his scar was sunken and whitened, and clearly the scar was from a knife wound.

"Let's just say I have had my fair share of experience with

death before."

Mason remained quiet, agonising moments passed as my muscles cramped up in anxiety and I pushed my free hand into my stomach to prevent the cramps. When I couldn't handle it any longer, I peeked up at Mason. He just nodded and didn't question me any further; I breathed out in relief.

"And me killing someone? Why aren't you running away from me screaming?" Mason asked tentatively.

"He was going to kill me, you saved my life," I whispered softly. I wanted him to know how grateful I was that he did that for me.

"He is not the only person I have killed," Mason revealed gravely. I wasn't expecting such an honest reply from him. I lifted my gaze to see him looking at me expectantly, with one eyebrow raised. Like he wanted to scare me. That wasn't going to work, not with me.

"I figured." He was quiet for a long moment and I didn't dare look back up at him, but I felt his heavy stare as he scrutinised me.

"It seemed like there is nothing I can say that will make you afraid of me." Mason sighed, and I could hear the agony in his tone. His words hit me straight in the chest, so that was what he had been expecting me to do this whole time. He thinks I'm afraid of him.

"There is nothing you can say," I confessed. Mason didn't reply and we morphed back into silence. Feeling confident that he had allowed me to touch him for this long, I gently grabbed the hair of his dark brown fringe and pulled it to the side to wipe the skin there. His hair was soft and my fingers streamed through the curled ends like it was sand.

My hand flickered through the hairs of his eyelashes and he

blinked making his eyelashes flitter down my skin. As I moved his hair to the side, I saw that he had another deep scar that ran from the skin on his scalp on his forehead down to his ear. So that was why he wore his hair over the side of his face to cover up his scars.

"Why are you helping me?" He questioned tenderly, but his eyes held a deep torment. I bit my lip as his stare caused my heart to squeeze and twist. I couldn't believe I was touching his hair. Reluctantly I released his hair and it fell back over his eye.

The knot between Mason's eyebrows and the crinkles around his eyes fell away and he glanced at me so softly and tenderly like I was a rare gem stone. My breath caught in my throat and I paused my movements on his skin.

"I don't deserve to be cared for. I was the murderer tonight, not the victim," Mason says hauntingly and the skin around his eyes scrunched up in pain as he admitted this.

"I don't believe that, you saved me." That soft stare of his intensified and I had to look away, just so I could breathe. "And I don't like seeing all those cuts on you, it makes me feel sick just looking at them, I had to do something," I explained.

I grabbed an alcohol swab and ran it over his cuts before placing a bandage over them. It distressed me when I noticed that he didn't flinch or show any pain at all from the alcohol soaking into his open cuts. I continued my work in silence until he was fully patched up. As I placed the remaining gauze back into the first aid kit, I felt an unexpected hand on top of my own, halting my movements.

Mason gently took an alcohol wipe from my hands and my eyes shot up to his in question.

"My turn," he explained. I frowned as I tried to figure out what he meant, but my confusion was soon forgotten when

Mason scooted himself even closer to me on the bed.

My heart pounded like a jackhammer and my body was sent into a frenzy. Mason reached up the alcohol pad up to my neck and waited with his hand hanging in the air as if asking for permission to continue.

I pulled my neck back, so he had full access to my skin. I wasn't capable of speaking at that moment. Mason touched the swab to my skin and it stung. I ground my teeth together to stop myself from making any noise. After a moment Mason released the swab and then gently placed a large band-aid on my neck.

"I'm sorry," he apologised softly, and his eyes shined with regret. His words shocked me but also sent warmth straight into the pit of my stomach.

"I didn't like doing that to you, I know that now," Mason explained further as he gently ran his finger over the patch on my neck. "It's not too deep, it won't scar."

I replied with a nod. Mason drew his lower lip between his teeth and it focused my gaze towards his mouth. He leaned in even closer to me, so our lips were almost touching.

"I truly am sorry. I won't ever do anything like that to you again. I know now that I don't like it. I don't like seeing you in pain." Mason's tone was fierce and his face was captivating. My body was a mess of sparks and elation from being so close to him that my mind wasn't thinking when I dipped my chin even closer to him.

The soft breeze of his breath caressed my lips and I closed my eyes to savour the sweet moment. Mason stayed there for a long moment completely immobile. My stomach flipped when he abruptly leaned even closer to me.

Our lips briefly made light contact. His touch was like a feather running along my lips, barely there at all. The warmth of the slight contact radiated through my entire body and took over my mind and soul. I began to move even closer but suddenly Mason withdrew.

I kept my eyes closed for a few moments longer, hoping he might place his lips back on mine. When he didn't, I finally opened my eyes to see him standing at the other side of the room. My chest deflated in disappointment but I stood up and followed him so I was standing right in front of him again.

He took a step back from me and his features became illuminated by the shadowed penumbral light from outside my room that shone around his head. My opened curtains allowed the string of light to dapple into the room. Mason's features were stoic, serious, and his eyes were filled with a pain that I hadn't ever seen there before.

"Why do you pull away from me?" I asked gently as I reached up my hand and touched his face. He flinched away from me when my fingers ran over his scar.

"This scar." He pulled his hair away from his face so I could clearly see the deep scar that ran down his left cheek and extended all the way to his collarbone. "My father did this to me when I refused to kill an innocent person," he revealed banefully. My jaw dropped and wrinkles creased my forehead in distress; I had always wondered how he had acquired that scar. I didn't realise it was something so horrific.

"I hated my father. He was pure evil. He used to kill people in front of my siblings and I and let their blood stain our clothes. He used to make us watch as he tortured and maimed human beings while teaching us exactly how to kill someone. He taught us how to torture someone for days without killing them. Then he would place that knife in our hands and walk out the room, leaving us to do whatever we wanted with that person," he exploded, all the words kept coming out like he couldn't stop them. He was trying to scare me and he was succeeding.

I was left staring at him wide eyed and my expression horrified. Sweat dotted my forehead and I focused on supplying oxygen to my failing lungs.

"Did you ever?" I started to ask eagerly, infatuated by his story but he sharply cut me off. He jumped away from me as quickly as a lightning bolt.

"That's enough," he bellowed but I didn't stand down. His story made me realise that his past had created something inside him that he didn't know how to switch off. I knew he had that demon inside him, the same one I had.

"You should try to fight it, the darkness," I commented softly. He stared deeply into my eyes for a long moment with a furrowed brow before he blinked, and his features became sour.

"My scars don't just reside on my skin, they run deep into my soul. You don't deserve to be with someone who's had the darkness scarred into their skin and soul." He answered my question before he turned his back to me, effectively ending our conversation. Without another look at me, he jumped out of my window and disappeared. The only movement he left behind was the billowing of the curtains blowing through the open window.

Chapter 9

As soon as I opened my door the next morning my grandma was right in my face.

"Where were you last night?" she barked indignantly with her arms crossed over her chest. Her curly grey hair was sticking wildly around her head.

"Why do you care?" I snapped, eyeing her in suspicion. I couldn't understand why she was so angry about something so meagre. Her hard expression softened as she perceived my confusion.

"I was worried about you," she explained with soft caring eyes. I stumbled forward as my muscles stiffened. I was always shocked whenever Grandma expressed any kind of care for me – I wasn't used to it.

"I went for a walk into town on my way back from my psychology session and got lost." I frowned staring down at my shoes as I lied. She was scrutinising me with narrowed eyes when I glanced back up. I kept my face impassive and after a moment she sighed in resignation.

"Please let me know next time if you're going to be late. I was worried all night." I lifted my head up with bewilderment lacing my features. I didn't know she cared. A strange sense of peace filled my chest and I relented.

"I will," I promised. Her rigid features fell into a relaxed smile and she trod a wary step closer to me. I ignored the feeling to step back from her.

"I love you, no matter who you are or what you are. Love is more precious than anything in this world. That is what my family has always preached and you are a part of this family," she admitted earnestly with a blistering intensity. I gaped back at her with a dumbfounded expression, she loved me?

"Ya'aburnee," she said gently as she kissed me on the head. "It's a word that has been in our family for generations. It's Arabic and means that I love you so much that I hope to die before you because of how difficult it will be to live without you."

My mouth fell open and I tried to say something, but I was completely stumbled by her words. My eyelids fluttered closed from the peace that settled in my heart. It was like I had finally been given something that I had been waiting my whole life for, love from family.

That thought snapped me out of it, there was no way this woman could love me only after a few weeks of knowing me. She must have an ulterior motive.

"Why are you telling me this?" I exclaimed in irascibility. She wasn't perturbed by my darkening mood.

"Because I want you to know that there is someone who will be hurt if anything happened to you." Her eyes held nothing but sincerity. I ran my hands down my face in disbelief – what she was saying didn't make any sense to me.

"You don't have to worry Gran, I can take care of myself," I mumbled airily. Her wrinkled eyes scrunched up even more as she smiled.

"I know you can take care of yourself. I just need to know that you are safe." She unclipped the chain of her necklace and handed her old stopwatch to me. "This was my mothers. I want you to have it," she offered. I glanced down at it to see it didn't

100

work properly, it was missing the hour hand. I knew Gran used it as a timer rather than a watch.

My hands dropped to my side as my muscles became lax, completely flabbergasted. This was her necklace that she didn't take off for a second.

"I can't accept that," I declined, shaking my head.

"You are a part of this family, Elora, and it belongs to you," she declared fiercely as she settled the stopwatch around my neck. Her face was set in determination and I realised that this meant a lot to Gran. I would wear it for her.

"Thank you," I replied humbly, and my words were choked. I moved to leave the room before things became too emotional – I couldn't handle that.

After that strange chat with my grandma I raced back into my bedroom expeditiously and spent the rest of the day planning how I was going to see Mason again.

***

Bright coruscating lights and screams of excitement wharfed into my senses as Grandma drove the jolting car up the hill towards the town fair. I laced my sweaty hands together and unlaced them in an attempt to curb my anxiety. Today was the day – the day of the town fair.

After the night Mason's lips touched my own, my obsession had intensified into something else. I didn't see him after that, not for two weeks and the angst of not seeing him was killing me. I needed to see him, and the perfect opportunity arose when I remembered that the fair that was coming to town. I posted a letter to Mason's mailbox asking him to meet me here. This gave him the opportunity to decide if he wanted to see me without projecting myself onto him.

The fair was assembled over the hill in a clearing within the woods just a few minutes out of town. My eyes were drawn to a dazzlingly lit Ferris wheel flashing with blinding lights that expanded over the night sky. There were multiple rides and stools spanning around the fair which was all enclosed by temporary fencing. The fair was buzzing with people – most of the town must be here.

"Where would you like to go first? Henrietta and Bill said they will meet me at the log cutting," Gran announced as we walked into the depth of the crowd. Gran was limping behind me; she was getting pain in her right hip.

People seemed to make way for Gran as she was well respected in the town. She greeted people by name that smiled at her. She was easily recognisable with her wildly curly grey hair wrapped in a pink head scarf.

"I am going to go explore by myself and then I can meet you later," I denied. I just wanted to meet Mason. Gran regarded me apprehensively with torn eyes, clearly hesitant to let me go alone.

"You know, to meet some people my own age," I added. That seemed to soften her up and the tight pinch between her eyebrows dissipated.

"Okay. Make sure you keep your phone on you," she compelled in her authoritarian tone.

"Will do." I nodded, a smile forming on my face and began to trot towards the Ferris wheel. That was where I asked Mason to meet me at eight o'clock. I found a small wooden cafeteria style bench just to the side of the Ferris wheel and sat down to wait.

My eyes scanned the faces around me, seeking that one beautiful face that I craved so desperately. People were looking at me strangely and most of them moved out the way to avoid where I was sitting.

The minutes ticked by sluggishly and my shoulders slumped as I started losing hope. Why would he come anyway? He had been avoiding me the last two weeks for a reason. Just because I asked him nicely doesn't mean that he would actually turn up. My chin dropped in defeat and I placed my forehead on the table in front of me in deep disappointment.

But just as I did the table shook under my head. I lurched my head up and my muscles froze into ice as my eyes set on someone sitting on the other side of the bench – Mason.

I shivered in delight and allowed my eyes take him in, letting them finally obtain their fill from being so deprived of him these last few weeks. Just from looking at him my body became alert like a million buzzing bees wired every nerve ending in my body.

His dark brown hair was styled neatly down the side of his face that just covered the corner of his eye and curled towards the ends. As always, Mason looked like he was sleep deprived from the dark shadows that sat under his eyes. But that just made his bright blue eyes stand out even more, especially with the gleaming flashes of the Ferris wheels lights shining into them. He was so beautiful. My mouth nearly fell open in desire.

"Hello, Elora," Mason finally greeted with a dark knowing smirk on his beautiful lips.

I stared at him with wide incredulous eyes trying to comprehend the fact that he was actually in front of me. My chest slowly started to fill with inundate happiness – he came to see me. I didn't reply for a second too long and he tilted his head to the side, and looked at me inquisitively.

"You came," I finally stuttered out. Mason tilted his head back and one of his lips turned up at the corner. His eyes lightening with a spark of amusement.

"I did," Mason confirmed with a full-blown smile. His nose crinkled when he smiled, and his smile pronounced the wrinkles around his eyes that looked like crow's feet.

My heart jumped by how handsome his smile was – that was the first time I had seen him really smile. I beamed back at him and my own smile grew on my lips until the elation inside me pulled it into a grin, his smile was infectious.

Mason stared at me wistfully as the grin took over my face for a second too long. I noticed his stare, and it caused my breath to catch in the back of my throat but as soon as he noticed my reaction, he moved his gaze away.

"I'm still trying to figure out myself just why," Mason admitted bluntly. He leaned forward over the table between us, closer to me. I blinked at him unable to look away from his eyes and swallowed the lump forming in my throat.

"I think I need to know why." His dark lethal eyes burned into mine. I still couldn't believe I was looking at him.

"Why, what?" I managed to breathe out. His eyes were scintillating, drawing me in.

"Why haven't you told anyone about me?" He asked quietly, vulnerably, looking down at his hand that was tapping the table. "About what you saw me do? I have been expecting a police car to pull up outside my house all week." I stared deeply at him quizzically as he admitted this. The answer came easily to me.

"Because you didn't do anything wrong," I blurted with a fierce sincerity. Instantly, outrage overtook Mason's features. His eyes flashed and his eyebrows knitted together tightly as his lips turned down at the corners.

"Are you kidding me? I murdered someone right in front of you," he raged in a whisper, throwing his hands into the air in frustration. His fierce reaction startled me, and I dropped my eyes away from his harsh stare and to my hands in my lap.

"But he was evil, he deserved it," I admitted quietly as I continued to keep my eyes away from his. My hands swirled into the floral patterns of my blouse, twisting it anxiously. Mason didn't reply for a long time and finally I moved my gaze up to his. He was staring right at me with a searching expression on his face, his eyes curious and his frustration gone.

"You see things so differently to everyone else," Mason whispered softly, so softly I almost missed his words. My stomach started fluttering.

"I guess that's why I like being around you and no one else does," I replied with a smug grin. Mason leaned back in his chair and folded his arms across his chest.

"Fair point," he agreed with a quirk of his eyebrow. My eyes brightened and I had to bite my lip to prevent an embarrassing giggle.

"So, what is there to do around here? I've never been to one of these before," Mason asked as he craned his neck to search through the mounting crowds.

"We can play some carnival games," I suggested joyfully, whilst also trying to contain my teeming excitement.

"All right," he agreed and lifted himself off the table. We started to walk side by side through the crowds. I noticed he walked with a swagger due to his long and lanky limbs; he was much taller than me, and my head only reached his shoulder. He was so close, and I felt the warmth radiating off him – I wanted to touch him.

The fellow towns people who recognised us stared mercilessly like they just saw two devil incarnates together and kept their distance from both of us. I glanced up at Mason to see if he was bothered by it, but he seemed to be lost in his own world as he looked into the trees beyond the fair. I still couldn't believe he was here with me, for tonight Mason was mine.

We walked in silence and finally we reached the part of the fair that housed the games.

"We should play the coin game. I remember when I was a teenager my friend Annalise and I used to play the game for hours," I gushed from nervousness. Mason gave me a sideways knowing glance like he knew his effect on me and that made my lungs palpate.

"Let's go play it then," he replied with a smirk and gestured with his arm for me to lead the way. My chest deflated in relief; he didn't think I was weird. I grinned and marched happily, swinging my arms beside me as we moved towards the coin game. Mason made a small noise from behind me that almost sounded like a chuckle. I swivelled my head around to smile at him over my shoulder, but I wasn't looking where I was going and ran into someone.

"Watch where you are going freak," spat a young man around my age who towered over me. I clutched at my watch necklace and my mouth fell open as I recognised him as the boy Melissa was fawning over that day at church.

The boy was bulky, and had dark blonde hair cropped into a buzz cut that accentuated his jutting chin that was clenched in anger. He was surrounded by a group of friends all around the same age as him. I recognised another member instantly by her dyed blonde hair and darker olive toned skin, Melissa the mayor's daughter.

Her hostile dark eyes glared at me and her hand was clutching the boy's hand who yelled at me. There was another guy there with long black hair pulled into a ponytail and a girl with a pointy nose that drew up at the end.

They all glared at me either in anger or disgust. I didn't care though. I was clenching and unclenching my fists to contain the fury that was brewing inside me at the nerve of this guy. How dare he embarrass me in front of Mason?

"Well maybe if you weren't such an obnoxiously large hippopotamus maybe I wouldn't have run into you." I snapped back in rage and indignation. I heard his friends gasp in outage and only then did I realise what I had said. I slapped my hand over my mouth, regretting my decision.

"Don't speak to me like that, you worthless criminal," the buzz-cut guy barked derisively. His words caused my ears to redden and my chin to start trembling as embarrassment streamed through me like a raging inferno. My resonating chagrin caused my temper to flare uncontrollably and I had to grind my teeth together.

His words caused an old pain of mine to be brought to the surface. His friends laughed at my expense and my mounting fury finally reached its boiling point and made me snap. I fronted him and without thinking about the consequences, I pulled my fist back and punched him in the face.

His face snatched back violently as the impact shocked through his jaw. He grunted in pain and blood started to drip down from his lip. I tried not to display the satisfaction this brought me, but I couldn't help the small smirk that surfaced on my mouth.

"You little witch," he fumed, and lifted a finger to wipe the blood away from his lip. In retaliation he stretched his own fist back and swung it at my face. I braced for the impact, squaring my feet to duck out of the way but was shocked into stillness when a hand reached out from nowhere, stopping the plummeting fist. The hand grabbed the guys swinging fist in its own, stopping it mid-air right before it connected with my face.

Mason growled in anger and took a menacing step out of the shadows to protect me. I gasped up at Mason to see his teeth bared and his nostrils flaring as he glared daggers at the blonde-haired guy. A rush of warmth spread through me as Mason tucked me behind him tenderly, my eyelids fluttering from his protective touch. Mason slammed his palms into the guy's chest with so much force his torso spun around as he collapsed into the muddy ground face first.

The demeanour of the group before us changed instantly as they set their now panicked eyes on Mason; they must not have seen him behind me. Mason's reputation preceded him – I had never seen such fear and dread cross their faces. The buzz cut guy shrunk back on his hands and knees into the safety of his friend's circle. He rose from the ground using the aid of Melissa and I could see his hands were shaking as Mason descended upon him.

"How dare you hurt her," Mason growled incensed. His hands were in tight fists at his side and his rage was written all over his face. Mason grabbed the guy by his shirt and planted a right hook into his jaw. Mason looked about ready to kill. He had that wild deadly look in his eyes again – the look that I had only seen when Mason was about to kill someone.

Mason continually punched the guy and blood began to drip down his face. Mason was doing some real damage. The long-haired guy tried to help out his friend, but Mason punched him in the face without taking his eyes off his opponent.

"Stop please, leave Brandon alone," begged Melissa, franticly biting down on her knuckles. The other girl with a pointed nose looked on in terror with her hand over her mouth.

I stood back just watching, fascinated at Mason's skills, but

I also perceived that the towns people around us were starting to notice the conflict and were watching in horror. I didn't want Mason to get into trouble or for him to kill Brandon in front of everyone. I took a step towards the crazed Mason and softly rested my hand onto his shoulder. Instantly Mason stopped punching Brandon and cut his dilated gaze up to mine.

"Mason stop. There are people watching." I warned him gently but sternly. The realisation dawned in Mason's eyes and he nodded up at me. I placed my hands around his waist and pulled him up and away from the bloodied Brandon who was cowering on the floor and already looked dead.

Mason was watching Brandon with a sinister smile on his face like he was enjoying him wince and wither in pain. I saw clearly the need in Mason's eyes to start hurting Brandon again from the darkening glare on his features and the twitching of his jaw.

"I need to get out of here," Mason suddenly proclaimed ominously. He faced me so I could see the savage look in his eyes and a vein pulsing in his neck. "Before I kill someone." He looked deep into my eyes and a jolt ran through me as I gazed into the dark eyes of a murderer and electricity buzzed in my stomach. As much as I loved it, I knew we had to get out of here now.

I led Mason by his hand between the thick crowds of people and through an opening in the gate, so we were alone outside the confounds of the fair. But Mason didn't stop – he released my hand and he continued to march forwards into the thick copse of trees where the woods began.

"Where are you going?" I yelled after him and he spun on his heels to look at me before he spoke.

"Into the woods." He paused for a moment. "Are you

coming?" Mason asked.

I hesitated, and he noticed this. He sighed, his eyes losing their light. Mason slipped his hood up over his face and turned around to walk into the dark trees without me. A sense of dread entangled me. Mason was leaving me again when I had waited weeks to see him.

But do I follow a murderer into the dark woods alone? A murderer who the last time I saw him he killed a man and then tried to kill me. Mason spun around once again to glance at me for a moment and I saw his blue eyes regarding me from afar to see if I was following him.

Through the side of his hood the resplendent light from the moon shined onto his jaw I saw his lips turned down at the corners and the disappointment on his features.

In reaction my heart jumped, sending butterflies through my body. Mason wanted me to go with him. And that thought unravelled me, I didn't even think about the consequences when I took a step forward into the shadows emitting from the towering trees above.

I followed a murderer into the dark woods alone.

Chapter 10

My hands wouldn't stop trembling from the adrenaline pulsing through my blood; my subconscious knew this was dangerous. I ignored the internal warning and quickened my movements to catch up with Mason. My boots crunched in the fallen leaves with growing intensity. The outline of Mason's dark hooded figure was barely visible in the distance due to the obstructive widening boles of the trees.

As I strode onwards the screams and laughs of the fair gradually dimmed and I was enveloped in the silence of the forest. Mason's shadow dipped below the level of the saplings as he moved over a hill, disappearing from my view. I hurried my steps to catch up, stumbling over roots in my frenzy.

I stopped dead in my tracks when I reached the bottom of the hill; the trees had thinned into a clearing and Mason was standing right in the middle. His back was rigid, as still as a bone, and his head was hunched over as he looked down at something in his hands.

Just from seeing his rigid posture a lump formed in my throat and after a moment's hesitation I courageously treaded up to him. This could be the point where I died, but I didn't care, I wanted Mason more than my life.

"Mason?" I asked hesitantly and then bit my lip as they wouldn't stop quivering. He didn't reply, and I warily stepped closer to him. It was then that I noticed something dripping onto the fallen leaves on the forest floor in splatters in front of him –

blood.

"Mason," I demanded sternly, fear tremoring my words. I grabbed onto his shoulder, my nails biting into the fabric of his black shirt. Only then did Mason finally turn around to face me and when he did a gasp of horror fell from my lips.

It was his eyes that hit me first and I knew something was terribly wrong. From the lambently shining moonlight through the sides of his hood I saw how desolate his eyes had become, like the ferocious eyes of an animal about to attack its prey.

Mason had one arm raised out in front of him where he had pulled the sleeve of his shirt up to his elbow. In his other hand he clutched his lethal knife which was covered in blood. When I caught sight of his arm a cold sweat rushed through me and chilled me to the bone.

My eyes were instantly drawn to the deep elongated cut he had lacerated along the skin of his forearm. Streams of blood dripped from the gash down his forearm through the webs of his fingers and splattered to the floor.

I clasped my hands over my mouth as bile rose at the back of my throat at the sight of so much blood dripping from the wound, from my Mason. My terror filled eyes searched up both his arms to discover that they were both covered in deep cut scars. He had cut himself more times that just this once.

"What are you doing?" I shouted in horror and Mason's feral eyes moved up to mine gradually.

"When I'm like this, I need to see blood," he explained. "Even if it's my own… it's the only thing that can calm me down." He lifted his hand gripping the knife up to his opposite forearm and held it to his skin, skimming the surface.

"Stop!" I objected imploringly, and reached out a hand to halt his movements, but he didn't listen to me. He sunk the

112

already bloodied knife into his forearm and I witnessed with wide panicked eyes as the blood spilt from the cut. It streamed down his forearm and dripped to the floor in gruesome splatters. All I could do was watch with my hands wrapped around my throat in blind panic, helpless to do anything.

I noticed that as soon as the blood started streaming from the wound that the tight muscles of Mason's jaw relaxed and that ferocity in his eyes started to dissipate. It was like seeing the blood, and feeling the pain of the knife sinking into his skin, was a drug that could decrease his anxiety and bring him out of his darkness.

I squeezed my eyes shut in a grimace as the sight of Mason doing that to himself caused my heart to break into a million pieces. When I opened them again Mason was still looking down at the wounds etched into his skin and his chest slowly stopped heaving. My stomach churned as I realised, he must have done this when I saw him at the church with blood dripping down his hand; he was angry at those people for tormenting me.

Following a few tense moments where I dared not to move a muscle, Mason gradually lifted his head up. His eyes connected with mine and it sent a dark shiver down my spine. His pupils were dilated which made his eyes appear almost black. It was like I was looking into a black hole of an emotionless monster.

In an unexpectedly flash, Mason leapt towards me. His body catapulted into mine and we both fell backwards until the air was propelled from my lungs when my back collided with a tree trunk. Mason's bloody hand gripped around my neck before I felt that all too familiar cold sting of his knife being placed against my throat.

A thrill hurdled into my stomach and my breathing quickened into gasps. I peered up into his eyes expecting to see

113

his dark fierce gaze but what I saw there was not what I expected, amusement. He was playing with me.

I angled my head away from the knife in annoyance and pushed his chest, but he wasn't having any of it. He touched the knife closer to my skin and its lethal blade skimming the hairs on my neck. I lifted my eyes up to his in defiance, straightening my back.

"You like it, don't you?" He asked seductively as he leaned his face down closer to mine. His brown hair fell down over his eye and slid against my forehead. He touched his lips to my cheek and my body started reacting to his touch like he had ignited a fire in my blood.

He twirled the tip of the knife in circular swirls along the skin on my neck. His eyes were alight with a playful gleam, but they also held a lethal glint behind the surface; he was enjoying this. The cold teasing touch of the knife caused goose bumps to emerge on my skin all the way down to my toes.

"Like what?" I managed to strangle out. Mason's sweet breath on my cheek sent tingles through me and caused my body to shudder. He tilted his head back, so he could search my eyes and when his vehement gaze locked with mine my stomach tried to jump out of my torso.

"When I'm like this, when I do this to you," he whispered into my ear, and I knew exactly what he meant. When he was in his darkly wild states, when he wanted to kill.

I nodded slowly. A smirk lifted one side of his mouth at his small victory before he touched his lips just to the corner of mine, almost a kiss but not quite. My eyes fluttered half way closed – I was lost in his spell and the darkness that was Mason.

"Aren't you scared that I will kill you?" He questioned puzzled, tilting his head to the side curiously. I loved it when he looked at me like that, like he was dying to know what I had to say next.

"No, I know you won't." My response was definite, I knew this the very first time he put a knife to my throat, I saw in it in his eyes and in the way his hands shook. To kill someone with a knife I knew you needed one hundred per cent conviction. When he looked at me there was never that savageness there that I saw when he had killed Kenneth.

Understanding radiated from his eyes at my words and they enticed me in. Without looking away, he lifted his other hand to follow the skin that rested above his knife that was still against my throat. The warmth of his fingers juxtaposed the chilled prickle of the knife causing my toes to curdle. He continued to run that finger all the way down my side until he hitched up my shirt near my hip and slid his warm hand all the way up the skin of my back. I closed my eyes as shudder ran through me.

Abruptly the warmth of his body left mine and he finally drew the knife away from my neck. The loss of his support caused my body to sink back into the tree behind me, digging my nails into the bark. I dropped my head as disappointment weighted heavily on my lungs from him moving away.

"I wanted to kill you, ever since you found out my secret. You know too much. My agony would be over if you were gone," he admitted as his stormy eyes seared into mine. His malicious words sent a creep through my flesh and I rubbed my upper arms to calm down. His eyes followed my movements and as he noticed my uncomfortable stance his eyes softened and the tense lines around his eyes fell.

"But you are right. I can't hurt you." He was looking at me gently and my chest filled with a deep breath of bubbling hope at his words. "I don't know how you knew so long ago. It just makes me feel physically sick," he continued, his tone was so soft like velvet and his expression was agonised.

"I have never felt anything like it before. This is the first time I have ever not liked hurting someone," he explained, in a whisper so quietly I nearly didn't hear him. His admittance made my heart squeeze in joy, I'm special to him.

"Why?" I asked timidly, looking at him from under my eyelashes to see him already staring at me intently with those gentle eyes of his. My heart skipped a beat when he took a step forward and rested his hand onto my cheek.

"I guess you are just so much like me," he started. "I can feel the pain you feel, because it's exactly what I have experienced myself." My eyebrows raised and my mouth was hanging open, completely astonished. He was an outsider too, and that was what drew me to him as well, but I envied him and admired how he was just so indifferent towards it all.

"The real reason I came here tonight is because I had to see you. You are so intriguing to me," Mason declared, and his words did something to me. I flushed and my heart filled with ardour and warmth. No one had ever said I'm intriguing before or anything even close to it.

"I thought you hated me," I counted avoiding his gaze, wrapping one arm around my waist. His hand dropped from my face.

"I did hate you, I never wanted anyone to know these evil things about me and you kept learning everything. And then I started to feel things for you, things which I never wanted to feel because I knew I needed to kill you, but I can't control how I feel. The fact that you try so hard to come closer to me. No one has ever tried to come closer to me before. Everyone just tries to run away." There was a tinge of vulnerability in his voice like he didn't want anyone to know that it actually affected him how he was ostracised.

"I will always want to be closer to you," I assured him, earnestly. Mason's chest deflated as he released a deep breath.

"I see that now, but I was shocked that first time when you saw me in the woods. When you tried to come closer to me when I was at my worst, when I was a murderer. I couldn't hurt you after that." He shook his head like he couldn't even picture it now.

"I thought if I was going to die then I wanted to kiss you first, even if that kiss was from my murderer," I recalled, avoiding his gaze. Mason touched his hand to my chin and tilted my face up to look him in the eye. There was a ghost of a smile on his lips like he found my explanation amusing and endearing. The sight of his smile made me feel all sorts of wonderful things.

"I didn't understand you. When I saw you that day at the church, I wanted to test it out to see if you would come closer again and you did. I must admit I'm a little addicted to it." He smiled timidly and I beamed back up at him. I couldn't believe that I had actually done something right for a change.

"I replayed that moment a million times in my head," I revealed as I glanced up at him tentatively. His skin around his eyes crinkled at the corners as his expression lit up.

"You took care of me the other night. No one has ever done that for me before. You're the only person that actually treats me like a human being, like I'm not a monster." He ran his fingers along my cheek softly and his touch left a line of fire in its wake.

"Why did you tell me to stay away from you?" I asked boldly, frowning as I remembered the pain I felt from after our conversation at the church.

"Because I didn't want to drag you into the darkness that is my world. I didn't want you to know that I am a murderer, but I

117

guess it's too late now," Mason explained. My tight forehead relaxed in relief at his words, so he pushed me away to protect me. I grinned up at him and bounced on my toes.

"I want to be a part of it," I exclaimed, breathless at the mere thought. His eyes widened and his blue irises sparkled from a ray of moonlight that shone through the awning of forestry above.

"You are one of a kind, Elora and I want to know more about you. If you're willing to be around a murderer," he declared ominously, running a hand through his dark hair like he was uncertain I would accept. I didn't even need to think about the answer to that question.

"Of course." The returning smile he gave me nearly knocked the breath out of me. We both grinned at each other for a moment before Mason tilted his face towards mine and took my hand in his.

"Let's get out of here. I want to show you someplace."

Chapter 11

Mason guided me through the woods, parting the branches of dense foliage for me. In the umbrage of the condensing canopy above the darkness transformed every tree stump into nothing more than a shadow.

I truly had no idea where he was planning to take me and I didn't know if I should be worried. Did he now think that because I knew about his murdering ways that I would want to join him? I didn't know if I was excited or frightened by that prospect.

As we reached the top of the hill a colossal structure came into view, but only partially because it was hidden behind overgrown shrubbery and was eclipsed by the gargantuan forest vegetation. Constructed from jaggedly placed white crumbling bricks that had been abused from the harsh sea weather, and covered in moss and climbing vines, was a very old and deteriorating lighthouse.

Its first landing structure was a few metres off ground level and the fence that surrounded the encircling concrete was decayed, and half of it had dissipated away along with the stairs that lead up to the landing.

I stepped closer to it and brushed a bloomed branch away to find a plaque embedded into the bricks dedicating the lighthouse structure to two men, Henry Edmington and Jeremiah King in 1918. It must have been abandoned many years ago.

"I didn't even know this existed," I revelled in fascination, swirling around to face Mason. A small smile lifted the corner of his mouth, revealing the crinkles around his eyes and he nudged me with his elbow. I couldn't tear my eyes away from his smile; he was just so enchanting.

Suddenly, he leapt into the air and grabbed onto the overhanging branch of a tree above. He climbed along the tree branch and jumped up onto the lighthouse's first landing. Without the stairs leading up to the landing, that was the only way up.

My eyes followed him cautiously, and I saw the light of the moon catch on a knife Mason pulled out his pocket. My breath hitched as my stomach twisted into knots.

"Oh relax," Mason whined. "We are just abseiling." A cheeky grin spanned the entire width of his face. It instantly caused the panic induced contortion on my forehead to melt away and happiness to bubble up in my chest.

"Abseiling?" I questioned sceptically, eyeing off the equipment with distrust. I glanced up at him from underneath my eyelashes, and he was crouched down on the lighthouse landing above, using the branch of the tree to stabilise him so he could lean down towards me. Our faces were so close I felt his breath swirl the hair that had broken free of my ponytail.

"Should I be scared?" I asked warily.

"Not at all, I would never let anything hurt you." He assured me with a knowing look and my heart skipped a beat. "And plus, I have done this a million times before." He used his knife to cut a rope that was hanging down from the tree and a backpack came falling down into his arms, and he pulled out a harness.

"Well, I am scared." I folded my hands across my chest. He laughed as he reached up to yank down a rope hanging from the lighthouse; he had already set everything up that he needed. He had a spark of excitement in his eyes as he looked at me. I placed my side bag from around my shoulder beside a tree stump – I didn't want it restricting my movements.

"How am I supposed to get up there?" I yelled.

With a closed mouth charmed smile Mason reached down one of his hands to me. I eyed him warily, but I placed my own hand into his. He lifted me up into the air and onto the landing easily.

"Thanks," I wheezed, the sound almost inaudible as he helped me to my feet and pulled me into him.

He smiled back and then stepped away, busying himself with strapping the harness around his waist and connecting it to the ropes on the lighthouse. I observed him with curiosity; I had never seen Mason smile this much.

"There is only one harness, so you will have to hold onto me while I climb." His explanation made my motions halt and my mouth to gape open.

"What if I fall?" I backed away.

"I will catch you," he stated confidently. As able as I knew he was, the chances of me dying far outweighed the possibility that I could climb a lighthouse without falling.

"Well as lovely as it sounds, I think I will just stay down here and watch," I refused with a smug smile. Disappointment caused Mason's features to fall and his once bright smile left his lips. I instantly began to reconsider my decision.

"Come on, Elora, live a little," Mason urged with stark intensity. I chewed on my lip as I deliberated and after a moment, I sighed loudly. He was right, what was the point in having a life if you're not willing to live it?

"You better not let me go," I conceded reluctantly, wrapping my hand around my wrist and twisting anxiously. A large grin broke out onto Mason's face and it suddenly felt like the sun just appeared out from behind the clouds, shining a brilliant aureate

121

like a blinding meteorite.

"I would never," Mason promised and then waved me over next to him. "Come over here." I did so languidly, still unsure. He watched me with eyes like a hawk and when I stopped next to him, he placed his hands on my hips and moved me, so I was right in front of him. A small chirp of surprise burst from my lips unintentionally.

"Wrap your legs around my waist." I blinked up at him, my mind no longer functioning properly.

"You, me to, what?" I stuttered, and gasped. Mason raised one of his eyebrows at me and grabbed both of my wrists placing them around his neck. My breathing instantly increased compelling my lips to part and my stomach flipped.

His hands lowered down my body until they rested behind my thighs and he guided me easily, lifting me up so my legs wrapped around his waist. I stumbled over my next breath and the next from how close I was to him. This was a dream come true.

"Don't let go," he warned with a spark of excitement in his eyes. He reached upwards and grabbed onto a brick in the lighthouse and started to climb.

My eyes were glued to his face, taking in every aspect of his features from this close distance. As I examined him; I noticed that there was a small drop of blood on his upper lip. I released one of my hands from around his neck to reach up to his face and touched my fingertips to his lip.

Instantly, Mason's head snapped down to gape at me as if I just shocked him with electricity. His movements halted on the brick he was clasping, as did mine on his lip. He just stared down at me with round eyes as if he was in shock that I was touching him. His feet dropped back to the ground again and my back slid down to rest against the wall of the lighthouse.

"You have blood on your lip," I explained. Mason was silent but didn't move his fixated gaze from me. Slowly I continued my movements and wiped off the blood with my fingertips. His pupils flared as his eyelashes fluttered and he didn't push me away. Feeling brave, I ran the base of my thumb over his bottom lip, and I felt them quivering underneath my skin.

Mason's chest began to rise and fall faster underneath mine as I touched him. Our eyes were locked, and it was like I was looking into an inferno of blue flames. I lifted my face up to Mason's and touched my lips to the jagged tainted skin of his scar that extended from his cheek down his neck.

He shuddered underneath me as I ran my lips all the way down his scar to his clavicle bone, revelling in finally being able to do this. I had thought about kissing his scar ever since I noticed he had it. I drew my lower lip along the scar back up to his neck and finally kissed him just under his jaw.

Mason's hand dropped from the brick he was still holding onto to curl it around my waist, scaling the lighthouse was completely forgotten. He moved his neck backwards, giving me complete access. My heart started fluttering in response and I smiled when I pulled back and saw that his eyes were closed.

I leaned forwards to return my lips to his neck but before I could, the ropes that Mason was attached to yanked him away from me as a strong gust of wind threw the ropes around viciously. The gust hit the ropes higher up the lighthouse, making the force at the bottom of them dangerously strong.

I clutched my arms around Mason's neck so tightly I could feel his rigid muscles tense as he fought against the ropes that were trying to pull him around. After a few tense moments, the gust eased, and the ropes stabilised. I breathed out deeply and sagged against him.

"We better head up now if we want to make it up there before the wind becomes too dangerous," Mason commented with a furrow between his eyebrows as he glanced up at the ropes disapprovingly, like he was annoyed at them for ruining our moment.

My lips pursed, I wanted to say that I didn't care about going up the lighthouse anymore. I just wanted his skin under my lips again. But then I remembered the happiness in his eyes when I agreed to this and knew that this meant a lot to him.

"Let's go then," I encouraged, with a small smile. Mason looked down at me for a long moment, his eyes smouldering as he gazed into mine. Finally, he nodded and started climbing the lighthouse.

When Mason lifted his feet off the floor the rope jolted as it took our weight and I tightened my hold around Mason's neck. This only brought me closer to him; I could feel his heart beating through his chest.

I tucked my chin onto Mason's shoulder – I was like a koala hanging onto a eucalyptus tree. I refused to move from that position as Mason gradually made his ascent up the lighthouse. As much as I wanted to, I couldn't close my eyes because watching was exhilarating. It was like we were in a glass elevator ascending through the tree tops. And the best part was that I felt every part of Mason against me, the flex of his shoulders and the tense of his stomach muscles as he pulled us upwards.

As we neared the top the salty wind started to whirl against my hair and finally, the foliage cleared as we broke through the crown of the trees. A stunning view of the ocean appeared and my jaw dropped open. Through the last remaining branches, I was able to see that the lighthouse was built on the edge of a massive cliff face. This gave an unimpeded view of the sea and how it extended for miles into the distance. The dark navy hue of the swirling waves generated the impression that we were miles above the ocean's surface.

In my awe I drew my head back to share this with Mason, but my words became clogged in my throat when I saw his face. Mason's lips were pursed, and his eyes were scrunched up in concentration as he climbed. When I caught sight of his captivating facial features I was overcome by a strange ache of yearning.

Sweat had formed on his skin and was slowly dripping down his temples. It made his dark hair stick to the side of his face and frame his long eyelashes. There was a small wrinkle in the middle of his forehead from how much he was concentrating.

"You don't look like a murderer," I commented with a husky voice. Mason's eyes cut to mine with a sharp look out of the corner of his eye.

"How do you mean?" His voice was hesitant but also curious with a line puckering between his eyebrows.

"You are too beautiful," I admitted.

Mason didn't reply and didn't look back at me, he just continued to scale up the lighthouse. But because I was watching him so intently, I didn't miss the slight tinge of red that tainted his cheeks. He was blushing. A wide smile overtook my lips as I tried to suppress a proud giggle. I made a murderer blush.

I couldn't take my eyes off the blush on Mason's cheeks, so I wasn't prepared when another gust of wind hit the ropes and jolted us to the side forcefully. Instantly, Mason wound his hands around my waist in a tight embrace, securing me to him so strongly it was almost painful. I clutched onto him so desperately nothing could tear us apart.

The strong gust gradually subsided as did the swaying of the ropes and I dropped my head into Mason's neck in relief. My heart was beating in my ears, and we were both silent as we caught our shaky breaths.

"It's getting dangerous up here. We better keep moving," Mason warned sternly. I nodded in agreement and tightened my hold on him.

Mason escaladed us to the top of the lighthouse and finally, we levelled out onto the gallery deck. Tree branches had overgrown onto the landing and wrapped around the railing like a snake. Mason brushed the stray willows out of the way as we climbed over the railing and onto the stable ground of the deck.

I clambered to my feet and grasped a hold of the railing in both hands tightly, anchoring myself to its stability. As I glanced up to the view in front of me my breath caught in the back of my throat.

My wide fascinated eyes could see everything; the ocean that expanded infinitely into the distance and a glade in the forest housing the town fair which was nothing more than specs of flashing lights metres below. The expansive view inland only stopped where the mountains that hugged our town spanned too immensely high to see beyond.

"It's beautiful, isn't it?" Mason spoke absentmindedly from behind me.

I closed my eyes, enjoying the feeling of the sea wind blowing through my eyelashes. I felt free like I was flying. There was nothing holding me back and I realised in that moment that being with Mason was like flying.

"Just who are you, Elora?" Mason asked me suddenly.

Chapter 12

My eyelids fluttered open, and I looked over my shoulder to find that Mason had moved up right beside me and was watching me intently, ardently.

"I don't know anything about you," he continued, and the skin around his eyes crinkled up as if this thought pained him. I returned my gaze back towards the raging waves of the ocean and noticed an immense rock that was cutting through the elegantly designed waves, dissolving them into nothing. They were not like the smaller rocks that allowed the waves to wash over them without disturbing its structure. The larger rock was me; I destroyed everything in my path.

"I am someone who is not normal," I stated, my speech laboured with poorly concealed sadness and my shoulders slumping forward.

"No one is," Mason countered, and placed his hand over the top of mine that was resting on the rail. Warmth spread through me like liquid gold from the small touch.

"What is your story? How did you end up in the dead-end town of Everbrook?" Mason asked, his eyes blazed with curiosity and I knew I couldn't refuse those eyes.

"From what my grandmother told me, my father who is her son, cheated on his wife and had an affair with my mother. When my father found out that my mother was pregnant, he wanted nothing to do with me as he wanted to stay with his wife. My mother was forced to raise me on her own."

Mason's eyes were fixated on mine as he listened to every word I spoke with intense interest. My own gaze was locked on our still touching hands. He saw where my eyes were directed and he interlaced our fingers. I closed my eyes from the heavenly touch and a whirl of pleasant emotions fluttered in my chest. My body almost heaved and shut down from what that small movement did to me.

"But when I was three years old, my mother became sick and she died. My father was forced to take care of me, but he sent me away to an orphanage. Then he disappeared from town with his wife and Gran has never heard from him since," I explained, my voice lowering as the small cracks of torment started to break away at my heart. I hated talking about my family; they caused me nothing but pain.

When I glanced up at Mason I wasn't prepared for his interest and the way his eyes did not leave my face. He gave me a small nod of encouragement to continue.

"I spent my whole life going in and out of foster homes. By the time I was sixteen I was over it all. I ran away and started living on the streets. Luckily, I made friends with another homeless girl who had been on the streets longer than me, so she helped me get through the cold nights. Her name was Annalise and she became my best friend," I continued, reluctantly now. There was a lump forming in my throat.

I quickly gave a sideways glance to Mason to see what he thought about me living on the streets. His face was inscrutable, but he did have a small crease in the middle of his eyebrows that looked like he was thinking hard about something. He saw my anxious look and placed his other hand onto my back and began running his hand down my spine soothingly, and it helped decrease my nerves.

"I spend a few months on the streets before a man who was on a charity bender for his company offered Annalise and I a job and a place to live. Things were good for another few years. The man who offered me the job became my boss and I started spending a lot of time with him," I confessed. My voice was hoarse from the rasp of the cold air that scratched the back of my dry throat.

Mason's sparked interest was palpable, he lowered his eyelids to look at me more clearly. I moved my gaze back to the destructive rock and ran my hand down my face with my free hand before saying my next words.

"That was when my first major obsession happened," I admitted, swallowing hard and biting my lip. Mason's features remained as stoic as ever; his only reaction was to inch his face closer to mine. I ground my teeth together as my chin started to tremble in panic. Until finally, he spoke.

"You're obsession?" He repeated, his forehead puckered in uncertainty. I released my lip from between my teeth in relief at his words. At least he didn't call me a freak.

"Yes, I was obsessed with him. I followed him everywhere – I had to know everything he was doing and be a part of it. It became unhealthy and he wasn't my only obsession," I recalled with shame.

"You see, I have a mental illness," I revealed, and I finally looked up to Mason cautiously to find understanding dominating his features.

"I know," he declared, in a matter of fact tone. I staggered a step backwards as the shock from his words were like a punch in the stomach.

"How did you know?" I spluttered out. A reassuring smile pulled up one side of Mason's mouth.

"I have had my fair share of experiences with mental illness and I know that it doesn't define who you are. You are not your illness – it's just a part of who you are." His words that were so passionately spoken caused my tightly coiled insides to slowly unwind. I smiled softly up at him with my eyes sparkling in awe; he understood.

"What is yours specifically?" Mason asked eagerly as he reached one arm over his head holding onto a stray tree branch and rested his head in the crook of his elbow.

"It's officially called Attachment Disorder, but my symptoms are well defined by something called Obsessive Love Disorder. My psychologist told me that being separated from my primary care giver, my mother, at such a vital stage in my development contributed to me developing it," I explained, and touched my index fingers to my temples to reiterate my point.

"Now, I become unhealthily attached to a man that I find attractive and become obsessed with him. I think that he is in love with me too when really he wants me nowhere near him." I glanced into the crashing waves as I remembered how I truly believed my boss wanted me too. Mason touched his fingertips to my chin and tilted it upwards, so I was looking right into his deep blue understanding eyes.

"So, this Obsessive Disorder where you follow a man around everywhere, it sounds familiar to me," he hinted, his lips quirking up. I blinked up at him guiltily. "You're obsessed with me, aren't you?" he asked animatedly. I held his beaming gaze as I answered.

"Yes." I watched his reaction closely and noticed his eyelids flutter closed for a moment. I didn't know what it meant but I felt like I needed to explain.

"But this time I can handle it; I've been getting better ever since working with my psychologist and taking medication. Plus, spending time in jail was like a hammer to the head," I gushed trying to rectify myself.

"Why did you go to jail?" Mason questioned, his lips parting in curiously. I grimaced but I knew it was time to finally tell him. I released his hand because mine had become sweaty with stress.

"When I said my obsession with my boss was truly out of control I wasn't exaggerating. I did some pretty stupid things just to learn more information about him. I used to listen in on his phone conversations, I stalked him, and I even broke into his house." I dropped my gaze in shame.

"When it was becoming really bad, I told Annalise, and she notified the police about it. She told me she was doing what was best for me, but I haven't spoken to her since. So, I went to jail for stalking, breaking in and entering my boss's house, and for plugging his phone," I divulged, digging my toes into the concrete floor.

"After my year sentence and I was released I had a criminal record, so I couldn't find a job. When my social worker managed to find my long-lost grandma, she kind of saved my life. Gran gave me a place to live and helped me find a job at the library," I finished and crossed my hands over my chest trying to prevent the churning feelings of insecurity.

"So that's my story." I raised my hands up in the air breathing out a sigh of relief that it was over. Mason was quiet for a moment longer and I finally squinted up at him to find his eyes were soft. I didn't understand what it meant – does he think I'm a freak?

"I thought you went to jail because you did something stupid like help someone rob a bank or something," he finally spoke, his right lip lifting up into a smirk.

131

"Well now you know the truth of how messed up I am. You can leave me now," I challenged.

"That's not going to happen," he objected fiercely, taking a step closer to me. I scrunched my eyes together as I quizzically looked at him in bewilderment, unable to understand why he was reacting so calmly.

My heart fluttered when Mason grinned with mischief. He grabbed my hands and twirled them behind my body. With my hands bound behind my back by his body he wound both of his arms around my waist as he hugged me from behind. He leaned his head down and placed it in the crook of my neck. His soft breath on my skin was so close it caused my skin to shiver. I didn't reply because I liked the feeling of the stubble on his cheek brushing my jaw and didn't want to say anything to make him move.

"You are so cute, you either don't talk at all or you never shut up," he observed, referring to how I just spoke for ten minutes straight and now refused to reply.

"And I love your hair," Mason proclaimed into my neck. "It's the colour of blood." He drew his head away from me, so he could observe my astounded features. I had never actually thought about that; he loved blood so of course he was drawn to me because of the colour of my hair, which I had dyed my natural ginger colour blood red.

"Why red?" He questioned, his eyes blazing into mine with a searing intensity. I turned around to face Mason and his hands slipped away from my waist.

"When I found out that my mother had died and she hadn't actually abandoned me. I dyed it the same colour as hers," I admitted. "Although, I am glad I didn't inherit how she had half an eyebrow missing." I laughed to brighten the mood, but it had

132

the opposite effect.

Unexpectedly Mason's face blanched, becoming wan as it drained of colour and he staggered a step away from me, grabbing onto the railing for support. His reaction caused my chest to tightened and my body rocked backwards in dread.

"She had half an eyebrow missing?" he panicked, running a hand over his mouth.

"Yes, what is so horrifying about that?" I perplexed with distress. Mason opened his lips to reply but was cut off.

A haunting scream echoed through the night from the direction of the forest below. Instantly my blood ran cold and my face paled in terror. The screech subsided into a haunting silence.

Mason turned to me and there was a strange new fear that had manifested in his widened eyes.

"You need to leave now," Mason ordered in blind urgency. Those words sent a chill through my bones and made my chin tremble.

"What is going on?" I questioned, distress evident in my tone. Mason didn't answer, he just stormed over towards a boarded door in the lighthouse and kicked it down. The wood cracked underneath his boot and crashed inwards to reveal a spiral staircase.

Mason faced me with foreboding on his features and grabbed me by the shoulders forcefully in both of his hands.

"The door at the bottom is unlocked," he explained evasively as he looked me straight in the eyes. His seriousness exigency caused my breathing to shallow.

"When you reach the ground, run as fast as you can back to the fair. Don't stop for anything or anyone," he warned darkly. His words made my heart start pounding and water to spring around the sides of my eyes. Another bone chillingly scream wailed from the woods again, but this time it sounded more frantic. Someone was in terrible danger.

"Why?" I demanded in full-blown panic mode now.

"Just do it," Mason yelled harshly, and his tone made me think that if I didn't do as he said, then I would be in store for something much worse than being yelled at.

"Go," he urged in a shout and that propelled me into action.

With one last anxious glance at Mason, I ran through the door and emerged into a caliginous decaying stairway that circled down the building. I sprinted down the stairs and when I reached the bottom, I swung the door open and flew through it like my life depended on it.

In the wake of the scream, the animals seemed to scurry away at any motion and the forest had an eerie ambiance brewing in the shadows. Before leaving, I grabbed my bag that I had left at the bottom of the lighthouse. I peeked one last glance up to Mason but was shocked when I saw nothing but swaying trees.

Sweat dripped down my temple and I clutched my knotted stomach when I realised that I was alone. Without a backward glance I took off back towards the fair. I manoeuvred my way through the trees and shrubs like a rocket, my frantic motions inciting the twigs of the trees to scratch my cheeks as I ran past.

My strides staggered and I slowed down my steps when I heard it again, a violent blood curdling scream. As I wiped the sweat off my temple, I emerged over a small hill and what I saw on the other side compelled my muscles to tense and paralyse. My eyes popped out of their sockets as my vision set on someone at the bottom of the hill.

It was a girl, a girl who was completely covered in blood. The blood was oozing from deep cuts that had pierced her skin and face, like someone had run a knife over her body. My knees tumbled and my hand clasped over my mouth as I gaped at her in mindless shock. Strangely she appeared more scared of me than I was of her from the way her eyes were wide in fear.

Suddenly, she snapped out of her trance and started running straight towards me. She moved so quickly and my body was frozen in terror, so I didn't have time to run. I was shaking violently as she grabbed onto my shoulders with her bloody hands. It was only then, at such a close distance, was I finally able to clearly see her facial features underneath all the blood and noticed her dyed blonde hair that was striking against her olive toned skin.

It was Melissa, the mayor's daughter.

"Help me," she agonised and shook me violently by the shoulders. Her words were pained like she could hardly croak them out of her throat due to it being so raw from all the screaming.

"What's going on? I will get you out of here," I reassured her as calmly as I could. I knew we were close to the fair.

In a flash her eyes darted from looking at me, to looking beyond me. Her features became haunted as she gazed at something behind me. Her terrorised and fearful eyes flickered back to mine.

"You can't help me. I will die anyway – Marlemore will find me," she declared lifelessly, with no hope for her survival. The name she spoke evoked a plummeting whirl in my stomach and sent my mind racing in panic.

"Marlemore?" I reiterated with wide eyes.

She regarded me gravely and, in her hysteria, she flailed her hands forward, grabbing for my side bag. She ripped it off my shoulder and started rummaging through it. She tipped everything onto the floor and finally her bloody hands made their way to a folded up old piece of paper.

"I can't tell you Marlemore's identity because then you will be killed." She hysterically glanced over her shoulder with panic-stricken eyes.

She opened the paper and I realised that it was the missing poster of the boy, Ryan. I squinted up at her perplexed with knitted eyebrows. She rammed the paper into my face and started pointing to the missing kid, smearing her blood-stained fingers onto the paper.

"This, it's the one," she slurred frantically. Who was the one? The missing boy?

Then unexpectedly she screamed and started chucking everything back into my bag including the poster. I didn't know what she was talking about; she sounded like she had gone mad.

She thrust my bag back into my stomach and with one last frantic look at me she grabbed my shoulders again. Her long-manicured fingernails sunk into my skin from her delirious motions.

"Run," she cautioned ominously before she sprinted off into the woods.

"Wait, let me help you," I yelled after her, but it was too late. She had already run back into the trees and I lost sight of her. I stood immobile with quivering limbs in the dark woods not knowing what to do.

After a moment of indecision, I decided to return to the fair and ask for help from the police. I jogged back with unsteady knees and after a few minutes I started to hear the blaring circus music and sounds of people screaming on the carnival rides. My tense muscles started to unfold and I breathed a sigh of relief when the trees cleared and the gates emerged.

I jumped over the fence and scanned my eyes through the crowds searching for Gran or a policeman. I nearly screamed bloody murder when someone touched my arm from behind. The hand spun me around and I came face to face with a murderous looking Gran.

"Where have you been? I have been searching for you for

136

the last hour," barked Grandma.

"I—" I started but was cut off when we heard a scream of horror cut through the fair.

We snapped our heads towards the noise and stopped to see everyone flocking around something in the distance near the Ferris wheel. My shoulders dropped and trembled as all the air left my lungs. Everyone started running towards where the scream originated and I followed suit.

While gasping for breath and clutching my lungs for support, I sprinted towards the commotion. Once I reached the back of the mounting crowd, I started to push people out of my way so that I moved in closer towards the heart. Another scream sounded and they started to increase in frequency among the town members. As I neared the front, I heard someone crying, the sound of hysterical misery and suffering.

Finally, I barged my way into the front of the crowd. When I caught sight of what was in the middle of the circle I nearly fell to my knees.

Melissa was lying on the floor covered in blood and cuts but this time she had a gaping hole through her head from where she had been stabbed through the skull. Her left arm was facing towards the crowd and this allowed us to see what had been cut into the skin of her arm with a sharp blade. With blood still dripping down from the corners of the words they read.

"*Love from, Marlemore.*"

I raised my shocked eyes up to Melissa's face to see there was blood dripping out of the corner of her mouth and her eyes were blank.

She was dead. She had been murdered.

Chapter 13

"All right everyone, stay calm and move out of the vicinity as quickly as possible," ordered Amanda, the chief of police, as she barged her way through the thickening crowd – her expression stern. When she reached the front, I noticed her eyes widen in shock as she saw the true gore of what happened to Melissa. But she covered it quickly, putting on a stolid face and professional demeanour.

Almost as if she shot off a gun everyone started dispersing and moving away from the scene before us in horrified whispers. The chief lowered to her knees in front of Melissa and checked her pulse; she glanced up at her colleagues with grave eyes and shook her head. She confirmed that Melissa was dead.

As the crowds dissipated around me, I was left frozen. My eyes were glued to Melissa's blank, unmoving eyes. I failed her; I could have saved her.

My whole body flinched in fright when someone touched their hand to my forearm. I squealed and spun around to find Gran looking at me with soft, compassionate eyes.

"Are you okay?" Concern radiated from her tone and her voice managed to calm me a little.

"No," I admitted honestly. In a nod of understanding Gran lead me away from the body. I glanced over my shoulder to see ambulance officers placing a foil blanket over Melissa's body. My intestines heaved up at the sight and I fell to the ground, placing my head in my knees. I desperately tried to keep the vomit down and after a few minutes, the spinning in my head decreased. Gran waited patiently beside me.

"Sorry, my head is spinning," I explained when I could see clearly again and Gran helped me up from the ground. As we moved back to the car, we walked past the chief of police who was interviewing Melissa's friends and I overheard a snippet of their conversation. It was the girl with the pointed nose and the boy with the ponytail.

"Kiara, has Melissa been acting strange lately?" The chief questioned the girl who was crying her eyes out.

"Yes actually, she has been obsessed with going to this factory for days now," Kiara answered in chocked sobs. My interest piked, a factory? Was it connected to her death? And could it be connected to Marlemore?

"Do you know what factory?" Amanda pressed with an upturned bushy eyebrow, jotting down the information on a note pad.

"No, I don't sorry," Kiara explained wrapping her hands around her torso. I twisted my head behind me but I didn't hear the chief's reply or the rest of the interview.

Gran held my elbow until we reached the car. She was extremely attentive until we were home where I locked myself in my room. My mind was completely filled with Melissa's hopeless eyes when she knew she was a dead woman.

I was so lost in the darkness of my thoughts that I gasped when I noticed a small piece of paper lying on my bed. That was not there when I left earlier today.

"Come to my house as soon as you can. Mason."

My heart started to pound in my chest and I rubbed the back of my neck. Mason wanted to see me. But why? I had a bad feeling in the pit of my stomach, this couldn't be for a good reason. But I couldn't ignore Mason, so I pushed away all the doubt that was infecting my mind and I jumped out my window into the cold night air.

I began jogging through the forest towards Mason's house. I had never been to his house before but I did figure out his address from Gran saying that he lived in the mansion on the top of the hill. I knew that there was only two hills' in our small town and the other was occupied by the church.

Unease was swirling in my stomach, but I refused to listen to the internal warning. If Mason needed me then I would be there. When I reached the hill, I ran all the way up the bitumen road and as I neared the crest, the road turned to stones. The lane was clearly not as frequently used as it neared the top of the hill.

Suddenly, I heard a horror filled scream echo through the forest. My blood ran cold as I snapped my eyes towards the direction of the noise, towards Mason's house. My muscles became taut when I realised something sinister was going on in there. I needed to find out what. I continued running until I reached the top of the hill.

A small gasp escaped from my lips as his house came into view. I glanced up into the darkness to reveal a colossal mansion. With wide eyes I glanced around in amazement; the mansion's style was archaic but still opulent – someone clearly still maintained it. Surrounding the entire property was a steel spiked fence that rose higher than some of the trees that enclosed it.

From the road a gravel driveway lead to a vintage gate that consisted of elegant wrought iron swirls and curlicues. The gate was connected by a lock in the shape of a lion's head roaring. The most noticeable feature about the mansion was how dark it was. A chill ran down the back of my neck in consternation as I thought about walking into the house.

Not one light inside the mansion was turned on, making it difficult to detect what resided at the end of the driveway. Just examining the haunting property set foreboding running into my toes. Its appearance was a clear warning not to come any closer. But Mason needed me.

I reached my shaky hand in front of me cautiously and pushed the gate forward. With a screech of disuse, the titanic gate creaked ominously as I opened it.

Moving stealthily, I slipped through the gate and gradually closed it behind me, grimacing as it creaked. I faced the dark mansion guardedly and ran a hand down my face to relax my puckered, tense forehead.

I crept towards the house, my steps crunching the gravel under my feet. I stepped up onto the veranda that encircled the mansion and peaked through one of the windows. But it was impossible to detect what was inside as they were boarded up with wooden panels and nails.

With tentative steps I neared the front door with a pounding heart and stopped before it, overwhelmed by its enormity. Its double doors were sculptured entirely of wood, its swing handle also carved into a lion's head. With sweaty palms I shakily raised my hand and softly knocked on the door. But there was no answer.

"Hello?" I yelled and knocked again but the house remained as inert as a corpse. I tried the door handle and luckily it was unlocked and swung open easily under my faltering grip. I stepped into the dark house and closed the door shut behind me.

My mouth fell open as I relished in the beauty that was before me. The house was nebulous due to the lack of lighting but I could see faintly due to multiple lit sconces that were protruding from the walls that were scattered around the room in various locations.

They radiated intermittent pools of an incandescent flickering glow from its candlelight, illuminating arbitrary features of the room. Before me was a foyer the size of a ballroom and located centrally was a grand staircase with swirling elegant handrails and red velvet carpet.

Its gloom set an ominous feeling straight into the depth of my bones. The house was deadly quiet and eerie like there hadn't been anyone living here for years and a shudder ran through me from the coldness biting my skin.

My attention caught on a hallway that was different to the rest of the house because it was illuminated by an electrical light. I stepped towards it to find a scintillating light shining through the cracks of a closed door.

Just before I opened the door, the most horrific agonising scream cut through the cold air of the mansion. With adrenaline fuelled fear pulsing through my veins, I sprinted straight towards the source which was a door that sat ajar on the opposite side of the room. When I emerged on the other side of the door my entire body became petrified and tensed up in terror.

Multiple sconces had been lit around the room immersing it in dappled shimmering light which made it clear for me to see what was occurring right in front of me. Bile rose in my stomach as my bulging eyes ranked over the scene before me.

I was in an open plan kitchen with a massive lounge room to its right that was overshadowed by a glass window running the entire span of the back wall. But the extravagance of the room wasn't what caught my attention.

Laid out on the island kitchen counter was a white sheet and above it was rows and rows of weapons. There was every horror inducing device possible, guns, knives of all shapes and sizes, shackles and endless objects I didn't even know existed. Behind all the weapons stood Mason and he looked absolutely frightening, like a fallen angel.

He was wearing a white coat over his clothes, but it wasn't white any more because it was completely covered in splattered blood. His expression was black as he picked up a lethal knife with precise movements. My hands were clasped over my mouth as my body shook violently, I wanted to run away but I was also shocked into immobilisation.

Mason didn't automatically lift his eyes to me like I thought he would have. It was like he was expecting me to be here or someone else. I watched slowly in mounting trepidation as Mason finally lifted his eyes to mine.

The first thing I noticed was how wild Mason's eyes were, his pupils had consumed his entire lens. I knew straight away what kind of mood he was in, murderous. When Mason recognised me, his face drained of colour and became ashen. For the first time since knowing Mason, I saw true fear take over his features.

"What are you doing here?" Mason raged hoarsely like there was something stuck in his throat. I didn't speak, I couldn't. Enmity glowered in his eyes from my lack of explanation.

"What are you doing here?" He bellowed, and he slammed his hands down onto the table. The emitting whack that resounded almost knocked me to the ground, making my knees shake. This was a new stage of angry for Mason, this was like how he was with Kenneth, not me.

"You told me too," I spluttered with knotted eyebrows. Mason's facial features scrunched up in loathing as he glared at me.

"I never said such a thing, are you deluded?" He spat with

such venom I staggered a step back from him. His words hit me as hard as a physical punch. I didn't understand his reaction and my eyes welled up with tears. Mason left me that note asking me to come here, unless someone else left that note. Which meant that I had just walked into Mason's home unannounced.

As that horror dawned on me, it was in that moment when I heard it. Another scream followed by the clanking of chains. The entire kitchen wall shook violently as another yell of torture sounded through the kitchen.

My eyes shot towards the noise and I saw that the fridge had been moved laterally to reveal a doorway that lead into an open secret room. I couldn't possibly imagine what Mason was hiding behind there, but it was something alive, something human.

"What is that?" I commanded forcefully, clenching my hands into fists as my anger sparked at how he was treating me when he was the one keeping secrets.

"Get out," Mason shrilled and pointed to the door behind me to leave. But the wall jolted behind him again as the sound of shackles reverberated through the passageway.

I didn't listen to him. I began to stalk towards the passageway to see for myself what was going on but as soon as I made my first movement Mason reacted.

He yanked his hand back and threw the knife that was already in his hand right at me. The knife flew through the air, heading straight for my face but just when I thought it was going to lodge into my skull it arched to the side. It narrowly missed my head and skimmed past my temple cutting through the side of my face, right next to my eye.

The knife landed in the wall behind me, leaving only a small indent in my skin. A droplet of blood fell down my cheek from the side of my eye leaving a trail of crimson in its wake. Mason didn't look surprised that the knife missed my face; it went exactly where he intended it to go. I was petrified into immobilisation, breathing heavily as I stared at him with wide fearful eyes.

"Leave now or that won't be the only cut left on your skin," Mason threatened callously, his eyes flashing. My body grimaced into the wall, wincing away from the knife. Tears welled in my eyes and one dripped down my face following the blood stain. I rose my eyes up to Mason, my eyes blazing with dissociation as I glared at him.

"You're a monster," I spat at him before I spun on my heels. I ran out that place that resembled hell as fast as possible.

I sprinted down the driveway and away from Mason and this darkness. I hurled open the gate and stumbled through onto the gravel road. But in my haste, I wasn't looking where I was going and as I raced out of the gates, I bashed into someone on the footpath walking past.

"Look out," some burly guy growled as he staggered a step away from me to correct his footing. He had dark skin and had tattoos all the way down both arms which only stopped where he had one hand missing. A few other scary looking guys surrounded him.

"Sorry," I spluttered and tried to dart past him hastily, but it didn't work. His eyes zoned in on my necklace and his hands impetuously grabbed onto the stopwatch that sat around my neck, the one Gran gave to me.

"What is this?" he demanded, flipping the watch over.

"A necklace." I yanked it out of his hand, taking a step away from him. He just smirked at me in return, revealing a diamond he had on one of his teeth.

"Give it to me," he commanded aggressively and closed the

145

gap between us once again. I stood my ground rising to my full height – I wasn't in the mood for this right now.

"No," I stated firmly and barged past him. But he raised one of his arms and my stomach smacked into his arm sending me staggering back into the gate. He drew a gun out of his pocket and my shoulders instantly tensed in response.

The man grabbed for the necklace and yanked it down so it ripped right off my neck. Redness rose up my neck and I clenched my jaw in rage from seeing Gran's necklace broken. Without thinking, I raised my arm and punched him right in the face so hard he collapsed to the floor. I had a moment of satisfaction as he grimaced in pain but I soon realised punching him was a terrible mistake.

All of his friends descended upon me, two of them grabbed my arms and held them behind my back leaving me completely restrained as I struggled against them. For the first time a small spark of fear lit up in my veins, after seeing everything I did inside that house, I felt fearless out here with these men.

The man with a missing hand stood up with his bloody lip now curled into a sneer as anger monopolised his features. He stalked towards me as he wiped away the blood from his lip. I allowed my mouth to curl up in amusement and pride at my work, but he didn't seem to feel the same way.

"You asked for it," he jibed before punching me right in the face. My head snapped to the side as pain radiated through my cheek to my entire body like I was shot. I yelled out as blood splattered from inside my mouth. I somehow managed to raise my head back up only to be greeted by another punch to the face, whacking my head back in the same direction.

I struggled against the men's hold that was restraining me and I managed to free one hand. I twisted out of one man's grip and ducked down before kneeing the other man. He fell to the floor, releasing my hands as he did so. After freeing myself from their grasps, I began to sprint off, but I was never a fast runner.

I heard the gun shot before I felt it sink into my flesh and the following burn that radiated through my pain receptors. I collapsed to the floor, yelling out in agony as I clutched my shoulder. My hands were covered in crimson liquid when I pulled them away, but I knew it wasn't anything serious.

The man with the missing hand stalked over towards me as well as his friends. One was short but strongly built with muscle and limping with tattoos all over his body and the other had a permanent sneer on his face. Those two men grabbed my arms again and yanked me upwards. I screeched out in pain as they hauled on the wound on my arm and pressed my back against the gate, holding my hands into the gate behind me to keep me restrained.

Toiling against the two men was eliciting no benefit for me because they were too strong and outnumbered me. The leader of the pack stood above me and delivered punch after punch until I couldn't stand the pain any longer. I screamed out in torment, for someone, anyone to help me. I finally gave into the thought that I was inevitably going to die.

When I saw a figure emerging in my peripheral vision, my heart soared with hope. I had just enough energy to twist my head to see Mason walking towards us. I sagged against the men holding me as relief washed through me like a wave. Mason was here. He would save me.

When Mason was only a few metres away he stopped dead in his tracks. He watched me intently, his head tilting to side as he observed the men throw punch after punch into my ribs and face like I was a punching bag. He waited there with a grave expression for an awfully long time while I glazed up at him like he was an angel, my saviour. But what was he waiting for? Shouldn't he be running over to help me?

Swiftly Mason spun on his heels, turning his back to me and walked away. Betrayal coursed through me, overtaking my mind and spirit and clouded my vision with tears. Mason just left me here to die.

It was then that I lost all my will and motivation to stay awake, to stay alive. I allowed my heavy eyelids to surmount over me and everything turned black as I passed out.

Chapter 14

My eyelids fluttered open to see a vivid image of Mason's face dominated by something intense and powerful. He was a clear vision of purpose as he stormed over towards me with a spark of silver hanging from his grip. The world around me shifted into blackness again, but I heard a cry of pain and the sound of flesh being cut open.

My vision returned in fragmented blurs and I saw Mason stalk up behind one of the men and cut his throat. The light left the man's eyes and Mason threw the body to the floor. I tried to keep my eyes open to watch what Mason was doing but I had lost too much blood and my eyelids were too heavy, and murkiness spotted my sight.

The ghastly noises continued on; I heard the crunch of punches being made as if a fight had broken out – it was five men against Mason. I forced my eyes open again to find that all the men that once surrounded me, were now lying on the floor with their throats cut open. The two men holding me up released me and I fell to the floor with a grunt of pain.

The men dropped, clanging into the gate with blood dripping down their necks, dead. I saw the man with one hand run off into the distance, but I took no notice; I only had eyes for Mason. He was standing right in front of me staring at the man as he ran off. Mason's eyes flickered down to me and shifted between us as if he couldn't decide who to go after first.

"Mason," I croaked, trying to speak but my voice was rough

as if my throat had been torn out. Mason's intense gaze snapped right down to me. His dark murderous eyes instantaneously softened as if they were melting gold as he glanced at me. He leaned down to touch his cold hand to my bleeding face and held my cheek softly as if I was a fragile piece of glass.

"I'm sorry," he whispered in my ear and his warm breath sent a beautiful chill down my spine. His hand left my face to pull a stray hair away from my sweaty skin before bending down and wrapping me into his arms. I couldn't take my eyes off him; he came back for me. Mason picked me up easily, tucking me into his chest as close as possible. The warmth of his skin sunk into my frozen flesh making me feel alive again.

With what little energy I had left I raised my hands up and wrapped them around Mason's neck as tightly as I could. Mason let his head drop so his nose rubbed against my cheek in a calming movement that made my stomach flip. I clung onto him like he was the only thing left on this earth. Mason walked me through the front garden and kicked the front door open, so he didn't have to let go of me.

The movement sent a jolt through my broken body and I couldn't help releasing a small cry of pain. Mason's muscles became rigid and he tightened his arms around me, so I was brought even closer to his body.

"Sorry," he apologised quietly. I couldn't move my mouth to speak but I didn't take my eyes away from his. He was looking down at me with his eyebrows pinched together and a deep care in his eyes that I hadn't ever seen there before. I wanted more of it. In that moment I needed more of it. He moved his eyes away from mine to walk us up the stairs and I tucked my head into his neck where it was warm and safe.

I didn't move my head away from Mason's neck, but I

noticed us going up yet another flight of stairs. Mason kicked another door open and then he gently placed me down onto a dark soft bed. I sunk right down into the mattress as Mason slid his hands away from under me once I was stable.

I noticed the loss of his warmth immediately and I reached out towards him desperately. It was as if in that moment when he wasn't touching me, holding me together, all the pain that was aching through my body returned with a brutal force. I managed to grab a fist full of his shirt and pulled him back to me.

He returned easily sliding onto the bed beside me, wrapping his arms around my body as if they were made to be there. I encased my own arms around his waist and rested my spinning head onto his chest. My body ached and cried out in pain, but the soreness was subsiding.

"Do you need anything?" Mason asked softly into my ear. I felt the light brush of his dark hair flutter across my skin and it felt just as intimate as any kiss could. All I needed was to look back into his worried blue eyes that were glued to mine and were searching me for any signs of pain.

"Just you," I murmured. Mason didn't argue with that, and he continued to hold me tightly. He leaned his head down and touched his lips to my forehead lightly placing a soft kiss there. Ardour rushed through me like honey at his affectionate touch and I closed my eyes to reveal in every second of it. His lips rested on my hair as he started running one of his hands down my back in a soothing motion that had an intense calming effect on my body.

I relaxed into him further, snuggling into his muscled body. I focused on the motion of his soft hands and it took my mind off the pain that was still coursing through my body. Surrendering to the weight of my heavy eyelids, I slowly drifted off to sleep in Mason's arms.

***

I woke up with a gasp of panic. I knew instantly that I wasn't in my room. My eyes scanned the area around me quickly to find myself in a large bedroom. There was a colossal window that was covered in opaque blinds cloaking the far wall and blocking out the morning sunlight. The room had a predominantly black layout with dark modern furniture and an obsidian covered king-sized bed in the middle of the room, which I was lying in right now.

All the events of the previous night rushed back to me like a tidal wave and nearly expelled all the wind out of my lungs. Melissa's death, Mason's secrets and his betrayal before he finally saved me. My hands shot to my neck to find that Gran's necklace was once again chained around my neck; Mason must have returned it there.

Firstly, butterflies swarmed in my stomach as I remembered the way Mason held me last night as I fell asleep, but then the reality of the situation dawned as I remembered Mason's betrayal. Last night when the only thing on my consciousness was the pain, I had no strength to push Mason away. But now that I had my wits back, I knew what I had to do.

Mason left me, he made the decision to turn around and leave me to die. Even though he eventually returned, his first instinct was to leave and that would always be the case. Mason could never love me like I needed him too. Look where trying to make him care for me got me? He yelled at me and then proceeded to throw a knife at me. Did I really want that for my future life?

That was why I needed to do what was best for me; for the first time in my life, I was going to put myself first. I couldn't do this any more; I couldn't see Mason any more.

I rolled over onto my side to find Mason still in the bed although he was no longer touching me. There was a distance between us now as he stared up at the ceiling with his hands folded over his chest, but his haunted expression made it seem like he was thinking about something a lot darker than just a ceiling.

Once again, his beauty nearly knocked the breath out of me. His dark brown hair sat curved on the side of his face like a curtain partially obstructing the scar that ran down his cheek and encircled his beautiful light blue eyes. Although, his eyes appeared to be anything but bright today.

He had black shadows under his eyes like he hadn't slept all night and his blue irises looked deeply tortured and blood shot. Using what little restraint, I had, I closed my eyes tightly and looked away from him. I placed up a steel barrier between my heart and him before rising from the bed.

Mason's eyes immediately snapped to me and he sat up rigidly as well mimicking my movements. He still had that tortured look in them as he scrutinised me. It only seemed to intensify the longer he stared at me. I must have looked as bad as I felt.

"Hi," I stammered, not really knowing what else to say to him after falling asleep in his arms after he left me to die. Mason didn't reply, he just continued to stare at me with an agonised expression. His eyes scanned every inch of my face and his expression of gloomy filled self-hate intensified.

He just continued to stare at me, not saying anything.

"Thanks for saving me last night," I acknowledged with a hoarse tone. I was still beyond angry that he turned to leave me, but he did come back and I would be dead if he hadn't.

153

Mason stayed silent, he just turned his head away from me and the corners of his eyes scrunched up tightly. I sighed and ignoring his stoicism, I tried to stand up off the bed but when a stabbing pain radiated out from my shoulder I had to sit back down again.

Mason finally reacted, rising up from the bed and walking steadily over to my side. He placed a hand around my waist, helping me up. Once I was stable on the ground, I took a step away from him and he noticed this, his eyes following my movements.

"How are you feeling?" Mason asked finally with a small voice and concern seared in his eyes as he inspected my wound. "I removed the bullet and stitched up your shoulder." I glanced down to my shoulder to find it patched over with a white bandage. I didn't remember him doing that, so I must have been passed out.

"I will live." I shrugged, although my shoulder was aching so badly that it felt like I might collapse from it. I knew my arm was going to cause me pain for some time after this but I knew how to handle it; I've been through worse.

Mason stared at me agonised, like I just stabbed him and I didn't know why. Out of nowhere he raised one of his hands and touched one of his fingers to the side of my eye. His light touch stung so I knew there must be a bruise forming there. He ran his finger over the bruise like a feather for one moment before letting his hand drop again.

"I'm sorry I let this happen to you," he apologised with a deeply repentant tone. My heart leapt for a moment at the affection in his eyes, but that jump of happiness was closely followed by stab of pain as I remembered what he did.

If my heart could have its way, I would go back to Mason

154

again and again no matter what he did to me. But I needed to be strong. I remembered how when I needed Mason the most all I saw was his back as he left me for dead.

"You walked away, you were going to leave me," I declared curtly, cutting straight to the chase. Instantly, Mason's eyes dropped from mine and he hung his head.

"Yes," he confirmed. My breath hitched painfully as his words cut me deep even though I already knew what he was going to say. I knew there was no point in asking my next question, but I did anyway, to see if he trusted me.

"Are you going to tell me what you were doing last night?"

"No," he answered bluntly. And that was all I needed to hear. I turned on my heels and moved to storm as far away from Mason as possible, but I was stopped when a strong hand wrapped around my wrist.

"Wait. Before you go just let me tell you one thing," Mason pleaded into my ear, and the desperation in his voice caused me to stop dead in my tracks. I spun around to face him and what I saw on his features was not what I had expected.

He was staring at me earnestly like I was the bright moon on a pitch-black night. It sent a jostle straight through my chest and I was left at his mercy once again.

"Fine," I huffed, crossing my hands across my chest. Mason's already intense eyes softened into honey as he searched my face, as if he was taking in every feature it held. He gently brushed his hand down my cheek and my breath hitched at his soft touch. His haunted deep blue eyes draw me in like a magnet.

"I love you," he admitted softly.

My entire being jolted as if I was struck by lightning; my heart squeezed and my stomach lurched into my throat like he had set off a cataclysmic reaction. Mason's words created all sorts of warmth and thrills of euphoria within me as my mind fluttered over that fantasy for a moment. The fantasy that what he had to say was true.

I froze as reality returned and I struggled to comprehend what he had just said. It didn't make any sense, he couldn't love me, not after what he did last night.

"What?" I spluttered, completely dazed. I staggered a step back from him, so his hand dropped to his side.

"I know you don't trust me after what I did to you, but I just need you to know," Mason explained sincerely. My eyebrows were pinched together tightly as I glanced up at him in utter bewilderment. But his features remained stoic and his eyes honest, he was serious. He actually thought he loved me, even after everything he did to me. An explosion of anger burned through my veins that I didn't even know existed and I jammed a finger into his chest.

"How dare you? Yesterday you yelled at me like you wanted to kill me and then you threw a knife at me and proceeded to leave me to die. Now, you tell me that you love me? What do you think love is?" I objected fiercely. Mason's features dropped into a grimace and he staggered a step back from me in a wince as if I just shot him.

"I know it sounds bad," he defended with pleading eyes and ran his hands down his face.

"Worse than bad, psychotic," I barked with callous. Mason pulled his hands through his dark hair strongly with both hands in deep agitation.

"I'm sorry, I just," he faltered as his voice fractured. Then he looked me straight in the eyes and his seared with desperation. "Things have changed since then. After seeing those men hurt you like that something changed. I wanted to kill them all and for

156

the first time I didn't want to kill because of my need for it, it was because they were hurting you. It made me realise that I do have feelings for you and these feeling, they are nothing like I have ever felt before. These are real," Mason proclaimed vehemently. I saw in his eyes that his whole heart and soul was trying to convey to me what he felt.

"You are strong and you aren't afraid of me. You are fearless and free and you fight for what you want, never taking no for an answer, and I love every part of you." Mason leaned closer to me so that our bodies were nearly touching, just how they were supposed to be.

"All my life I have never felt anything even close to love but what I feel for you, when I'm around you, it's an emotion so strong it's overwhelming. I thought it was hate that I was feeling but it's not. I can't bear the thought of anything happening to you, or the thought of you dying." He shivered, with horror plain to see on his features.

"When I turned around to walk away, I realised then that that was it, you were going to die. And I couldn't bear it. I would have done anything to keep you with me," Mason explained.

His words were slowly breaking the steel wall I had put up between him and my heart, and I was melting inside. This was everything I ever wanted to hear him say, everything beyond even my wildest dreams. The worst part of it all was that I couldn't even relish in it because all I could see in my mind was his back as he left me for dead.

He was just going to do the same thing again and again and it's just going to leave me broken beyond repair. I didn't trust him and I knew what I had to do next.

"I can't do this. I need to do what is best for me," I stated with finality as a tear dripped down my cheek. The heartbreak was clear in Mason's features but he didn't fight my choice. He just brought up his hand and softly wiped my tear away.

"I understand, I know I messed up and I can never tell you how sorry I am." Mason's eyes were brimming with regret as he clasped my hand in his. The warmth of his skin seeped into mine and I wanted to stay there forever.

"Just know that I will always be here if you need me, always," he promised, and my heart melted further. My tightly bound muscles were relaxing into him and I knew I was giving into him. So, I steeled my heart and pulled my hand away from him.

Agony rose in his eyes and crinkled the skin around them. The sight of his pain that I had caused made my heart hurt like someone had just stabbed a jagged piece of glass through it.

I closed my eyes tightly, blocking him off from me and turned away from him. I left the mansion with a heavy heart and a strong sense in my chest that leaving Mason was a terrible mistake.

Chapter 15

"Firstly, I would like to thank everyone for gathering here today. I know it was late notice, but it was imperative that we had this meeting," announced the chief of police, Amanda. She scanned the crowd with lowered bushy eyebrows that resonated a stark severity.

The seriousness of the situation kept the entire town silent. I was sitting next to Gran with my spine held up stiffly – we were situated on the furthest bench from the front in the church where we were congregated for a town meeting.

"As you all know, the beloved town mayor's daughter was murdered last week in cold blood. Most of you saw the remains of her body and saw that this murder was orchestrated by someone who called themselves 'Marlemore'," she announced darkly, lifting her nose to narrow her eyes at the town.

I gasped quietly, and just from the sound of that name my hands shook. I noticed similar reactions in those around me; the name set a fear alight within everyone in this town. I noticed Brandon, Melissa's boyfriend, was standing on the stage beside the chief of police and I saw his body start to tremor. I pressed my mouth into a firm line in distaste as I remembered the horrible words he spoke to me at the fair.

The chief's stern gaze sunk into us as she flickered her eyes around to each of us accusingly. The whole town remained so quiet that you could hear the crickets outside as what she said resonated within the masses. There was a murderer in our town.

"But this horror has not been new to us in recent months. We have also had a teenage boy, Ryan, go missing and now I can confidently affirm that these two crimes are related. From my investigations, I believe that the same person is responsible, Marlemore," she declared, her expression grave. I tucked my coat closer around my shoulders in unease.

"The reason that I am holding this urgent meeting is because we have had another person go missing in the last week. One of our own, officer Kenneth Milton," Amanda explained hauntingly. Hushed horrified whispers broke out in the crowd. I looked down to my hands that were clasped in my lap avoiding everyone's eyes. I knew who the murderer of officer Kenneth was. I saw him murdered before my own eyes by Mason. I kept my lips tightly pressed together.

"It is imperative we find out who this murderer is." Her tone had turned dire and grim as she spoke her words carefully. "If anyone has any knowledge of what happened to Melissa, you need inform me as soon as possible. You could be the difference between life or death. Because Marlemore will strike again until they have got what they came for. No one is safe," she warned, leaning forward over the lectern towards the crowd to accentuate the seriousness of the situation.

A shiver slithered through my limbs; she was right, because no one was safe. Any one of us could be murdered at any moment.

"I'm regretful to inform you but there is a murderer among us – someone in this town is trying to kill us," she denounced inauspiciously.

I noticed those around me wondering their eyes to those sitting next to them, as did my own. I glanced towards my fretful grandmother who had a pink handkerchief up to her mouth in horror. Then I moved my gaze towards my left, where Belle my boss was tightly clutching her child into her chest with one arm and clutching her girlfriend's hand with the other. I looked around at the rest of the town. No one looked like a murderer, but I guess you never know what people are hiding.

"We need to find this murderer soon or I fear that Melissa will not be the last death that will occur in this town," Amanda warned mournfully. The town became quiescent and soundless from her haunting words.

The silence was only broken by the squeaking sound of the church doors opening. It caused all of us to jump in our seats and snap our heads towards the back of the room.

I recognised the dark curve of Mason's hair immediately and it caused all my nerve endings to ignite. He was dressed in dark jeans and a white t-shirt that made his eyes stand out against the light colour.

It was a shock seeing him, and I wasn't prepared for the way my heart reacted to his presence. I hadn't seen him since that night and it had been a long week trying to stay away from him. I tried all manner of distractions, such as dancing classes and I even went out to dinner with Belle and her girlfriend.

Mason sauntered in casually as if he hasn't just walked in late when we were talking about a murderer. Everyone in the town glared at him accusingly, and I knew what they were thinking. They thought he was the murderer. And I was the only one who knew that they were right; he was the murderer of one of those people.

He placed himself on one of the back seats in the last row opposite to where my grandma and I were seated. I noticed a few people shuffle away from him as he sat down, as if they thought he was going to pull out a knife and cut their throats right here in the church.

The chief called back our attention as she gestured to Brandon who was still standing beside her and she wrapped an arm around his broad shoulders. I noticed Brandon didn't look like he had taken Melissa's death well. His eyes were puffy and his face was as white as a sheet.

"My son was Melissa's partner and he is doing everything he can to help with the investigation. I need everyone else to be brave like my son and come forward to give a statement if you have had any close relations to Melissa in the last few weeks," the chief urged. I kept silent in my seat, but that wasn't the only reason I couldn't move my eyes higher than my knees.

I felt Mason's eyes on me, and they were boring straight into the side of my head like they were lasers setting my skin alight. He didn't move them from me for the rest of the meeting.

I fervently tried to retain my attention at the front but I couldn't stop my eyes from flickering to him. Each time he was looking right at me and a jolt would ignite through my stomach like a jumping jack when I caught his blue stare. All I could think about were his words, I love you.

It caused a warmth of euphoria to swirl through me and remembering those words made his stare so much more meaningful. But I refused to move my eyes to him. It was strange having our roles reversed. Weeks ago, I would have done anything to look at him whereas he wanted nothing to do with me.

Luckily the meeting ended relatively quickly. Everyone stood around talking about the horror these last few weeks had become, including my grandma as she spoke with Bill and Henrietta.

Gran watched me out of the corner of her eye. She had been

162

especially attentive towards me after that night I ran into those men. I had been able to cover my bruises relatively easily with makeup, but I think Gran still suspected and noticed the way I hobbled around from the bruises on my ribs.

I didn't want to hang around and deal with the feelings that Mason was evoking within me as he stood crossed legged leaning against the back wall staring at me. I decided to wait for Gran by the car and started moving towards the back doors. But in my haste to avoid Mason I tripped over a tile which was jutting out on the floor and staggered into a pile of crates, one lodging itself onto my foot.

My cheeks burned red as I stood motionless and trapped with my leg in a crate at Mason's feet. We locked eyes and I saw a light of amusement in his which made me huff. But Mason didn't move, he just watched me as I tried to yank my foot out repeatedly but to no avail.

Shockingly, I felt the warmth on his hands as he rested them on my ankles. My eyes shot down to him as he kneeled in front of me. He was staring up at me with a look of pure devotion. My skin started blazing from where he touched me as he slowly twisted the crate off my foot carefully like I was a porcelain plate.

My heart squeezed as he ever so slowly released my ankle from his grasp. He stood from the floor gradually but he was so close to me that his chest slightly brushed against mine as he rose. I shivered in longing.

When he reached his full height, he stared deep into my eyes with a small smirk on his face. I was soaking in every feeling he created within me which was more intense now that I knew that this was not just all in my head, and he cared about me too.

"Hi," Mason breathed finally. His breath fluttered across my skin like a velvet touch from a feather causing goose bumps to break out on my arms.

"Didn't I tell you to stay away from me?" I replied apathetically, resting my hand on my hip. He raised an eyebrow at me.

"No," he stated confidently.

"Well I am asking you now." I crossed my arms. Mason leaned closer to me and my stomach pushed up into my throat.

"You don't seem genuine in that request," he challenged, as our eyes locked in a silent standoff. His fluorescent blue eyes were so distracting; they were so light, so pretty.

"I am certainly certain exactly what I am requesting, thank you very much," I stuttered in disorientation. Mason's eyes seemed to brighten up as he watched me struggle and his lip turned up at the corner like he was hiding a smile. Damn him.

"Your body's reaction to me suggests another story." He gestured his chin down to my chest which was now touching his and he hasn't moved a muscle. Unconsciously I had been moving my body towards his.

"What do you know about my body?" I shot back.

"Not as much as I would like to," he breathed seductively. My blood was heating up rapidly due to his presence and words. I needed to get out of here now.

"It was nice talking to you, but I best be off," I declared as I shambled away from him, but I was stopped as a hand wrapped around my wrist softly.

"Don't go," he pleaded into my ear and his desperate tone broke my heart. All I wanted to do was turn around and bury my face into his chest, but I knew I couldn't do that.

"Don't speak to me again. I need distance," I stated but it sounded more like a request. Mason just tilted his head to the side as he looked at me inquisitively.

"Please," I reiterated, allowing all the emotions I was feeling to leak into my tone. He dropped his eyes and they became soft like a calm lake in the summertime.

"Okay. Anything for you, my love," Mason agreed with a nod of his head. He let his eyes search my face one more time before he took one more step closer to me. He placed his hand onto my cheek and the warmth of his skin and calloused hands send a shiver through my body.

He moved his hand lower and ran his thumb over my bottom lip. A rush of heat spread through my entire body and my heart started skippering, longing for his lips to touch that spot. His fingers lingered for a beautiful moment before leaned forwards instead of away. He kissed the top of my head and contentment streamed through me like liquid silk. His lips lingered there for a moment before he was gone. My heart jumped in my chest as if it was trying to run after him.

I glanced around shakily to find he had already moved into the crowd. It took me a few moments to regain my bearings and ability to move. I exited the church with my mind in a haze and as I stepped out into the cold wind it blew my hair fiercely around my head.

Behind me I heard the other town members follow me out from the church and the herd moved out together like frightened sheep. I hurried over to the car and just as I placed my hand onto the door handle, I heard a snap of a twig within the trees beyond. My eyes shot to the sound, towards the dark canopy of the woods that encircled the church.

And what I saw between the umbra of the tree trunks caused panic to grip a hold of my stomach like it was wringing my insides like a towel. My eyes rounded as I watched a man being held by a knife to his throat by someone whose face was covered by a dark hood. The rest of the attacker's body was covered in a black cape, contorting it into a black sinister shadow. But I knew who it was instantly, Marlemore.

It happened so quickly, so fast I didn't even have time to move a muscle. The dark figure of Marlemore stepped out of the shadows. I recognised the man who was being held captive by his blonde buzz cut and his eyes that held such a tormented agony when he stood before the town not moments earlier. Brandon.

Brandon's terror filled eyes locked onto mine as it happened. The shadow pressed the knife into Brandon's neck causing blood to stream down from the wound. I watched immobile in blind terror as the light slowly left Brandon's eyes and he lost function of his body. He slipped to the floor, dead. With my hands on my mouth and my breathing non-existent my eyes darted towards the shadowed figure to find the yellow light of its eyes were staring right back at me.

But before I could process that information, the dark figure lurched towards me with murder in its eyes. The crunch of the gravel underneath Marlemore's boots was all I could hear as he advanced. I tried to move, to spark my muscle fibres with a conduction but my tendons had stiffened up. In less than two second, hands wrapped around my neck and started squeezing the life out of me.

Immediately, my eyes drew out of their sockets and my neck muscles constricted under the strain causing my breathing to cease. I couldn't see into Marlemore's eyes as they were covered from the hood that just touched the bottom of his eye-socket and the darkness of the night disguised his facial features, but I heard something. In the quiet of our struggle, it was a hushed noise, a ticking.

"This is for you, Elora," spoke Marlemore in my ear

sinisterly and the sound sent a tremulous shudder through me. The voice was deep and electrically amplified to sound as horrifying as possible.

I managed to open my mouth to release a piercing scream, that echoed hauntingly through the night. My scream did its job; everyone who had gathered around the church snapped their attention towards us. The first thing I heard was Mason's voice.

"Elora!" he yelled at me with pure terror lacing his tone in a way I had never heard from him before. He started sprinting towards me at full speed.

At the sound of Mason's voice, my muscles tensed and my body prepared to fight. I was not going to die now, not now when Mason loved me. Gathering all the fire I had left in me, I twisted my body out of Marlemore's grip and elbowed his neck so that he loosened his hold on my throat. I was then able to take a few steps behind him and kick at the back of his knees so he lost his balance and stumbled away from me.

I gasped for breath and without thinking about my broken lungs, I swirled on my heels and sprinted towards Mason as he ran to me. I heard the crunch of oncoming boots as Marlemore sprinted up behind me. With my arms reached towards Mason I was just about to run into his arms, but Mason did something unexpected.

He rushed past me and placed his body in front of mine, so he was blocking me from Marlemore. It happened so fast I didn't even notice what was occurring until I saw the silver knife sink into Mason's chest. He placed himself between the oncoming knife that was meant for me. My heart stopped and my worst nightmare became a reality when I saw it sink into Mason's flesh.

But just as quickly, Mason counteracted the stab as if he wasn't even wounded and pushed his forearm out in front of him, which sent Marlemore flying out from under his feet. Marlemore kept a hold of the knife and it slid back out of Mason's body with blood covering it.

My stomach curdled to the point where I felt nauseated and I darted my wide panicked eyes to Mason. He was looking down at his chest and inspecting his wound. There was just a small cut on his left pectoral muscle just under his clavicle and the sight of the insignificant flesh wound allowed me to breathe again. Mason was okay.

Marlemore retreated, moving back into the shadows but I didn't care, I only had eyes for Mason. I grabbed his face with both of my hands as I fretted over him. He leaned his cheek into my hand and closed his eyes like he was savouring the moment. Even though he had just been stabbed, my touch to him was more important. It made my heart skip a beat.

"Are you okay?" I gasped with a raspy breath.

"Fine," Mason insisted, opening his eyes with a tight smile. I searched his storm raging eyes for any signs of pain to find none.

I opened my mouth to ask how he wasn't in pain when another blood curdling scream cut through the night. Without us noticing, the other town members had raced over to us.

Someone must have seen the blood on the ground that had spilt from the woods. My face fell as I remembered Brandon's dead body. Without another thought I started dashing back towards Brandon's body.

"Elora," Mason called after me but I kept running. I maneuverer my way through the branches of the woods until I finally reached his body. Blood was dripping down from the cut in his neck by the gallons and the cut was so deep I saw his veins. His eyes looked up into the canopy of trees above, blank. It was too late; he was already dead.

My lungs deflated, and I allowed my head to fall in grievance as I mourned over his body. I had failed to save Brandon too. It was then that I noticed something sticking out of his jacket pocket, something unusual. It was a yellow handle and it stood out in the dark night due to its bright colour.

I grabbed it and pulled it out from Brandon's pocket to find that it was a handle of a gun. I stared at it for longer that I should have but I felt a strange sense of familiarity. Then I remembered Marlemore's words.

"This is for you, Elora."

Suddenly it hit me like a battering ram.

No. I dropped the gun like it was poison and crawled away from it as far as possible, my hands clenching into the dead fallen leaves. It couldn't be could it?

With deep anguish puckering my forehead I stepped back over to it and looked down at the base of the gun to find the shape of a snake engraved into the metal. My entire body seized up and blazing fear shot through me as realisation hit me in the stomach in full force.

How does Marlemore know?

Chapter 16

The incessant dripping of the rain against the roof of the cottage set my bones on edge. It had started pouring when I began making dinner. I made a pasta and left a portion there for Gran. She was helping with the aftermath of Brandon's murder at the church. It was almost midnight and she still hadn't returned home yet. I was lying on the couch shivering, waiting for her to return. I couldn't sleep in the house alone, not right now, not after what happened.

After finding the gun on Brandon, I hid it in my pocket before Mason found me shaking violently over Brandon's body. The chief of police pronounced her only son dead at the scene and I couldn't stay around to watch the agony on her face or listen to her tortured screams. Mason gave me a lift home on his motorbike and he offered to stay with me but I declined. I knew this upset him because his shoulders and face dropped but I needed to be alone to think through this new revelation that Marlemore knew my secret.

Giving up on Gran's return, I took a diazepam, a fast-acting anti-anxiety medication to help me sleep as I was feeling close to a panic attack. I switched the lights off in the living room and closed the curtains. I checked outside to see if Gran might be there and that was when I noticed a hunched over figure sitting out in the rain at the end of the porch. My veins lurched alive throughout my entire body. I knew who it was immediately.

What was Mason still doing here?

I grabbed my raincoat and moved out into the drizzling rain through the front door. Mason was sitting on the end of our stone cobbled porch staring into the dark forest beyond my house. He was leaning back against a pillar and he had one of his knees pulled up to his chest and his chin was resting on his knee like he was huddling for warmth. The pouring rain was dripping down his face and had soaked into his clothes, but it didn't seem to bother him.

"What are you still doing out here?" I exclaimed with a sigh, my words breaking through the silence of the night. Mason jolted before he quickly spun his head around to look up at me. We locked eyes for a brief moment and then he jumped up to his feet to stand in front of me. I had to take a step back from him because he stood so close. His dark brown hair had stuck to the side of his face from the rain making a curtain around his blue eyes.

"I couldn't leave, not after what happened. I just need to make sure you're okay," he breathed, and his words made a lump form in my throat. He was waiting out here in the freezing rain just to make sure I was okay. The elation of this realisation was followed by a stabbing pain bursting that bubble.

I hated this, why did he do this to me? Why did he have to make me push him away when all my heart and soul wanted was to be with him?

"You can leave, I'm fine," I snapped as my frustration at this situation festered into my attitude towards him. Mason's eyes widened for a moment at my harsh words before he returned to his normal stoic expression.

"What if something happens in the night?" he deflected, folding his arms across his chest. He was so stubborn.

"Nothing will happen Mason." I gave him a flat look to convey my disinterest in his argument. I could take care of

171

myself.

He exhaled deeply and glanced up at me with tired eyes. He was so worn out, there were deep black circles resting underneath his eyes, he looked as if he hadn't had any sleep for weeks.

"Why won't you let me help you? Why won't you let me in?" He looked at me with defeated eyes and it was like he was finally allowing me to see the vulnerability he felt and it made my chest ache. Which then sparked into anger because he was the one who caused this. How dare he make me feel guilty?

"Because you will just leave me again. You are so unpredictable," I rebuffed, throwing my hands into the air. His constant change in attitude towards me was causing me too much anxiety, he goes from telling me that I'm beautiful to throwing knives at me.

"Haven't I shown you that I've changed?" Mason argued as he raked his hands through his dark hair.

"You haven't changed. As soon as the going gets tough you will leave," I declared with finality. Mason took another step towards me causing my breath to hitch. He was so close that the aureate fluorescent from the porch light shined into his blue eyes allowing me to see the white specs in them.

"I promise you I will never leave you again. Not if something threatens to kill everyone I know or destroy this whole world. I will always choose you," Mason admitted fiercely. His words made my breathing catch in my throat as my heart hammered.

"Why won't you give me a chance?" he pleaded. I remembered the last time I let someone in, I remembered the back of Annalise's black braid as she betrayed me, sending me to jail. My next words came out more forcefully than I intended as the lingering heartbreak exploded to the surface.

"Because everyone I have ever let in has left me. I can't have you and then lose you. I wouldn't be able to live through that. If I don't let you in then I can't lose you," I exclaimed, my emotions and fears bursting from within me.

My eyes welled up with tears and one stray droplet fell from my eye, but I wiped it away quickly. Mason blinked, stunned into silence and a few rain droplets fell from his long lashes. He raised one of his hands and took mine in his, intertwining our fingers. It made my heart warm.

"I'm sorry that happened to you, my love. But I can assure you I will never do the same," he promised as he touched his hand to my face for one moment. Just the small touch caused my quivering muscles to relax.

"You have left me before, how can I have any trust that you won't do it again?" I counteracted, revealing my fears to him. Mason ran his hand down the back on his neck raking at his skin.

"I can't begin to tell you how sorry I am for that, but there was a reason for it and it wasn't because I wanted you to suffer." His eyes were pleading with me to believe him. My stomach swirled with hope, that his explanation could be true.

"What is it then?" I asked. Mason's eyes dropped from mine and my hope diminished with them. He scuffed one of his feet on the pebbled floor.

"I can't tell you."

I dropped his hand as both of mine balled up into fists at my side, how dare he ask me to let him in when he won't even let me in?

"Again, with all the secrets and lies. How do you expect me to be with you if you're just going to keep lying to me all the time?" I boomed.

My insinuation shocked Mason, his head jerked back and he staggered a step away from me as if I just shot him in the chest.

173

He squeezed his eyes shut and it took him a moment to gather himself. I spent that time trying to rein in my anger, taking deep breaths. I focused on the pitter patter splashes of the rain on the roof.

"You're right," Mason admitted with repeated nods of his head. "You're all I care about in this world. Before I had nothing to live for, nothing that I really loved and no one that loved me. But you changed everything. My existence became such a different place since meeting you. You're everything to me," he explained as his fierce eyes stared straight into mine.

Tears welled up in my eyes again at his beautiful words. No one has ever said anything like that to me before. I didn't know what to believe any more. Why was I pushing him away again?

"Why are you telling me this?" I stuttered as a tear fell down my cheek.

"I just want you to know that I could never leave you," Mason vowed, and brought his hand up to wipe away my tear that had already mixed in with the rain droplets falling from the sky.

"Just give me a chance, please."

In deep aggravation, I ran both my hands through my hair and pulled it into a knot at the back of my neck. I felt myself slipping, slowly giving into him and his words that made me feel truly loved for the first time in my life. But my fretting was cut short when Mason suddenly turned livid, his body stiffening.

His pupils dilated turning his eyes dark and hooded. His hands became fists at his side and his jaw muscles tensed under the strain he was applying against them. I squinted my eyes up at him completely baffled by his sudden change in demeanour.

"What is that?" he growled as he pointed to my neck. Instinctively I brought my hands up to my neck which made it

174

sting as if pressing down onto a bruise. That was when I realised what it was, it was from Marlemore's hands as he tried to strangle the life out of me. It had bruised badly already.

Mason's eyes carefully inspected every inch of my neck and rage flashed in his eyes when I flinched away from the pain.

"I am going to kill him," Mason spat in resentment. He lifted a hand out to reach for me but then realised that if he did so then I would be in pain and dropped his hand.

"It's fine, I'm okay. It will heal in a couple of days." I waved it off with a flick of my wrist. But Mason wasn't listening to me, his fists had started to become white from him pressing down so hard on them. I was beginning to understand the warning signs when he would switch into one of his dark moods – the mood when he needed to kill, to see blood.

"He will die for doing that to you."

"Relax Mason, it's okay," I placated conciliatory, trying to calm him, but I wasn't getting through to him. His eyes snapped up to mine and the darkness that resided there sent a chill down my spine.

"I need to kill him," Mason declared, taking a step away from me and his eyes flickered around wildly searching the forest as if Marlemore was in there.

"I need to kill something," Mason barked and reached into his pocket. The first thing I saw was the flash of silver and then his knife emerged. My eyes widened in fear as he yanked up one of his shirtsleeves. I knew what he was going to do next.

Nausea radiated through my body and I bit down onto my knuckles, I couldn't watch this, not again. Just the thought of it made my heart feel like it was tearing into two pieces. Panic streamed through my veins and I flinched when Mason brought the knife up to his skin and began to add pressure. The smallest

175

drop of blood drew from the cut and the sight spurred me into motion. I didn't know what I was doing but all I knew was that I needed him to stop.

I threw myself at him and wrapped both my arms around his neck, pulling his head down towards mine. My lips flew straight to his and I kissed him with all the emotion and fear I was feeling inside. His knife immediately dropped to the ground with a clatter. His lips stayed rigid against mine for a moment before the surprise wore off and he kissed me back. And boy did he kiss me back.

His lips pressed into mine, overpowering my lips as he dragged his bottom lip over mine and pulled it into his mouth. His arms cradled me against him, wrapping around my waist as his lips moved against mine forcefully. My blood charged beneath my skin, steaming up like I was on fire. I moved my lips against his in response with similar vigour, running my hands through his dark hair. His lips were so soft and he kissed me like I was the most precious thing in this world. Not at all how I imagined a murderer to kiss.

Kissing Mason was even better than I had imagined. I couldn't believe this was actually happening. His hands slowly ran down my back touching me like I was glass. His kiss was filled with so much passion, drawling alive everything I felt for him and every nerve ending in my body.

Our lips came apart at the same time, but they were still touching as we both caught our breaths. Mason pulled back further and stared down at me. His features had a strange sense of calmness to them and his eyes were stunned, as if he couldn't believe what had just happened.

My strategy worked, there wasn't one spec of the previous darkness there, he no longer needed to hurt himself or kill someone else.

"I better head inside," I mumbled as I unwrapped my hands from around his neck.

"Okay." He didn't argue this time.

With shaky hands I fumbled with the door handle and finally walked into the cottage. I didn't dare look back at Mason as I closed the door behind me. With my heart still hammering in my chest I brought my hands up to my lips and touched the skin that was just on Mason's.

I just kissed a murderer and I absolutely loved it.

Chapter 17

"Are you feeling okay?" Gran asked quietly from behind me. I jumped, throwing dish washing liquid into the air and nearly dropped the plate I was cleaning. I didn't hear her enter the room. As she walked into the kitchen, she tiredly pulled on her dressing gown. Gran arrived home well after midnight looking haggard. Only when she was home, did Mason leave his post on my porch.

"Yeah, just a little shaken from yesterday," I lied, she didn't need to know that I was drowning in anxiety.

"Me, too. I have never seen such horror in my life," she exclaimed as she rubbed her tired eyes.

"What is going to happen now?" I asked sombrely.

"They are bringing in more qualified investigators from the city," she revealed, taking a few steps towards me. "You need to be extremely careful from now on, Elora. This murderer seems to be targeting young adults and I fear that you could be next," she warned and I saw her fear for me in her damp eyes.

"I will be fine, Grandma," I assured her.

"Please make sure of that because I don't know what I would do without you. Our family have always lived by the saying that love is the most precious thing in the world and that could not be any truer for how feel about you, Elora. You are the most precious thing to me," she declared fiercely. Her words caused my heart to warm in a way I had ever experienced before – this is what love from family feels like.

"I promise, Gran." I gave her a small hug and a smile. A tear fell down from her eye and I knew it was because I had hugged her voluntarily.

"Believe in yourself and trust your instincts," she proclaimed.

I just nodded back to her; I didn't want to say anything because it would have been laced with too much emotion. For the first time in my life, I had a real family. She truly loved me; my family loved me for just being me.

I scurried into my room taking deep breaths, trying to recover from the emotions. As I closed the door, a few strands of my hair swirled around my face from the slight wind blowing through my open window.

Instantly, my body became rigid because I didn't leave my window open. My blood started pumping through my ears and with shaky hands I locked the door behind me. As I looked back towards my room, I saw a figure standing by my window. I flinched violently in fright and my hand flew to my heart.

"You are right," Mason started ominously. He was once again covered in rain and his dark clothes camouflaged him into my curtains. I just stared at him with wide eyes in bewilderment, how did he get in here?

"How can I expect you to let me in if I won't open up to you about my own life? I don't want to keep lying to you, Elora. Come to my house at midnight tonight and I will show you everything. No more secrets," he promised.

Then he turned on his heels and jumped out of my window just as quietly and quickly as a ghost. Mason left no room for me to answer his question. He was giving me time to think.

My quick breathing didn't slow down for a long time after Mason left my room. He wanted to open up to me, and he wanted to tell me everything. I kept staring at my billowing curtains

179

where he been moments before. It was only until I snapped myself out of my stupor that I saw he had left something on the windowsill for me.

A red rose.

But it wasn't just a rose, it was a red rose covered in blood. I picked up the rose's stem and a droplet of blood dripped off the rose like a wilting petal. Mason was warning me that even something as beautiful as a rose has a dark side that can hurt you. He wanted me to know what I would be walking into if I decided to meet him tonight.

He was warning me that every rose has its thorns, and those thorns can make you bleed.

***

I whirled the rose's stem around in my fingers. I was sitting on my windowsill seat as I stared out of my rain-streaked window towards the forest beyond pensively. I watched as the rain droplets trailed down the glass like miniature streams. Twilight dawned without my notice and the night transcended and I still hadn't come up with an answer to Mason's proposition.

I knew that every bone and fibre of my being wanted to go to him, to always be with him. But there was a part of me, the rational part, that told me to stay away. He had hurt me before and it would be so easy for him to do it again.

My heart wouldn't be able to take it, being rejected again. I already knew what it was like to lose loved ones – I lost my parents, and I lost every foster family I had lived with. The one boyfriend I ever had left me because he thought I was too obsessed with him and I lost my best friend Annalise from betrayal. Going through that again would break me. But wasn't love worth the risk? How would you gain anything if you weren't willing to give it a go?

Mason had given me this choice to decide if I wanted to see the real him. But he had also given me the power to end him, I could so easily betray him. I could go to the police with this information and tell them to follow me to wherever he was taking me and that would be that. He would be in jail for the rest of his life and he knew that.

He trusted me enough to place his whole life in my hands, and that was the ultimate sacrifice I needed him to make for me. He finally trusted me with his secrets and therefore I would place my trust in him. Gran told me to trust my instincts and they always drew me to Mason.

I allowed the beautiful red rose to fall from the constraints of my fingers. It landed on a few droplets of water that had leaked through my windowsill. The blood on the rose and the water combined to create a beautiful mess. I had a feeling that was exactly what tonight was about to become.

Because I was going to give a murderer my broken and battered heart.

***

Mason's mansion was inumbrated due to the fog that lined the top of the hill and from the lack of lighting that failed to illuminate the mansion's architecture. I was hesitating in front of his house as I was overcome by a wave of fear that shuddered down my spine from the vast desolation of the mansion.

Nobody knew I was here. I had said goodnight to Gran earlier in the night and locked my door behind me, so she wouldn't become worried about my departure. I was also hesitating because I was one hour early from when Mason asked me to arrive. I knew it was a bad idea to arrive earlier than Mason asked but I couldn't wait.

I pushed the gates open but froze instantly when I heard a noise echo through the forest. A haunting scream bellowed through the quiet reticent of the night, originating from the darkness that engulfed Mason's home. My blood ran cold and turned my hands clammy at the thought of walking right into that horror. I was finally going to find out Mason's secrets.

With shaky hands I raced to the house and opened the front door – it creaked portentously beneath my touch. I crept into the house, which was darker than usual as the glowing lanterns that usually lined the walls were unlit.

For a moment, I stood immobile not sure what to do before I remembered the secret door Mason had open in the kitchen the other night. That had to be where Mason was keeping his secrets.

I tip-toed into the kitchen and instantly knew something was out of place. The fridge was no longer in its normal position, it had been moved a few metres out of its nook beside the cabinetry. I had seen the passageway behind the fridge open up when I had arrived unexpectedly the other night but right now it just looked like a normal wall. How did it open?

I placed my ear to the wall and cringed back fiercely when I heard it, the screams. They were emitting from the other side of this wall. Flames burned through my veins; I needed to see what was going on. I fished my hands along the wall and unexpectedly my hands rested upon a latch which I pulled open.

A portion of the wall unclasped from the rest of the wall and swung backwards revealing a dark passageway. I had to scrunch my hands into fists to stop them from shaking as I stepped inside to find a small empty room with shackles bolted to a wall. That must have been were Mason had someone chained up last time I was here. I cautiously moved towards the posterior end of the room where the floor morphed into blackness. When I glimpsed closer, I saw that the floor dropped away into a rusting metal spiral staircase.

There was only opaque darkness below, but the screams blasted from within. My stomach twisted into knots and I inhaled a deep breath to repress my epinephrine filled body that was telling me to run the opposite way. I descended the steps into the basement with my hands gripping the railing so tightly my knuckles turned white. As I entered the basement my muscles stiffened as I remembered something that Gran had said to me about the Blackwell family.

It was in the basement of this home that Mason's father committed his murders. Gran said the entire floor of the basement was covered in many different people's blood and the entire back wall was covered in torture weapons.

I blanched; did I truly want to go down there? All I knew was that I needed to know what Mason was doing. Shakily I descended multiple steps into a place where no one could hear me scream.

When I faced the room at the bottom of the stair's the hair on the back of my neck rose and my breathing stopped as I gasped in terror. The floors were still lined with dried blood. No one had cleaned it up since the killing's years ago. The room was large and rectangular shaped, but visible as along the side walls ran lanterns casting the room in a shadowed gloomy semi-darkness.

My hands flew to my mouth in horror as I realised that the rumours that Gran relayed to me were true, the entire back wall was full of deadly weapons. Knives of all shapes and sizes, guns, swords, pole arms, chains, flamethrowers and many more torture

183

devices. But it wasn't the weapons that nearly made me fall to my knees in shock and terror, it was what lined the vertical walls.

Human beings were shackled and chained up to the walls like animals. Three were hanging limp, passed out and the other two were barely awake, their limbs randomly convulsing. But they all had one thing in common, they were all covered in deep cut wounds. They had all been tortured. With quavering steps, I moved closer to one of the men hanging limp and nearly choked on my own saliva when I recognised him.

It was the man that punched me and tried to kill me outside Mason's house, the man with one hand. Looking closer I recognised most of them as the men from that night, the strongly built one with tattoos and the guy with a permanent sneer on his face.

That meant Mason didn't kill them that night. He had just incapacitated them so he could bring them down here and torture them, but why?

I couldn't even hear myself breathing as my pulse was pounding so loud in my ears; my entire body was alight with terror but also something else. Something dark, something electrifying. Every nerve ending was sparked alive and every sense was overactive, absorbing every last gory detail of Mason's life.

A scream bellowed through the air piercing my ears and I snapped my head towards the back of the room. I squinted my eyes in the direction of where the scream originated to see a white sheet blocking the view of one of the cubicles that housed another human that was chained up. Behind the white sheet a lantern illuminated the shadow of someone as they paced.

I jammed my elbows closer into my body to stop my shaking as I staggered towards the back of the room. As I walked, I passed

184

another person who was chained up to the wall but this one wasn't unconscious or barely alive like the others. This one was fully awake.

Before I could process this fact, the chained man screamed at me with wide manic eyes and surged forward to pounce at me. He strained against his shackles bounding him to the wall. I jumped back instinctively as my fight or flight response smashed through my veins. I fell onto my back, my hands breaking my fall as I scrambled away from the horrific sight before me.

The chains clanged around him as they snapped him back, preventing him from touching me. But he yelled and screamed at me like a mad man, struggling against the chains. My breathing returned to me when I realised that he was bound.

It was only then that I finally had a close look at his features. And what I saw before me was not a man but a monster. What was so horrifying about him was his entire face and body was marred by rippling burn scars. The disfigurement had reclassified his human features, so his nose and mouth were now hole's in his skin that were like melting plastic. The erosion of his face caused his eyes to pop out of his head. Blood coated his face and the rags that were his clothes. I didn't want to look at the horror of the man chained in front of me, so I quickly hurried towards the white sheet.

"Don't go in there," warned the chained man that looked like a walking corpse. My footsteps froze and I warily turned my gaze back towards the monster to see his black eyes boring straight into me with a wicked gleam. My chin began trembling as my body shook uncontrollably.

He chuckled wickedly which soon morphed into another scream as he tried to surge at me again. I wiped my hand across my forehead and clenched my sweaty hands to pull myself together. The secrets Mason held down here were far beyond even my wildest imagination. I needed to find Mason and leave this place as quickly as possible.

A menacing scream screeched from behind the white sheet and I heard Mason's voice as he said something in a hushed tone to whoever was being tortured. With deep flesh creeping anxiety shaking my knees, I lifted my hand up to move the white sheet out of the way. And what I saw before me sent a shock deep into my bones, deep into the heart of my very being. I clasped my hands over my mouth to prevent voicing my horror with the scream that was building in my throat.

Mason was dressed in his usual all black attire and he was completely covered from head to toe in red blood. He was like a fallen angel, so beautiful yet covered in darkness. I couldn't help the way my eyes absorbed every inch of his being and the slight thrill of attraction that shot through my body towards him. The power that radiated out from him was causing my heart to skyrocket.

A man was chained to the wall by shackles bounding his wrists and ankles. Mason held a knife up to him and he pressed it forward digging deeply into his torso muscles. Blood dripped down from the wound in waves, gushing out like a dam had been broken. But it wasn't the fact that Mason was torturing someone that sent my jaw dropping in stupefaction. It was who he was torturing.

It was Brandon, Melissa's boyfriend and the police chief's son. The man who I watched be murdered right in front of my eyes. And yet here he was alive and screaming as he was tortured. But how was he alive? And why does Mason have him? And why was Mason torturing him?

I shook my head uncomprehending; nothing made any sense.

I couldn't feel my body any more as the adrenaline was sending too much blood around my veins.

"Tell me or else I will kill her," Mason seethed as he stalked over towards another body that was chained up beside Brandon. The head of the other prisoner had lulled forward and it was only when Mason pulled its head up by their hair and placed a knife to their throat, did I see who it was.

My scream lodged itself in my throat, suffocating me when her eyes fluttered towards me and sent an ice chill down to the base of my spine. My stiff legs stumbled an involuntary step back, no it couldn't be. I saw her die; I saw her dead body. I looked into her eyes and saw nothing but an empty corpse.

It was Melissa. Her brown eyes looked straight into mine as if she was pleading with me for mercy and that was all the confirmation I needed. She was alive.

"One last chance," Mason taunted and when Brandon didn't respond Mason kept his word. He plummeted his knife straight into Melissa's chest. My heart stopped and my breathing choked, the shock winding me as if I had been punched in the chest. Blood squirted from the puncture and splashed onto my face. Gradually Melissa's body became limp. The entire time her eyes were still connected with mine and I watched as the light left her eyes and she slowly died, again.

Mason just murdered her. There was no containing my horror any more and the scream that left the confounds of my mouth screeched louder than any other that had been made that night. Horror overtook my being causing my body to convulse as I watched her dead body hang there. I allowed her to die again.

Following my scream Mason instantly released Melissa's head and lurched as he turned around, snapping his attention towards me. The colour drained from his skin as he looked at my horror-stricken face.

"Elora," he whispered, his tone was distraught and imbued with a deep pain. I pierced him one look of betrayal and he tried to reach for me. Panic rushed through my blood and I allowed my fight or flight response to take over. I bolted as fast as I could away from him and this evil place.

In the dark I sprinted up the stairs and through the door at the top into the kitchen, all I could think was escape. Lactic acid burned the back of my throat as I ran towards the forest beyond the house, the best place to hide. I dodged trees and branches that flicked my way, jumping over stumps and streams. But I could hear him gaining on me. I allowed myself a glance behind me for one moment to see his dark figure not centimetres behind me.

His footsteps inched closer impetuously and then a force whacked into my body. It sent me flying towards the leaves and dirt-covered forest floor. Mason landed on top of me, his body restraining more than painful. He flipped me around and restrained me by placing my hands over my head. I screamed but a hand was placed over my mouth, a hand covered in blood. I squeezed my eyes shut as I accepted my inevitable fate, I was going to die. I was going to be murdered by the man that I loved.

Mason's breath feathered my ear and his stubble scraped my cheek before he spoke calmly in my ear.

"Let me explain."

Chapter 18

"I know what it looks like but there is a logical explanation," Mason continued conciliatorily. I gradually lifted my gaze up towards his face with a darkened glare set on my features. We locked eyes and something passed between us, like an electric shock buzzed through my body.

"You're a monster," I spat. "You're a murderer." He flinched back from my hostility and the skin around his eyes scrunched up in pain.

"Elora, you know I would never hurt you. You know this." His eyes became wide and pleading, almost innocent. His words and tone hit something in my heart. I did know that he would never hurt me, but he did hurt others. I searched his familiar blue eyes deeply; they were surrounded by splatters of blood. I felt nothing but love and calmness when I looked at him.

"Then explain yourself," I demanded as I threw him off me and stood up to my full height.

"Can we go somewhere more private?" he countered as his eyes warily scanned the trees.

"Fine," I huffed, brushing my clothes free from dirt.

We didn't speak as we walked through the caliginous forest but even in the darkness, I felt safe walking beside Mason, like I could breathe easier. When we reached his house, I followed Mason through the dark hallways until we walked past the one door with an electrical light shining from behind it. I stopped dead in my tracks.

"Why is there a light on in there and nowhere else?" I asked, questioningly glancing up at Mason.

"The house has no lights on because I like being in the dark," he muttered evasively, not even stopping to look at me. I crossed my hands over my chest and didn't follow him, annoyed that he avoided my real question. He looked back over his shoulder at me and sighed. "I will explain everything in a moment but just know for now that I don't want you to go anywhere near that room," Mason explained curtly and began walking off again. I frowned at his blunt evasion but followed behind him again, I wanted answers.

Mason continued on through the house until we reached a gargantuan arch with wooden double doors. Mason opened the door into a sitting room. The extravagance of the antiqued design within the room made my mouth fall open, my eyes immediately drawing to a magnificent fireplace that expanded across the posterior wall.

There was a grand desk situated in one corner and a set of leather arm chairs in front of the fire. One of the chairs seemed to only be for decoration and the other ostentatious wingback chair had a blanket over it and the beige colour was fading as if it was used daily.

The fire was ablaze, casting a warm golden incandescence over the room as the burning embers released whips of smoke up the chimney. The flickering light from the fireplace made the room the brightest in the house. I instantly felt cosy and secure in here. Mason gestured for me to sit in the lavish wingback arm chair and a warmth rushed into my cheeks; this must be his chair.

"Take a seat, I will be back in a moment," he muttered so low it was almost a whisper and he took off down the corridors. I started into the fire lifelessly until Mason entered the room again after a few minutes with fresh clothes on and smelling like soap.

He didn't say anything as he sat on the chair opposite mine and proceeded to stare at me intently. His hands were in fists at his side as if he was trying to contain an intense emotion, like he was scared of what I thought of him now that I knew his secrets.

"Explain," I demanded as I crossed my hands over my chest.

Mason ran his hands down his face before his eyes slowly lifted towards mine. He looked so tired. His eyes were ringed with red and those constant black bruises that hung under his eyes were darker than ever. The glistening light from the fire blazed onto the side of his face, elucidating the strong line of his jaw from its glow. Even in his exhausted state he was still dazzling, he was always so heartbreakingly handsome.

"You really want to know everything about me?" he cautioned, warning easily transparent in his tone.

"Yes," I encouraged unperturbed with a nod of my head.

Mason suddenly picked up a fake, decorative bundle of red roses that was sitting in a vase on the stool next to his chair. He twirled it around in his hands as he gazed down at it sombrely in deep thought. His eyes snapped up to mine and they were filled with a bleakness obscure as glass.

"Fine but I am warning you, beautiful things get destroyed when they are around me." He crushed the fake roses in his hands with a vexatious crunch. The bundle crumbled into dust and the flakes tumbled to the floor through his digits. A lump formed in my drying throat in trepidation but I wasn't leaving until I knew all his secrets.

"Okay, I will start at the beginning," he spoke quietly, uncertain of himself. His back was rigid – he was anxious.

"My father was a cold-blooded killer. He got away with it

191

for years and not one person in this town suspected his true nature. He was the chief of police, a saint in everyone's eyes," Mason recounted with a sneer on his lips.

"My siblings and I were brought up in this madness. Killing was a normal everyday occurrence for us." As Mason recalled, he had a permanent crease between his eyebrows as if it was painful for him to talk about this. My stomach swelled with nausea at the thought of Mason being raised in this darkness and my fingers twitched with the urge to grab his hand.

"Marcus and Masie, they were all I had. Our mother was around but she was a shell of a human. The town thought we were home-schooled but really we were being taught how to murder," he declared with haunted eyes and there was a manic gleam in them.

"Every day we had lessons. My father taught us everything he knew. And he knew a lot about killing as he used to be in the army." Mason's hands were gripping the armrests of the chair tightly as if this was the only thing keeping his anger in control.

"He taught us exactly how to torture someone until they were on the brink of dying. He taught us how to clean up after our crimes, so no one would suspect us." I shivered as I thought about just how dangerous Mason was, he was the ultimate killer.

"That's why when Marlemore stabbed me I knew exactly how to position my body, so it wouldn't hurt me. I know this because my father would torture us. That's why I don't feel pain any more; I was desensitised to it when I was younger," Mason admitted, his tone was detached like this didn't even affect him any more. Bile rose up in my throat and I clasped my hands over my mouth as I listened to the horror that Mason was put through as a child.

"Mason," I whispered aghast, my voice tinged with agony. I

scrunched my eyes together as I tried to not think about that horror. Mason's eyes flickered to me for a second and I saw the torment there before he looked away, like he couldn't look at me while he explained the horror of his life.

"When I was fifteen years old, he locked me in a room with someone he had kidnapped, placed a knife in my hand and allowed me free reign to do whatever I wanted." I was left staring at him wide eyed and my expression horrified but I also scooted closer to the edge of the chair in anticipation of learning the result of that scenario. Mason's haunted eyes flashed to mine and I knew before he even said it what he did.

"You killed them, didn't you?" I surmised.

"Yes," he admitted. My pupils dilated as my blood rushed to my head as I stared into his eyes, the eyes of a murderer. Mason moved closer to me on his seat as well and the heat of the fire wasn't the only thing warming my skin.

"I absolutely hated myself for it. I couldn't live with myself knowing that I had ended this person's life. I refused to kill innocents after that," he explained. I always knew that Mason didn't kill just because he wanted to, that there was always a reason behind his murders.

"My father despised me for it but accepted I would never kill. My brother Marcus went through the same test when he was old enough and he only killed to prevent my father's wrath. Years went by in this same fashion, until my younger sister was put through her test," Mason ended ominously and his tone was laced with dread.

"Masie was an angel, she was kind and caring, not like the rest of us. She didn't let the horror of our lives affect her gentle soul." Mason smiled and it was the first genuine smile I had seen on his face all night. She must have meant a lot to him.

Mason's eyes turned cold as they glazed over with darkness. His jaw clenched tightly and the cords in his neck became rigid.

"We were all there, when he forced her to kill for the first time. And she couldn't do it. My father became furious, he was so angry that he tried to kill her." Mason grimaced and shut his eyes tightly as if thinking about that night was torturous. My hands reached out towards him unconsciously.

"I couldn't stand to watch it but I was useless. They were in one of the cells and no matter how hard my brother and I tried, we couldn't help our sister. But before my sister died something happened that none of us were expecting." Mason's eyes flew open and the hair on the back of my neck raised.

"My dead inside mother snapped. Seeing her daughter being killed awoke her out of her stupor. She threw my brother and I the keys to the cage before she attacked my father. But there was no ending a mad man. He killed my mother instantly," Mason seethed as he angrily jumped out of his chair and faced the fireplace.

"My brother and I were too late. He murdered my sister right in front of us," Mason bellowed and smashed his fist into the wall, sending plaster flying into the air. I gasped in my seat and shuddered away from his outburst.

Mason stared at his demented knuckles as the blood dripped down from his hand. I noticed his tight jaw and black eyes start to soften as he watched the blood.

"I will never forget the sight of the light leaving her eyes. She deserved a better life," he continued tremulously and with a downturned gaze. Mason was staring into the fire with his shoulders hunched over holding onto the mantle.

My heart was pounding in my chest as if it was trying to reach out towards Mason and soothe him. I couldn't sit here and

194

watch while he was in so much pain, so I rose from my chair and lightly touched my hand onto his shoulder. His stiff muscles gradually relaxed underneath my touch. Mason grabbed my hand and kissed it softly.

My stomach started swimming with butterflies with the knowledge that I was able to soothe him. He slowly released my hand and we both returned to our seats.

"After she died, Marcus and I fought against my father. We overpowered him together and chained him up before I tortured him." Mason smiled wickedly and an evil gleam entered his eyes.

"It was only during that time I realised how much I loved hurting him. I wasn't thinking when I set my father alight. The fire became out of my control and the whole house was engulfed in flames," Mason recalled. So that was how the fire started, Gran said it was a mystery to the police how it began.

"We left my father to burn in the flames. The police arrived soon after asking us all sorts of questions. We weren't charged as we told the police that it was all my father's doing," Mason explained.

"After that my brother and I were free. Marcus couldn't live in this town any more, so he moved far away. I tried doing the same and moved to the city to start a new life. But I was only gone for a few days before I realised killing had become something I needed, something I craved. It had become a part of who I was," Mason revealed ominously with a disgusted scowl on his face at himself.

A chill ran through my bones as I recalled him in that dark mood and knew exactly what he was referring to, his need to see blood.

"It was then that I knew I had to do something about it." I watched the pure hatred on his features at himself and I realised that Mason was not evil, he was not a bad person, he just had a bad life. The people in his life failed him, just like how I was failed. Even though he wanted to kill people, he refrained from killing innocents. I couldn't control the doe eyes I made when I looked up at him.

"I tried to reconnect with my brother but I couldn't find him, he had disappeared. So, with no family left I returned here and even though there were terrible memories for me, it was the only place in the world where I felt like I belonged." Mason spoke with a strangled voice and gestured towards the grand mansion around him.

"I'm sorry Mason," I sympathised as a tear fell from my cheek. Mason gave me a sad smile in return before leaning towards me and wiping the stray tear from my cheek.

"I returned to the basement to find the police has taken away all the bodies. But what I wasn't expecting was to find that the wall where I had been torturing my father had been flipped. Although he was still chained to the wall, he had managed to turn on the switch that spun the walls around. That feature was made if the torture basement needed to be concealed. So, he was saved from the flames and the eyes of the police. When I turned it around again there he was, alive."

My breath caught in my throat, that evil man was still alive?

My vision clouded as my mind reeled and continued to connect the dots. My eyes widened when I released that Mason's father was the crazy man chained to his basement covered in scars, burn scars.

"At first I was furious that he was alive but then I realised it was a good thing. I tortured him for hours that night and I finally felt like myself again. I could hurt someone and I didn't feel bad about it. I decided to keep my father a prisoner down here, so I could torture him whenever I wanted to." Mason smirked. I realised that this was the origin of the screams that the town heard coming from Mason's house, it was Mason torturing his father.

"That man chained in your basement covered in scars is your father?" I deciphered and Mason nodded slowly.

"Yes. I knew that if I was going to keep my father alive then I needed to take every possible precaution to prevent him from escaping." Mason shivered at the thought and I followed suit.

"I keep him chained in the basement, but I also have injected a tracking system under his skin. If he even went past the perimeter of the house the system would kill him instantly. I have the lights in the house connected to the same system. So, they will all turn on as an alarm to alert me if the tracking system ever fails or if he escapes from the basement." I nodded as the revelations clicked into place. That is why his house is always dark.

"But soon it wasn't enough, just torturing him, I needed to kill. So, I decided to hunt and kill people like my father, evil people who deserved it," Mason revealed and he spoke with such a colloquial tone like killing was just a daily chore.

Mason's malevolent eyes flickered to mine and drew me in. I stared back at him without blinking, infatuated by his beauty. He inched closer to me, standing up so he was right in front of my chair and the closer he was to me the more my body would react to him. My breathing became gasps and my skin twitched with the need to touch him.

"You see, Elora, I like seeing people in pain. I can't live without it," Mason admitted with a frown on his lips. His deep guttural voice reverberated through his chest and I felt it, as he was so close to me. He was the most unique man I had ever met in my life. He loved seeing people in pain, yet he also hated hurting people that didn't deserve it.

My every nerve ending was alive just from being around him, from being near such enticing darkness. He was my beautiful broken murderer who loved me.

"I'm a monster," he denounced darkly with downturned eyes. "A sadistic murderer." He was right, he was a murderer but I didn't care and I wouldn't have him any other way.

"I know who you are Mason and I don't care. I still want you," I proclaimed and reached up to place my hand onto his rough scarred cheek. "I want every part of you, even the dark parts." Mason's expression flashed with disagreement but also sparked with interest.

"I could hurt you at any moment. Would you like it if I hurt you?" He looked at me with that wild look, those dilated pupils and it sent my pulse hammering. Mason grabbed my wrist and squeezed tightly causing pain to burn through my arm until I gasped. He immediately released my wrist with a snap, his features twisting up in discomfort.

I didn't care what he did to me, I leaned even closer towards him so that our foreheads touched. He inhaled a deep shocked breath at my closeness.

"You don't want to hurt me," I asserted as I stared back at him defiantly, I was so sure of that fact. He pulled away from me and his lips turned down at the corners.

"You are right, you are the only person that I hate seeing in pain. I don't understand it." He ran his fingers up from my wrist along my skin and wrapped his hand around my elbow, squeezing. He kept doing that, testing me to see if I truly trusted him, or to see if he trusted himself. I wasn't scared of him hurting me, I wasn't scared of death. I was only scared of a life without him.

"I am not afraid of you," I declared formidably and he tilted his head to the side as he searched my features.

"I knew you were different, from the very moment I saw you on the bus," Mason admitted suddenly, standing up to his full height in front of me. I tilted my chin up to look at him to see a small smile on his face that was filled with affection.

"That day on the bus when that lady was hurt, I saw you smiling," I remembered. Mason walked back over to his chair and lowered himself back down again.

"Yes, I was returning from an interstate trip for my security company but I was also searching for a murderer unsuccessfully. Marlemore was killing in the city before the murders started in Everbrook. I was agitated, so when I saw that woman in pain it relaxed me." One of Mason's lips turned up at the corner. "I knew you saw everything, that was why I pushed you away. No one could know my secret or even suspect anything," he proclaimed darkly.

"I told you to stay away from me but you didn't and the closer you got to me, the closer you were to learning my true nature. And that made panic consume me and as that panic intensified the more desperate I became to get rid of you." I remembered the first time Mason tried to kill me because I saw him covered in blood in the woods.

"That night when I first saw you in the woods, were you killing someone?" I asked tentatively.

"Yes, someone who needed to be stopped," Mason confirmed and his eyes flashed with fury. A shudder ran down my back as I was chilled to be bone from his admittance of murder but I wasn't scared.

"What about those men that attacked me? I thought you killed them but they were shackled up in your basement?" I asked. Mason's gaze became wary and his lips pressed into a line but he answered.

"I didn't kill them because they work for Marlemore. I was torturing them for information. Although they haven't been particularly talkative yet," Mason grumbled, with a frown. My breath hitched in my throat. They were working for Marlemore? No wonder I nearly died that night.

"You said before that you only torture and murder evil people," I stated.

"Yes," he agreed, nodding his head slowly.

"Then why were you torturing Melissa and Brandon? Why would you kill innocents?" I demanded grimly and Mason leaned further forward on his chair ominously.

"Because they were not innocents," he revealed sombrely with cold calculating eyes and a raised eyebrow.

"What?" I spluttered, stunned. I didn't understand, if they were not innocents then that could only mean one thing.

"They were both working for Marlemore."

Chapter 19

My jaw dropped open as I comprehended what his words meant.

"Mason, nothing is making any sense. I saw both of them die. How are they even alive?" I exclaimed dubiously as I ran my hands through my hair in frustration.

"That's because they were never dead, they were just made to seem like they were dead," Mason explained with a dire expression.

"How?" I demanded. Mason stared at me for a moment longer, his eyes calculating before he walked over to the fire and grabbed a tinderbox that rested on the top of the mantle.

Mason sat back down and opened it to reveal an array of papers and trinkets inside. He grabbed one piece of paper and held it out to me. I took it from him cautiously and inspected it, flipping it over in my hands. It was a lab test of a blood sample, and it revealed elevated levels of a substance called Tetrodotoxin.

"Marlemore injected them with a poison called Tetrodotoxin. It slows their heart rate down, so it virtually becomes non-existent, but they are still alive. And only if they are injected with the antidote a monoclonal antibody will they be able to recover. If not, they die a slow, painful death. Marlemore made their wounds look fatal but really it was all staged," Mason proclaimed.

I slapped my forehead with my hand, I didn't even think to check Brandon's pulse after I found his body.

"But I figured it out," Mason continued. "When I first saw

Melissa, I knew that the puncture wound to her head wouldn't have killed her." He spoke with a professional tone as if he wasn't talking how someone was brutally killed but rather an aspect of his job.

The next thing Mason gave me from the box was a hand full of pictures. The first was of Melissa's dead body on a metal table. I shuddered as I saw her cold corpse lying there unblinking. The next picture showed her face completely clear as Mason had washed away the fabricated gash wounds.

"Melissa's body was taken by the police; how did you get it?" I asked sceptically as I glimpsed up at him with an interested gaze.

"When she was being taken from the scene of the crime to the morgue, I stole her body from the police van. Obviously, the police covered that up to prevent large scale panic. I examined her body to discover that she had taken the poison and I injected her with the antidote. But it was too late for her, the poison had already spread to her brain, she had such severe brain damage she was practically brain dead," he explained. The air left my lungs as I realised something.

"That night I saw you here torturing someone, was that Melissa?" I speculated. Mason glanced at me with one raised eyebrow as if curious as to how I knew that.

"Yes, I was trying to torture information out of her, but it was useless, she was lost to the world. I failed but I was better prepared for the next murder. When Brandon was killed and I followed you through the woods to the body. I injected him with the antidote before the poison reached his brain," he admitted with downturned eyes, another thing he didn't tell me that night.

"But the antidote takes time to take effect, and in that time, Brandon was already pronounced dead and his body taken to the morgue. He was still passed out when I retrieved him in the morning, I stole his body and brought him here. When he woke up, I started torturing him for information. I tried to use Melissa to entice him into speaking, but he was adamant in keeping his mouth shut. That's why I killed Melissa because she was already dead inside. I was putting her out of her misery." Mason's hands gripped both of the chair handles tightly as I regarded him closely. He tilted closer to me as if he was afraid I would run away from him again.

Everything started clicking into place, so when I saw Mason murder Melissa again in the basement, he wasn't really killing her because she was already brain dead. But then why was she already dead inside? Why did Marlemore poison them?

"But why kill them by poison, why not just stab them? Why show the entire town their fake dead bodies?" I wondered puzzled. Mason's haunted eyes snapped to up mine and glazed over inscrutably, covering a seriousness associated with that question.

"I am not sure but there is one thing I do know. Melissa and Brandon had no injection marks on their bodies or any signs of a struggle. From that information the only conclusion that I could surmise is that they took the poison willingly," Mason theorised.

I tapped my fingers on my chair, Melissa was terrified of Marlemore that night at the fair so Mason's statement didn't make sense. But what I didn't understand was how Mason knew all this.

"How did you know they were working for Marlemore?" I pondered, resting my chin on my hand. Mason handed me an old scrunched up piece of paper that he had tried to smooth out unsuccessfully. On it read a list of names, none of whom I recognised other than Melissa and Brandon's.

"I had been following one of Marlemore's men for weeks, and he had been leaving me threatening notes. Eventually, I found him. He was a police officer named Kenneth – I'm sure you remember him. Before you arrived, he finally told me the names of Marlemore's other men which I wrote down," Mason explained. I recalled the reason Mason was torturing Kenneth, it was about a note.

"What were the notes about?" I questioned curiously. Mason pulled out a bunch of cards that had been written from cut out magazine words to reveal taunting messages.

"This was the first note I received and what I was referring to that night." Mason handed one to me.

I picked it up to read the sinister words, *"I know that your father is still alive and, in your basement, what would happen if I told the police?"*

I gasped, no wonder Mason was so desperate to find who sent them. Mason would go to jail if the police found out. I examined the card closely. The posterior side was clear but what did stand out was that there were random specs of white dust dotting the card. I picked up another card to find the same white dust but this one read something much more sinister.

"If you don't do as I ask, then your brother will die."

I snapped my wide eyes up to Mason, tilting the card in his direction questioningly.

"That was another reason why I tried to kill you when we first met, I couldn't risk you telling the police what you saw because if I went to prison then my brother would die. Marlemore is holding him hostage to force me to do what he wants."

My hand flew to my mouth and I fiercely grabbed Mason's wrist with my other hand, giving a squeeze of reassurance.

"We will get him back," I promised. Mason nodded back

sadly before he changed the subject.

"I also received a note the day Melissa died – if I didn't start working for Marlemore myself then he was going to kill someone. I refused to give into him but only when I heard that scream through the woods, I realised how serious he was in his threat." Mason's eyes were narrowed as he glared into the sparkling fire. I bit my lip, so that was why Mason bolted down from the lighthouse so quickly, because he knew Marlemore was about to kill someone.

"Why is Marlemore doing this to you?" I wondered, perplexed.

"It all started when I began to hunt him, I heard that he had been orchestrating killings in the city. One night I came close to learning his identity. That was when the massages started," Mason seethed, and his eyes were in slits as he tried to contain his anger.

"Marlemore wanted me to release my father but I will never do it nor will Marlemore ever be able to release him without me," Mason smirked confidently as he pulled up his wrist to show his watch that I had never seen him without. "This is the only way to deactivate the tracking system, along with a password that I will never tell a soul." I reached forward to touch the skin around his watch, it was such an ordinary looking piece of jewellery you would never think that it had any importance. I noticed Mason's eyelids flutter against my touch and I pressed my hand into his skin harder, running my palm up his forearm.

"You don't know how nice that feels," Mason admitted softly. I smiled as I continued running my hand up his arm and wound it around his biceps. "Which brings me to you," Mason declared, his tone suddenly softening. His eyes lifted to look into mine, brightening up with a new playful gleam. He pushed himself closer to me on the chair and glanced at me like I was a puzzle to be solved. Until abruptly he stood up.

"Come with me," he insisted grabbing my hand.

He led me along the back veranda and into the trees beyond. I didn't know why we were going into the forest but I trusted him. So, I blindly followed him through the dark woods with our hands tightly clasped.

We reached a clearing and the capon of trees above started to dissipate to reveal the moon's light shining through the treetops. We stepped out onto a ledge and from the sound of the waves crashing into the rocks below I knew that we are on a cliff. The wind whipped through my hair and I run a hand through it to stop the stray crimson strands from blocking my vision. I glanced at Mason in uncertainty, what were we doing here?

"Have a look," Mason gestured down to beyond the cliff face. Hesitantly, I moved towards it until both my feet were on the very edge. I looked down towards the oblivion below. It was high, but I could see the dark waves crashing upon the rocks below, gashing in the wind.

Mason came up behind me, I felt his presence before I saw him. He could kill me so easily, just one push and I would be at the mercy to the waves below. My breathing accelerated and my lungs heaved up and down. Mason placed one arm around my waist as he pulled me back into his chest. His whole body was against mine, the strong muscles of his chest curling around my back and the warmth of his body seeping into mine.

Then I felt that familiar chilled pinch of the cold blade of his knife against my throat. His warm breath was fluttering on my neck as he breathed in deeply and his lips touched my ear causing shivers to run down my spine. Slowly he added pressure, so a small drop of blood started dripping from the wound on my neck.

His body stiffened as he caught the sight of my blood. My own body was pounding with adrenaline and a fire that only he could ignite. I was on the brink of death and I had never felt so alive.

I didn't move, I didn't fight him. His knife dug in deeper and I flinched against him, my first show of pain. Immediately, Mason took the knife away from my throat and released me completely. My body instantly was rushed with coldness as I lost his body heat that was blazing through me just moments before. I stood there frozen facing the edge of the cliff and raised my hand towards my neck.

My fingers wiped against the blood there and I lifted it up in front of my eyes to inspect the damage. Blood had coated my skin and drizzled onto the palm of my hand. I was hypnotised by it, the sight of my blood.

I heard a growl behind me and spun around on my heels to face Mason. He was frowning down at his hands that held the knife, the knife that was covered in my blood.

"With anybody else that would have been easy, but with you. I hate it," Mason fumed. He threw the knife to the ground and glared at it in disgust. His wild eyes gradually rose up to mine before he spoke his next words.

"Everything changed when I met you."

Chapter 20

With my bloodied hand hanging by my side and blood droplets dripping down my neck I listened to his sweet, loving words that were completely contradictory to his actions.

"That first night when I saw you in the woods and I nearly killed you, that was the first time ever that I didn't like seeing someone in pain. I didn't understand it," Mason explained softly. He looked at me with a ferocious intensity that set alight my nerve endings. The tips of my fingers tingled where the blood had trickled and I knew why he cut me, another test to see if he liked it.

"When I saw the pained look on your face when Melissa and her mother were tormenting you at the church, I didn't know why but I had to intervene." Mason took a step closer towards me as I stood on the edge of the cliff, my breath hitched.

My heart skipped a beat as Mason reached up a bloody hand and intertwined our fingers together. His bloody hand and my blood covered hand laced together. Two broken pieces finally come together to make an imperfect but functioning whole piece. I stared down at the mess that we both were and finally for the first time in my life I felt like I belonged. This felt *right.*

"You cared about me then?" I stuttered in disbelief. Mason smiled back at me warmly, the gesture lighting up his blue eyes.

"I found myself worrying about you. If Marlemore knew about my other secrets, then he could know that you meant something to me and could use you against me." Mason shuddered, and a frown furrowed his eyebrows as if this thought pained him.

"That nearly became a reality the night you found me torturing Kenneth. He realised you meant something to me and so I had to kill him. I was horrified at what I was willing to do for you. I gave up valuable information I could have tortured out of Kenneth by murdering him for you. And what made it even worse was that you saw everything," Mason explained with dark eyes. His tone made it sound like it was the ultimate disaster I had witnessed this.

"And because of that you had to kill me," I surmised. Mason nodded slowly, hesitantly like he was trying to gauge my reaction before I made it. Even though I knew this already it still hurt and I slipped my hand away from his and crossed my arms. But because Mason was already standing so close my forearm brushed upon his chest.

Mason glanced down at me with hooded eyelids and that look sent a bolt of electricity through me. I didn't move away from him though. We stared at each other in silence for an extraordinarily long heated moment before he broke it.

"I went to your house that night with every intention to kill you. No matter my feelings for you, if you told anyone about me then no one would be able to put an end to Marlemore," Mason described hauntingly as he ran his finger along the cut on my neck. The blood had started to clot and dry from the wind, but it was still raw, and the movement caused my features to scrunch up in pain. And just as I winced Mason flinched back instinctively, like he physically could not watch me in pain.

"I couldn't do it." His lips pressed together into a sharp line and my heart responded to his statement, beating faster in my chest.

"Why? What makes me different?" I asked earnestly. Mason's eyes dropped from mine like he was embarrassed to admit his next words.

"When I'm around you all my dark thoughts turn off, I don't think about all the ways I can kill you like I do with everyone else. The voices in my head, they don't tell me to kill you like they tell me to kill everyone else." Mason ran a hand through his hair and clutched at the end pieces. My forehead lifted as I looked at him bewildered; I didn't know that he heard voices.

"You hear voices?" I gasped as my eyes opened wide, shocked. Mason's shy eyes skittered to mine for a moment before they flickered away again, embarrassed. In that brief second our gazes connected I saw the deep embedded agony there.

"The darkest monsters that I have fought in my life weren't the real kind but the ones in my mind," he described horrifically as his hands scrunched into fists at his side. My stomach flipped as I thought about that and I stared back at him with wide empathetic eyes.

"I told you I have had my fair share of experience with mental illness. The voices have been there ever since I was a kid. But right now, I hear nothing. You have no idea how peaceful this is," he continued with a gentle voice and he let his hands fan out by his side, closing his eyes. He breathed in deeply as the wind blew the dark strands of his hair away from his face. Pride swelled up in my chest that I was the reason he looked that peaceful.

"You mean the voices you hear in your head don't speak at all when I'm around?" I questioned curiously, whirling both my hands around his bicep and looking up at him adoringly. Mason nodded, opening his eyes and gazing down at me with a closed mouthed smile. I stepped back so I could see more of that smile.

"When I'm near you it's like falling out of a blazing inferno that was burning my skin and into a cool lake. But then when you leave, I'm back in the inferno. The more I am near you, the more addicted I become to it, to you," Mason admitted, staring deep into my eyes and I felt that familiar buzz on my skin that only Mason could create. Like there was an electrical current running between us, pulling us towards each other.

"After that night at your house and you took care of me, there was no way I was ever going to hurt you ever again. I didn't care about the risk of you telling the police about me or that my brother was going to die. I was a fool to think that killing you was the answer. I should have known that hurting you was never a possibility for me. I decided to avoid you after that, I was trying to keep you safe and out of my dark world where being around evil murderers was a common occurrence. But when you asked me to meet you at the fair, I couldn't stay away any longer especially knowing that you wanted to see me too." He reached up his bloody hand and softly cupped my face. I closed my eyes, loving the feel of his skin against mine.

"You were obsessed with me too, this whole time," I marvelled, leaning my head closer into his hand.

"That night when you told me about your obsession with me was probably the best night of my life. I had never felt so calm knowing that maybe I could have this peace forever. You gave me a small taste of heaven – a small taste of what it's like to be normal."

Mason ran his thumb along my cheekbone softly and my eyelids fluttered from happiness. But that small moment of bliss was shattered when Mason's finger ran along the small scar near my eye that he placed there. My jaw clamped shut and my body stiffened in his arms. Mason's face fell along with his hand.

"Then why did you throw a knife at me when I came to your house that night?" I accused harshly. Mason's eyes flashed with fear for a moment as I stepped away from him.

"I was furious because I was terrified," Mason responded desperately, grabbing my shoulders in his grip, pulling me back to him. "I had sent a message to Marlemore that night explaining that I knew Melissa was still alive, and I had her. I wanted to lure him out to capture him. I had invited all of his evil murderous men to my home and then there you were right in the middle of it all. I was so panicked I couldn't think straight and then you weren't listening to me, you weren't leaving. The only way I could think for you to get out in time was to yell at you, to hurt you, and it worked," he revealed with a set jaw and intense eyes, willing me to listen, to understand.

The breath left my lungs in a silent gasp as I realised that all of those men were outside Mason's house that night because Mason had invited them there. And I was right in the middle of it all because someone sent me a note. Only now I knew it was Marlemore who sent it.

"Or so I thought," Mason continued darkly, bringing me out of my panicked thoughts. "You ran into Marlemore's men and I knew they were going to kill you. I watched as they hurt you and it made me feel so physically sick that I needed to vomit. I realised in that moment when they were hurting you that I would have done anything to make sure that you were never in pain again, including giving into Marlemore's threats. If he had you and started hurting you then I would have done anything, I would have given him my father, I would have killed and maimed hundreds of innocent people. I would have let someone else take control of the murderer that I am." He glanced up from underneath his lashes and stared at me with a vulnerability I never

212

thought I would see on his face, "for you."

Mason took a step forward so our chests touched and it sent a wave of desire running through me. My stomach fluttered and my lungs heaved pulling me forwards, closer to him.

"You are my ultimate weakness, my beloved, Elora," Mason announced earnestly as he stared deep into my eyes. From the light of the moon, I saw the tiny specs of white that glowed deep in his irises, nearly camouflaged in their dazzling blue iridescence. Tears welled up in my eyes; this was everything I ever wanted to hear Mason say. But there was still one nagging thought in the back of my mind.

"If you cared about me, then why did you leave me to die?" I murmured disheartened, breaking the sparks between us. Mason sighed and glanced away.

"I knew when they were hurting you that it was too late. Marlemore knew how much you meant to me. He would torture you, torment you, and destroy you to force me to do what he wanted. I thought that if you died, I wouldn't have to worry about you any more, and no one would be able to take control of me. If you were dead, then I would never have to watch what was happening to you ever again. So, I decided to leave you, I decided to let you die and along with you my ultimate weakness would be gone," Mason declared.

My heart squeezed at his painful yet beautiful declaration. Although it was a dark and twisted means to make sure I was never hurt again, it was still in Mason's mind a way of ensuring I was not in pain. To him, even leaving me to die was a show of his love for me. The tight knitted crease between my eyebrows started to relax when I realised that everything Mason had ever done to me was because he cared for me.

"But that was a grave mistake," Mason continued, oblivious

to my revelations. "When I truly did walk away, when reality hit me that you were going to die. I have never experienced such an agonising feeling in my life. The thought of you being dead was a hundred times worse than the thought of you being hurt. That is why I came back to save you," he revealed with a vulnerable expression, his eyes wide and jaw clenched. I couldn't take my captivated gaze away from him.

"I thought that you left me because you didn't care about me," I admitted, my mind still reeling.

"Ever since I realised that I hated seeing you in pain Elora, all I have ever wanted was to keep you safe. Which meant keeping you away from me. So, you didn't learn my secrets, so I didn't have to hurt you. But everything changed that night you fell asleep in my arms after those men broke you. I decided that there was nothing more in this world that I wanted than to be with you. I wanted to protect you honestly by being by your side, not following you in the shadows."

Excitement bubbled up in my stomach sending my pulse racing. Mason truly cared about me.

"You understand my darkest parts and accept them as apart of who I am. I will do everything in my power to make sure that you are okay, until the day that I die. I am yours," Mason declared passionately. I reached my hands up and placed one onto his chest above his heart and I felt it plummeting in his chest.

"Mason," I whispered in yearning. His lips brushed my cheek before he leaned his forehead against mine. As my heart skipped a beat, I finally realised that this was not an obsession. With Mason everything was real and so much more intensified than with any of my other obsessions. With Mason I have been able to push him away if it meant what was best for me and him. And everything I felt, he felt too. For the first time in my life this

214

was love.

"I love you," I whispered passionately. The truth of those words resonated in my soul. I loved him, and I always would. Mason tilted his head back, so he could search my eyes. He must have seen something in them because he closed his eyes tightly. The edges of his eyes crinkled up at the corners from a smile that surfaced on his lips and he inhaled a huge breath as if savouring the moment.

He leaned his face closer to mine and every inch he neared sent my breathing rate skyrocketing. His breath was fanning on my skin and just when I thought he would kiss me he opened his eyes and they bore into mine with a stark intensity. Just from that look alone, my stomach leapt in foreboding.

Suddenly Mason's fingers wrapped around my throat and he pushed me backwards so my back hit a tree. He held me in place by holding my neck and his lips came down onto mine forcefully. He kissed me passionately for a long moment and my muscles sunk into his demands, giving my body to him. I felt his smile against my lips as he pulled back from the kiss.

"Show me," he tested, gasping against my lips. He grabbed my shoulders and spun me around before pushing me forwards so I was right on the edge of the cliff face. I tensed and curled my toes against the small rocks that were biting into the bottom of my feet.

The waves below were treacherous and stormy as they crashed upon the rocks of the cliff face unrelentingly. My vision cleared as my muscles streamed with oxygen to fuel my escape as I realised how close I could be to death. Mason leant down and strapped a metal collar around both of my ankles. Once they were clipped on, he stood up and pressing his body right into mine. He placed his hands onto my hips, holding me against his chest, sending heat swirling into my circulatory system.

"If you love me," Mason whispered, his lips trailing along my ear. The warmth of his breath on my neck and the stubble on his cheek sliding along my skin sent shivers through my body.

"If you trust me." Mason spoke into my other ear which caused goose bumps to rise on my skin. I angled my torso even closer to his, pushing back into him as I closed my eyes. But suddenly his warmth was gone, leaving my body vulnerable.

"Then jump," he finalised sternly, nodding towards the cliff face before me. My muscles stilled; Mason wanted me to jump off the cliff. I glanced back at him fearfully to see a stoic enigmatic expression on his face, he was serious about this. There was not a spec of the love and affection I saw on his features not moments ago, he had placed a wall up against me.

He needed me to show him how much I loved him. I guess when you grow up around lies and broken promises, you learn not to believe words but actions. I needed to prove to him that I loved him, and I had to do that by placing all my trust in him. I needed to jump off this cliff.

I turned my eyes back towards the cliff face and placed both my feet right on the edge. My toes were hanging off the edge allowing the wind to whip up through the webs of my digits. With wide eyes I nervously looked down at the water to see it was resonating only darkness below. The cliff was high, so high I wasn't even sure that I would survive the fall into the water.

And if I did make it into the water, there could be rocks right below the surface. Then the waves were so wild and untamed that they would suck me under instantly. The chances of me surviving this on my own were minimal. But I needed to trust Mason.

My only other option would be to refuse to jump but then Mason wouldn't believe I loved him. I would go back to a life without him. With that thought in mind I plucked up all my courage and decided to place my faith in Mason.

I closed my eyes tightly as I tried to rein in the terror that was causing my muscles to stiffen, compelling me to move away from the edge. I spun around to face Mason and he was standing there with his hands tucked into his pockets and hood pulled up with a void expression. But I saw his eyes scanning me through the depths of the hood, I saw the deep desire in there to show him how much I loved him.

With my eyes locked on his blue ones that were smouldering with a dark intensity, with excitement and hope. Just from one hopeful look from him I knew that I would do anything for him. I inhaled a deep breath, allowing my muscles to relax and I dropped backwards away from the top of the cliff gracefully. Then I was falling.

Instantly, panic flooded my system and my arms flung out for something to grab onto, but it was too late. A scream slipped from my lips as I started plummeting towards the ocean below at a frightening speed. The wind forcible whipped at the skin on my face and my stomach dropped aggressively with the nausea of falling.

Abruptly I was already at the level of the waves and my limbs solidified turning to rock, bracing for my death. I sucked in a huge breath as I fell into the dark waves of the ocean and my body was jolted fiercely as I hit the water. I was overcome with shock from the ice-cold water as I was pulled under and swirled around by its currents. I began sinking down into the depths of the plummeting waves.

I flailed my arms out trying to stop myself from sinking but the momentum was yanking me down, into the dark depths of the water below. I moved my arms harder, but the wave's forceful currents were unrelenting, sending my body spinning. My blood was slowly depleting of oxygen which caused my muscles to become weak and my lungs to burn like I was on fire inside. I couldn't see through the dark waves and I had no idea where the surface was. I was going to die down here.

Suddenly an arm wrapped around my waist and pulled me upwards, Mason. I allowed him to tow me, kicking my legs to aid him. Finally, we reached the surface and Mason kept one arm safely wrapped around me to keep my head above the water. I gasped wildly for air and spluttered out ocean water that I had swallowed.

Mason hauled me along towards the rock face as I coughed for air. He towed me into a small alcove, which was hidden from the mammoth waves crashing behind it, setting a calm to the water. When the burning in my lungs lessened, I moved my eyes up towards Mason who was still holding me tightly. He saved me.

He was staring me with those dilated fierce eyes of his. I didn't have time to prepare before he pushed me into the wall of the rock face and he pressed his body into mine. He had one arm tightly wrapped around my waist and the other tenderly landed onto my cheek. He must have had one of his feet on a rock because he easily supporting both of our weight.

"You did it, you do love me," Mason growled approvingly, and his eyes flashed with something intense. He was looking at me like I was a crowning jewel. He pressed his lips into mine forcefully, devouring my lips, pulling them into his. I smiled as I saw just how happy he was that I did this for him. Even though I nearly died, he kept his word by saving me.

"You are crazy, but I love you." I grinned against Mason's lips and pulled my head back so I could see his face. "I would rather risk my death than live a life without you," I avowed.

Mason's eyes were awed as he gazed at me, dazzled. He moved his hand from my cheek towards the back of my head where his hands laced into my hair. His lips smashed into mine and he kissed me with vigour. His lips were warm against mine and I kissed him back fiercely responding with the same intensity.

My heart was galloping in my ears and I wrapped my legs around his waist, wrapping myself around him. My body was on fire, even though we were in freezing cold water. His hands stopped on my cheek.

"Will you stop pushing me away now?" Mason's lips didn't leave my mouth as he asked this, his lips moving along mine enticingly. He wanted me to let him be a part of my life. The only reason I didn't before was because I wasn't sure how sinister his secrets were that he was keeping from me. But now I knew everything.

Mason loved me, and he saved me from the dark depths of the waves. He just proved to me as much as to himself that he wanted me alive. And that he wanted me as much as I wanted him.

"Yes, my beloved murderer," I affirmed as I ran my hand down the jagged skin of his scar on the side of his face and kissed him deeply. I loved Mason with everything in my being and now I knew that he loved me, that he always had.

Now we can finally be together.

Chapter 21

I kept my eyes squeezed shut, I didn't want this dream to end. My arms were encircled around Mason's waist as I sat curled behind him on his motorbike. The wind whipped through the strands of my hair sending them billowing away from my skin.

Last night after we jumped into the ocean, we made our way back to his house. After changing into fresh clothes, we lay on the couch snuggled up and I fell asleep on Mason's chest. When I woke up in the late morning, he was still there wrapped in my arms and I couldn't believe it was all real. Mason made me breakfast and offered to take me home on his motorbike.

The ride home was peaceful. I rubbed my cheek against Mason's neck and he took one of his hands off the handlebars to entwine his fingers with mine for a moment.

My happy bubble burst when we neared my cottage, my heart stopping as fear debilitated me. I knew something wasn't right the very moment I set eyes on the cottage. As we drew closer my jaw clenched in dread, something was wrong.

The front windows were smashed and had been left in jagged shards scattered over the path. The front door was hanging open on one hinge as if someone had kicked through it. There were black tire skid tracks on the drive and continued on to skid through Grandma's beautiful flower garden. Terror overtook me as if someone was squeezing on my intestines.

Grandma.

We skidded to a stop and I jumped off the bike like it was on fire. I ran into the house and my veins pulsed as horror tightened my muscles from the devastation of my home. The cupboards were opened, and all their contents were thrown onto the floor. The dining table was upturned, and the couches were tipped onto their sides.

My wide eyes landed on bloodstained streaks on the floor leading towards the front door. My head spun and I stumbled backwards as I realised that Gran was missing.

"Grandma!" I screamed in shrilled panic. I raced into her room to find it empty. I rushed around the entire house screaming her name repeatedly. I felt like someone had ripped a hole in my heart. This couldn't be happening.

I only stopped when I ran into something hard. Mason gripped my shoulders in his hands steadily.

"Elora, she isn't here," he whispered softly, painfully, with his lips pressed together. Suddenly I noticed Mason's face become ashen and his features dropped into a horrified expression when his eyes focused on something behind me. I spun around to find my kitchen window covered in blood. But the blood wasn't in random splatters, it was a message.

"I have your Grandma now."

Everything in my body shut off then. The room started spinning around me and Mason grabbed me as I lost control of my limbs, sinking to the floor.

Tears started forming in my eyes and a sob released from my chest. Mason's eyes softened, and he pulled me into his chest. I wrapped my arms around his waist holding onto him for dear life as the reality of the situation dawned.

My grandma had been taken.

***

The first wail of the police sirens nearing in the distance was a faint echo. Mason had called the police to report my grandmother's disappearance and we waited anxiously for them to arrive. We knew it was risky getting the police involved but we needed all the help we could to find my grandma.

I paced back and forth around the broken house, the crunch of glass shattering beneath my boots.

"What could Marlemore want with my grandma? She's an old woman, and nothing like the others he has been killing, just teenagers," I stressed as I raked my hands through my hair.

"We will find her, I promise," Mason reassured sincerely, placing a comforting hand on my shoulder.

But it all doesn't make sense. The fact that Marlemore took my grandma made me feel like we were missing something; he wanted something more than just letting Mason's father escape.

"Unless…" My shoulders hunched and my stomach rolled as I flickered my gaze towards my room, towards the draw in which the gun lies that Marlemore left for me.

"Unless, he was trying to get to me," I whispered forebodingly. Mason stood up, his expression turning dire, and a hunted look entered his eyes that I would never be able to forget.

Before Mason was able to respond, the police cars pulled into my drive with a skid of their tires, the sound of the brakes screeching reverberated through the smashed windows of the cottage. My eyes darted to the front door to see the chief of police storm into the house with a sombre serious expression on her face.

"What has happened here?" Amanda exclaimed in consternation as she searched the surroundings. I watched as the horror of the situation sunk in, her eyes bulged and her large nostrils flared.

I was surprised to see her here after the death of her son. I could see what the death had done to her; her eyes were red ringed and stray strands of her hair had been pulled out of her usually neat high ponytail. If only she knew just where her son truly laid, and his murderer was right in front of her.

"I returned home to find the house a mess and that written on the walls." I pointed towards the bloody wall spelling the words that made me feel like a knife was sliding through my heart.

"Marlemore," she gasped and then her eyes turned to stone, fury clenching her jaw.

"We need to find my grandma before it's too late," I panicked.

"We will do everything we can," she assured me, with an authoritative tone I couldn't help believing.

"What do you know so far about Marlemore?" I asked desperately. I needed to know more information if I was going to find Gran.

Amanda's bushy eyebrows lowered and her eyes became wary as she looked at me like I was trying to pry information out of her that I shouldn't know.

"We are still investigating the murders. More highly trained officers will be arriving tonight to assist."

I ground my teeth together – I should have known the police would be useless. Mason and I will have to save Grandma on our own. I heard Mason huff in annoyance and the chief's wary gaze flickered to him.

"Mason," Amanda greeted with a curt nod of her head.

"Morning, Chief," Mason replied with narrowed eyes. They greeted each other like they have had many ill-natured confrontations before.

"I didn't see you there. I guess this makes things easier," she replied gruffly.

"I am sorry to do this, but the evidence is incontrovertible," Amanda announced, and Mason raised one of his eyebrows. "Mason due to your family history, we were able to gain a warrant to have your home searched and we found a sample of blood on your car. It has been confirmed that the blood belonged to Melissa Williams." My hands flew to my mouth as a lump formed in my throat, my mind swirling with terror. Amanda nodded at her other police officers who began restraining Mason.

"Mason Blackwell, you are under arrest for the suspected murder of Melissa Williams," Amanda declared, following with his rights. My breathing became panicked pants and my stomach swarmed with the need to vomit. This couldn't be happening.

My horrified eyes closed in on Mason's as my entire world crumbled around me. Defeat was plain and clean in Mason's eyes; he had no means to defend himself against the accusations placed against him because they were true. Even if what he did was to save us all, it was still wrong in the eyes of the law. He still murdered Melissa.

Tears filled my eyes as I reached for Mason. I saw the yearning in his eyes as he longed to reach me. I ran up to him and grasped my hands onto his upper arms.

"Mason, I can't do this without you," I cried, desperate. Mason managed to shove off one officer from his arm and reached up to cup my face.

"Everything will be okay. I will get out as quickly as I can," he reassured me. But I didn't believe his words. I don't even think he did.

"Stay safe, my love," he whispered in my ear so only I could hear, and then the officers pulled him away and his hand was yanked from my face. His fingers lingered for as long as possible before finally his hand dropped.

"Mason!" I yelled after him and tears splattered onto my cheeks, pooling on the end of my chin. They handcuffed Mason and pushed his head into the police cruiser and the last thing I saw was Mason mouthing three words to me.

"I love you."

A sob burst from my chest as I realised that Mason was going to prison for the rest of his life. My heart shattered at the thought of never being able to be with Mason again. I didn't want to live that life, I refused. With resolve settling my heart into stone I knew what I had to do. If I was able to capture Marlemore then Mason will be released.

"Elora, I must ask you to return to the police station to give a statement," the chief stressed. I didn't look at her as I said my next words.

"Yes of course – I will just get changed." She nodded and allowed me to pass her.

I locked my bedroom door behind me. With shaky hands I grabbed the gun out of my chest of draws and held it out in front of me. From just one look at the gun, it sent my head whirling with dizziness. It couldn't be a coincidence that I was given this gun and my grandma was taken.

I searched the gun for anything unusual; I pulled the slide back and then yanked the slide lock into place. I checked into the barrel for any ammunition to find one lone bullet in there with my name written all over it. Dread made my body shudder with a cold sweat from seeing my name. I emptied the bullet out but I was unable to open it.

I knew what I had to do, whatever message had been left for

me was inside the bullet and to release it I needed to shoot the gun. With resolve cementing in my mind, I was able to focus on one goal. I was going to bring an end to this monster on my own.

I stashed the gun into my bag before I jumped out my bedroom window and landed swiftly on my feet. I ran towards our back garage that housed Grandma's car, and luckily the police didn't notice my escape.

I drove Gran's car into the depths of the woods where I parked and stood in front of a tree stump with the gun hanging in my hand. I glanced down at the lethal object and a quiver of fear shot through my veins so paralysing I dropped the gun to the floor.

I inhaled a deep breath to calm my nerves; I had to do this for Gran. My hands shook violently as I grasped the gun in both of my hands tightly. Ignoring my terror, I aimed the gun and closed my eyes as I pressed down on the trigger. The thunderous noise shattered around me, sending a tremor through my limbs as the gun fired. I opened my eyes to find a letter sticking into the tree from a small spike.

I plucked it out of the tree and unravelled its rolled-up form to reveal an elegant handwritten letter.

"The answer you seek is in the place where all the answers become clear –

Be sure to follow your heart to where the thorns lie.

In order to enter you will need to face your deepest fear.

Only then will you find the place where they all will die."

It was a riddle. My heart sunk as I re-read the words that made no sense. My hands balled into fists as I realised Marlemore was playing me, trying to send me on a wild goose chase. If Marlemore wanted me to solve this riddle, then I wasn't going to. I shoved it into my bag forcefully but as I did so I saw another

226

piece of paper in my bag.

It was the poster of the missing boy, Ryan. The exact piece that Melissa had shoved into my face that night she died. The smudge of the blood that had stained the paper was still evident from when she ran her fingers along the picture of the boy. The words she spoke that night still haven't left my mind.

"This, it's the one." Melissa was trying to tell me something important about this boy. He was the one she tried to say, that meant this boy was the key.

He was different to the other murders. He went missing while the others were injected with poison and had their bodies displayed for the entire town to see. I needed to find out more about him and I knew exactly the right place to find my answers. The Library.

I hurled back into the car and drove frantically like a mad woman towards the town centre. I barged into the library not thinking about the racket I would make through the quiet silence the readers were immersed in. Belle lurched away from her computer as if I had just shot her. Guilt streamed through me and I gave her an apologetic smile.

"Sorry, Belle, I didn't mean to frighten you," I announced in a small voice. I stood in front of her while she quickly pressed buttons on the computer to close the page she was working on before looking up to me with a tense expression on her face. As I looked closer at her, I noticed that she had dark black bags under her eyes and her usual smile was absent. She looked worn out. These murders must be taking a toll on her too.

"No worries, Elora. What are you doing here, isn't today your day off?" she asked with her eyebrows pinched together in confusion. I searched her face again as I considered my response. I didn't want to worry her any more with the knowledge of my grandma.

"I'm just here for some research. Do you mind if I use your computer quickly?" I gushed.

"Sure," she muttered, before logging out and handing it over to me. I pulled up a search engine and typed in the full name of the missing boy. The first few links that appeared were the news articles about his disappearance. I clicked on the first one.

It detailed how the last place he was seen was at the markets in town and it explained how the last place his phone tracked him to was right in the middle of the forest. The closest landmark to the location was the old asbestos factory that was shut down forty years ago. My eyes stopped on the word factory as it jolted my memory.

My eyes burst wide open as I remembered something Melissa's best friend told the chief of police. She said that Melissa kept talking about going to a factory, and that she was obsessed with going there. This couldn't be a coincidence.

No, it wasn't. I remembered when Mason showed me those notes Marlemore sent him. They were covered in a white dust like whoever was making the note was writing it on a table covered in dust, but not dust, asbestos.

It's the perfect place to make sure no one comes snooping and the police would never suspect the factory because who would live in a place that was going to kill you?

A shudder ran through me to the bottom of my toes as I realised that I knew where Marlemore was plotting his murders and even possibly where he was keeping my grandma.

I knew the location of Marlemore's lair.

Chapter 22

Foreboding sunk into my bones as the dark clouds overhead descended. Rain droplets bucketed down from the sky splattering onto the roof of Gran's car, beclouding my vision of the road ahead. All that was visible before me were the shadows of dark ominous pine trees that were only found deep in the forest, spanning metres above my head like an iron cage.

The factory was far from any main roads or from any civilisation. The tress thinned to open into a clearing and my throat dried when the old decaying building emerged into view.

This was the place where an evil murderer resided; my hair stood on end as a chill ran through me. I parked the car and shut off the engine which made the forest eerily quiet. The only noise tangible was my shallow breathing and the rain splattering on the roof.

The building in front of me was clearly abandoned. It was a large warehouse spanning multiple stories high with a large chimney protruding from the roof. The exterior walls were cracked and crumbling, and the paint had stripped from the weather that had eroded it, turning it into the original red colour of the bricks. It looked exactly like a place where someone was going to kill you. I couldn't let fear derail me now. I needed to be brave and investigate; this was the only way to get my Mason back and save Grandma.

Steeling my mind and straightening my back, I stepped out into the pouring rain. I ran up the stairs towards the entry and swung open the creaking rusty door into the factory.

The ajar doors revealed a warehouse with enormous machines reaching to the top of the factory ceiling. It was filled with conveyer belts and large tubs where the asbestos materials were made. I took a few cautious steps inside stiffly with locked knees. I looked down to my feet and I noticed my black converses were covered in a white layer of dust.

"This is the place," I whispered to myself. This was the exact same white dust that was on the letter to Mason. I glanced around the warehouse with speculative eyes and noticed small particles of dust floating through the air. My heart started pounding viciously as I realised that Marlemore could be here right now.

Before I had time to process that thought, I stepped forward and the ground disappeared from underneath me.

I screamed wildly as I plunged through the air, my stomach rolling. My arms flailed around trying to grasp onto anything until I finally hit the floor onto a pile of a bagged substance. The air was propelled from my lungs with a gasp as I landed. After a moment, I gained control of my limbs again and rose from the floor. I glanced up to the roof to find the old decaying planks of wood I was walking on collapsed under my weight and sent me into the basement.

The room was dark, but my eyes soon adjusted, and structures started to form before me. With a gasp of realisation, I knew instantly that this place was Marlemore's lair. My flesh creeped as I searched around me. The room spanned the entire width of the factory's layout upstairs.

In one corner lay a minuscule bedroom set up with a narrow single bed, a portable wooden wardrobe, and a large desk covered in papers and skewed notebooks like someone had been busy at work. I inspected the work to find written on one of the pieces of

230

paper was a list of chemical equations written by a man named Henry Edmington and co-written by Jeremiah King. It didn't make any sense to me, so I placed it back down and continued searching the room for clues.

The entire back wall was covered by a roller door. I shuddered to think what was behind there. The only entry into the basement was a door that was just behind the location where I fell through the roof. Next to the door was a chest of drawers that looked more like a pirate's chest of gold. The only thing that had character in the room was a small rocking chair in the corner of the room that was a faded green colour and covered in black decorative swirls.

I took an involuntary step back as random memories flashed across my mind and my breathing spiked erratically. I didn't understand my reaction – it was like some deep part of me recognised that chair. But from where? I couldn't place where I had those memories from and the thought was nagging at my subconscious.

My revelations were cut short when the chest of drawers shuttered violently as if something had just kicked it from the inside. I flinched back violently, staggering away from the chest. My eyebrows knotted together as I treaded a few careful steps towards it. I reached down and tried to lift the lid but just before I could, a loud bang shattered the silence around me.

"What are we doing here, Brett?" spoke a deep man's voice with an Italian accent from the other side of the door. I clutched at my chest as my stomach twisted with dread, sparking my muscle fibres alight. Could that be Marlemore?

Without another thought I sprinted towards the scanty wardrobe to hide inside it. I opened the door by its rusty handle with violently shaking hands. I breathed easier once I slipped through into the tiny space, sliding in between coats and shirts.

"Marlemore told us to wait here," another man's voice answered from behind the door. A key slid into the lock and with a click the door jerked open. I peered through the small gap between the wardrobe doors as men came swarming into the room.

Shock disoriented me and made my head spin and my body shudder as I recognised the faces of the men. They were the men that attacked me outside Mason's house, the men that worked for Marlemore.

There was the dark-skinned man with one hand, the short bulky man with tattoos, and the man with a permanent sneer on his face. But how could they be here? They were locked up in Mason's basement. Unless, Marlemore released them? It was possible now that Mason was in jail.

"I hope Marlemore has someone for us to kill," grumbled the man with an Italian accent and permanent sneer on his face.

"I'm sure he will, Jacob." Spoke the voice of the man whom I know now is called Brett. He was the dark-skinned man with the missing hand and their leader. His dreadlocks were tied up scruffily in a bun and the sight of him sent fear into the depths of my heart.

"Why don't we do something fun while we wait," smirked the shortest one with too many tattoos. There were more of them here then when they attacked me – almost ten men kept waltzing into the room.

The others nodded and cheered their agreement. Brett stalked towards the roller door and yanked the doors open so they crashed and rumbled as they slid apart. I gasped and slammed a hand over my mouth as my wide eyes took in the horror before me.

Chained to the wall was a man-hanging limp, his face hanging towards the floor and covered in blood. I realised with a jolt that I recognised the man from his long grey hair parted with a widow's peak. It was the friendly old man from the markets and Gran's friend, Bill.

The innocent old man was unconscious but was woken by the noise of the roller doors and one swollen eye gradually opened. His eyes widened in terror and he flinched away from them. My jaw clenched in indignation; why the hell are these men torturing an innocent old man?

Brett turned to search through the wall beside Bill which was filled with deadly weapons at his disposal. Brett picked up a knife with a sinister smirk and a dark gleam in his eye as he stalked back over to the helpless man. Brett grinned back at the other men before he cut the knife into Bill's chest in a long gash.

Bill screamed out and the horrific sound made my stomach coil and convulse. The other men cheered in encouragement and some others picked their own weapons. Brett lacerated along Bill's face this time and blood went flying through the air.

I dry heaved at the sight and fury set my blood alight. I refused to watch as they tortured an innocent man. I reached behind me in the cramped space to search for some kind of weapon.

But my searching reached an abrupt end when my hands grabbed onto a solid piece of flesh. I knew what it was immediately – decaying human skin. My stomach rippled with nausea as I turned around slowly to face the horror behind me, the horror that was inside the wardrobe with me. The air was sucked out of my lungs when I saw a dead bloodied body dangling from a hanger behind me.

The body was of a young man. I didn't recognise him

through his sunken cheeks and decaying flesh, but it wasn't the dead body that horrified me to the depths of my soul, it was the way his open dead eyes looked right into mine. His eyes were red and blood shot. It was like all the blood vessels in his eyes had burst and the blood had pooled in his irises and dripped down from his eyes like tears. His whole body had been mutilated by cut marks from a knife; he had been tortured before he died.

I pulled the top of my shirt over my mouth and stumbled a horrified step back away from the blood-curdling sight. I forgot about the small space I was in and my back slammed into the door of the wardrobe with a loud bang. I had to slam my hand over my mouth to prevent a scream that was threatening to surface.

But, I was too late. All the men snapped their attention in my direction. With narrowed eyes the short man with the tattoos stalked towards me. He tilted his head to the side as his dark eyes looked right at me through the wardrobe doors. If they found me, I would have no hope against them. They would kill me instantly.

My tremoring hands and legs shook the wardrobe beneath me. The man twisted the wardrobe handle with a click and started to open the door. The light from outside the door shined through the widening crack touching my cheeks.

"All right men, that's enough," ordered a voice in an authoritative tone. Instantly my body relaxed – it was a subconscious reaction. Whenever I was in the presence of the person with that voice, I was calm, I was safe.

Mason.

The man's hand froze on the doorhandle and he yanked it back as he glanced at Mason. Fear was evident in his black eyes and in his tight shoulders. Relief released my coiled muscles as I sagged against the side of the wardrobe when the man's attention was diverted from me.

As the relief wore off, I frowned and shook my head from the confusion that stewed in its place. Mason was supposed to be in jail. Unless he was released somehow, but then why didn't he come straight to me to help me find my grandma? Why was he here? And the most important question – what was Mason doing in Marlemore's lair? He was speaking to the other men like he was in control of them.

"Yes, boss," spat Brett in a condescending tone. Brett's nefarious eyes glared at Mason with a scornful expression.

Mason ignored Brett's clear resentment towards him and strolled in with a confidence that made all the other men back away from him. I narrowed my eyes and pressed my lips together as I watched Mason like a hawk.

Mason's features were apathetic, his face wiped clean of all emotion. But his eyes were pained, he hid it well, but I knew him so deeply I saw it hidden there. His dark brown hair was unkept and hanging over his eyes and his cheeks were red; he looked dishevelled from stress.

"I have a job for you all in the city," Mason declared. I didn't understand what Mason was doing, these were the men that had attacked me, and he had chained in his basement. My heart splintered, trembling my chin as I realised that Mason must have let them go, not Marlemore.

"Not tonight, mate. Tonight, we work on this one," Jacob objected, his features sneering and he nodded his head towards Bill. Mason's eyes flickered towards the broken and bloodied Bill chained to the wall. I wanted with every bone in my body for Mason to walk over to Bill and set him free.

Mason gave one agonised look over his shoulder towards the door that was right next to the wardrobe I was hiding in before turning his back to the others with a determined expression set on his features.

"Fine, let's get this over with," Mason conceded and stalked over towards Bill. My heart rate picked up in trepidation – I didn't want to face the possibility that Mason was here for malevolent purposes.

Mason strode towards the horrifying wall of weapons and searched through them all until his fingers set on his weapon of choice. He had to tweak his thumb and finger together to pick it up. It was a tiny syringe.

Mason stared at Bill intently for an exceptionally long moment; his eyebrows were folding together tightly as if he was thinking though something deeply and it was paining him. A part of me ached from seeing such torment on his features but my betrayed side had more dominant rage filled emotions.

"Please don't," begged Bill, and as he spoke blood spilled out from his mouth and gargled his words.

Mason stared at him for a moment longer before he made his decision. Without another thought he plunged the syringe straight into Bill's chest. I jerked forward and strained out my arms as if I could stop the movement from my position metres away.

Everything went quiet then, and everyone watched the liquid flow into Bill's veins. Bill watched with his mouth hanging open in horror. He didn't make a noise; it was as if he was so shocked, he had lost the ability to scream. But my eyes were plastered onto Mason. Mason's stoic expression was faltering, like he couldn't hide his emotions any more they were so strong.

The torment was shining through his features by the way his jaw was clenched tightly and how his eyes were squinted creating a crease at the top of his forehead.

The quiet that cascaded the room ended abruptly as

everything changed. Bill screeched out a gut-wrenching sound of pure agony and his body started convulsing against the chains that bound him violently. His eyes were tortured as they started being torn apart by what looked like tiny cuts turning his irises red, just like the body's behind me.

The blood vessels slowly started tearing around his eyes causing blood to trickle down from his eyes. Cut marks started manifesting on his skin like he was being tortured by an invisible knife cutting through his body. Blood dripped from all over his body and face from the materialising cuts.

I couldn't blink. My eyes were frozen open and I covered my ears with my hands, shuddering fiercely. I couldn't stay in the shadows any longer – I couldn't watch this. This was something worse than torture, and the noises coming out of Bill's mouth were like shards of ice piercing my soul.

I opened the wardrobe door with a creak but just as I was about to step out Mason grabbed something out of his pocket, a knife and plunged it into Bill's chest. The screaming stopped.

Bill's head sagged back against the chains and his body morphed into stone as the convolutions ended. His tormented eyes slowly lost their suffering and then lost their light. He was dead.

Mason just killed him. I was left staring with wide darting eyes and with my mouth hanging open at the scene in front of me. It couldn't be true. Mason only killed evil people. He would never kill an innocent.

"It didn't work. Let's get out of here," Mason ordered with a voice no one would disagree with unless they wanted to die. Mason began turning around and it willed my petrified body into motion. I staggered a step back and allowed the wardrobe door to slide over me again, concealing my presence.

Mason stormed out the room without looking at anyone and the door slammed behind him. The other men grumbled and groaned their disappointment but followed Mason nonetheless. When the last man left the room, I stumbled out of the closet and away from the dead body that was shunted in there.

My knees gave out, and I didn't have the strength to comprehend what I just had witnessed. My throat ached painfully for Bill; his body lay before me as still as stone.

Mason just murdered an innocent man. I couldn't deny it any longer because the facts were right in front of my eyes and incontrovertible. Mason was working for Marlemore.

As I accepted the horrific truth, an echo of Brett's voice rang in my mind – he said 'yes, boss' to Mason. Could that mean that Mason was these men's boss? These men who I knew were working for Marlemore. Could Mason be Marlemore?

I sagged onto the wardrobe and curled my head into my knees as betrayal sunk into my mind. Mason has been lying to me.

Chapter 23

My mind was numb as I drove through the misty forest back towards the town. Twilight had dawned, and the clouds were obsidian black as a storm brewed beneath the surface. The darkening trees around me were dark ominous shadows that swayed heavily from the strong wind.

My tires threw up mud as I turned corners. I knew exactly where I was going. As I lay helpless on the floor of Marlemore's lair after Mason left, the pain of his betrayal started to consume me and I finally realised what the riddle meant.

My deepest fear – I feared nothing more than losing Mason. But not just losing him, losing him because he didn't love me, that my obsession was real. That he was using the fact that I loved him for his own intensions. My deepest fear was that Mason was Marlemore.

I knew I had to confront Mason. I needed the truth. Before I left, I grabbed a box full of bullets from the back wall of the lair to re-fill the ammunition in my snake gun and strapped more guns around my body.

When I arrived at Mason's house, I stormed up to the front porch to find the door was locked – Mason must still be out. I stalked over to the grand windows at the back of the house and plucked my gun from my pocket. I pulled down on the trigger with a bang.

Glass shattered everywhere. The tiny shards flew through the air with destructive force as the thunderous noise of the glass shattering echoed around the empty house. The once beautiful colossal window lay in shards around me. I took a shaky step into the dark house; there were no candles illuminating the nebulous hallways. I came to an abrupt halt once inside. If Mason wasn't here, then where would I find my answers?

I stepped into the front room and my eyes flickered around the house. As I peered down the aphotic corridor, I saw an exceptionally faint glow of light gleaming from the distance. I remembered the room with the only light on in the house and how Mason told me that he didn't want me to ever go in there.

I followed the light – I wanted answers. I stopped outside the door as a shudder wobbled my knees, turning my complexion pallid. I ignored my fear and turned the handle until it clicked, and the door swung open wide.

My eyebrows pinched together in confusion as I searched around the room in dismay. I wasn't in a room that was going to be my worst nightmare but rather in a library.

Suddenly I was reminded of that bloody riddle.

The answer you seek is in the place where all the answers become clear.

So, where do you go when you need to find information? I thought about the place where I went to find the answers about the missing boy.

A library!

More specifically, this library. I had a feeling that whoever left me that riddle wanted me to find out about the secrets Mason had been keeping from me. I pulled the riddle out from my back pocket and unfolded the worn-out creased paper.

Be sure to follow your heart to where the thorns lie. I searched around the room, trailing on anything that looked remotely like a place where thorns would lie. But instead my eye caught on the location where the light was resonating from. At the far back wall of the library there was a single light bulb that hung down from the ceiling on a string that was brightly lit. Its fluorescence shone directly downwards onto a large painting.

My eyes were drawn immediately to the people in the painting. There were five people – a woman with long blonde hair and dead eyes, a prestigious looking man in a police uniform but with evil crazed eyes that I recognised, and three young children. This was Mason's family.

My heart flipped as I set eyes on a boy that had the exact same blue eyes as Mason. It was then that I knew where my heart lies. It lies with Mason.

With closer inspection I noticed the frame had a shape carved into it with fine elegant precision. It was a rose stem and branching off it was hundreds of thorns. My eyes burst open in realisation. This couldn't be a coincidence. The stem originated at the bottom corner and spiralled within the frame to stop at the top corner. The thorns were mostly bunched at the bottom of the stem and I ran my hands over the frame of the painting following the stem downwards.

My heart started pounding as suddenly my hand rested onto a small latch underneath the frame. I clicked it. The picture frame swung open to reveal the wall behind it that had a small electronic keypad and screen attached. I pressed the on button and in green capital letters it said, who is Marlemore? I stumbled, I had no idea who Marlemore's true identity was, but I bet that the writer of the riddle knew.

In order to enter you need to face your deepest fear.

I already knew my deepest fear. I was terrified that Mason was evil, that Mason was Marlemore. That had to be it; I flipped open the keypad and entered Mason's name into the machine.

I inhaled a staggered uneasy breath and pressed enter. My heart shattered as the machine flashed green and the wall jolted which slowly opened to reveal a dark room. My lip trembled, and I wiped my sweaty palms onto my jeans as a cold sweat ran through me.

Only then will you find the place where they all will die.

I tried to prepare my already damaged heart for what I was about to find. I held my breath as I stepped into the dark room. As my eyes adjusted to the darkness the horror in front of me began to materialise.

I was in a small room with black walls and bare tiled floors, and the dark atmosphere inside the room set my teeth on edge. The only visible structure was at the back of the room where there were multiple glass cages like trophy cabinets. The cabinets were large and enclosed a space big enough for a human body to hang inside, and that was exactly what was in there.

My hand slapped over my mouth to quieten the blood-curdling scream that left my lips and my knees buckled underneath me. My knees landed into a slimy liquid, blood that had dripped out from the bodies hanging on the walls in their glass cases like dolls hung up for show.

In the first enclosure hung the body of the missing boy, Ryan. He was dead, and there was no hope for finding him now. My skin crawled as I saw that, like Bill and the man's body I found in the wardrobe, Ryan had blood dripping down from his eyes and cheeks from lacerations all over his skin. I swallowed the lump in my throat to prevent the vomit from heaving out of my stomach.

My eyes skittered painfully along to the next hung up body, Melissa. Her face and body were also bleeding, and her dead lifeless brown irises stared straight into mine just like when I

242

witnessed her being killed twice. Next to Melissa, was the body of Brandon. His buzz cut head lolled at an unnatural angle.

My eyes fell onto the very reason my knees buckled underneath me and all the energy was sucked out of my muscles. The last body was my grandma's.

"No!" I screamed, the sound piercing the walls around me filling them with pure agony. I jumped up and slammed my hands onto the glass wall that she was hung up inside.

"Grandma!" I bellowed at her, willing her to wake up. No matter how hard I slammed my hands onto the wall her eyes never opened. She was dead. My heart started splintering into tiny pieces. My only family was gone.

I was in a crypt. A place where Mason stored the bodies of those he had killed. I realised as my eyes flickered across each dead face that these were all the people that Marlemore had murdered, and now I knew that Mason had killed all these people. I spluttered out a cry of torment as I realised the truth. Mason was the murderer.

Suddenly, my grandma's eyes flung open and her body violently spasmed. A scream caught in my throat as I watched her body jerk around. Her movements slowly relaxed and her eyes set on me. I watched as realisation dawned in her eyes and horror gradually entered them, but it wasn't horror for herself, it was fear for me.

"Run," she screamed silently. My heart started to beat again as a relief so strong washed through my body it almost felt like I was floating. My revelations were cut short when a noise reverberated through the entire house of a slamming door. Someone was here.

"Run!" she bellowed again, her eyes flickering to the door and back to me. I stood immobile not knowing if I should risk rescuing her or running. If I saved her now, we would most likely be caught but if I ran and came back later with a proper plan and help, she would have a higher chance of survival. With an agonised look back at my grandma I whispered to her that I would be back.

I squeezed my eyes shut painfully and sprinted out of the heinous room. My footsteps echoed as I ran down the dark corridors and just as I was about to escape out the back door something caught my eye in my peripheral vision. My head snapped to the right to see a dark shadowed silhouette of a man standing in the doorway staring straight at me with a knife hanging by his side. My heart pounded as I saw him – Mason.

Instantly, my flight or fight response kicked in and I flew. I swung open the back door and sprinted through the garden into the forest. The rain instantly saturated me to the bone and the strong whips of the wind sunk into my cold skin. I heard the crunch of leaves and increasing reverberation of footsteps on my tail as I dodged tree branches. He was gaining on me.

My feet skidded to a halt when I reached a clearing and I emerged at a familiar cliff face. My eyes flittered around me in panic as I realised that I was trapped. With the tension palpable in my muscles, I turned around to face my pursuer. My hands clenched into fists at my side as I spun into the darkness to see Mason emerge from the confounds of the mist of the forest. I looked into the beautiful dark face of the man I loved.

He looked dishevelled; his hair was sticking to the side of his face and the rest stuck up at odd angles. His clothes were drenched from the rain and his black boots were slick with mud. His eyes were wild, and I couldn't comprehend what was going on inside them. The black circles under his eyes were more prominent than ever. They were almost black and ringed with red from the blood vessels that were protruding from under his skin. His red lips trembled, and his jaw was set into a hard line.

As I looked into the eyes of a murderer my traitorous heart still jolted and fluttered at the sight of him. My stomach filled with warmth and all I wanted to do was fling myself into his arms.

"Elora," Mason growled in warning. His words snapped me back to reality. My eyes narrowed as I remembered the body of my grandma and what he did to Bill.

"Stay away from me," I insisted, but it was released as a broken whisper. Mason's eyes became wary but he didn't listen to me. He took a step closer, so our bodies were almost touching. I still had the gun placed securely in my back pocket. I thought about using it, but the thought was so agonising that I realised that no matter what Mason had done, I could never hurt him.

In a whirlwind, Mason's strong arm encircled around my waist and he pulled into his warm chest. My body fluttered with ecstasy at his touch, at his familiar and enticing embrace. I fought against its allure and tried to struggle away from him, but it was futile. He placed a hand around my throat and my body instantly stilled into glass as fear paralysed me.

Was the man that I loved going to kill me?

Chapter 24

My body was alive with suffocating fear but also electrocuting attraction. Mason's beautiful face was dangerous; his unkept dark hair was falling across his face and his red rimmed blue eyes stared down at me hooded, but filled with blazing emotion. I jerked my arm free and slammed my forearm into Mason's stomach, but his grip remained unyielding.

"Relax, Elora, I am not going to hurt you." Mason's soft voice breathed down my neck steadily. His familiar voice calmed me, and his breath sent seductive shivers down my spine. I did as he asked, and it left me frozen against him with the only sound emitting between us being the panicked gasps of my breathing.

Mason spun us around, so he was the one closest to the cliff face and then released me. I wasn't expecting it and I stumbled back a few steps until my back hit a tree trunk, the same one he kissed me against. I placed my shaking hands on the tree and gripped the bark with digging fingernails. Mason stared at me darkly. His eyes were burning into mine like he was trying to tell me something important. A tremor wracked through my muscles as he took a cautious step towards me.

"You are the murderer," I declared as I stared into his piercing eyes.

"Yes," Mason agreed confidently. "I killed the missing boy Ryan, I killed Melissa, and I killed Brandon." My breath caught in my throat as horror sent my lips trembling.

"You are Marlemore," I whispered in defeat. Mason's eyes

flashed, and his features set in an expression of defiance. My eyes focused on the knife he still had hanging by his side. He waited until our gazes locked once again before speaking. His eyes were filled with vulnerability.

"You don't truly believe that, do you?" he countered in distress as if the very thought hurt him to the core and my heart pounded with hope. His eyes bore into mine with an intensity that pulled on my heartstrings. It was like an invisible string was pulling me to him, and it always had no matter what he had done.

"I am not Marlemore," he asserted fiercely with a strong set jaw and serious gaze. My tight muscles unclenched as I started to believe him and I realised what a good liar he was. My hands balled into fists – did he think I was a fool?

"Don't lie to me. You kidnapped my grandma," I objected, stabbing a finger into his chest. His eyes softened and he ducked his head, so we were at eye level.

"You know me, Elora," Mason implored. He raised his wrist warily and touched his soft hand to my cheek, cupping it lovingly. My eyes fluttered closed for a moment from the warmth of his touch and my anger dissipated. Why was I allowing this? He was a murderer of innocent people.

But I knew the answer instantly, as I looked deeply into his captivating blue eyes that glistened from the reflection of a portlight that shined on the ocean. I loved him, no matter what he had done and I would do anything just be near him. He leaned his face closer to mine and I didn't stop him when he pressed his lips to my cheek.

My body shuddered in contentment but also fear from allowing a murderer this close to me. It was a strange combination that sent my heart and mind into a frenzy. The warmth of his skin against the fear induced cold chill that ran through my veins was electrifying.

"You know deep in your heart that I would never do anything to hurt you," Mason implored as his lips moved against the skin of my cheek. He pressed his body into mine and I felt a stab of the knife in his pocket sticking into my skin.

Why was a murderer kissing me so lovingly? He should be killing me now I knew his secrets.

"Everything I have done has been to protect you." Mason's declaration and the clear love for me that was shining in his irises sent my heart skippering in hope, but I pulled away from him forcefully as flashes of my gran's imprisonment glimpsed across my vision.

"I know everything, Mason. I saw you kill Bill at Marlemore's lair!" I shouted, my voice quivering with rage.

"I know," he admitted with down cast eyes. I blanched and my eyebrows pinching together in confusion.

"I knew you were there. That was the only reason I was there," he revealed ambiguously. I glared back at him, but pressed my lips together, perplexed.

"You're not making any sense." I shook my head repeatedly trying to understand him.

"Let me start from the beginning," he proposed. I stared at him warily trying to find a spec of untrustworthiness on his face but there was none. I nodded back conciliatorily.

"Ever since the night I discovered Marlemore's deceit about Melissa's death, Marlemore asked me to work for him. Naturally I refused." Mason started to pace in front of me, his hands winding together then apart. My muscles were shaking, and my knees were wobbling but I was listening intently.

"That night you were attacked by Marlemore at the church I needed to do something to make sure you were never targeted

248

again. So, I agreed to work for him if he left you alone. Marlemore agreed." I grinded my teeth and locked my jaw, I could protect myself.

"Why would you do that?" I snapped, my voice nearly a growl. His eyes flickered up to mine suddenly as if bewildered by my anger, confusion clear in his eyes.

"Elora, surely by now you must understand how much you mean to me? I would do anything to make sure you were safe." His eyes pierced mine and I did understand how much I meant to him because I felt the same for him. "And besides, this would have been the only way to find out Marlemore's identity and take him down," Mason revealed with a shrug.

That was a smart plan, gain information on Marlemore and take him down from the inside.

"Why didn't you tell me this?" I growled angrily, trying to hide the hurt from his lack of trust to confide in me.

"Because, my love, Marlemore made me swear not to tell you or else the deal was off," Mason admitted sincerely. I ran my finger against my chin in agitation, why would it matter to Marlemore if I knew that Mason was working for him?

"That doesn't explain how you got out of jail." I crossed my hands over my chest.

"That was another deal. While I was locked in my jail cell, Marlemore appeared and showed me a video of you inside his lair with his men heading right to you. I knew that they would kill you, so I needed to get out to save you. Marlemore offered to release me but only if I gave him my watch." Mason gestured to his wrist which had a stripe of pale white skin, untouched by the sun because he never took his watch off.

My eyes widened as my stomach swirled in dread. Marlemore could now release Mason's father. Mason just gave up everything for me just like he had feared. Mason released a monster for me.

"I made it to his lair in time just before they found you in the wardrobe." The stark relief was evident on Mason's face even now. My mouth gaped open; everything I saw Mason do he knew I was seeing. I tilted my head to the side to examine him as if a different angle would reveal the reasoning for his actions.

"I knew I couldn't take them all on by myself. So, I decided to play along with their game and then try and lure them out, and it worked." Mason shrugged nonchalantly.

"You killed Bill to protect me," I outraged. The thought that Bill died so that I was able to escape made me sick to the stomach.

Mason's eyes filled with fervour as he stopped pacing and faced me. He grabbed my chin in his hand and tilted my head up, so I was staring deep into his eyes which were burning lucently into my own.

"Elora, what would you do for someone you loved? Would you kill an innocent human being? Because I would do anything for you," he vowed darkly, moving his lips closer to mine so I felt his breath on my skin. My stomach knotted in horror and I shook my head repeatedly at what he was insinuating.

"But no, I didn't kill him," Mason elaborated, his tone and expression serious. "I injected him with a new strain of poison that Marlemore has been creating and testing. I was shocked myself at what happened to Bill." Mason visibly shuddered. "That knife I stabbed him with wasn't actually a knife. I only made the syringe in the shape of a knife, so the guys wouldn't become suspicious. What I actually stabbed him with was an antidote. Bill will be waking up any moment now." Mason grinned at his intelligent deceptive idea. I swayed from side to side, mind blown by this revelation.

"But I saw all those bodies hanging up in your house like trophies, including my grandma," I accused but uncertainty was evident in my wavering tone. Mason's austere eyes softened as he ran a light touch of his finger across my cheek.

"Marlemore must have placed her in there to frame me, I swear to you. I would never hurt you," Mason proclaimed, gnawing on his bottom lip. I searched his eyes with a vulnerable gaze and my broken heart started beating as a fixed entity once again when I saw the honesty there.

"Did you kill Ryan?" I asked, my stomach contracting with the anxiety of his answer. If he truly killed that innocent boy I could never forgive him.

"Yes. I killed him." My insides turned to ice and its jagged sharp edges cut into my soul. Mason must have been able to see the horror on my face because his expression became frantic and he clutched my wrists in protest.

"But not for the reason you think. As you know, Marlemore kidnapped my brother and has been blackmailing me. That first night you saw me in the woods I was trying to find Marcus. I had learned that he was being kept somewhere in the forest. I was trying to search for clues when I ran into this boy stumbling around the woods lost. I thought he was just a drunk kid," Mason explained, ominously.

"He seemed dazed like his eyes couldn't focus on anything. Then cuts started appearing on his skin, dripping blood down his face and from his eyes like tears and he began screaming in agony." Mason shuddered, and the distress was plain on his face.

"He stopped screaming and when his eyes focused, he glared murderously at me. To him I was the monster that was hurting him," Mason explained with a dangerous glint in his eyes.

251

"Through the haze he tried to kill me, but I managed to restrain him. I was going to take him back to my house to investigate what kind of drug he had taken, but then we heard someone else walking through the woods." Mason turned his head slowly, so his gaze fixated right on me, "You."

My skin quavered as my blood ran cold, Mason never did explain why he was covered in blood that night.

"The boy became insane again. He started pursuing you and he was just about to attack you. Without thinking I threw my knife at him. I didn't mean to kill him – I just needed to stop him. Even then it was instinct for me to save you," Mason whispered, and I felt his body heat radiating into my skin from his close proximity.

"I wrestled him to the floor and he bled out in my arms," Mason continued. My breath caught in my throat as I realised that I nearly died twice that night.

"I thought that you had seen me kill him, and I needed to make sure you didn't tell anyone. I was going to threaten you or kill you into silence. But I soon realised that there was no way I was ever going to hurt you myself. As soon as you leant towards me and not away, I couldn't hurt you. I didn't want too." His words cracked through the ice wall that I had built up around my heart.

"I was intrigued by you. I didn't want anything to happen to you even then." Mason softly placed a crimson stray hair that had blown free from my pony tail behind my ear.

"Why did you keep his body?" I asked.

"To study him, I placed him into that glass cabinet because it preserves human flesh by releasing a chemical into the chamber. I needed to find out what poison Marlemore was giving them that was turning people into monsters, so I could create

252

antidotes. And I succeeded," he explained. I rested my head in my hand as the truth sunk in. Mason only killed the missing boy to protect me. Marlemore was the one who turned him into a monster.

"The riddle, everything was just a sick game to frame you," I realised dumbfounded. "This poison, what is it exactly?" I inquired with pinched eyebrows and ran my hands through my hair in agitation.

"I don't know but it's what Marlemore has had us all working on. We were sent on missions to capture innocent people to test them on. We would inject them with the poison that sends them into blinding agony and they would start attacking people around them. But my colleagues never knew I was injecting them with the antidote after." Mason's lip turned up in revolution before his eyes became severe.

"But recently the poison has changed. Marlemore has been creating new strains and it has greatly evolved since he injected the missing boy with it. I have been working hard to create antidotes for them all."

"What could Marlemore want with a deadly poison?" I speculated with a confused shake of my head.

"This poison is not just deadly. It doesn't just kill you it's like you're internally being sliced by knives trying to cut through your skin to the outside. Anyone injected with it will tell you anything if they were tempted with the antidote." Something clicked inside my mind and my head snapped so suddenly towards Mason that my neck muscles screamed in protest.

"How do you know that the poison feels like knives are stabbing you from the inside out?" I asked with foreboding lacing my voice and a quiver to my words. Mason's eyes slid to mine; they were riddled with guilt.

253

"Because I was injected," he exclaimed woefully and his words shattered my world apart. He was looking into my eyes earnestly as if to comfort me when the pain of his words hit. My lungs cramped up and twisted into knots sending the breath out of me like I was winded.

"What?" I spluttered confused, barely containing my mounting anguish. Mason grabbed my hand in his and placed our entwined hands onto his heart.

"When I took that knife for you after the town meeting, something started happening to me. This low stabbing pain began gnawing at me from the inside and it became progressively worse. I must have been injected with such a small dose and its effects are slowly working its way through my system." He pulled down the top of his shirt, so I could see just below his right collarbone where the knife pierced his skin.

I gasped in horror; his chest was black. The stab wound was like a poisoned heart and spreading away from it were veins, but the blood in the veins were black.

"Mason," I choked, my hands flying to cover my mouth. It all made sense, the reason Mason had been looking so tired. The bags under his eyes and the red rim around them that looked like all the blood vessels were about to burst.

"You're dying," I whimpered, and a tear fell from my eye.

"I realised later that night when I was waiting outside your house. As soon as your Grandma was back, I went to find Marlemore to accept his offer to work for him. I needed to ensure your safety when I was gone so I made a counteroffer that I would only work for him if he left you alone. He agreed." A strange sort of sound left my lips, a whimper. Mason's features crumpled up with anguish as he looked back at me and he reached forwards to cradle my cheeks in both of his hands.

"Can't you use the antidote you used on Bill?" I queried desperately. Mason shook his head minutely as if any sudden movements would frighten me.

"I tried, but I must have been injected with something different, something more advanced," he stated hauntingly, ripping my chest apart. His hands left my face to run through his hair.

"We will figure this out. We will find a cure," I declared forcefully, straightening my posture in determination.

"Why is Marlemore doing this?" I questioned in a cry and between my clenched teeth in quiet agony. The only sound tangible was the waves crashing up against the cliff as Mason and I thought this question through. But the silence didn't last long.

My eyes squinted as a resplendent light flashed on from the mansion like a spotlight illuminating the rigid textured lamina of the leaves in the trees. I heaved in fright and clutched my hand in Mason's shirt as we snapped our attention towards the mansion to find it gleaming with luminescent light.

That could only mean that Mason's father has escaped from the basement. A cold sweat ran through me as I realised that Marlemore had just released Mason's father.

"I think we are about to find out."

Chapter 25

Mason grabbed my hand into his and we sprinted back up to the house. I didn't even feel the twigs that dug into my skin as I whipped past branches from the panic streaming through my veins. When we neared the mansion, something caught my eye at the front of the house. Something embedded in the trees that wasn't there before. I squinted my eyes at it and yanked Mason to a halt.

"Stop!" I yelled at Mason sternly. He glanced back at me with urgency on his features. I pointed towards the copse in the forest and I heard Mason's gasp of shock. It was a police car.

My hands started shaking as my brain started ticking over, and everything fell into place. With fumbling hands, I dug into my pocket where I stashed the poster of the missing boy. As my eyes scanned the old poster, I realised something that I didn't see before.

The place where Melissa had smudged her bloody finger over the poster when she was telling me who 'the one' was, wasn't smudged over the picture of the missing boy. It was smudged over the small words in the corner that asked anyone who had seen or heard about the boy to contact the chief of police. The blood on her fingers was smeared right over the words – chief of police.

She wasn't talking about the missing boy she was talking about the chief of police. As horror sunk into my veins, I finally realised who the identity of Marlemore was. It all made sense, the person who was first at both murder scenes and who had checked their pulses and pronounced them dead. Making sure no one else performed that task and managed to pick up on their faint heart rates.

The man Mason tortured, Kenneth, was also a police officer and the chief of police's right-hand man. So Marlemore wasn't a man like we had been deceived to believe from the boyish name. Marlemore was a woman.

"Mason," I wheezed, and he turned his head towards me with a bewildered, critical expression. "Marlemore is Amanda, the chief of police."

I watched numb as Mason's his eyes began to seep with something dark and lethal. But neither of us had time to discuss this further because the front doors to the mansion swung open and out stalked a hooded figure. Marlemore.

She was clapping slowly, mechanically.

"You figured it out. I'm impressed," spoke the voice of Marlemore that was deep and electronically altered to sound sinister, to sound like a man.

Marlemore pulled the hood off slowly to reveal the true menacing identity of Marlemore. The plump stern features of Amanda, the chief of police, smirked down at us. Her light blonde hair was pulled back tightly as if trying to thin out the wrinkles that lined her forehead. My jaw fell open in stupefaction.

"Hello, Mason and, Elora, we finally meet face to face. It has been a good game of cat and mouse between us," leered Amanda in her womanly voice. Which was so different to the voice of Marlemore that haunted my nightmares. She must have turned off whatever machine she was using to alter her voice.

"What have you done with my grandma?" I barked viscously

and pounced at her, but Mason held me back by grabbing the back of my arms.

"All will be revealed in good time," she jested evasively, smiling at the way Mason had to hold me back. Then her eyes darted to the trees beyond us.

"Grab them," she ordered sternly, losing her joking tone. A dozen of Marlemore's men had snuck up behind us – we were outnumbered. Brett pushed Mason away from me and secured my wrists in handcuffs using only his one hand. I struggled against him violently, as revolution pulsed through me.

"Get your filthy hands off me," I spat at Brett, but he ignored me, only increasing the handcuffs tightness in response. Mason was in a no better state than I was. They had five men needing to restrain him as he fought against them valiantly, but even he was no match for five strong arms.

I recognised two of the men holding Mason, the short bulky man with tattoos all over his skin, and Jacob the Italian guy with a permanent sneer on his face. They started pushing us up the stairs of the mansion and into the house, passing a smirking Marlemore. I blinked rapidly from being in the house with all the lights on, I could now see the layer of dust that lined the windowsills and furniture.

They yanked us into the kitchen where the back-glass wall was in shatters over the floor. They dropped us down forcefully into chairs and my hands were secured to the back of the chair with the handcuffs. I struggled in the seat, but I was tied down too strongly. Mason was secured like me, but he wasn't struggling; he was glaring viscously towards the doors that Marlemore was walking through. Behind her galloped the horrific face of Mason's father. He had a grin plastered onto his decaying face and the few patches of hair that grew on his burnt head were pointing out at odd angles.

Cold ice slid through my blood as I realised that she had released him from his chains in the basement. When Mason's father's eyes set on us, they lit up with a menacing gleam and he laughed loudly, and the sound made the hairs on the back of my neck rise.

"You don't know what you have done by releasing him," Mason growled darkly in warning.

"I know exactly what I have done. I know a lot more than you think Mason," grinned Marlemore. I refused to call her anything other than the murderous name that she had chosen for herself.

"But why? You killed your own son," I questioned baffled, unable to remain silent. She laughed wickedly and there was true delight on her callous face.

"He wasn't my son, silly girl. I just found him off the street and adopted him before I moved to this horrific town, so people would think that I was a normal chief with a nice family. He was more than happy to repay me for my kindness by working for me." Marlemore's eyes glinted with cruel excitement as she revealed her brilliant plan.

My stomach rolled with disgust. How could she use an innocent, desperate boy that way?

"I realised it was the perfect idea to make sure no one suspected me, killing my own son. Especially when the police investigators from the city were about to arrive. I wouldn't have been able to cover up my activities as easily as I do now." She smirked viscously. My upper lip curled up in loathing at her.

"But you were there that night when Marlemore killed Brandon. I saw you standing by the church when Marlemore attacked me," I opposed. Marlemore glanced at me from the

259

corner of her eye with a snide smile on her lips and then slowly strode over to me placing her hands onto my shoulders. I noticed the yellow outline to her teeth from the close distance and shrunk away from her.

"Do you think I would be foolish enough to attack as Marlemore myself? People would notice if the chief of police disappeared. I had one of my followers dress up as Marlemore and attack on my orders," she revealed, raising her nose in the air in conceit.

"Now, enough chat." She squeezed my shoulder painfully, making a cringe form on my lips before she walked off. I heard Mason growl threateningly in the corner. Marlemore's snake like eyes shot to him.

"I need something from you," Marlemore demanded of Mason. Mason just glared back at her, baring his teeth.

"Walter, take Elora out the room. He won't say anything if she can hear." Marlemore's eyes focused on Mason's father with the demand and I realised that was Mason's father's name. There was a gleeful giggle in the corner and Mason's father jumped up in the air in delight.

"No," I protested in revolt.

"If you do anything to her, I will never tell you anything and I will kill you all slowly after I have killed everyone you care for," Mason threatened. The deadly glare emitting from his features promised suffering to anyone who didn't listen.

"I have no intention of hurting Elora, we made a deal," reassured Marlemore with a condescending roll of her eyes. But before Mason could react, a bang clashed as someone barged in through the doors of the kitchen. In shock we all snapped our attention to the doors to see Belle sprinting into the room with hysteria on her features. Her eyes were locked on mine.

"Elora, I need to warn you." Belle screamed as she ran towards me. But she didn't finish her sentence as Brett whacked Belle over the head with the hilt of his gun from behind. Belle passed out and her body fell to the floor with a crash and thud. As she fell something dropped from her hands and skidded underneath the couch. We were all left stunned and staring at her fallen body in compete bafflement. What did Belle have to do with any of this?

"Stupid girl," Marlemore tufted under her breath in a nasty tone. Then she turned and nodded at Mason's father. "Get Elora out of here," she commanded.

Walter advanced towards me and unlocked my handcuffs, yanking me up from the seat by my hair.

"Don't hurt Belle," I yelled as Walter pushed my struggling arms from the room. Marlemore just grinned maliciously back at me causing a new shot of fear to eat away at me. I glanced back at Mason with wide eyes filled with terror and dread. What was going to happen to us?

Mason kept a stoic expression on his face, but his eyes were scrunched up at the corners expressing the panic he was feeling at our separation. I didn't take my eyes away from his and we only broke eye contact when the doors slowly closed behind me.

My throat dried as I lost sight of Mason and I was dragged through the corridors of the mansion. Through the biting cold air of the dark corridor we heard the echoes of a blood-curdling scream. Terror so intense swept through me that it caused my knees to buckle as I recognised that voice, Mason.

Walter had to start dragging me along as I stumbled and tried to get back to Mason. Mason's scream sounded again, and I realised with a jolt of agonised panic that Marlemore was torturing Mason for the password to release Walter.

It was then that something cracked inside me; I needed to end this monster and save Mason. I thought about the guns that I had stashed under my clothing and moved to grab one, but a hurricane of terror froze my muscles and it left my hands hanging by my sides uselessly.

"What a pitiful way to die. Now you will never know what's inside the clock," Mason's father giggled senselessly as he suddenly released me, making me stumble to the floor in the lounge room. Walter placed his hands over his head and started laughing to himself. Ignoring his hysteria, I bounded up from the ground when he wasn't facing me and attacked him from behind.

I wrapped my hands around his neck, squeezing it with my forearm. Walter choked wildly, not expecting my attack. I continued squeezing until he passed out and I let him collapse to the floor. Without looking back, I sprinted back through the corridors towards Mason. My feet skidded to a stop at the doors of the kitchen, which had been closed and locked shut.

I cursed and searched for another way in. Beside me I noticed a small hatch in the wall next to the doors which must have been where the old cooks would have passed food through to the serving staff. Slowly, I inched the small latch open and relief washed through me when it opened silently. I peeked through to see Marlemore standing with her back to me. She was facing Mason who was still tied down to the chair. Beside Mason, restrained to the chair I had previously occupied, was Belle – her head lolling over her shirt, passed out.

Mason was covered in blood. It had gushed down his body and splattered onto the floor. Deep sores were embedded into his skin and the blood oozed out from his shirt were Marlemore had cut through. I dry heaved from the pain that twisted my chest from seeing Mason hurt so viscously.

262

Marlemore plunged a knife deep into the top right of Mason's chest, exactly where his previous wound was where he was poisoned. Mason screamed out a sound of pure agony and something inside me snapped. I moved to jump through the small latch into the room.

But just before I did, I noticed Mason lock eyes with me beyond Marlemore's form and he shook his head infinitesimally. My muscles froze, and I rocked back onto my heels backtracking my movements. It was then that I remembered about Mason's brother; if Marlemore died now then we would never find out where she was keeping Marcus.

"What is the code Mason?" Marlemore ordered, her nostrils fairing on her large nose.

"I am not scared of a knife," Mason jibed sardonically gesturing towards the knife hanging from Marlemore's grip. He was trying to make it seem like he was not fazed by the torture, but I could see the pain wrinkles around his mouth and eyes.

Rage broke out on Marlemore's face and she punched Mason hard in the jaw. His head jolted back aggressively, and he spat blood onto the floor. Mason raised his head again gradually with a smirk on his face, there was blood running down his chin but he wasn't even reacting to the pain.

"If you don't tell me, I will kill your precious Elora," Marlemore growled with a menacing curl in her lip. I was shocked at seeing such a predatory look on the usually warm hearted and strict face of the chief of police.

"I know," Mason breathed in defeat as he lowered his head.

"What is it?" Marlemore barked.

"I will tell you on one condition," Mason counteracted. Marlemore raised her bushy eyebrows.

"You tell me why you are doing this," Mason suggested.

Marlemore was quiet for a long moment, rubbing her chin as she considered.

"Fine," she conceded, looking directly at Mason with a mocking smile. "When I was a child, I lived a great life. I had never felt like I belonged somewhere so much in my life. But that all changed when my brothers betrayed me and left me to die," she started and as she spoke her eyes never left Mason's face.

Mason's jaw was clenched and he was glaring back at her, but I saw him following her every movement vigilantly. With a smirk Marlemore brought her hand up to her large and bumpy nose. Abruptly she ripped the entire nose off and it fell to the ground. It was a wad of fake cosmetic skin.

I choked on my saliva as my breathing stunted; she was wearing a fake nose. I still couldn't see Marlemore's face as she continued ripping off other fake pieces of her face and wrinkled skin. She pulled off added lines to her jaw and peeled off her bushy eyebrows. She took her contact lenses out and then finally removed her blonde wig. The only remains of her hair were small tuffs of random black hairs growing in awkward positions.

Mason gasped in horror as he looked at the new person in front of him. Marlemore removed the last lines of fake skin to reveal deep burn scars all over her head and down her neck, scars that were exactly the same as Mason's fathers.

"You see, brother, some things aren't always what they seem," she declared ominously, in a lighter voice than Amanda's that had a squeaky undertone. It was a voice I recognised but couldn't place from where.

"Masie," Mason stammered, his mouth was hanging open and his eyes were wide as disbelief had stunned his features. My hands flew to my mouth to stifle a gulp of shock and my gaping jaw. Mason's sister was alive?

"No, I watched you die. I watched him stab that knife into your heart. You bled out on the floor – I watched the light leave your eyes," Mason objected vehemently. Mason was shaking his head furiously and he kept blinking in incredulity.

Marlemore stood in front of Mason so she could glower down at him venomously. The veins in her neck were rigid and she was almost hissing at him with her teeth bared.

"It was a game. We wanted to see just how far we could push you and Marcus until you snapped. It was fake blood and I acted dying. It was fun watching you both withering on the floor trying to save your precious sister. You see, I was never like you or Marcus; you were both weak with how you refused to take innocent lives. I have always loved killing," she admitted macabrely.

"You had never killed anyone before," Mason fought back in a shout. Marlemore rolled her eyes.

"I wasn't the perfect sister that you thought I was. I only made it seem like I was because I didn't want to face you both after telling you that I loved killing. I knew you would both hate me like you hated him. I loved the power that murdering gave me," she explained in a low malicious voice.

She picked up her bloody knife and twirled it around in her hands expertly. She flung it into the air and it flipped and twisted, splattering blood everywhere in its wake like she was a circus performer. She caught it easily, displaying her expert skills with a knife.

"But what we weren't expecting was our mother reacting the way she did, and then everything went wrong. I tried to get up to calm you all down but, in the struggle, someone knocked me out. I woke up being burned alive. I managed to escape out the flames through the secret tunnel. I didn't return after that because then

265

you would have known that I betrayed you," she revealed, and her words made my flesh crawl, chilling me to the bone.

If Marlemore was Mason's sister, then she was just as lethal as Mason was. How were we ever going to defeat her?

"But I couldn't give up the killing, and I knew I couldn't use the name Masie any more because if you ever heard it, you would know it was me and you would try to stop me. That's how I became Marlemore," she declared ominously. A cold chill settled at the base of my spine sending my blood icy.

Finally, Marlemore turned around to face me and I caught sight of her face. It was in that moment that the ground crumbled underneath me. The burned face that confronted me was that of my old friend from the streets, Annalise.

Chapter 26

The world shattered around me. Everything that I believed to be true was a lie. The woman in front of me looked different to the Annalise I knew. Annalise had a full head of black hair, which must have been a wig and her skin wasn't scarred.

She must have used cosmetics to cover that up too, but this girl was unmistakably Annalise – the girl I considered my best friend once. If Annalise was Marlemore then we were facing someone so much more dangerous than a girl who liked to kill people. She couldn't be here; she couldn't be alive. I killed her.

My legs gave out underneath me and I stumbled sideways onto the wall. I clutched onto the railing on the wall for support and my eyesight became blurry as visions of the moment Annalise betrayed me and sent me to jail flashed in my mind.

The moment when she revealed her true nature and killed my boss, the man that I was obsessed with, right in front of my eyes. I had placed that time behind me, but everything that I had repressed came gushing back to the forefront of my consciousness. I was the only one who knew the truth about how evil this woman truly was.

Piercing red anger seared through my veins as my eyes fixated on Annalise. Resolve pounded my soul like a battering ram, and I knew what I had to do. I couldn't repress my instincts any more. There was only one-way to save Mason and my grandma from this monster. I slid out the guns strapped to my legs and without shaky hands this time I clutched the gun with the snake engraved onto the side, my gun. I didn't feel fear at holding the gun now; it was steady in my hands.

My eyes sliced towards Marlemore. She was descending upon Mason with her knife and the rage that ignited within me sent me over the edge. I straightened both guns out in front of me and pulled the triggers. They shot right through the lock to the door. I outstretched one leg and kicked the double doors open with shattering force. They slammed open with an exigent crash and gushing wind in its wake.

Everyone's heads wrenched towards me in shock as I stormed in. I only needed to aim for one second before I shot the short bulky man with tattoos who was restraining Mason's shoulders, straight into both of his hands that were holding Mason down. Blood splattered out from his wounds and he fell to the ground with a thud.

The two men standing guard at the door were the first to emerge from their stunned stupor and raised their guns to shoot me, but I was quicker. I ducked out of the trajectory from one shot and it plunged into the man beyond me standing guard. As I rose from my crouched position, I slammed the hilt of my gun into the temple of the man who tried to shoot me. In five seconds both guards were incapacitated.

Marlemore's men started charging at me. I aimed the gun and fired it at a man in the leg who had started running at me. A stocky man grabbed me from behind around the waist but I elbowed him in the face. His hands released me as I spun around and kicked him in the chest so hard he fell back and slammed his head on the floor with a whacking thud. To be sure he was down, I shot him straight through his humerus in his arm.

I straightened up to find two more men lunging at me. I raised both my guns towards them and simultaneously shot them both right in their shoulder joints. They fell to the ground with a crash and blood started to pool around their crippled bodies. The rest of Marlemore's men realised that they were no match for me and held back, aiming their guns at me. I didn't care about them I just wanted Marlemore. It was interesting that they weren't shooting at me; Marlemore must have given them orders to keep me alive.

I noticed Belle stirring from unconsciousness and the ticking noise of her pacemaker was louder than ever. I pointed the gun at Belle and shot her right in the chest with a pestilent bang. Her eyes closed again, and she slumped in her seat, blood dripping down her shirt in gruesome splatters. A horrified gasp sounded to my right and I knew it was Mason. I ignored the stab of pain I felt in my chest at hearing that noise of betrayal.

With both my guns held offensively out in front of me, I levelled in on Marlemore's smirking face. Fury ignited within me making my jaw clench from seeing her smug features and I gripped the guns harder turning my fists white.

"It's good to see you back, Elora," remarked Marlemore snidely. I stepped forward so the gun pressed into her forehead, causing her skin to dent inwards from the pressure of the gun. My fingers itched to pull the trigger, but I needed to know where she was keeping Mason's brother before I killed her and I needed a confession from her so Mason would not be sent to prison.

"I don't want any part in your games, Annalise," I spat in disgust. She just laughed wickedly, there was an evil malignancy in her eyes showing her sinister enjoyment.

"Did you like the gift I left for you? I kept your gun for you all this time," she sung with a villainous grin. I glared back at her with venom in my eyes as I realised what she had done. She left my old snake gun that I thought I killed her with on Brandon –

she wanted to frighten me by bringing back my troubled past.

"Elora, you just killed Belle," Mason exclaimed with hysteria in his voice. I glanced at him fleetingly with guilty eyes. His expression was wide and frantic, and he was straining in his chair to reach me.

"I'm guessing you didn't tell him about your past," chirped Marlemore happily, stepping away from my gun. I ignored her and raised my gaze to Mason.

"No, I just incapacitated her. The place where I shot her won't kill her. Trust me I know what I'm doing," I explained, gushing. But Mason just stared at me with betrayal in his eyes. I couldn't stand it. I had to move my gaze away before the pain became unbearable.

"What?" Mason spluttered, confused and I hurried to explain myself.

"Belle is passed out. This is all just another game Marlemore is playing." I snapped my head towards the smirking Marlemore who was leaning against the wall with one elbow behind her neck lazily watching our interaction with zest.

"I am not stupid, Annalise. I know you have had Belle working for you too. It was her that night Marlemore attacked me. I heard a ticking sound. The very sound of Belle's pacemaker," I growled. The light in Marlemore's eyes faded as she realised that I knew the truth.

"You ruin all the fun," she sulked rising from her lazy position.

"How did you make her do it?" I demanded. "I know Belle, she is not evil. She would never work for you voluntarily." I still had the gun pointed at Marlemore's head; I wanted so badly to pull the trigger, but I needed answers first. Marlemore grinned cruelly, accentuating her scarred cheeks.

"As soon as I threatened her little children's lives, she did everything I asked. The perfect opportunity arose when she was alone in her library – I broke in and then left with a new allay close to you," she explained as her vastly mouth turned up at the corners. It made her scars more evident as they pulled back her lips making her gums visible. She was a horrific sight to behold.

"But why Belle? You could have had any of these men do your dirty work for you?" I demanded, tilting my gun higher.

"Why not? It's all just part of the fun isn't it?" She cackled, callously. I grinded my teeth together to contain my anger.

"You're evil, how could I ever have thought of you as my best friend?" I sneered disgustingly at her. Four years we were friends, how could I ever have been fooled by such an act?

"How do you know each other?" Mason questioned. Shock was evident on his features as his eyes flickered between us.

"Do you remember the girl who lived on the streets with me, Annalise? This is her. She is the one who told the police about my stalking and then proceeded to kill the man I was obsessed with." I narrowed eyes at Annalise, distrustfully. She grinned her scarred derisive smile back at me proudly.

"I broke into my boss's house and planned on telling him how I felt about him but instead I was faced with Annalise trying to kill him. She wanted his position; she wanted more power and she killed him for it. I was so angry I turned my gun on her and shot her dead. It wasn't in self-defence, I murdered her because I wanted to," I revealed quaveringly, my voice cracking. My breathing became gasps as everything in my body tried to stop me from speaking the truth.

"She isn't the sweet and innocent girlfriend you thought her to be. She is a murderer too," declared Marlemore derisively, snickering. I cut her a piercing glare.

271

"But just as she did with you, she faked her death with me too. But how?" I demanded Marlemore with an unbelieving shake of my head.

"I wore a bulletproof vest. There was a possibility our boss had a gun on him and would have defended himself," Marlemore explained, shrugging. It made sense, after I shot Annalise, I was in such a state of panic I hauled her body into the lake beside my boss's house. I threw my snake gun in the lake along with her body. Then I rang the police and told them that Annalise killed my boss; they found her handprints on the gun that shot him and I told them she ran off. They never found her body – now I know why.

I was taken to jail and arrested for breaking and entering into my boss's house. With the evidence they had that Annalise gave them about my stalking, I was sentenced to a year. I went to jail gladly. I wanted to be taken away from the horror that my small stability in life had turned into.

"That's the reason I have never been able to pick up a gun since. I was terrified of what I would do with it, of what I was capable of doing with it. I was terrified that I would kill someone else with it like I killed Annalise," I explained as a shudder ran down my arms.

"I understand, Elora, you know just how much." Mason smiled sadly. There was no judgment from him in his eyes and a weight lifted from my shoulders. My heart swelled with love for him. Mason was the one person in the world who understood me.

"But how do you know how to use a gun?" Mason questioned with pinched eyebrows.

"When I was a kid, my third foster father taught me how to use it. I had a natural ability with them. When I lived on the streets, Annalise and I used to shoot food out of people's hands

272

to eat. Turned out one of the men I shot at was a military officer. But he didn't send us to jail; he saw my skills with a gun and instead he hired us. From when I was sixteen until I went to jail at twenty, Annalise and I were trained up in the army to become snipers."

"Why didn't you tell me this?" Mason agonised, and the hurt was evident in his eyes. My heart pulled towards him like I was being tugged from my chest.

"I was forbidden by the military to ever speak of it again or I would be sent to prison for the rest of my life. I was bound to a lifelong contract. And I couldn't tell you about killing Annalise because I couldn't even face it myself, let alone tell you. It is something that I have suppressed in my consciousness and I never wanted to bring it back up again," I explained desperately, reaching out towards him. Mason's eyes and pinch between his eyebrows softened and he started leaning his head towards me too.

But our moment was cut short when Mason's father stormed into the room with wobbly, lateral movements. Blood was dripping down from the deep gash that had split his head open from falling to the ground. He plonked himself down in the couch like he was about to settle into watching a movie.

"As much as I enjoy your domestic squabbling, I have more important matters to attend to," Marlemore piped up coarsely with a disgusted curl of her lip. She turned on her heels and stalked over to her father. She took something out of his hand and then moved to leave the room.

"You are not going anywhere," I objected. "If you don't tell me what you need with my grandma, I will kill him," I warned her, aiming the gun at Walter who was sitting happily on the couch.

Marlemore looked over her shoulder to smirk at me devilishly with an excited glint in her eye. She spun back around and stalked over towards where the broken window lay in shatters over the floor.

"Lock them away," she ordered her men belligerently. With a final smirk at me she jumped through the broken window and into the garden swiftly.

I gaped after her retreating form. I didn't understand – I thought she was trying to release her father. Why was she running away from here without him?

Six dangerous men started to descend upon Mason and I with the intent to kill. Mason was still handcuffed to his chair. Jacob, along with another tall man were the first to move as they rounded upon Mason. Fear churned in my blood for Mason, but it was trivial.

"You didn't really think that I could be tied down by handcuffs, did you men?" Mason gloated and displayed both his hands in front of him with the handcuffs hanging on one wrist – he was free. His trusty knife was gleaming from his fingertips. I couldn't help the smile that surfaced on my lips at Mason's skills.

Jacob growled and pounced at Mason. This propelling motion spurred on the others causing mayhem to break loose as they attacked us. I avoided the attack of two men by falling to the ground and spinning around on my heels until they were in front of me.

I rose again to punch one man in the face from under his chin and kicked his legs out from under him. He fell to the floor with a hiss of pain and a bloody nose. As I was following through from that punch a man with a blond ponytail whacked my elbow and yanked my gun out my grip.

Balling my fists, I twisted out of his grasp on my elbow and

274

swung my arm around trying to whack him in the face with my other gun. He ducked it swiftly, his blonde hair sweeping out of his ponytail. But as I was attacking, I felt a bullet plummet past the side of my head, I had only just moved my head to the side in time to avoid it.

While still trying to fight off the ponytail guy who had his grip on my elbow, I aimed my gun at the man who tried to shoot me and pulled the trigger. The bullet landed exactly where I intended it to and hit him through his knee joint. Huffing out in frustration at the man with the blonde ponytail who wouldn't let go of me I shot him in the leg, incapacitating him.

I noticed Mason fighting the rest of the men in the corner with only his knife. I gasped in panic when I realised that Mason was unaware of Jacob who was silently stalking up behind him. Jacob pointed a gun at Mason's head and began to press down on the trigger. But I was quicker; I shot Jacob's finger that was pressing down on the trigger just before his gun fired. Jacob screamed out, and the gun fell from his hands as blood spilled from his now demented finger.

He lurched his eyes up to me. His sneer deepened as his expression became livid with rage. I smiled smugly back at him, as relief washed through me at knowing Mason was safe. But my smirk enraged Jacob; he growled loudly and surged at me. As he ran, I shot him in the other hand, but he didn't stop his advance.

With his demented hands outstretched and dripping with blood he tried to grab my throat with feral flailing fingers, driven by rage not skill. He must have been dizzied from lack of blood because it was too easy to whack him in the face with the hilt of my gun. He crashed to the floor.

With an unexpected detonation, a gun fired from the back of the room and my eyes instantly flashed in that direction. I noticed the man with the blonde ponytail crouching behind the couch in the far corner clutching his leg in one hand and in the other he was aiming a gun at me. The gun that he just fired, I didn't have time to move out of the trajectory of the bullet that was plummeting towards my heart.

Suddenly strong arms wrapped around my waist and I was pulled back into a warm chest. I felt the wind of the bullet spiralling through the air swish past the skin on my face as it missed me by millimetres. I looked behind me to find Mason's panicked and fervent gaze staring intensely down at me. We locked eyes for a long moment allowing the relief to pass through us.

My eyes were drawn away from Mason's as I perceived someone running up behind him with a knife outstretched. My eyes flashed in warning. Without even turning around Mason extended the back of his leg out and the attacking man tripped over Mason's ankle, losing his balance. Mason released me to duck low and as the man plummeted to the ground, I punched him in the face. Then Mason swirled around and grabbed the falling man around the neck and slit his throat with his knife. Blood gushed from the wound and he gargled a bloody scream.

Behind me I heard another gun shot. I knew it was the man with the blonde ponytail again. Curling my lip and growling, I angrily turned around and shot him in the shoulder so he fell to the floor, passing out. I stalked up to him and yanked my gun out of his now still fingers.

Mason was fighting the last man still standing but he had it under control. He didn't need my help, so I sprinted to the broken window and glanced out to see the remnants of the shadow of a figure running towards the police car. Fury alighted within me, and my hand balled into a fist around my gun.

I shook my hands to release my anger and steadied my gun as I crouched down to aim it at Marlemore's retreating form. From one hundred metres away, I fired at the shadowed form of Marlemore as the gun ricocheted violently in my hands. I heard Marlemore's surprised howl of pain as she lost her balance from shock and fell to the floor clutching her shoulder.

Pride swelled within me causing a smirk to form on my lips as I realised, I hit her. I still had it. My aim had always been perfect. But Marlemore's form rose again, and she looked back to glare at me before disappearing behind a tree. I clenched my jaw together to hold in the growl – I only wounded her. The police car's engine started up with a loud rev and Marlemore sped off into the night.

"She got away!" I yelled and angrily slammed my gun into the wall. I spun around to run back to Mason but stopped short when I bumped into his chest. Mason was already behind me watching me shoot Marlemore. I glanced up at his face to see an awed expression on his features as he looked down at me like I was a chest of gold.

"I am unbelievably pissed at you for not telling me about this side of you, but right now I'm too attracted to you to care," Mason breathed. Then he wrapped one arm around my neck and brought my lips to his. His kiss was desperate and filled with fire.

I kissed him back for a heated moment before pushing him away.

"Mason, my grandma!" I stressed with wide fearful eyes, but my tone was breathless from his intense kiss. She still might be here.

"Right, I will check on her," he agreed seriously but still breathless and sprinted towards the library.

The kitchen floor was lined with bodies skewed at wrong

angles and surrounded in pools of blood. My eyes skittered towards Belle. She was still passed out in the chair from my gun wound and I was beyond relieved that my plan saved her. I shot Belle in hopes that if she was incapacitated then Marlemore would forget she was there and leave her out of this. I knew Masie and I knew she would kill Belle for trying to warn me.

I shook Belle's shoulders trying to wake her but she was out cold. I needed to know what Marlemore was after and I had a feeling Belle knew. I didn't understand why Marlemore would just leave without her father. The code to releasing her father was what she was trying to torture out of Mason minutes ago.

I wished I could have asked Belle what she was going to tell me when she came sprinting into the room. My eyes widened when I remembered that something had fallen from Belle's hands when she ran in. I sprinted to the couch and fished my hand under it, searching the ground. My hand rested on a book and with a racing heart I pulled it out. I recognised the book instantly, *Everbrook's secret*.

My mind started ticking over everything that had happened in the past few weeks since I moved here. I realised now that Belle gave me this book for a reason. Maybe even back then Belle was trying to warn me.

With a jolt of pure fear, I realised the truth. I knew what Marlemore was after.

Chapter 27

The thunderous wind whipped my hair away from my face as we sped through the dark night at a frightening speed. The electrifying velocity was exactly what I needed, I twisted the accelerator, willing it to move faster. We needed to save my grandma, and to do that we needed to get to the church.

I had been in a state of blinding frenzy ever since Mason ran back into the living room with panic overtaking his features.

"Your grandma is gone," he explained grievously, and I crumbled, my soul filling with guilt and agony. I knew what Mason was going to say before he said it, because I knew what Marlemore wanted. Kidnapping my grandma wasn't just a ploy to turn me against Mason, Marlemore needed her. I sprinted towards Mason's garage and jumped onto his motorbike. I revved the engine loudly and as soon as Mason slide on behind me I sped off.

The town was deserted; they were all too terrified of Marlemore to venture out at night. The village felt like a ghost town. As we sped to the top of the hill towards the church, the first thing my eyes noticed was the police car that was parked out the front. My suspicions were correct – Marlemore was here.

Lightning coruscated through the night sky illuminating the dark grandiose building in front of us. My eyes drew towards the clock tower that became lucent in the fulmination of the flash. I skid the bike sideways to a stop and stones flew out from under the wheels in protest. My hands trembled as we leapt off the bike and I looked up at the ominous building with its large windows spanning each bordering wall all the way to the top of the two-story high ceiling. Mason took my hand into his and gave me a small squeeze.

"We are in this together," he promised, smiling reassuringly. The warmth of his hand and in his eyes caused my quavering body to calm down. I smiled back at him and just looking at his soft features steadied my accelerated heart rate. Our boots crunched into the wet stones under our feet as we rushed up towards the building. With sweaty palms I pushed open the double doors into the church.

The church was dark inside. It was so caliginous that I needed to narrow my eyes to see the penumbral light that was emitting from the spotlight in the garden that radiating through the coloured windows that spanned up the walls. I couldn't see much other than the shadowed silhouettes of the benches and the stage.

My eyes flickered around the room searching for something out of the ordinary. We took a few cautious steps forward and the sound ricocheted off the tiled floors. As we neared the front of the church closer towards the light, I noticed a small stain of blood on the tiled floor. My throat dried and my posture became rigid because I knew whose blood that belonged to, Grandma. I fell to my knees in front of the drop of blood.

I tried to calm my breathing so I could think clearly and my eyes searched around the small stain of blood looking for anything unusual. My sight was drawn to a tile that jutted out higher in the ground compared to the rest of them. Another splatter of blood rested right on top of that tile.

I realised that this was the tile that I fell over when I was ignoring Mason the day of the town meeting. Could this tile possibly be the way to enter into the vault? I remembered the details of the book on how to get inside the vault and knew what I had to do next.

"Can I have your knife?" I asked Mason resolutely. His forehead wrinkles scrunched together in worry, but he dug into his pocket and gave it to me anyway. I glanced down at the sharp sparkling silver edge and sunk the knife into the skin of my wrist. Blood bubbled up from the cut and slid down my wrist in a stream. Mason gasped and yanked the knife out of my hand.

"What are you doing?" he objected in alarm with a clenched jaw and arched eyebrow. He was looking at me like I had gone insane.

"To enter one must give a drop of their own blood," I explained as I placed my bloodied wrist over the tile. A small drop of blood streamed from my wrist falling through the air until it splattered onto the tile.

Expeditiously, the tile dropped into the ground as if it had been released from a harness underneath and collapsed into a hole under the church. Following in its path the tiles surrounding it fell into the ground as well. Mason and I staggered a few steps back to prevent from also descending into its depths. Within it revealed a small circular hole in the ground leading into a pitch-black tunnel.

Mason clutched me around the waist and pulled me back into him as I heard his gasp beside me, "The book is true."

My own mouth fell open as I watched the entrance to the vault reveal itself. Everything written in the book was true and wasn't just a myth to bring tourists to the town.

So, that also meant that the deadly machine inside was real and my grandma was in mortal danger. Ignoring the fear that was pulsing through my veins like a tornado, I cautiously dangled one foot down into the black hole until it rested upon a stone step. Leaning down further into the ditch my eyes adjusted to the dark and before me materialised a spiralled stone staircase.

"Stay behind me," Mason whispered as he followed me down the hole and tucked me behind him. With Mason leading the way we walked down several stories worth of steps. As we reached the end of the staircase it emerged into a dark tunnel.

The tunnel was illuminated by sconces lining the walls that someone had already lit with fire. Decaying and crumbling stone cobbled bricks lined the floor and the compounding restriction of fear weighing down my chest was magnified by the fact that the tunnel was only held up by a few metal beams. The only feature in the tunnel was a metal door with a spiral shaped black frame at the opposite end of the tunnel.

As I stepped further into the darkness, my jaw gaped when I realised that there was someone laying on the floor by the spiral framed door. Instantly I recognised Grandma's wild curly grey hair and light pink frilly robes. Horror paralysed my breathing and my hands flew to my mouth.

For one terrifying moment I thought she was dead all over again. But then her eyes opened and focused right on mine, making my stomach leap. Her eyes widened when she saw me, and panic riddled her aged and worn out features. She placed her hand on the floor in front of her trying to push herself up but her limbs gave out on her and she collapsed.

She looked up at me from the floor, her expression dire and fatigued. She began saying something but all that was released from her mouth was a breath of air and a croaky low mumble. Warning was written on her features and without thinking I ran to her, my feet pounding on the stone cobbled floor.

As I ran, Gran raised a languid hand out in front of her with an exhausted cringe on her face. I fell to my knees in front of her and placed my hand to her cold face, which was slick with sweat.

"Grandma, are you okay?" I panicked, my hands fumbling over her trying to find where she was hurt.

"Trap," she croaked with wild eyes. My eyebrows knitted together for a moment, trying to comprehend her words.

"It's a trap," she finally gasped out using all her remaining energy. Realisation dawned and my muscles tensed in trepidation.

I spun around on my heels to face Mason and when I saw what was occurring behind me my stomach twisted in dread. Mason was running over to my grandmother and I with his panicked gaze only on me, but he couldn't see Brett who had snuck up to the side of him. Brett raised a gun above Mason's head and slammed it down forcefully onto Mason's temple.

"Mason!" I screamed in warning, rising from the floor and reaching my hand towards him, but it was too late.

With a loud crunch, Mason tumbled to the floor and his body collapsed, sending a ripple of nausea through me from the intensity of his fall. My shocked wide eyes were fixed on Mason's passed out form so I didn't notice when a dark figure in a hood sneaked up behind me until it was too late. The only thing I felt was the cold tip of a knife being placed against my throat. My spine straightened instantly as my body tensed from the attack.

"You figured it out again. I'm impressed," Marlemore's rasping patronising voice spoke in my ear. The cold wind of her breath made my flesh creep with a shudder of fear. My eyes were glued to Mason, trying to see if he was moving at all, but he was passed out cold. Brett kept his gun aimed at Mason's temple ready to kill him at Marlemore's order.

I only realised now that Brett was missing from the latter parts of the scene at Mason's house. He must have gone back to steal my grandma in that time. Brett grabbed Mason's knife out of his hand and then searched him to retrieve all of his other weapons.

"Everything is working out just as I had hoped," Marlemore snickered. Her arrogant tone coupled with the way she hurt Mason made my cheeks redden and my teeth grind together in fury.

Agilely, I placed my hand on Marlemore's elbow and slammed her arm down that was holding the knife. I ducked from under her swinging arm and then yanked the knife out of her hands, so that I was now facing her with the knife pointed at her throat. The tip of the knife brushed against the flesh of her neck as she craned her head away.

"Try to hurt me and my men will kill Mason and your grandma," Marlemore threatened and instantly my hand wavered. Marlemore snatched the knife back out of my hands.

"Let my grandma go," I growled, both my hands hanging by my side in fists helplessly.

"I can't do that because I need her," Marlemore countered in a dangerous tone, her eyes narrowing into lethal slits.

"Give me all your guns and weapons," she demanded, holding out her hands. With a sneer I did as she asked.

"Why do you need my grandma?" I snapped. My hands were shaking with anger.

"This was never about releasing my father or tormenting Mason." Marlemore shook her head in disagreement. "No, this was always about you, Elora," she declared hauntingly. A weight dropped onto my chest and I stumbled a shocked step backwards.

"Me?" I stuttered, "What do I have to do with this?" I

questioned in complete bewilderment, frowning.

"You are more special than you know," she revealed with eager eyes as she circled me, still holding the knife between my eyes.

"I have been planning this for years. Do you think it was mere coincidence that we happened to be friends when we were younger?" She spat with a scowl on her face as if our friendship was a disgusting reminder. My mouth dropped open and my heart shattered at her words from the knowledge that our friendship was all a lie.

"No, I planned that too. I was never homeless; my family was rich. But I never cared about riches. I only cared about power." Her chin raised an inch in conceit as if she was above me.

"What I have been trying to obtain will give me the ultimate power. It was something my father and I were working towards when we still lived in the mansion. Father had been planning it for years, long before we were even born. That is why he moved to this town," she explained.

"What are you after?" I demanded.

"The machine that releases a deadly poison in the form of a gas cloud. My father knew the rumours of the machine that circled this town from a book published many years ago was true. Imagine the power we would have if we had the ultimate weapon in our hands. Every single government would be at our knees – we would rule the world," she revealed maliciously.

The severity the situation we were in dawned and settled in my stomach, churning my insides. If Marlemore was to succeed in her endeavour to obtain the destructive device then the world as we knew it would never be the same. World wars would break out, countries will be turned against each other, and Marlemore would hold the power of the world in her hands.

"But after I believed my father was dead, I couldn't complete the mission without information only he knew, so I tried to gain power by a different avenue. I joined the army and began blackmailing and torturing those who were high up the ranks to force them to do what I wanted. But I found that every decision I tried to blackmail them into making would need to go through a higher authority and I was sick of it. I decided to return here to try and enter the vault on my own." As she explained she paced in front of me. I watched each of her steps warily ready for an attack.

"I broke back into the mansion to find all the plans on how to enter the vault my father had uncovered. That was when I discovered that my father was still alive." Her eyes widened in elation.

"He told me about your family and how to enter the vault," she explained with malignity flashing in her eyes. My own eyes narrowed suspiciously back at her.

"What does my family have to do with this?" I demanded.

"You see, Elora, you and your grandma are descendants of Henry Edmington – the genius who created this machine and locked it up when he believed it was no longer needed. Only you two together can enter the vault." I gasped and clasped my hands over my mouth as my muscles froze. I didn't want to believe it but deep down it made sense. Grandma was the owner of the church and it had been in her family for years.

"But Grandma didn't know about this, she had this place officially searched for a vault and it was proven there wasn't one," I objected fiercely. Marlemore cut me a look from the corner of her eye and one of her lips curled up.

"No, she didn't have it searched. She just told everyone she did, so that people would stop searching. So that nobody found out it actually existed."

I glanced down at the still form of my grandma, her eyes were closed, and her chest was slowly rising and falling. Just looking at her calmed my heart rate, her curly grey hair reminded me of curling up into a warm chair by the fire. She was my home.

A wave of fury ignited within me so fierce I have to clench my hands together to prevent myself from attacking Marlemore. My eyes moved to Mason's unmoving form and light headedness rippled through me at the sight of him so defenceless. I needed to save them both. It was up to me now.

"After my father told me the truth, I tried to find you. And after much searching, I discovered you living on the streets. When I found you, I knew things were going to be a lot harder than I originally thought." She cringed.

"I needed you to return to Everbrook, but I knew you would never return to the family that abandoned you unless you were forced to. That was why I told the police about your stalking and sent you to jail as I knew you would be left with nothing after. Then when you were released, I sent your social worker your long-lost grandma's address, so your only option would be to return to this town." She grinned horrendously, proud of her own devilry brilliance.

I stumbled backwards and had to use the wall for support. My whole life was crafted by Marlemore, so I could open this vault for her. It made my head spin with the impossibility.

"To enter the vault, you need two living descendants of Henry Edmington to break past the defences that have sealed the poison machine within. One to open the vault and the other person to activate the machine. You see, Henry never wanted the weapon to be released unless the world was in mortal strife and everyone on the planet was going to die anyway, and this had to be the last option. To enter, someone in his bloodline needs to give enough of their blood to kill them," she divulged in a haunting tone and her forehead plucked as if she was pondering on a particularly difficult mystery.

"There had to be no hope for the survival of this family member without the machine's interference so if they voluntarily give their life to release the poisonous gas then it would prove that they would have died anyway. They need to give their life to release the poison." She steepled her fingers together as she paced in front of me.

"Your whole life has been shaped for this moment, Elora. You will not fail. I have made sure of it," she announced maleficently. I ground my teeth together to rein in the rage and I glared at her with venom in my eyes.

"Now, I need your grandma because she is the one who needs to die to open the vault." Marlemore waved her hand through the air as if this was a minor inconvenience.

I clutched my stomach as all the air was blown out of my chest. It felt like I was punched in the gut. I wasn't going to let that happen, this madness ended now.

"No," I objected fiercely and leapt at Marlemore, my hands aiming straight at her neck. I slammed her head against the stone wall with a violent force. Her head snapped back, and a stomach-curdling crunch emitted from the back of her head. But she didn't display any of the pain I inflicted on her, she just smirked down at me mischievously with her scarred mouth.

"Now, Elora, be nice or else I will kill Mason. Brett just connected a bomb collar around his neck." Marlemore grinned with a sardonic glint in her eye and gestured over towards Mason. I looked over to see Brett had Mason's passed-out form in an iron

288

grip headlock and there was now a black strap around his neck. My limbs tensed and I shrunk back as terror so extreme plummeted through me.

From seeing Mason in such a vulnerable position red-hot rage welled up in my chest and I squeezed Marlemore's throat harder for a moment, so her face drained into a pale hue from lack of oxygen. But the promise was set in her strong features, she wouldn't hesitate to kill Mason.

With a defeated sigh, I slackened my grip on her neck. Her body crumbled to the floor with a satisfying crack and she inhaled a deep gasp of air. I hung my head in defeat – I would do anything to save Mason.

"You stay away from him," I barked in fury, my top lip curling up in anger and I pointed my finger down at her.

She grinned up at me maliciously from the ground with blood dripping down from the top of her head. Even in her beaten-up state she still managed to rise off the floor in a confident swagger. She faced me again with a malevolent quirk to her mouth.

"Evie Emsworth, would you please kindly place your hand onto the door and allow it to kill you slowly," Marlemore ordered Grandma macabrely, without looking away from my eyes. Her desolate eyes were the exact shade of blue as Mason's. It made me sick to see such evil shining in those eyes.

My stomach dropped to the floor and my shoulders curled forwards as panic took over my body. I darted my gaze over to Grandma with terror-stricken eyes to see that she was already looking right at me. She had risen from the floor and was limply holding onto the handle on the door with all her might. A resigned look had settled on her features.

"Don't do it, Grandma. It is not worth our lives to let the

machine fall into her hands," I implored, trying to reason with her.

"I thought you might be noble like that. You heroes make me sick," Marlemore spat and then pulled out a device from her pocket with a red button on the top.

"That is why I planted a bomb in the heart of the town. If you don't give your life, Evie, then I will kill every single living soul in this town." Marlemore smiled happily, sadistically.

"You wouldn't because you will be blown apart too," I disagreed fiercely.

"No, Henry didn't want his creation being destroyed by the bombings going on during the war, so he made this place inside a bomb shelter," she explained. My shoulders sunk in defeat; she had a plan for everything.

"You wouldn't," I seethed in objection, my tone dangerous.

"Try me," she smirked viperously, her broken smile revealing a missing tooth and scarred gums. One of her eyebrows raised in challenge. When I said nothing, her eyes turned to settle on my grandma.

"Just think about all the children you will be killing. Think about those families that will be torn apart – your best friends will die. Every single person that means anything in your life will be dead because of you. Can you live through that Evie?" Marlemore taunted Gran. My grandma's features welled up in pain as she imagined this.

"You will perish in hell where you belong," Gran seethed to Marlemore and then her eyes shifted to mine. "Elora, I believe in you," she declared strongly and the look in her eyes was fierce and brave. From that look I knew what her words meant, that she trusted me to stop this.

A tear fell from my grandma's eye as she squeezed them shut

and then pressed her hand onto the metal door. My heart lurched in my chest causing a horrified expression to settle on my features. I didn't have time to stop her, but I flung myself towards her anyway.

Instantly a needle plunged into my grandma's wrist and started pulling her blood from her veins. Her eyes started to droop, and her knees gave out from under her as she sagged onto the floor. I crumbled to the floor next to her and cradled the back of her head to keep it supported. She stared into my eyes as she tried with all her strength to raise her hand to my cheek.

"Stop her," Gran whispered in my ear. Her strangled words echoed through my mind repeatedly causing something to break inside me. I couldn't watch this; Gran was always so strong and fierce. Now her words were that of defeat, she had accepted her death. A tear slid down from my cheek and fell into Gran's curly hair.

"Don't let her release the machine," Gran spluttered between choked gasps.

"I promise, Grandma, on my life," I declared fiercely stroking her whitening face. I tried to blink away my tears, so that I could see her face as clearly as possible.

"You are good, Elora. You have always been good." She pressed her cold hand to my heart. "In here." Although her hand was cold, I had never felt such a warmth run through me at her meaningful words that meant everything to me. My family just confirmed what I needed to hear all my life, that no matter what I had done in my past to survive, I wasn't a bad person. My heart constricted and shattered apart in my chest and it felt like I couldn't breathe through the pain swallowing me.

"I love you, Grandma," I cried sincerely. For the first time in my life, I finally had a family to love and who loved me back.

And now she was going to die.

"I love you more than you know. Tell Mason to take care of you, he has my blessing," she whispered back, through choked breaths. Her words made my heart burst apart and I cried out a sob.

"Use the necl—," she spluttered her final words before her throat constricted and clogged up leaving only a mumble of distorted letters. Her eyes that usually held so much sparkling love for me slowly became still and lost their light. Her head dropped as the life left her body. My grandma died in my arms.

"No!" I screamed, the agony ripping apart my chest. I clutched my grandma's head to my heart as if holding her tightly enough would keep her with me. The first person I ever truly loved and who honestly loved me back was now gone.

"Grandma," I sobbed, and my tears spilled down my cheeks. I didn't even notice as the last of her blood was extracted from her veins.

The vault door clanged and swung open revealing the deadly machine inside.

Chapter 28

My grandma's body hung limp in my arms. I clutched her desperately to me sobbing into the sky, the grief consuming me. Suddenly familiar and warm arms wrapped around my waist securely. The touch was so unexpected that it made my numb, broken heart feel again and swell with love.

Mason had awoken and incapacitated Brett who was now lying still on the floor. Agony was embedded in Mason's eyes from seeing me in so much pain. All that mattered to me was that he was here in the moment when I needed him the most. I flung myself into his chest and he stroked my hair soothingly. My fingers were so deeply wound into his shirt a bulldozer couldn't tear us apart.

"I'm so sorry," Mason whispered into my ear, and I dug my head into his neck. Knowing that his heart was still beating was the only thing that kept me sane.

"Wasn't the first thing that I taught you when living on the streets was to never show others your weaknesses?" Marlemore sneered into my ear. A surge of hot iron flames ignited through my veins and turned my vision red. I softly placed Grandma's body on the floor and stepped out of Mason's hold.

"I am going to kill you," I growled, the sound emitting from deep in my chest. My red ringed eyes left my unmoving Grandma's form to trail up to glare up at Marlemore with a deadly hatred. I jumped at her with clenched fists preparing to punch her in the face.

"Not so fast," she yelled, raising her hands and lurching back from me. She gestured to the trigger in her hand and towards the small bomb collar that was still secured around Mason's throat. My muscles froze and shut down, losing their fire. Marlemore smirked victoriously from the power she held over me.

"Follow me," she directed, leading the way through the vault door. I glanced back at Mason with broken eyes and a sense of understanding settled in my stomach. Mason placed his hand into mine, securing me to him. Strength surged through me from the mere proximity of him. Taking a deep breath, we walked into the deadly vault.

My breath caught in my throat as we emerged into the vault because it wasn't a vault at all but an expansive underground cave. My eyes searched around in awe. Flowing through the middle of the cave was a small stream; the sound of rushing water was the only noise in the room. The stream ran continuously into the distance further than my eyes could see. The flowing water was spinning a small funnel beside the stream. This was the resource they needed to create the machine – a secure underground power source.

Marlemore walked over towards an antiquated sconce lantern that was drilled into the cave wall and used her cigarette lighter to spark the candle. As she lighted more sconces the cave gradually enlightened with a resplendent lambent shine. I was able to see that everything man-made in the room had clearly originated from many years ago.

My eyes fell onto the machine; it was made from old rusting metal, and shaped like a cylinder with a large circular window on its anterior. I stepped up to it to see that on the top of it held a minuscule keypad and screen which was currently obsidian, dead. Situated just below the keypad and nestled into the metal was an old archaic clock. I glanced at it distrustfully –why does it need a clock?

"Place your hand on top of it," ordered Marlemore with a tilt of her gun towards the machine. I warily glanced up at Mason and he nodded back at me in encouragement, releasing my hand. I placed my shaking hand on top of the machine right over the clock face.

A red laser shined from inside the clock and scanned my hand print. Nothing happened for a few moments – the only thing I could hear was the fear-filled pounding of my heart in my ears. Then the black screen shined a flowing primitive computerised pixilation of one sentence which was continuously followed by another across the small screen.

"Roses have thorns,

This passion can only be concluded by the antagonist of living,

Time is ticking towards what it forewarns,

Using two words you must decipher what is missing,

What is the most precious thing in the world?"

I ran my hands over my face in an exasperated breath as I realised that it was a riddle. I was sick of riddles.

"What is this supposed to mean?" I barked at Marlemore with a sidewards glare.

"You have one shot at answering the riddle or this whole place comes crumbling down on top of us," she explained from the safety of the path just outside the vault. Her form was a dark shadow through the veil of the vault door.

"Is that why you sent me that riddle in the gun?" I deduced. It finally made sense for why she made me decipher that cryptic riddle in Mason's house.

"Yes, I needed to test you to make sure you could solve this one," she confirmed.

"But why a riddle?" I queried.

"It is supposed to be a riddle that only someone in Henry's family would know the answer to. That is why I needed you to live with your grandmother and your true family before I attempted to enter the vault. You needed to learn information that would not have been gathered any other way," she advised with an impatient tone. I clawed my hands through my hair in agitation and inhaled a few calming breaths as I thought the riddle through.

Roses have thorns,

Well roses are a symbol of love and affection. The first sentence meant that love had thorns – that love hurts. The next sentence –

This passion can only be concluded by the antagonist of living,

Meaning this passion can only be concluded by the opposite of living, which is death. So, what passion leads to death and pain?

As the first sentence just told us love has thorns – love hurts, love kills, leading to your death. But then my mind hit a roadblock.

Time is ticking towards what it forewarns,

What does time forewarn? I guess what the forward motion of time inevitably leads to, death. Then –

Using two words you must decipher what is missing,

What is the most precious thing in the world?

The two words must be love and death.

Suddenly, my memory was jogged by something my grandmother told me a long time ago. It was the first time she told me she loved me. She said that our family have always lived by the saying that the most precious thing in the world was love.

That must be it! I thought with elation rising my chest. I typed the word love into the machine, but my hand hovered over the enter button.

That was way too easy; love is too obvious. Anyone could have deciphered that just from the riddle and it doesn't take into account the pain of losing someone you love to death. Why would Marlemore have me live with my grandmother for months just to determine this word? No, it must be something more specific than just love – something more in tune with my family. Then I remembered.

Grandma once told me an extremely old word that had been in our family for generations. The word meant that you love someone so much that you would rather die than live without them because life would be unbearable with them gone. I wracked my mind to remember and suddenly with a jolt, I remembered the word.

"Ya'aburnee," I whispered under my breath in realisation. I typed the words into the old keyboard with sweaty hands and pressed enter.

As we waited my knees shook underneath me. The machine sounded a deafening clang and slowly the clock lid sunk into the depths of the machine to reveal a small chamber inside. I peaked in to find a notably old revolver. I staggered a step backwards and I gnawed at my lip. Why would I need a gun?

I glanced back at Mason with a wary look and he understood. He moved towards me to wrap an arm around my waist. But suddenly Marlemore's face became dangerous and she pointed her gun right at Mason's face.

"Move over to that black tile, Mason, and stand on top of it."

"Why?" Mason defiled, his lips curling.

"Do as I say, or Elora dies." Marlemore pointed the gun at

me. The responding glare that Mason directed at her was the most lethal expression I had ever seen on his face, but he did as she demanded.

"What is this for?" I asked Marlemore, running my palm along my puckered brow and glancing down sceptically at the weapon.

"Pick it up," she ordered. I looked to Mason with wide eyes to see that he was still glowering at Marlemore. I dipped my hand into the machine cautiously and picked up the significantly aged revolver gun. I didn't like the look of this; it reminded me of my old life as a sniper in training.

What unsettled me the most was that Marlemore was the reason I had that past, and it all must be for this moment. As soon as the gun was released from the pressure magnet on the machine something emerged from the wall in which Mason was standing in front of.

The wall flipped on its axis to reveal chains. Marlemore clamped them around Mason's wrists, so that he was tied down to the wall. With an enraged growl, Mason tried to break free but Marlemore gestured the gun in my direction and Mason allowed her to restrain his ankles too.

I started shaking in panic and I instantly dropped the gun and began to move towards Mason to release him. But I was stopped when Marlemore stepped into my path, blocking it.

"Don't move another step or else I will detonate the bomb," she threatened and I staggered a step backwards.

"What are you doing with him?" I screamed as I pushed her in the chest with both hands.

"The machine's last defence," she explained with hurried words. "This machine will kill and destroy millions of lives, therefore, to release its power you need to destroy the most precious thing in the world to you. This sacrifice is meant to be a test to ensure that this person you love dearly would have died from whatever is threatening your world even if you don't release the poison."

I raked my hands down my face as pure terror sank into the heart of my being. Something snapped in my chest and broke me in half like I was a mere piece of string. My eyes darted up to Mason and I saw the horror reflected in his own iris's. My legs willed me to run over to him, to hold him to me forever. I couldn't lose Mason, not after losing Gran. I wouldn't survive it because I would have nothing left to live for.

"Henry made sure that living in a world without the thing you love most is worth releasing the horror inside," Marlemore revealed. Her own features were stoic; she displayed no emotion about killing her brother. My breathing stopped and I gasped for air as red-hot fear seared through me.

"But how does the machine know that Mason is the person that I love the most?" I asked desperately, hoping for any way out of this. I didn't understand how such an old piece of technology could know who I loved the most. Marlemore eyed me vigilantly as she explained.

"As smart as Henry was, he couldn't create a machine that could read minds, but he was a genius. He knew that someone would only come down here with you to assist you in releasing a poison that could potentially kill them unless they loved you and trusted your judgement. And most likely you would love them in return." She shrugged her shoulders like it should be obvious. Henry's cleverness was genius – the plan was plain but brilliant. There were flaws but, in the end, I guess it truly worked.

"Pick up the gun, Elora," Marlemore demanded. I just glared back at her defiantly, crossing my hands over my chest.

"Pick it up or I will kill the entire town," she screamed fiercely, and spit flew from her enraged mouth. I flinched back from her, frightened by her sudden ferocity. My posture sagged and I dropped my head into my hands as defeat weakened my muscles. I had no other choice but to do this.

With trembling hands, I lifted the gun from its rusty hangings. I stared at it, investigating the intricacies of its vintage design, and trying to figure a way to turn this around onto Marlemore. And then I realised that all I needed to do was literally turn around and point the gun at Marlemore which I did. Marlemore just smirked back at me.

"I thought you might try that." She pressed down onto the red button that set off the bombs. My very soul sunk to the floor and I surged towards Marlemore in blind horror. But nothing happened, no bang, no cries of death.

"It won't blow up yet but if my finger releases the pressure on this trigger, it will activate the bomb." Her eyes flickered to Brett to share a smirk as he had regained consciousness and was now standing next to Mason.

I cradled my hands to my chest in relief, but the horror of my next choice was devastating and capable of destroying me. I couldn't kill this whole town just so that I could keep Mason.

I moved my eyes to Mason to find him already staring at me deeply, ardently. I knew the look that was in his eyes, he was searching my face like he was never going to see me again. The force of the emotion that rushed through my chest just from that look nearly sent me falling to the floor.

"Do it, Elora, shoot him," Marlemore whispered hauntingly, like the devil on my shoulder.

"Shoot him. He is already dying, Elora, is it truly worth everyone's lives in this town for a man that is already dying?"

she questioned. I rose the gun up and pointed it directly at Mason. My hands shook violently and I willed myself to press the trigger, but I couldn't do it.

My hands lowered, and I bowed my head in resignation. There was only one option left; I placed the gun at my own temple. If I wasn't here, then Marlemore had no reason to kill everyone in our town.

"No!" Marlemore and Mason screamed in synchrony. Mason wildly flung himself against the chains in an attempt to reach me but all it did was make his wrists bleed. Marlemore's eyes were wide with panic as she lurched at me.

"I am going to kill Mason and the entire town anyway if you do that in anger. You know me," she threatened with a ferocity that made the hairs on the back of my neck stand on end. There was no winning, she was right. I knew her well enough to know she would kill everyone in spite.

"Think this through, Elora, are you really going to kill yourself for him? For the man that killed your mother," she revealed with a deadly tone. Her words echoed through the room, sending shockwaves of trauma tremoring through me.

"What?" I spluttered, my hands holding the gun falling to my side.

"Mason never loved you," she taunted with narrowed eyes, flickering them towards Mason. My gaze flowed suit.

"Don't listen to her," Mason defended. Marlemore's head cut towards Mason and she growled at her brother.

"Shut it," she snarled at him and then gestured to Brett. "Get him to shut up," she ordered. Brett placed his hand over Mason's mouth tightly so that he couldn't speak a word.

"All Mason ever cared about was using you to get you to open this vault. Do you think that my father wouldn't have told

301

him about it too?" Her accusations rung through my mind, torturing me.

"Yes, he was the one who killed your precious mother," she explained, stalking between Mason and I. How dare she accuse Mason of such treachery? But then her words were intriguing me. I thought my mother died of an illness when I was three years old.

"There is more to your parent's story than you know. My father knew that Henry's descendants lived in this town, but he had no idea who they were. He discovered where the vault entrance was and found a trace of an immensely old drop of blood that was previously used to open the vault. He had obtained the DNA of Henry." I leaned forward. I was taking in every single word she was saying like a vacuum.

"Through DNA testing on new births, he discovered that you were a descendant and deciphered that your mother was also one. But he was mistaken about your mother which I only learned a few years ago that it was actually your fathers' line. A few months after your birth he kidnapped you and your mother. He needed you both to open the vault, but you were too young. For three years you both lived in the room that is now my lair." Her words started to sink into my mind with a nauseating shock and revealed why I recognised the small room in Marlemore's lair.

My knees gave way out from underneath me from the revelation and I needed to grab onto the machine for support. Deep down I knew her words were true.

"But your father was an issue that my father underestimated. He was an undercover police officer who had moved away from Everbrook and into the city when he was younger but he was sent back to his home town to investigate the many murders that were occurring in Everbrook by my father. Your father was never

302

married to that woman – it was only a cover. He fell for your mother and they had you. He was going to give up his job and his cover marriage to live with you both after he had completed his assignment," she revealed in a blubbering baby voice like she believed the very thought of love was childish.

"My father didn't expect that yours had the resources to find you. After three years your father managed to rescue you, but he didn't save your mother because my father realised in time and took your mother to a safer location – our house. Your father sent you to an orphanage far away, so that you could never be discovered by my father again. Then he embarked on a vain suicide mission to save your mother."

Everything she was saying was crumbling down the very foundation that I thought my life was based upon. If there was one thing that I always knew about myself it was that my parents didn't love me and left me voluntarily. I cupped my forehead in my hand as my head was spinning.

"But what he didn't know what was while your mother was locked up in our house she ran into Mason. Mason couldn't help killing a poor woman chained up in my father's basement. When your father tried to break into the basement to save your mother, my father killed him instantly," she concluded with her hands clasped together in superiority. There was a dark sadistic enjoyment in her eyes. My hands were in fists at my side and I was overwhelmed with different conflicting emotions.

"Mason has been lying to you this whole time. He was working for me because he wanted half of the glory with me. I showed you the truth when he killed your grandmother's friend, Bill, with the poison," she revealed tauntingly. I glanced over at Mason, his eyes were pleading with me. I knew that look. But then did I even really know Mason?

303

"If you still don't believe me, watch this."

She pulled out her phone from her pocket and played a recording. The video was of Mason in the woods and next to him was the dead body of Melissa. Mason had blood on his hands and was writing on Melissa's arm, love from Marlemore. My eyes nearly popped out of their sockets; I couldn't believe my eyes.

Mason dragged Melissa's body through the woods. The person recording was following behind silently. Mason dragged her body towards the back entrance of the fair and dumped her underneath a secluded part of the fair below the Ferris wheel. I stumbled back a step from the shock coursing through my veins.

"The evidence speaks for itself." Marlemore stood right in front of me and her grubby hands grabbed me by the shoulders, her grip painful.

"I am the only person who has ever cared for you. I was your best friend. I didn't need to spend four years with you in the army but I liked our life. I took care of you," she reasoned with deep wide innocent eyes. I looked back at her and I saw the girl that used to give me half of her food rations.

"I only killed your obsession because I knew that he would never have loved you back. I was doing you a favour." Her words were enticing and I wanted to believe them.

"Forgive me, Elora, for sending you to jail but you have to understand that it was for a good reason. Now you can join me in ruling the world," she apologised sincerely and threw her hands up in the air.

"Are the people's lives in this town really worth the life of a man that deceived you?" She whispered into one of my ears.

"You know how to use the gun, Elora," she implored malevolently into my other ear.

"Kill Mason and we will be gods." Her voice held a finality

and I knew I had to make a choice. I glanced over at Mason; I would do anything for him. I would die for him and I would kill him for him. I knew this was what he wanted; I could see it in his eyes.

With my mind firmly set, I raised the gun. My hands quivered violently and my vision was blurry from lack of oxygen because I couldn't breathe properly. With accurate precision, I aimed the gun at Mason.

Looking straight into the eyes of the man that I loved with all my soul; I pressed down on the trigger. The shot fired straight through the air in the perfect trajectory as Marlemore made sure it would and plummeted straight through the left side of Mason's chest.

Chapter 29

There was no time for shock to display on Mason's features before his body collapsed and slumped against the chains. The machine registered that the bullet was now inside Mason's chest – effectively killing the person that I loved the most.

The machine lit up, shining a florescent gleam and activated with an ominous clang. I refused to acknowledge the hole the has been ripped apart in my chest and the pure panic streaming through my veins, I needed to end this first. I glanced down at the machine to find that instructions had appeared on the screen.

"Please verify identify to activate poison release."

"You need to place a drop of your blood onto the receiver," Marlemore announced. I glared at her with seething hatred and a muscle twitched in my jaw. It was the only display of outward emotion that I showed but inside I was screaming in torment. I glanced back at Mason's still form in bone chilling distress.

"Before I do this, tell me something," I challenged. I still needed to know where she was keeping Mason's brother and I needed to clear Mason's name as the police still believed he was the murderer. Her eyes scrutinised me before she sighed in exasperation but nodded her head.

"I guess there is no harm, I can take your blood easily enough." I didn't like the sound of that but I continued anyway.

"Don't play me any more. I know that you have been framing Mason this whole time," I declared with an emotionless voice. The sadistic smile dropped from her lips.

"You are smart, Elora. In fact, I would call you a genius." There seemed to be something akin to pride on her expression, pride at herself for what she had turned me into.

"Why were you injecting people with poison?" I demanded.

"Because I didn't believe it was possible to enter this vault. I needed a backup plan." She paced in front of me running her hands through what little wisps of hair she had left.

"I tried to re-create the poison myself. That was why I made the fake identity of Amanda and became the chief of police. I needed the information the police had on Henry's company and the access it granted me around town." She shrugged before continuing.

"I found out that the library had the information on Henry's company that made the poison and I broke into the library to steal Henry's work and to start blackmailing Belle. In Henry's laboratory notes I found a sample of the first batch of the poison – the less potent version that was used in World War One. But it was useless to me as I needed the potent version created in World War Two and a way to release it in the form of a gas if I wanted my plan to succeed. Using that sample, I tried to create the more potent version unsuccessfully," she explained. I clicked my tongue in realisation, so that was what all those notes were on her desk in her lair.

"So, you injected that missing boy with the poison you created?" I surmised with a disgusted curl of my top lip in revolution.

"Yes, unfortunately for him he was wandering in the forest at night and was an easy target to test my first batch on. But it sent him mad." She frowned in dismay. I gritted my teeth together disguised at how she could destroy a young innocent life.

"How did you make Melissa and Brandon take that poison

307

and frame them?" I asked, my nostrils flaring.

"On my orders they took the Tetrodotoxin poison voluntarily. I wanted them placed inside Mason's house, so that they would be my inside ears. I needed to find out how to release my father."

I ran my hands down my face as I realised that she was playing Mason this whole time. When Mason thought he was discovering Marlemore's secrets, he was actually doing exactly what she wanted. I remembered that Mason and I were in his house when Mason explained to me how to release his father. That was how Marlemore knew about Mason's watch, because Brandon was listening.

"But I didn't tell them that I was using them in the hope that Mason would figure it out before they lost their minds from the Tetrodotoxin. They thought I would give them the antidote in time. I knew Mason would figure it out because our father loved using that poison so we both could recognise the effects it caused." Her lip arched up to reveal a decaying scarred piece of skin in her mouth.

"Why did Melissa change her mind and try to tell me who you were?" I questioned, curling my hands together and then apart.

"Just after Melissa injected herself that night, she learned that I was using her and there was a chance that she wasn't going to survive. She tried to run to the fair to tell everyone my secret, but I caught her in time," she sneered. The twist of her features caused the scars around her mouth to be more prominent, I shivered away from her in disgust.

"But Melissa died, unfortunately for her." Marlemore spoke with a sympathetic tone but then she rolled her eyes as if it was a joke. "Therefore, I needed another person that I trusted with the information about my father's survival to get inside Mason's basement. So, I staged Brandon's murder in front of the town for two purposes. I knew that police investigators were arriving in town and I needed to protect myself from an investigation. And who would suspect the distraught mother of the boy who was murdered?" She beamed in pride at her malicious plan.

"Secondly, it was essential that Mason was in attendance so he could give Brandon the antidote in time, so that Brandon could infiltrate Mason's basement. And by that time Mason had captured all my men, and Brandon would be able to release them." Marlemore tutted under her breath as if all the effort was such a hinderance to her. "To ensure I had an alibi as Amanda, I forced Belle to dress up as Marlemore and pretend to kill Brandon." Marlemore grinned showing her decaying gums and yellowing teeth.

"Why were you trying to release your father? Why didn't Mason just kill him?" I asked with knitted eyebrows. I still didn't understand why she did all this to release her father and then left him back at the mansion.

"That is why I kidnapped Marcus, our brother, and threatened his life, so Mason wouldn't kill our father. Mason is weak and he would do anything for those he loves."

She was right; he would do anything for those he loved, including dying for them. My heart ripped apart again and I clutched my stomach willing my mind to focus on the present.

"I needed the information my father knew about entering the vault. He told me most of what he knew the first time I found him alive in the basement but there was one vital piece of information he refused to tell me unless I helped him escape," she continued explaining, clenching her jaw in annoyance at her father.

"And then earlier tonight just before I left the mansion, my

309

father thought that I had already released him and he told me the truth. After that I didn't need him any more." I remembered Mason's father giving Marlemore a piece of paper before she left.

"What information did he tell you?" I questioned. Marlemore halted in her tracks and looked at me knowingly with a calculating gleam for a long moment.

"The antidote to the poison," she declared finally. Time stopped. My heart stopped with it and then started again at double the pace. There was a cure.

"There is an antidote?" I stuttered, amazed. My eyes became wide in disbelief and euphoria. Marlemore nodded cautiously as if she was unsure if telling me this was the right choice.

"How else do you think I am going to be safe from the poison cloud?" she rolled her eyes callously. "During World War Two, Henry worked on an antidote to protect the allies because the reason they couldn't use the poison as a weapon, like they did in World War One, was because they had no way of containing the poison cloud when it was released. They didn't want a repeat of the Spanish influenza, but by the time he created the antidote the war had ended." My mouth gaped in shock; this wasn't included in the book.

"If the poison cloud was released into the world now and I had the only antidote, world leaders would give me anything for it – they would give me power," she boasted, displaying her gums through holes of dead flesh. Her eyes sparkled with delight at the very thought.

"But why frame Mason?" I challenged. I didn't understand why she placed all that effort into making me think Mason was the murderer. She gave me a flat unimpressed look, but there was amusement deep in her eyes.

"I needed to turn him against you so that you were able to

kill him tonight." She took a step closer to me and her eyes flashed knowingly. "I know you, Elora, your anger is much stronger than your love. If you thought you were betrayed by Mason you would kill him in spite like you did to me a year ago," she jabbed.

My jaw clamped together; she thought she knew me but she was wrong. I knew she was evil, but with Mason deep down I always knew he was good, that he was mine.

"Why did you place that riddle in the gun?" I coaxed.

"I knew you had stopped using guns and I needed you to overcome your fear, because I needed you ready and able to shoot Mason tonight," she explained. My hands balled up into fists at her wicked games.

"But Mason is already dying – you poisoned him," I pondered the meaning of that. Why inject Mason with a poison that would kill him when she needed him to open the vault?

"That wasn't supposed to happen. That knife was meant for you," she declared. I staggered a step back in shock. "I placed the sample poison from Henry's notes onto the knife to test a theory, but Mason got in the way." Her mouth twisted into an angry sneer. I pressed my lips together to keep from screaming out at her.

"What theory? Why would you inject me with the poison if you needed me alive for this?" I burst with urgency. She tilted her head forward as she examined me, and a curve lifted the side of her mouth.

"Do you really think I am going to tell you all my secrets?" she taunted and skipped over towards the machine.

"You evil bitch," I bellowed at her retreating form, stomping my foot.

"Yes, I am. Now please place a drop of your blood onto the

311

machine to end the world as we know it," she ordered with an overly sweet tone and that in combination with her callous words made me see red with fury.

"No!" I objected fiercely. She looked over her shoulder at me and I caught sight of her smile fading.

"I thought you might say that," she snarled and suddenly lunged back at me as stealthily as a cat. Her knife was outstretched aiming for my chest, but I ducked to the side and the knife missed her target cutting my arm instead. I gasped as the knife cut through my flesh and created a stream of blood that rushed down my arm. I gaped down at it panting, and back up to Marlemore's smirking face and the horror sunk in. She now had my blood and the means to activate the machine.

She turned around to move towards the machine, but I leapt after her. She was expecting my attack and dodged my reaching fingers with an elegant spin. She stuck one foot out behind her which tripped me over and then whacked her hand into my chest, so that I slammed to the floor. My breath was knocked out of me and I lay on the floor clutching my chest, winded and gasping for breath. Marlemore towered over me and plunged the knife down towards my chest, aiming to kill.

Abruptly, her hand stopped in mid-air as someone grasped onto her forearm. She tried to yank her hand from their grip, but to no avail. With confused acrimony filled eyes she turned around to face my saviour and astonished shock flashed on her features. I tilted my head up to see the smirking face of Mason grinning down at me.

"Hi, love." He smiled at me and his beautiful face shined down at me, causing my heart to explode as if he was the sun. He was alive. Relief so strong rushed through me it caused my head to fall back down to the floor again as a huge weight was lifted from my chest.

He had a white bandage expertly strapped around the left side of his chest where I shot him and blood from underneath had started to leak through the bandage. Brett was also passed out on the floor and was no longer an issue – Mason had taken him out. Our plan worked.

"No," Marlemore whispered in disbelief. Her eyes widened in unease and her lower lip quivered, displaying her first signs of fear. Her eyes flickered to Brett's passed out form and those fear lines deepened.

"You can't get rid of me that easily." Mason grinned.

"Mason," I whispered in relief. His eyes moved to mine and something deep passed between us. All my anxiety dissolved like melting gold just from seeing his stunning blue eyes alive and shining with love.

I had never been so terrified then I had in those minutes between when I shot him and seeing his face alive. I thought that maybe I might have missed, or that maybe I accidentally had actually killed him. I couldn't go to check on him because then our plan would have been discovered.

Mason quickly grabbed the bomb switch out of Marlemore's hand. He was careful to swap her finger pressing down on the button for his and then he threw Marlemore away from me. As the air filled my lungs once again, I rose from the floor and carefully took apart the bomb switch while Mason held down the detonation button. My shoulders sagged in reprieve when the bomb was disabled and the whole town and Mason were safe.

"What is going on?" Marlemore screamed, her mutated scars smearing back through her cheeks. Mason moved up to her and held both of her hands behind her body.

"Do you really think I didn't have my own plan?" I scoffed.

Marlemore's features distorted in disgust as if she couldn't believe such a betrayal.

"Your biggest weakness, Annalise, is that you don't know how to love. If you cared at all about your brother, then you would know that he has dextrocardia. Meaning his heart sits on the opposite side of his chest. The place where I shot him was just a flesh wound. I knew that the machine would activate because the receiver only needed to detect that the bullet was inside his flesh on the left side of his chest," I explained.

"How do you know all this?" she barked as her face contorted and twisted with rage into a wretched sneer.

"Because, Marlemore," I growled in a deadly condescending tone. "Threats don't always cause people to give you their full devotion," I leered.

"Belle knew what you were planning, and she tried to warn me. She gave me the book, *Everbrook's secret*. I read it and learned exactly what I needed to do to get into this vault. I knew that I needed to kill the person that I loved the most."

Rage slowly brewed in her eyes and her features twisted into a snarl. She bared her teeth at me.

"So, before we came here Mason and I created a plan. I taught him how to perform an occlusive dressing onto his wound to prevent blood loss and I determined exactly the place I needed to shoot Mason so that it didn't hit anything important. I knew it was risky, that is why I didn't want to do it but it was our last resort and it worked." Mason's eyes locked with mine and I could see pride shining in them.

"Now, I am going to end this," I announced. I took Mason's knife out of his hand and descended upon Marlemore. I inhaled a deep breath and then plunged the knife into her chest. But before it could sink into her flesh, she was already gone.

314

Once again, we underestimated her power. She managed to kick Mason's feet out from underneath him and then jabbed her elbow into Mason's gun wound. He released her with a yell of agony as his gun hole wound was ripped apart. A moment later she rose up from the floor with her palm outstretched and yanked back my elbow of the hand that was attacking her. Her jab was so forceful that my arm whacked back causing the knife to clatter to the floor. It took Mason and I a moment to process what had happened before Mason grabbed the fallen knife and we both surged at her.

Mason attacked her throat and I went for her torso, but she blocked both of us simultaneously. Using her shin to stop me and the opposite forearm to block Mason. Then she twisted away from Mason's attacking hand and used her free leg to strike me, kicking me so hard that I slammed back onto the floor. She landed on two feet and jumped up again to punch Mason. But Mason didn't react to the pain and instantly struck back, slicing the knife at her neck which she barely managed to evade by bending her back to the floor and catching her body with her hands on the floor behind her.

The knife sliced into her stomach causing blood to stream out from her wound. She clutched at her laceration and I grabbed my snake gun from her pocket in her moment of weakness. She snarled and spun around to strike me, but I ducked out of the way. I skidded away from her sliding on my back along the floor and aimed the gun at her chest. I pulled the trigger, but she reached her hand out in front of her causing the gunshot to plummet straight through her hand instead.

Her features winced in pain, but she displayed no other signs of agony from having her hand blown apart. She ignored the gaping hole in her hand and ripped out another gun from her pocket which she used to shoot me in the arm.

"Ah!" I screamed as the bullet lodged into my deltoid muscle. Mason growled and attacked her with his knife, but she dodged him easily and cut through his chest.

She was good, nearly impossible to beat, but Mason and I were the perfect match for her as I knew all her gun skills and Mason knew all her knife skills. But she performed the one manoeuvre that she couldn't be defeated by. She used us against each other.

With rage infused movements I ran towards Marlemore, aiming to strike the gun from her hand while Mason rushed at her from the opposite side. But she suddenly ducked and fell to the floor between us in the extreme last moment, so that Mason and I ran straight into each other. Our heads bashed together with a loud clang and pain streamed through my body, incapacitating me.

I held my head as it spun and my vision became blurry. I only saw a streak of a blurred smear rush past me towards the machine. Marlemore pressed something on the machine and the small clock face clicked. She pulled out the clock from the machine which was now the manoeuvrable size of a small wall clock. Marlemore opened the back of it and placed someone inside which looked like batteries.

Ingenious, Henry was an absolute genius. He only needed the large machine and flowing water to create power to turn the machine on in 1940's and he would have made the machine able to be adapted to modern batteries when they were invented. Now the machine had energy from a portable battery, it was mobile. My vision cleared just as Marlemore lifted her eyes from the portable deadly machine. Her eyes were alive with excitement and her mouth lifted up into a sinister smile.

I growled deep in my throat and lunged at her, as did Mason. But she easily evaded us and sprinted out the vault door. With a drop of my blood on her knife, she exited the vault with the poison machine in her grasp and the means to release it.

Mason grabbed my hand and we sprinted like we had never sprinted before in pursuit of Marlemore. We reached the top of the stairs and emerged back into the church. I was breathing violently and my heart was racing a million miles an hour.

We both searched the church with frantic eyes trying to spot where she had gone. Our gazes darted up when heard a door slam shut above us where a set of stairs led onto the roof. Mason and I glanced at each other before we both raced up the stairs and swung the metal door open, dashing out into the vicious wind.

The storm that was still raging outside had grown fierce; the wind ripped through my clothes, throwing me off balance. The sky was covered in dark black clouds and rain was pouring down sideways. I hugged my jumper tightly around my waist as the lightning set off a lucent ominous flash through the sky followed by a deafening roar of thunder. The deadly weather was like a warning of what was about to transpire.

I noticed a dark figure standing at the very edge of the roof of the church, right beside the grand clocktower. She faced away from us and towards the rest of the town.

"Annalise, don't do this," I reasoned delicately, moving towards her slowly.

"There is nothing you can do to stop me," she refused. The small strands of hair that still grew in patches around her head were billowing in the wind.

"Yes, there is," I objected as I aimed my gun at her and shot her silhouette. But nothing happened, I was out of ammunition.

My stomach lurched, creating a lump in my throat as I

realised that I was helpless. With no other options, I ran towards her aiming my hands for her throat. My motions spurred her on and she tipped her knife with my blood on it downwards, so that my blood dropped onto the machine activating the release of the poison.

I glanced up at her with wide horrified eyes as a wisp of the poison in the form of a black cloud dispersed from the clock and rushed towards me. A grin of victory plastered on Marlemore's face – that horribly scarred face was going to be the last thing I ever saw. But at the very last moment before the gas hit my airways, someone flung their body in front of mine and breathed in the poison. Mason.

Horrified, I watched as he gulped in a deep breath and inspired all the poisonous gas into his lungs.

"No!" I screamed in protest, but my screams were drowned out by the enormous clap of thunder that ricocheted through the sky. Mason fell to the floor and I caught him as he collapsed, both of us sinking to the ground. His eyes scrunched up in pain as he tried to look at me.

"Run," he whispered in urgency. Mason just gave his life for me.

"Pity," clucked Marlemore with fake sympathy. I was too shocked and distracted to notice Marlemore stalk up behind me and punch me in the face. Agony ripped through my jaw as my cheekbone broke and my torso dropped to the floor. Mason was still in my lap; I clutched him to me, refusing to let go of him.

"There is nothing you can do, Elora," Marlemore yelled over the sound of the rain with an evil twist to her mouth.

"Now I am going to take over the world." She laughed viscously and raised the clock into the sky in victory. She slammed her hand down onto the clock and instantly the poison was released into the atmosphere at a frightening velocity. The black poison cloud replicated the dark storm clouds above, like the clouds in the sky had descended down and immersed us into its deadly storm.

With an agonising motion, I forced myself to let go of Mason and crawl backwards away from the black cloud as it descended upon me.

My back hit the edge of the roof and I stalled as I couldn't move any further. The dark mist engulfed me and with no other option I breathed in the black particles. Its deadly effects streamed through my veins, poisoning my blood.

There was no longer any hope to stop the deadly poison cloud as it contaminated the air surrounding the church and began to spread down the hill like black mist towards the rest of the town.

Chapter 30

Nothing happened. I lay sprawled on the floor gasping, expecting my airways to seize up and agonising pain to ricochet through my body, but I was completely fine. Warily, I inhaled a deep breath of onyx poisoned air and my lungs expanded normally. The gas didn't poison my blood. But how was that possible?

With shaky and unsure motions, I pulled myself up from the ground. I couldn't see in front of me due to the dark cloud that was obstructing my vision. I didn't know where Mason or Marlemore was, but I did know one thing – I was finally going to put an end to this.

I knew for sure that there was an antidote; therefore, Henry probably would have also created a way to reverse the effects of the poison cloud. But how? I wracked my hands through my hair, willing my mind to think. A stabbing pain in my chest nearly knocked the breath out of me as I realised that Gran would know.

Then I remembered when she took her last breath, she tried to tell me something. She said, "Use the necl—" What could that mean?

I ran my hands through my hair again, pulling at my necklace chain in anxiety. It sounded as if she had only spoken half a word, like there were a few more letters to complete what she was saying.

Then it dawned on me and my eyes widening as I stared down at my necklace. Gran meant to say necklace. The stopwatch necklace she gave me that used to be her mothers, passed down for generations. It was Marlemore's men who attacked me outside Mason's house trying to steal my necklace, maybe because Marlemore knew it was important and told her followers about it.

Gran said that this necklace would keep me safe. She would have suspected that the disappearance of Ryan could be someone trying to plot to break into the vault and she gave it to me to keep it safe. Or so I could stop them.

I gasped into the obsidian air, comprehending that it must have something to do with the clock that sat on the top of the machine. Therefore, I needed the machine that was currently in Marlemore's possession. I squinted my eyes as I searched around in the darkness for any sign of Marlemore's figure.

I noticed a movement in my peripheral vision and glanced to the side to see a darker silhouette through the penumbral black cloud. As stealthily and quietly as possible I snuck up to the shadow and pulled my gun out of my pocket. I raised it over my head and with all the force plummeting through the hilt of the gun I whacked the back of Marlemore's head.

Marlemore yelped as a sickening crunch resonated from her head and she collapsed to the floor, passed out. I crouched down to yank the machine out of her hands.

The face of the clock was obstructed by the misty haze of gas so I raised it closer to my eyes and gradually the clock face materialised. Instantly I noticed that this clock was missing the second, minutes hand. With fumbling fingers due to my hands still being covered in blood, I grasped my stopwatch from around my neck.

With a shocked gulp, I remembered that my watch was missing the hour hand. It was like the two clocks were connected; they each had each other's missing parts and when placed together created a fully functioning clock.

I ripped open the plastic lid that covered my own stopwatch and then gently with agile fingers pulled off the minute hand. It un-clicked from its original position like it was made to do so. I placed the minute hand on the machine's clock bearing where it clicked on easily.

Suddenly, through the onyx shadowed clouds, I saw a crimson light shine up from underneath the clock face gleaming through the digits.

"To reverse what has been done you need to turn back the time," the machine read.

My mouth fell open as I realised that my theory was possible – I could destroy the poison cloud. With shaky hands I turned back the time on the minutes hand. It ticked each minute it reversed until finally it returned to the twelve o'clock mark. For a few silent moments nothing happened. The only perceptual sound was my erratically beating heart.

Abruptly, from the location where the black poison cloud emerged previously in the clock, a new blood crimson gas bloomed and released. The red cloud spread through the air quickly, almost like it was transparent and didn't need the air particles to move through.

It devoured the atmosphere surrounding the church and dispersed down towards the town rapidly, dissipating the black cloud as the two gas's combined. My vision gradually began to return to me so I could see the small rain droplets of water as they fell from the sky as if cleansing it.

I glanced down at the machine to see that it now read, "this will self-destruct in t-minus ten minutes."

My heart leapt into motion as I panicked and threw the clock, ditching it into the forest beyond us. But my throw was weak and

I doubted it put us out of the explosion range. Mason and I had ten minutes to get out of here before it detonated. I spun on my heel to run after Mason but was stopped unexpectedly as I bumped into something.

And that something whacked me in the side of the face with agonising force and all the air exploded from my lungs. The dark cloud cleared enough for me to see a fist as I fell to the floor. I felt my attackers rage in the brutality of the punch. My lip cracked, and blood trickled down the side of my chin.

I spun around on the floor just in time for the veiling black cloud to dissipate in front of me and gradually reveal the livid form of Marlemore towering over me. Her features were set in a ferocious snarl and she had a gun aimed right at me. I looked up at her from the floor helpless with no weapons at my disposal. She was going to kill me; I recognised that look in her manic eyes.

"You ruined everything!" she shrieked incensed, rage twisting her features into a sinister sneer. There was blood trickling down her forehead from where I whacked her.

Her steel gaze was shaken from me when we heard a bloodcurdling scream emanate into the night. My heart sunk, and it felt like someone was tearing apart my chest when I recognised that voice, that scream. The obscuring cloud cleared further along the church roof to reveal Mason's still form sprawled across the floor, screaming. I flinched and curled my hands around my stomach when it filled with pure dread. The release of the red gas didn't infuse Mason with the antidote. He was still poisoned.

"Why isn't he cured?" I demanded of Marlemore, my voice cracking in terror.

"The poison has already entered his bloodstream – he is a dead man," she gloated laughing, her eyes were glowing in happiness with the pain she could inflict on me. She glowered over at her brother like he was filth.

"And now you will die along with him," she sneered, and her eyes narrowed threateningly. She laughed manically as her head tilted towards the sky before her eyes focused on my face again. She repositioned her hands, so they were both holding onto the trigger and she pointed the gun right between my eyes. I stared down the barrel of the gun and noticed that she was about to kill me with my own gun.

I tilted my chin upwards and looked death in the face, I was going to die valiantly. The corner of Marlemore's mouth turned up in triumph as she pressed down on the trigger. The gun fired with a bang, and the bullet catapulted from the gun. But the bullet didn't speed towards me, it sped towards Marlemore's head.

Marlemore only had a second to realise that the gun had fired the opposite way that she had intended. I saw as horror and shock started to manifest on her features before the bullet shot through the middle of her skull. Blood splattered and streamed out from the wound in her head and her eyes lost their light as the life drained out of her. Her body collapsed to the floor and she lay there motionless. Dead.

Marlemore was finally dead.

My plan worked. I knew that she would take my guns off me when I arrived, and I knew that if I disarmed her from her own gun then she would be forced to use one of my guns. And one of those guns I brought with me was a novelty gun which I took from her own lair – designed to manipulate your opponent. Allow them to think they gained the gun off you and then trick them into shooting you, but the gun actually shoots the person pulling the trigger.

With stiff limbs that only looking death in the face could

cause, I pushed myself up from the floor and stared down at the bullet that had dug a hole into the middle of her forehead. I turned away from her blank familiar eyes and felt nothing but relief. In the end, Marlemore was played at her own game.

When I was certain that she was no longer a threat, I spun around to run back to save Mason. As I turned away from her, I jumped in fright and gasped out a shrill cry of shock when I came face to face with another figure. Mason.

Standing at his full height, Mason towered over me ominously. A bolt of lightning erupted behind his dark figure and his body was like the moon in a penumbral lunar eclipse. The flash of scintillating light illuminating the planes of his features and what I saw emitted fear into the very centre of my bones.

My muscles tensed with terror and I brought my hands around my stomach to hold together my shaking abdomen. The Mason before me was not my Mason. He was glaring at me with pure loathing and the sight of that glare set my teeth on edge. Blood was dripping down from the corner of his eyes like tears. The whites of his eyes were red with blood where the blood vessels had been ripped apart with deep carvings.

Cuts had manifested all over his face and skin which were dripping with blood. I watched aghast as more cuts appeared on his skin like he was being lacerated with an invisible knife. What was left of his irises were black as his pupils had dilated fully. The dark circles underneath his eyes were more prominent than ever and the corners of his eyes were sprouting blackness in the outline of his veins. It was like his blood had turned black and it was visible through his skin. He looked like a monster.

But what made my heart shatter into pieces was the way that his eyes were burning with agony. His body tremored violently like he was on the brink of a seizure and his jaw was locked tightly as if he was holding in a scream of torment. Mason was being tortured from the inside, like he was being cut apart by a million knives from the inside out. The potent version of the poison had infected his bloodstream.

"You are doing this to me," Mason growled in a deadly tone that sent shivers to the base of my spine. My features contorted as I realised that he truly believed that I was the one inflicting this pain on him. His head tilted to the side as he glared at me and then it snapped back to its original position as if he was fighting hard against something inside of him.

"I'm not," I promised dulcetly, holding my hands out in front of me in a calming gesture.

"Mason, listen to me," I reasoned directly. "You have been poisoned. I never hurt you and I never will," I spoke vehemently but softly, staring deep into his eyes. I saw the turmoil there, swimming underneath those black irises that were shining with hate on the surface.

"You are causing this pain – make it stop," he screamed, and the sound nearly broke me. He tilted his head up towards the sky, allowing the rain to pelt straight onto his face as he screamed a sound of agony into the wind.

"Mason, I am not doing anything to you. It's the poison." I took a cautious step closer to him, but he snarled back at me and I rocked back onto my heels. I glanced at Marlemore's form hopeful that she might still be alive and could tell me antidote. But her body was now surrounded in a pool of blood.

"If you won't do it willingly, then I will force you to make it stop," Mason snarled with a horse tone, the screaming had caused his throat to constrict. His head tilted downwards and he looked at me from underneath his eyelashes glaring at me with intense loathing. His black and bloody eyes set on me and the look he

326

gave me sent my blood running cold in fear – he wanted to kill me. My Mason truly wanted to kill me.

I walked towards him gently, stopping for a moment between each step until I reached him. This was reckless, confronting a murderer, but I had to get through to my Mason. I reached my hand up hesitantly and touched my fingers lightly to his cheek. He flinched away from me violently, but I perseveringly placed my hand back there again.

"Mason, I love you. I would never hurt you," I whispered passionately as I ran my hand down his cheek affectionately. He looked deeply into my eyes and he stayed still for a long time where I held my breath hopefully. But I noticed that his pupils stayed dilated and covered in blood, there was none of that familiar blue that I loved so dearly visible.

Suddenly, Mason screamed out a blood-curdling shriek of torment. His body convulsed violently, and his eyes started being gashed apart and dripped with more blood like his insides were being torn apart. He stopped screaming and his deadly glare settled on me.

After a breath he pounced at me, wrapping his hands around my throat and began to squeeze the life out of me. I gasped for breath around his strong hands constricting my throat and tried to move out of his grasp, but he was too strong. His black eyes glared into mine with loathing as he lifted my body off the ground by my throat, blocking off my airways entirely. My feet dangled fretfully and fruitlessly trying to touch the ground.

With a surge of energy, I drove my knee into Mason's stomach. He released me immediately and I collapsed to the floor gasping for air, my throat red and raw. But as I tried to get my breath back Mason had already recovered from my attack. His body slammed into mine on the floor and his hands snaked around my throat.

They squeezed painfully, turning my vision blurry from lack of oxygen. I was going to be murdered by the man that I loved. I gazed deep into his eyes and strangely he stared back, and the pain induced crinkles around his eyes started softening.

"Mason," I croaked breathlessly, with the last of my air. Just as my vision started to become dappled with darkness, I noticed something deep in Mason's eyes. A flicker of blue, of that beautiful blue. Abruptly, the hands around my throat were gone and the air was rushing into my lungs.

I gasped violently and coughed as my body inhaled all the oxygen it could. Bewildered, I glanced up at Mason who was still lying on top of me. His eyes were focused on me, but his head was tremoring around at every angle. Impetuously, his head stopped moving and he blinked a few times which wiped away the blood in them and then he looked back at me with his blue eyes.

"Run," Mason whispered impedingly. My eyes widened in shock; my Mason was speaking. He was fighting it, the poison. I didn't even know that was possible.

"Get away from me, Elora." He blue eyes glanced deep into mine, his words pleading. But I didn't have any energy left to push his body off mine; I was still pinned underneath him.

"I can't fight this for much longer," he bellowed wretchedly. And suddenly his head tilted back as he released a blood-curdling scream and cuts began forming on his skin again. He screamed into the sky and then his head flung back to settle on me once again, his eyes black.

His hands wrapped around my neck and squeezed painfully but only for a moment before relenting. Mason's head snapped to the side as he fought what was infecting his mind. He bellowed out a sound of torment.

"Kill me," he screamed beseechingly and grabbed both of my shoulders in his hands. His frantic blue eyes bore into mine desperately and when he spoke his next words, they shattered my heart.

"Elora, you need to kill me, or I will kill you," he declared, and the urgency in his words were frightening. I stared back at him bewildered, but surely, he must know I could never do that?

He turned his body limp for only a moment. It was a moment where I could wrap my own hands around his neck and snap it. I thought about doing it; my hands inched up to encircle his neck but then every moment I had with him played through my mind. Everything we shared had bonded us to a point where I could no longer live without him. My hands slackened and I lovingly stroked my hands down his neck instead of snapping it.

"No," I objected resolutely. "I would rather die than live without you." I wrapped my hands completely around Mason's neck and instead of saving my life and killing him, I hugged him and pressed my body against him. I pulled myself closer to the man that was trying to murder me, allowing him to kill me. His black eyes flashed for a moment.

"We are in this together, if you die then I die," I resolved with finality. Mason screamed but this scream was different. This scream was so much more tormented as it was filled with Mason's emotional pain as he knew we were both going to die. The screaming stopped, and his onyx hate imbued eyes settled on me.

His hands wrapped around my throat and squeezed until my airways were blocked. My vision became hazy, and my body started to shut down, my muscles weakening. But with all the power left in me, I stared into the eyes of the man that I loved.

Mason was staring back, and I felt him there – the man that I loved was in there staring back into my eyes as we both died. I knew at that moment that if I was going to die, then I was going to die kissing his lips.

With the last of my energy, I propelled myself closer to Mason and planted my lips on his, but what made my heart squeeze and try to burst out of my chest was when Mason kissed me back. He fought against the poison enough to regain control of his lips so we could have this one last moment together, so that he could comfort me as I died. His lips kissed me passionately as his hands strangled my throat.

He was killing me as his hands squeezed my windpipe to death, but he was also kissing me lovingly with his lips. I had never experienced such an intense and thrilling love filled moment in my life. This was my Mason kissing me and the poisoned delusional Mason killing me. He was pushing through the pain just so he could kiss me back, while he murdered me.

My lips parted from his slowly as I lost the energy to move them any more, but I felt his lips again as he inched them back to mine trying to keep our lips together. But with my oxygen deprived muscles I became limp in his arms. I was dying kissing his lips and it was the best feeling in the world. I was happy dying with my Mason – I was content. But then suddenly something happened.

Mason bellowed out a roar of fury, his hands leaving my throat as he threw his body away from mine with a tremendous amount of force. I gasped and spluttered into the rainwater as my lungs filled with air. Mason screamed on the floor near me but he never came close to me. He was fighting the poison and he was winning.

My kiss must have given him a stoke of fire, something to

fight for. I crawled over to him slowly because I was still coughing erratically. His scream drowned out until finally he made no more sounds. His body stiffened and stopped moving altogether. My heart crumbled as I realised what was happening, the poison was going to kill him.

"No," I wailed into the sky as I clutched Mason to me. I wrapped my arm around him and plastered my other hand to his dripping face. The plummeting rain from above wiped away the blood that had tricked down Mason's cheeks to reveal his beautiful features. His blue eyes stared up at the sky with no light in them. He was dead.

"No!" I wept in torment. The pain that was tearing apart my chest felt like a torture I had never known before. I couldn't live without Mason. I sobbed as I clutched him to me, pulling him into my chest. I held him so tightly a bulldozer couldn't have torn us apart.

I couldn't breathe; my breaths were painful pants as my sobs overcame me. Tears were streaming down my cheeks and mingling with the rain. I wanted to tear my heart out, so that I never had to feel this pain again. I felt like I was dying without Mason. I wanted to die. How could death be any worse than this?

"Mason come back to me – please don't leave me," I sobbed into his ear as I tucked my head into his neck. He was still warm, and I could imagine that he was still alive and hugging me back. That helped calm down my quivering muscles for a moment as I breathed in his scent.

When I could finally breathe evenly again, I glanced down at my beautiful Mason. With my fingers I stroked the planes of his features, his strong jaw, his arched dark eyebrows and until finally, they drew along his lips. For a final goodbye, I reached my face down gently to touch my lips to his one last time. His lips were already parted and as I kissed him it felt like I was truly with him. I started to move away but the agony that tore into my chest was too much to bear and I pressed my lips harder to his.

As I was pressing my lips so forcefully into Mason's I felt my cut lip from earlier puncture and start to drip with blood. The blood dripped from my lip and into Mason's mouth as I kissed him. I pulled away from him agonisingly and stared at his features which were obstructed by the tears streaming down my face and the rain that stuck to the ends of my eyelashes. As I blinked my eyes to rid them of the droplets, so I could stare deeply at my Mason again, I heard something.

A deep gasp. I snapped my eyes open and they widened in shock as I saw Mason heave oxygen into his mouth. His eyes burst open and fell onto me. It felt like I was hit in the chest with a bullet as I saw that Mason's eyes were the colour of a light blue ocean again.

"Elora?" he whispered coarsely, his eyebrows pinching together in confusion. Euphoria built up in my chest and I yelped out in relief.

"Mason, you're alive." I hugged him with every last piece of energy that was left in my body. He clutched me to him in return and ran his hand down my back soothingly as I cried into him. I leaned my head away from him to grab both of his cheeks, searching every inch of his face and marvelled in the way his eyes searched mine in return.

I couldn't believe it; he was truly alive. His eyes were blue again and the dark circles and black veins underneath his eyes were gone. Hastily, I ripped away the top part of his shirt to see that the knife wound to his chest was no longer black.

Mason was completely cured. I realised with a shock that I must have cured Mason. That was why I wasn't poisoned when the gas cloud hit me because I already had the antidote streaming through my veins. My blood was the antidote, Henry's blood that was passed down through the generations and I just gave Mason the antidote through my kiss.

Now Mason was alive.

Chapter 31

I clutched at my throat in panic as I remembered that the machine was about to self-destruct. Mason was still breathing heavily and his eyelids kept repeatedly fluttering closed.

"We need to get out of here," I stressed as I wrapped my hands around Mason's waist and tried to haul him up from the ground.

"What?" Mason breathed, his voice was only a croaked whisper due to fatigue and he glanced up at me with heavy-lidded eyes.

"That machine is going to explode at any second," I explained frantically. With a nod of understanding Mason wrapped his arm around my shoulders and helped me raise him to his feet. He was already wheezing as I lugged him along the rain coated roof and my muscles began burning from exertion.

With hurried steps, we made it down the stairs and broke through the doors of the church. We hobbled down the cobblestone path and instead of taking the long winding road down the hill, I continued forward into the thickness of the trees. Mason was slowly losing consciousness and with adrenaline fuelling my motions I carried most of Mason's weight. I wasn't losing him now.

"Mason come on, keep going," I begged of him. Mason seemed to find some unknown strength and propelled his legs faster. We were in the depths of the trees when we finally heard the ear-splitting detonation. The resounding bang of the explosion ricocheted through the night, blowing the forest apart and setting alight the church.

I screamed as the force of the bomb's trajectory threw Mason and I off our feet, slamming us into the forest floor. Debris from broken bark of trees and the church building whacked into my back and a heat flew over my skin. Mason landed on top of me, lying over me protectively.

After a long beat of squeezing my eyes shut tightly, I slowly lifted my head to examine our surroundings in bewilderment to find that we were safely out of the bomb's firing range.

Mason groaned painfully and rolled onto his side and off my body. It was with a sinking heart that I discerned that Mason wasn't in as such a good state as I was. Pieces of wood had lodged into his back and blood was dripping down from those cuts in splatters. The fabric of his shirt had singed away due to the waves of heat that had exploded from the bomb and had scarred his back red and raw.

"Are you okay?" I gasped in horror and reached out to help him but stopped, hanging my arm in fear of hurting him further. He was still covered in lacerations and blood from the poison.

"Yes, I just need to rest," he assured with a small voice, closing his eyes tightly.

"We need to get you to the hospital," I fretted over his wounds, but he placed a reassuring hand on mine.

"I am sure an ambulance will be here any second to investigate the huge explosion. Don't worry, they will find us before we can get to the hospital anyway," he reasoned with his eyes closed from exhaustion. I knew he was right but the worry that was infecting my mind was hard to ignore.

"Come here." He smiled and gestured to his chest. Still apprehensive, I glanced towards the direction of the town and accepted that Mason was right. He needed to rest. I looked back at Mason to see him gazing at me desperately, like a lost boy.

"Please, Elora, I need you," he pleaded. It was heart wrenching seeing Mason usually so strong this reliant on me. I rested my head onto his chest and he wrapped his arms around my waist, pulling me into him. He closed his eyes and tucked his head into my hair. I looked up towards the church above us that was engulfed in lurid gleaming flames, burning down the clock tower to dust. The flames had taken over the forest beyond the church and the rainfall was too insubstantial to prevent it devouring the trees foliage.

We lay there for an immeasurably amount of time watching the coruscating blaze engulf the forest and the church.

"You saved me, Elora," Mason spoke fiercely. "If you hadn't refused to kill me then I wouldn't have fought so hard to fight off the poison." I rested my own hand onto his, smiling up at him lovingly.

"My love, haven't I already proved to you that I would rather die than be without you? There was no choice for me," I admitted. His blue eyes searched mine vehemently.

"Thank you." Gratitude was shining in his eyes but also something deeper, awe. I dropped my eyes, I didn't deserve thanking, not when he went through that agony for me. And not just once, he went through that twice for me, when he took the poisoned knife that Marlemore tried to stab me with. Thinking back to that night with the knowledge I knew now, I finally realised why Marlemore tried to poison me.

"Marlemore said to me that when you were cut with the poison coated knife it was actually meant for me. She was trying to test out her theory then, to see if my blood was the antidote," I deduced. Mason was still looking deeply into the fire with his eyebrows knitted together.

"Henry must have injected the antidote into his own bloodstream which changed his DNA and it contained an antigen that was passed through generations, so no one in his family could ever be harmed by the poison," I concluded. I picked up Mason's fingers and ran my hands down his palm calmingly. He was listening to me intently; his eyes were watching my fingers as they moved along his skin.

"You are related to a psycho genius," Mason joked, but he was right, now I knew where my interest and intuition in biomedical physics came from.

"Maybe that is why you are such a good shot," Mason continued and I looked up at him guiltily, remembering his expression when he found out my secrets. My tight shoulders softened when I saw that he was looking at me with pride and admiration.

My heart swelled with how accepting he was of this dark side of me, of my keeping this secret from him. He must have known what I wasn't keeping it from him voluntarily, my mind literally would not even allow me to think of it. I snuggled into his chest and as I relaxed, more questions about the night came into my mind.

"How did your father know what the antidote was?" I asked Mason inquisitively.

"My great grandfather was Jeremiah King," Mason revealed gruffly. My head darted up and towards Mason to stare at him wide-eyed. Jeremiah King was the man who co-wrote those notes I found on Marlemore's desk. That meant that both of our descendants worked together to create that poison.

Suddenly as I was reminded of those pages something struck a chord in my mind. When I was reading those pages, I heard a crash in a box like there was something inside it. Maybe that crash inside the box was Mason's brother.

"Mason, when I was in Marlemore's lair I heard this box jolt as if someone was in there," I blurted with an increasing pitch from mounting joy. Mason's gaze snapped to mine, his eyes lighting up and widening in hope.

"You don't think?" He whispered in ebullience, but he still didn't have the strength to lift his head off the forest floor. I placed my hand onto his chest and looked up at him with my chin resting just above his heart.

"I think that could be where she was keeping your brother," I surmised.

"Elora, you are a genius." Mason smiled widely and grabbed both my cheeks and kissed me on the forehead. I grinned goofily back up at him – it was infectious seeing him happy. Suddenly my happiness was ripped apart as something from my unconscious punched a hole in my chest. I had to drop my eyes from his and the smile was wiped off my face. I pulled my head back, so Mason's hands dropped to his side.

"What's wrong?" Mason's tone turned dire. He knew me too well.

"That video Marlemore showed me of you writing on Melissa's body, what was that about?" I questioned, nervously intertwining my hands together on his chest and looking down towards them. My heart was beating rapidly in fear that his words could take a sinister turn.

Mason touched his hand to the bottom of my chin and tilted my head upwards to face him. His eyes were burning with the sincerity of his words.

"I found Melissa's body in the woods and I honestly thought she was dead at first. Marlemore didn't want anyone knowing about the crimes she had been committing so I thought I would let everyone know. I needed help to find my brother in time, I couldn't take down Marlemore on my own. So, I thought if the whole town and police were investigating her then we could take her down together," he admitted with a grimace, like remembering what he had to do was a torment in itself. I listened to his words with hopeful eyes.

"But only after I left her body at the fair, I noticed that her skin wasn't turning the usual colour that a dead body became. So, I decided to steal her body back to study it myself," he explained formally, like stealing dead bodies was nothing more than a job.

The tightly built-up and coiled air released from my lungs in a sigh of relief. Marlemore was lying again to turn me against Mason. She just never realised the intensity of our bond; it was like another sense that drew me to Mason. I trusted Mason but there was still more information I needed to know.

"Why did Marlemore say that you killed my mother?" I inquired fretfully, pushing myself up on his chest so I could see his face. Mason avoided my eyes and dropped his gaze as if ashamed.

"Because I did," he admitted crisply. My throat constricted sickeningly and the air started to whisk through my lungs at a rapidly expanding pace.

"Please explain," I demanded, my voice cracking in mounting trepidation. Mason didn't look at me as he explained.

"I was young, barely eight years old. I was helping my father clean out the basement of bodies one night when I heard someone begging for help." Mason's tone was sombre, almost strangled, like he had been dreading to tell me this for a long time. It was hard to listen to, but I swallowed the lump in my throat and prevailed through.

"I investigated it to discover a woman with red hair and half an eyebrow missing chained up. It was only the night on the lighthouse when I realised that woman was your mother." I squeezed my eyes shut tightly.

"She begged me to kill her. At that time, she thought that she was a descendant of Henry and that if she died then my father would no longer need you to open the vault as she had no other living members in her family. Then he wouldn't hunt you down," Mason revealed. Finally, his guilt riddled eyes turned to me.

"Did you kill her?" I challenged sourly.

"I didn't know how to kill. I was still too young." He shook his head violently like he was trying to clear the memory.

"She asked me to leave her a gun, so she could kill herself," he admitted, running his lacerated hand through his hair. "I did as she asked, I thought I was helping her. She killed herself with the gun I left her. It was all my fault she died. It was only a few hours later a man arrived trying to save her." Guilt and mourning scorched in his eyes but that was all I needed to hear.

Mason was not evil. He would never kill an innocent person in cold blood. He didn't kill my mother. He just gave an already dying woman a final wish, to save her daughter's life. And those words gave me the information that I needed to place my parents behind me, now I knew both of them died to save my life.

"You didn't kill her. You gave her what she wanted. You helped her save me." I smiled warmly. "Even back then you saved me," I revelled as I stroked my hand down his rough face and over his deep scar that ran down his cheek. He softly moved my hand off his cheek as his eyes flashed.

"Elora, I didn't save you. Look what I did to you," he denounced tautly and referenced towards the cuts and black bruises surrounding my neck. I brushed it off with a wave of my

340

hand.

"I don't care what you did to me, that wasn't you." I reached for his face again, but he shook his head out of my grasp.

"These cuts were me. I did that to you. No poison," he stressed, running his finger down the scars on my neck from when he cut my throat with his knife. His tone was brittle causing his voice to break halfway through.

But to me these cuts were what made our love stronger; despite all odds Mason never was able to kill me, no matter how much he needed to, no matter the price it cost him. They were a reminder that we belonged together. That I had always embraced and accepted Mason's dark parts because I had those dark parts in me too. I understood him, I knew what it was like to be ostracised and to murder someone even though you didn't want to.

"Mason, these cuts are a part of our story and the beautiful journey it was falling in love with you. I wouldn't change it for the world." Mason's tear-filled eyes bore into mine and I felt in my heart just from that look how much my words meant to him.

"And I know that you're different now. You love me now, you didn't then," I defended. Mason's eyes flared darkly, and I was suddenly reminded of when they did the exact same thing when he was strangling me to death.

"Are you sure about that? Because not minutes ago I tried to kill you," he snapped, resentment clear in his tone at himself. His jaw was locked tightly, and his hands were clenched into the fallen leaves by his side. I knew I needed to calm him down or else he would pass out. His complexion was a pale sickly shade and his eyes were bloodshot.

"That wasn't you." I shook my head calmly. Mason's eyes narrowed with angered disagreement but suddenly he closed his eyes tightly and inhaled a deep breath.

When he looked back at me again, his expression was pained and the silent agony on his features was difficult to witness. He reached out a hand towards mine that was still resting on his chest but then stopped as if he wouldn't allow himself that small comfort. But I grabbed his hand and held it tightly in my own. His eyes rose back up to mine and just from that look, my heart skipped a beat.

"Elora," he whispered my name softly, like it was the most precious thing in the world. "In those moments when the poison had taken over my mind and I thought that I needed to kill you to make the pain stop. I had never wanted to kill someone so much in my life. It felt real, and it still does," he croaked, tormented.

"It was agony to push myself away from killing you. I am afraid that at some point that might happen again. What if that lack of need to kill when I am with you begins to fade and I want to hurt you?" He looked like he was on the verge of tears but there was no water in his eyes. I shook my head in disagreement.

"You fought the need to kill me when you were poisoned. If that does happen when it is just you, then you would easily be able to fight it," I assured. And even if there was a possibility that he wanted to kill me in the future, I would still choose being with him.

"You are right. I would do anything for you." His blue eyes gazed into mine and they gleamed shimmeringly from the reflecting light of the forest fire. "When I was poisoned, I knew that you wouldn't be able to kill me. I knew I needed to fight it myself. All I wanted to do was give into the poison but for you, I fought against the agony." He forced a smile but then his expression turned grim. "But I see it whenever I close my eyes, the image of my hands around your neck as I slowly murder you.

342

I don't know how I am going to live with myself; I deserve to die. I want to," he admitted wretchedly.

His tired and broken eyes looked right into mine, like I was the only thing keeping him grounded to this earth. Tears welled in my eyes and I had to take a deep breath to fight the constricting feeling bearing down on my chest. My Mason wanted to die.

"Mason, you have to learn how to live with yourself because if you die then I will die too," I objected fiercely. I held his face tightly between my hands, as if by holding him tight enough I could prevent him from breaking apart between my fingers.

He must have seen something in my expression because he closed his eyes and smiled softly. He knew I was telling the truth because I had already proved it to him before. Mason was all I had left now. I had lost Gran, my only family. If I lost Mason too, I would be left with nothing worth living for.

It seemed like a huge weight lifted off Mason's shoulders. Maybe I just gave him a reason to keep living, something to fight through life for. When he opened his eyes again there was a fire in them that I hadn't seen there for a long time.

He grabbed my hands from his face and then rolled me over, so he was resting on top of me. His face was inches above mine and one of his hands tangled into my hair.

"Elora, I love you, more than life, more than pain. From here on out I will do anything for you. I will go through a life filled with pain and depression. If you want me to stop hurting and murdering evil people, I will. I will be whatever you want, whatever you need," he declared sincerely. His words were like a seal of peace for me; he would truly give up everything that made him Mason for me. As much as I wanted him to be good and righteous, I knew deep down that he needed this darkness to keep him sane.

I had already accepted that darkness that resonated deep within his soul. That was what made our love so strong, we fit perfectly together and accepted each other as we were. Being together made us better people than we were apart.

"I want you to be yourself," I proclaimed with pure honesty.

He nodded back slowly and then leaned his head gradually down to mine. His lips brushed against mine softly and goose bumps rose on the back of my neck. He kissed me like he was sealing a promise to himself with a kiss.

My entire body ignited into an inferno and set alight from his kiss. I never thought this moment would ever happen again. I thought this was lost to me when I believed that he was dead.

It was a miracle that we both survived through the night and I was able to be with Mason now. I felt all the pain and suffering and loss we had both endured in that kiss. We were clutching each other like lifelines. He was my air, my oxygen. He was my reason to breathe through all the pain that was buried deep in my soul.

I pulled away from him as a sob wracked through my body. Horrific images of my grandma's crumpled dead body flashed in my mind as she died. My lungs constricted painfully and I gasped out, clutching my chest.

"My grandma is gone," I wept, and that knowledge ripped me apart. My family was gone. But she didn't die in vain, she died saving millions of lives, including mine. I made a promise to myself in that moment that her sacrifice would not be forgotten.

"I am so sorry, my love," Mason whispered consolingly, his features replicating my own from seeing me in pain. I buried my head into his neck and cried out the pain and sorrow I felt inside.

"She is in a better place now." Mason gently wiped away my tears. He was right – I just knew it.

"When I was a kid and locked in a cage, the only thing I knew in life was murder and blood," Mason began sentimentally. He inhaled a deep breath and his voice staggered. This was hard for him to admit.

"The only reason I knew that killing was evil was because I found a bible hidden in our house. It helped me see that everything my father was saying wasn't true and that was why I refused to kill innocents. From then on, the bible became a source of solace and goodness in my life, just like how you have become for me now. I hope that the peace it once brought me will help me bring that peace to you now."

Then Mason recited bible verses to me. His meaningful words and voice were so calming that my sobs lessened in severity just so I could hear him as he opened up a hidden part of his life to me. A part he had never told anyone before. So, this was why Mason was always calmer after he went to church and why he endured through the ostracisation of the town just to be closer to something that made him feel at peace.

Listening to Mason's beautiful and calming voice made me realise that although the agony of losing my family would torment me until the day that I died. I knew that I would be okay, that I had something to live for as long as I had Mason by my side. With his voice lulling me into serenity I watched the scintillating flames engulf the clock tower.

Epilogue

Blood started trickling down my finger. I yanked my hand away from the red rose bush and its thorn that had cut into my skin, drawing blood. The rose stem that I had just snipped off from the plant fell from my fingers and landed onto the cobblestoned path, covered in my blood.

"Do you think these tomatoes are ready to harvest?" my daughter asked happily. I wrapped my hand up in the end of my shirt sleeve to cover the wound and directed my attention to my daughter.

"My grandmother used to tell me that they are ready to harvest when they have turned bright red all over," I explained cheerily, smiling as I remembered when Gran first told me that I could harvest these exact tomatoes.

"They look very red, mum." My daughter grinned, showing her dimpled cheeks. I kissed the top of her head.

"They do. I think they are ready to harvest, my lovely." My daughter clapped her hands joyfully and began work wrenching them off the plant exceedingly ungracefully.

As I harvested the tomatoes with my daughter it reminded me of my first meeting with my husband. I glanced over at Mason who was chopping wood with an axe by the entrance to the forest. Our son, James was fetching him pieces of wood from the leafy verdant trees beyond.

My eyes were caught for a moment on Mason's beautiful face as he concentrated on the task he was performing. His dark chocolate brown hair was falling over his eyes and peeking out from the concealing strands of his hair was the deep scar that ran down his cheek. Due the strenuous nature of the activity Mason had taken his jumper off and it displayed all the scars down his arms from his own knife wounds and the cuts from the poison. I shuddered as I remembered watching him acquire those scars.

It was impossible to think now that there was a time when I nearly lost Mason. My eyes glazed over as I stared up pensively into the towering misty mountains above and thought back to that horrible night when I nearly lost everything.

The police, ambulance, and fire brigade arrived not long after the bomb exploded. They extinguished the flames, managing to save the church but not without damages. The police found us in the woods after much shouting from me. We were both taken to hospital and Mason needed to stay there for a few weeks.

When we were recovering in hospital, we explained to the police everything that had happened and the truth about the chief of police and Masie. And because I had recorded Marlemore's confession through my phone the police believed us. Although I did cut out any parts that would have convicted Mason and I of any crimes.

As soon as we were released from hospital, we returned to the vault to make sure that the poison machine was truly destroyed and sealed the vault off forever. Mason buried my grandmother's body right beside her church. After that traumatic experience we returned to my grandmother's cottage. She had left everything she owned in my name.

Mason asked to live with me in the cottage which we now call home. He didn't want a life in that horrible mansion that held such dark memories. Mason and I both suffered from terrible nightmares and PTSD ever since that night; sometimes Mason wouldn't even sleep for days. He told me once that on bad nights he feared that if he went to sleep then he would lose control or be sent back into that poisoned delusional state and try to kill me.

Mason returned to the mansion to kill his father and went back to Marlemore's lair one more time to release his brother. It was a massive relief to find his brother in that chest. I knew how much saving his brother meant to Mason – he had a new light in his eyes after embracing his brother again. Marcus didn't stick around town but we still kept in contact with him, visiting him once a year.

Belle and I still worked together at the library. We are close family friends now after what we went through together. I don't know what I would have done if I had lost Belle too. Mason ended up joining the police force. He shut down his surveillance business because he didn't like leaving me for long periods of time whilst he travelled to gain business. Mason told me that he only set up the business so he could use the video surveillance to find evil people for him to kill. Mason wanted to make amends for what a disgrace his family had turned that police force into.

After a few years of living together, I became pregnant with our first child, Evie. Mason was horrified because he didn't want his dark world to interfere with our child's innocence. But in all honestly, I believed that he was terrified that the way he didn't like seeing me in pain wouldn't be passed onto his child and he would want to hurt them. That the voices in his head will tell him to kill them.

He broke up with me during that time, thinking he was doing the best for our child. It nearly killed me, but I stayed strong for our baby. Mason moved back into the mansion and even though we weren't together, he was always there when I needed him.

Mason returned for her birth and he realised that we both needed him and he had no compulsions to hurt her. He loved her like he loved me. Three years later we had our boy, James.

Only then did Mason finally ask me to marry him. Once our family was settled, we became more integrated into the town. Everyone accepted us into society once they realised that Mason and I saved the town and that Mason wasn't Marlemore.

I ensured a large shrine was placed up at the entrance to the church, thanking my grandma for her sacrifice. I held a memorial at the church, explaining to the town exactly how Gran gave her life for us. Years later we were living relatively normal lives, but there was still one secret that we kept that no one could ever know.

A darkening storm cloud had whisked over the mountain and the last of the days light casted a dimming gloaming over the cottage, adumbrating the evening shadows. Blood started to trickle down my finger from my cut and a shudder ran down my spine, but it wasn't from the coolness of my blood or the icy wind. A crunch of a leaf sounded from the forest next to our house and instantly my back straightened, alert.

In rushed motions, I called my children and brought them inside into the warmth of the cottage. They both sat in front of the television with their tomatoes by their side. The sound of Mason's wood chopping eerily quietened and I hurried back outside to check on Mason and investigate the noise. I closed the door gently and locked it behind me.

As it clicked shut, a hand wrapped around my waist and my neck was pulled back as a knife was placed at my throat. My body tensed, and I angled my neck away from the knife. After an initial jolt of fear from feeling the cold tip of a knife scrape my throat, I released a breath of relief. I tilted my head to look behind me to reveal the deadly intent face of Mason.

His pupils were dilated, and his face was so close to mine that I felt the jagged air of his breath as he exhaled. He inched his face even closer, so he could run his lip along my cheek until it rested at my ear. Goose bumps rose on my skin.

"In the woods, to your right," he whispered. I knew instantly what he meant. In a lightning fast movement, I spun my body around and kneed Mason in the stomach. He buckled over and I snatched the knife out of his hands. With Mason on his knees in front of me I plunged that knife into his chest. He crumpled to the floor, his body turning rigid. Without looking behind me, I spun on my heel and began to walk inside again.

But as I reached for the door handle, I heard the swish of a gust of wind behind me that wasn't there before. I tilted my head to the side just in time as a knife swung through the air. It missed my head and sliced through the skin of my outstretched wrist and lodged into the wood of the cottage door.

I felt the warm liquid of my blood start to trickle down my wrist from the cut and through the webs of my fingers. If I hadn't just moved my head then I would be dead right now. I was prepared the second time the knife struck. I heard it as the knife plummeted through its trajectory towards me. I spun around and caught the hilt of the knife just before it was about to sink into my skull.

Without a moment's notice I flickered my eyes up and threw the knife back towards my attacker in retaliation. The knife found its target easily and sunk into the shoulder of a man hidden in the trees behind the cottage. The knife drew right through him into a tree stump rendering him immobile.

I yanked the other knife out of the cottage door and descended upon my attacker, with my hands in fists by my side.

I didn't know how he found us, but he was going to pay for it. I stalked up to my attacker that was pinned to the tree – his head was bowed in defeat as he tried to contain his agony. I ripped his head up by his hair when I reached him and placed his knife at his throat.

I recognised him instantly, his name was Adrian Green, he was a mass murderer and leader of multiple gangs. He was the man that Mason and I have been trying to hunt down and kill for months now. But somehow, he managed to find us first.

"How did you find me?" I barked with venom as I slammed my forearm into his throat. He just grinned back at me, revealing yellowing teeth.

"I must admit I am surprised. I thought you two were partners." He tilted his head to the side inquisitively, gesturing to Mason. I bared my teeth back at him.

"Now that you know where I live, my bodyguard was of no need to me any more," I lied nonchalantly, waving off his comment. "How did you find me?" I reiterated punching him in the face. His gleaming eyes lit up.

"It wasn't hard and now I know you have a family," he taunted. Panic settled in my stomach turning my entire body cold, this was my worst nightmare.

With fear and rage turning my vision red, I dislodged the knife out of his shoulder and stabbed it into his other shoulder. He screamed out in agony, but it wasn't enough. He deserved pain beyond death for threatening my family. I yanked the knife out to stab him again expecting his agony, but I wasn't prepared for his retaliation.

He ducked out of my advance and kicked my legs out from under me so I fell to the floor on my knees. He knocked the knife out of my hand and grabbed me around the throat. He pulled my body off the floor by my throat, dangling me in the air and threw my head against the tree. I gasped wildly, the pressure on my throat was starting to constrict my oxygen supply.

"Let go of my wife," Mason spat as his figure towered over Adrian from behind. I heard the sound of a knife sinking into flesh and then I was released from Adrian's hold. I fell to the floor gasping and glanced up to see that Mason had Adrian around the throat with a knife. With shaky limbs I stood to my full height and my eyes locked with Mason's to find his eyes filled with that wild darkness of his need to kill.

Our plan always worked, make it seem like we had turned against each other just so the other can strike when our prey was preoccupied. Using a plastic knife to fake the others murder. This is our secret.

We spend our nights hunting down and murdering evil people. Mason tried to become a better person for our family, but I knew that he would always need the thrill of killing to sedate his dark side. We tried not to kill our prey and mostly passed them onto the police but sometimes when I knew Mason needed to hurt someone, I would let him torture them.

Only if it became life or death, then I accepted murdering as a hazard of the job. We used Mason's mansion for our base of operations and that was why I was so horrified that this evil man had found us here, at our family home.

I cut my gaze to Adrian, so we were at eye level. I sneered into his disgusting face.

"I am going to kill them," Adrian provoked with a sinister tone. My heart stopped beating.

"I am going to tell every single person that you placed in jail and the families of those you murdered that you have children." He grinned wickedly, enjoying watching the blood leave my cheeks as agony started tearing my heart apart at the mere thought.

I glanced up at Mason horrified to find his face was also drained of colour.

"I am going to make you listen to them scream as I torture them," Adrian tormented. I couldn't handle his words any more. The vision he painted flashed in my mind and I could hear it, just as clearly as I heard Mason's tortured screams from my memory every night. With Adrian knowing the location of our home it could so easily happen. But I refused to allow it; my children were innocent, and they would never be hurt by the darkness that Mason and I are.

Mason's features were incensed and he increased the pressure of the knife on Adrian's throat and blood began gushing from the wound. With my mind a haze of fire, I pulled the knife out of Mason's hand and then plunged it into Adrian's heart.

The light left his eyes and he turned limp in Mason's grip, dead. Mason chucked his dead body to the ground. I closed my eyes tightly trying to block the image from my mind, I had never murdered anyone before.

A warm hand wrapped around my wrist that was still clutching the knife and it was only then that I realised my hands were shaking violently. Mason gently detached the knife from my paralysed grip and it clattered to the floor. My vision was locked onto the blood that stained my tremoring hands, the blood of a man I just murdered.

"You did the right thing, for our children," Mason reassured me, but I wasn't listening. My eyes were frozen to my blood covered hands.

Mason intertwined our fingers, both covered in the blood of the man I murdered. His touch was able to ground me back to

353

reality and it helped me remember that I was not in this alone. I glanced up at Mason and a shock of fear shot through me causing my knees to shudder and a gasp to wheeze from my lips.

Mason was staring at me with dilated wild eyes and for a chilling moment I was reminded of the time when he tried to kill me with those eyes – when he placed a knife as red as a rose to my throat. My body and soul sung with a thrill that was only alive when a dark Mason was attacking me. Like my body thought I was about to die but my mind knew that Mason could never hurt me.

The darkness in his eyes was only present when he wanted to kill or hurt something. I knew it was there because he wasn't able to kill Adrian – I had done it instead of him. Just standing there and staring into his murderous eyes caused thrills to shoot through my body setting every nerve ending alight.

Without looking away from my eyes, Mason gently raised my wrist in his hand. My heart was beating wildly in my chest as I watched him, unsure of how he was going to react. Was he going to finally lose it and try to kill me? His eyes were fixated on my wrist and filled with an intense darkness as he looked there. That was when I remembered that I was cut and bleeding there from Adrian's attack earlier. Mason slowly tried to clean my hand of blood but my cut was still bleeding.

Mason tilted my wrist to the side and my blood started streaming down my hand as he pulled it back. Neither of us took our eyes away from each other. Very slowly, causing my stomach to jump into my throat, Mason lowered his face closer to mine. My heart stuttered just like how it did that first time I met him, electrified with enticing fear. With his darkness filled eyes and soul locked on mine, he gradually inched his face towards my wrist.

He gently touched his lips to the cut on my wrist, kissing it softly. His lips burned my skin causing electric sparks to run up my spine. His tender touch decreased the pain I felt there and my eyelids fluttered. With a gasp, Mason pulled his face away from my hand and I saw my blood stained onto his lips. The sight sent a hot flutter to scorch through my veins. The feelings that he evoked in me as he tended to my wound were like nothing I could ever have imagined. This dark man that liked to see other people in pain, wanted to take my pain away.

Once again Mason showed that no matter what he was faced with, no matter how dark the inside of his mind was, he would always do what was best for me. And just this simple act of not hurting me when he was in this dark state, proved to me just how much he loved me.

I knew that we were both not normal and as much as our mental illnesses had caused us so much pain in our lives, they were the reason we had this happiness and love now. If I had not fought so hard for Mason and fought through the dark parts of my life, then I would not be alive for the beautiful parts.

I remembered what it felt like to be obsessed with Mason when we first met, the torment of desperately wanting him to be mine but not being able to be near him. It was like a miracle now looking up into his eyes that were staring lovingly back into mine. Mason was dark and dangerous and everything I imagined loving him would be. I knew in my soul that this was where I belonged.

Mason's bloodied hand intertwined with mine. The blood staining both of our wedding rings. I looked up into his face to see his eyes burning with a sadistic darkness. I knew my husband well enough to know that he wanted to kill in that moment, but he chose to look after me instead. Mason loved me more than murdering, more than his need to see blood.

"No one can know our secret – you made the right choice murdering him," Mason declared.

I glanced towards the cottage and our children, who were oblivious to what had just occurred outside. A tremor of terror shook through me at the thought at them finding out about our secret or our enemies finding out about them. My eyes drew lower to the cobblestoned path and towards the red rose stem that I had dropped earlier that was covered in my blood and I was hit with a painful reminder.

Mason warned me about this, that even something as beautiful as a rose has thorns and has a dark side that can hurt you. That the beauty of being with him also meant that my life would have a dark side, and that dark side can make you bleed.

I looked down at the cut on my wrist that was still dripping with my blood – the actualised consequence of Mason's warning and the wound that was caused by Mason's obsession with murder.

I revelled in the sight of our hands clasped together even though they were both covered in blood and savoured the dark thrill that accompanied being with Mason. I knew that I was willing to take that risk of being hurt, but I refused to allow my children to be subjected to that darkness and with that thought in mind I realised that Mason was right.

No one can ever find out what we become in the dead of night – murderers.